the Sisterhood of the Rose

The Recollections of Celeste Levesque

JIM MARRS

www.**sisterhoodoftherose**.org

Published by:

The Disinformation Company Ltd.
111 East 14th Street, Suite 108
New York, NY 10003
Tel.: +1.212.691.1605
Fax: +1.212.691.1606
www.disinfo.com

Library of Congress Control Number: 2009929854

ISBN: 978-1-934708-29-3

Designed by Greg Stadnyk
Frontispiece art by Sherry Vicars

Distributed in the U.S. and Canada by:
Consortium Book Sales and Distribution
34 Thirteenth Avenue NE, Suite 101
Minneapolis MN 55413-1007
Tel.: +1.800.283.3572
www.cbsd.com

Distributed in the United Kingdom and Eire by:
Turnaround Publisher Services Ltd.
Unit 3, Olympia Trading Estate
Coburg Road
London, N22 6TZ
Tel.: +44.(0)20.8829.3000 Fax: +44.(0)20.8881.5088
www.turnaround-uk.com

Distributed in Australia by:
Tower Books
Unit 2/17 Rodborough Road
Frenchs Forest NSW 2086
Tel.: +61.2.9975.5566 Fax: +61.2.9975.5599
Email: info@towerbooks.com.au

Attention colleges and universities, corporations and other organizations:
Quantity discounts are available on bulk purchases of this book for educational
training purposes, fund-raising, or gift giving. Special books, booklets, or book
excerpts can also be created to fit your specific needs. For information contact
the Marketing Department of The Disinformation Company Ltd.

Managing Editor: Ralph Bernardo

10 9 8 7 6 5 4 3 2 1

Printed in the United States of America

ACKNOWLEDGEMENTS

JIM MARRS GRATEFULLY ACKNOWLEDGES THE editorial assistance of Gary Baddeley, Maritha Gan and Pat Turk as well as the encouragement and support of his wife, Carol, and many others who offered their opinions of this work.

CELESTE LEVESQUE WOULD LIKE TO acknowledge the support and encouragement of Merrily Smith, Hazel Chandler, John Todd Miller, Karla Bass Hoffman, the late Karen Neves and "the many members of the Sisterhood who have come into my life to move this story forward."

CHAPTER 1

British Honduras
April, 1940

GISELLE TCHAIKOVSKY FELT A VAGUE apprehension as she watched the new twin-engine, twin-tail Beechcraft Model 18 lift off the packed-dirt runway at the airfield near Belize City. As it gently lifted in the warm humid air, the dark cowling and yellow paint of the craft made it look like one of the brightly-plumed toucans inhabiting the verdant jungle not more than 50 yards from the chain-link fence at the end of the runway.

She turned and pulled a large straw hat over her blonde hair to block the brightness of the midday sun. Squinting in the intense light, Giselle saw the only sign in evidence was a badly-faded, hand-painted board hung over a decrepit wooden shack. "*Aeropuerto Belize*" was its message.

Scanning the tiny reception shack, two run-down hangers, and the freestanding control tower, she knew that once again civilization as she knew it was far behind her. This small military airfield near the base of the Yucatan Peninsula was a far cry from the hustle and bustle of the Miami airport she had left just two days ago.

But she was used to caring for herself in the Central American jungle. After all, she had just spent the past several months there on an archeological dig site prior to her brief return to the States. She had no apprehension over the primitive condition.

The apprehension came when she found no sign of Jim or the guides. It was not like Jim to be late, especially since they had been apart for almost three months. She knew the yearning to be with him that she felt, so she had a pretty good idea of how he must be missing her in return.

Trudging toward the seemingly deserted reception area with her baggage in tow, Giselle stopped to light a cigarette and tried to muster up some good humor. After all, she thought, how fortunate it was that there was this small military airfield in British Honduras. She well knew it was only one of a handful of landing spots anywhere near the Yucatan.

She recalled the length of time it had taken a year earlier when she and Jim had traveled by train from Mexico City and then by pack animals to reach this same area. A slight frown creased her forehead. It was caused by both the blinding sun and from recalling their harrowing adventures in the jungle.

She also felt grateful that on this trip a powerful business associate of her father in Miami had agreed to her use of his private plane and pilot. She knew it otherwise would have taken days, perhaps even weeks, to reach British Honduras by train or ship.

And the stopover in Havana had been great fun. Papa Hemingway had been in residence, writing a novel based on his experiences in the recent Spanish Civil War. When Madrid fell to the Fascist-supported Franco in the fall of 1938, Hemingway saw the handwriting on the wall and returned home. He now fought for the Popular Front strictly with his typewriter rather than a rifle. Giselle had taken the opportunity to contact him. He seemed overjoyed to encounter Giselle again and invited her for dinner with some cronies.

Giselle smiled as she recalled the appreciative look in Papa's eyes when they met in the hotel lobby in Havana. The first time they had met had been in Europe in the early 1930s during one of her dance tours. Giselle had been but a mere teenager. The great Ernest Hemingway, even then a literary legend thanks to his popular books on the "lost generation" of the Great War, had been kind and gracious but had shown no particular interest in her as a female despite her reputation as a world-class ballerina. One of the disappointments of being a child prodigy was that older men rarely saw past her accomplishments on the stage. This was perhaps a good thing she had decided. Between her Aunt Gez acting as chaperone and a teenage love affair with her dance partner Michel, Giselle had been kept from the advances of her older admirers. This undoubtedly had saved her considerable heartache.

It was a much different story during her recent stopover in Havana. Now that Giselle was a grown woman, Papa had exhibited a more personal interest in her. His eyes constantly appraised her ample cleavage and shapely legs. He had been more than happy to renew his acquaintance with the young American dancer and was quite surprised to learn of her recent work in archeology. Giselle had patiently explained how her disaffection with the tumult of the ballet tours led her to another profession.

Papa and his friends had turned Giselle's melancholy longing for Jim into two nights of welcomed distraction, a whirlwind tour of Havana's top nightspots filled with laughter and frivolity. Her smile widened as she thought of Papa, his eyes glistening with scotch, regaling her with his exploits in Spain and ranting how another war was approaching.

Of course, he had tried to accompany Giselle on the flight to British Honduras, exaggerating every potential danger that might await her. The British authorities could not protect her outside the area of Belize City, he had warned. She had been forced to be quite firm in her refusal of his offer. She had dreaded the thought of fighting off his advances the entire trip. There had been a bleary early-morning farewell and Giselle had slept during the entire flight to the Yucatan Peninsula.

Now she was here and no sign of Jim.

With a small sigh of irritation, she dropped the cigarette in the dirt and ground it out with the heel of her high-top riding boot. Leaving her luggage at the door, Giselle strode into the reception shack to find only an old woman slumped on a wooden bench and a fat man in a brown uniform draped over a counter. Both were sound asleep.

Tapping the counter, Giselle assumed her most polite tone and said, "*Excusa, Señor...*" The man jumped as though a coral snake had suddenly crawled up his arm. He backed into a desk spilling several piles of official looking forms.

"*Madre Dios!*" he exclaimed, frantically attempting to recover the flying forms.

Giselle merely gave him a slight smile, simultaneously apologetic and sultry. "Oh, I am terribly sorry, *Señor*. An important man such as yourself must have much more pressing business than the safety of a poor lone woman traveler, and an American at that."

The swarthy man shifted his attention from the papers on the floor to Giselle. His small dark eyes narrowed in sudden appreciation of the slender woman standing before him and he broke into a broad smile.

The pair stood looking at each other, both wondering what to say next. Giselle felt uncomfortable to feel the man's piggish eyes sweep over her body, lingering at the shape of her hips in the tight-fitting white denim pants.

She was relieved to hear a roaring noise from the road that echoed through the small reception area. As one, she and the official moved to the door and peered down the road at an approaching cloud of dust.

As the weathered Ford pickup slid to a dust-raising stop, Giselle recognized it as the one Jim had bought three months earlier when she left for the States.

"Jim!" she cried, her eyes widening with eagerness and anticipation. Grinning broadly, she pushed past the gaping airport official and ran to the driver's door. She was stopped short by the sight of the short, dark driver climbing down from the cab. Two unfamiliar men squatted in the bed of the truck. They viewed her with dispassionate eyes.

"Miguel," said Giselle softly, "Where's Jim? Has anything happened?"

Miguel, who had been with Giselle and Jim earlier that year when they had discovered one of the greatest archeological finds of the century, hung his head.

"*Si, Señorita*, there is trouble, *mucho problema*," he muttered as if he felt guilty for not providing Giselle with a happier homecoming.

Placing one hand on her hip and cocking her head slightly, Giselle peered into Miguel's face. Deadly serious, she formed her words slowly, "Miguel, everything will be just fine. Now tell me what has happened."

As though a dam had burst somewhere inside of him, Miguel began to speak, his rapid delivery almost becoming a babble.

"*Señorita* Giselle, when *Señor* Peter heard you were returning, bad things began to happen. He changed. He turned the peasants against *Señor* Jim and the rest of us and began collecting a gang of bad men including *banditos* and renegade headhunters. *Muy malo*! He said he had a duty to perform and nothing would stop him. Oh, *Señorita*, we believe he plans to take the treasures of the temple."

"Peter!" gasped Giselle. "Oh, Miguel, you must be mistaken. Peter has been with our expedition from the beginning. I helped deliver his child. He would never do anything like that."

Miguel merely shrugged, not wishing to dispute his employer.

"He wouldn't take the treasure!" snapped Giselle, more to herself than to Miguel. "We all agreed that everything would remain in place until it could be excavated properly. That's why we all agreed to secrecy concerning both the find and its location."

"*Si*, I know, *Señorita* Giselle, but things have gone very wrong. There has already been one attack on our camp. One of the men was hurt. *Señor* Peter denied it and we couldn't prove it, but both *Señor* Jim and I think that *Señor* Peter was responsible. That's why *Señor* Jim stayed behind to guard the treasure. That's why he sent me to get you. We have had to hire some men as extra guards." He motioned to the men in the truck bed. Only then did Giselle notice that both men had old but deadly looking bolt-action rifles lying next to them.

Giselle stood still, her mind racing. She now understood the apprehension she had felt on the return trip and why she had felt a pressing need to hurry back. But what possibly could have happened to Peter?

She recalled the arduous jungle treks with Peter Mantel and his wife, poor Katrina, pregnant and uncomfortable the whole way. Peter was the stereotypical scientist, right down to his slight German accent. He was cool and levelheaded, always making detailed plans for every aspect of the journey. Giselle had always admired his meticulous planning and his reserved demeanor. It made him somehow unapproachable and thus mysterious and attractive. But he had always been there for them, pulling his weight and adding a good balance to the reckless enthusiasm of both she and Jim.

What had happened?

Giselle knew that the answer would not be found at the small airport with its one dusty dirt runway and single sleepy administrative officer.

"Miguel, *por favor*, get my bags," she said peremptorily. She pointed at the small pile of luggage sitting near the shack's door. "We're returning immediately. Do you have enough gasoline?"

"*Si, Señorita*," responded Miguel, brightening as he realized that Giselle had taken the heavy weight of decision-making from him.

Amid the sudden activity, the airport official said to no one in particular, "*Perdone*, but there are regulations to be met, forms to be filled out..."

He suddenly realized that the luggage had been tossed in the bed and that Giselle was climbing into the passenger side of the truck as

Miguel turned the ignition switch and hit the floor starter with his foot. The dirt-encrusted truck coughed to life and began to pull away.

"*Oye*! Wait, you can't leave until these forms..." the official's voice died away as he stood watching the truck disappear back down the road, this time the dust cloud diminishing into the distance like a film run backward.

Miguel drove the truck south for many miles before stopping to pour gasoline from a jerry can. After filling the gas tank and consuming a light snack of tortillas and beans washed down with homemade tequila, the truck turned west onto a narrow rutted track that knifed through the lush green foliage. Giselle knew they were nearing the border with Guatemala.

They passed palm and cacao trees woven together in a tangle of undergrowth that housed an amazing variety of life. There were various species of insects, bats and even predatory animals, including jaguars and ocelots. Towering overhead was the jungle canopy, composed of tall trees with spreading branches more than 150 feet off the ground. These were covered with climbing plants such as orchids and bromeliads. They all reached high striving for light and moisture as the dirt on the rocky forest floor was shallow and poor. The canopy was home to a diverse number of howler and spider monkeys, parrots, toucans, macaws and multi-colored butterflies.

The monotony of the jungle scenery coupled with the heat put Giselle into a sleepy reverie despite the bumping and jarring. While her body relaxed during the long drive, her mind wondered at this turn of events.

Her thoughts again turned to Peter Mantel, handsome Peter with his impeccable manners and that slight guttural accent which had always intrigued her. He was tall and blond with sharp features and piercing pale-blue eyes that always seemed to quickly analyze everyone and everything around him. His knowledge of archeology and many other subjects had captivated Giselle. She had often thought that if Peter had not had his young wife with him and if she had never met Jim, she might well have developed a real attachment for the quick-witted scientist. What could have caused Peter to suddenly become a problem, if Peter indeed was the problem? Could it be that someone else had found out about their discovery?

Still puzzling over the matter, Giselle settled into the bench seat of the truck and soon was falling into the same restless sleep she had experienced on the airplane.

In spite of her reverie, Giselle was somehow aware after several hours that they were getting close to the dig site when there was a sudden, loud report.

"Damn! I really don't need a blowout this close to camp," she thought, rousing herself. But then there was another. And another. The truck began swerving madly within the narrow confines of the jungle track. Her mind was racing, trying to understand what was happening.

Something clanged off the side of the truck near her head and Giselle realized they were under attack. Instinctively, she reached for her travel pouch but realized it was a useless gesture. Not expecting trouble, she had not taken the gun she had carried for so many of the previous months.

When two more slugs impacted her side of the truck, she knew that their attackers were off to their right. Clinging to the thin metal door of the truck, she furiously searched her memory of the area and yelled to Miguel over the roaring of the engine and the explosions of gunfire, "Veer to the left! There's a stream over there!"

Just as the truck wheeled to the left, a small object flashed past Giselle's face and embedded itself into the upholstery by her left shoulder. Holding tightly to the doorframe for support, she pulled the object loose with her left hand. It was a small wooden arrow. Set in carved notches were clipped pieces of parrot feathers.

Holding the point close to her nose, Giselle recognized the bitter odor of curare, a fast-acting poison that paralyzes the motor nerves. Natives of the region had used it for centuries. Her countenance was grim. These people are not playing games, she thought, tossing the arrow out of the cab.

Miguel was desperately swerving to and fro, more to avoid hitting oncoming trees than to dodge the bullets and arrows raining about the speeding truck. "Over there!" shouted Giselle pointing toward a brighter area of the jungle foliage ahead.

The truck careened wildly through the dense greenery throwing torn branches, stems and leaves in every direction before breaking into an open area formed by a small stream which flowed down a steep hillside. Over time it had cut a rocky swath through the jungle.

As the truck bounced along the streambed, the fusillade of gunfire and arrows slackened considerably. "Stop here," ordered Giselle. "The camp can't be more than 100 yards over there." She pointed off to the right.

Climbing hurriedly from the cab, she called to the two men in the back. "Okay, boys, here's where you earn your pay. You hold them off while I find reinforcements."

As the armed pair took up positions behind the truck, Miguel moved to her side, and placed a hand on her arm. With a look of genuine concern in his eyes, he said, "Here, *Señorita* Giselle, you may need this." With his other hand he offered a heavy and lethal-looking .38-caliber Smith & Wesson Police Special. She gave him a grateful smile, still wishing she had kept her pistol with her.

Grinning and flushed with adrenaline-driven excitement, Giselle grabbed the steel-blue revolver and yelled *"Muchas gracias*, Miguel! *Vaya con Dios*!" She sprinted for the cover of the jungle's leafy shadows.

As Giselle made her way through the thick foliage toward the camp, she kept a sharp lookout for anyone lurking in the undergrowth. But nothing moved.

Rapidly, but warily, making her way through the dense underbrush, Giselle found memories of this place pushing into her consciousness. She thought back to the day that she, Jim, Peter and Katrina along with their guides had discovered the vine-enshrouded temple buried deep in the primeval jungle of this part of British Honduras. That was little more than three months previously, in late 1939. It seemed much longer to Giselle after her recent activities in the States trying to retrieve part of their find.

What profound and prolonged feelings of joy and success they had shared at their discovery. Once the excited celebration had come to an end, along with their meager supply of tequila, the small archeological expedition had set up a base camp equidistant from the stream and the hidden temple and had immediately begun to excavate the structure, careful to catalog and photograph each step of the process.

In her mind's eye, she could still see the magnificent blazing blue emerald-like stone that she had discovered in a particularly secluded niche within the Temple. It was the largest of its kind she had ever seen and its purity was remarkable. Although she was not certain what it was, she knew at once that it was worth a small fortune. Now, as she crept through the jungle foliage, she realized she should have been better prepared to protect it.

It was the blue stone that had prompted her return to the States just after New Year, 1940. It had taken nearly a full three months to clear up the mess brought about by the benighted officials of the Smithsonian. She was still angered that they had allowed a wealthy financier to purchase the stone for his own private collection.

"I don't care if he is Joseph P. Kennedy!" she had screamed at the institution's director upon her arrival. "I don't care if it's John D. Rockefeller himself, the stone belongs to the public. That's why I had it shipped to the Smithsonian."

Then she thought of the Skull of Fate, another of the spectacular treasures found in the long-forgotten pyramid temple. She now realized she should have taken it with her. But she knew that neither Peter nor Jim would have agreed to let it out of their possession. Both men were clearly fixated on the mysterious ancient artifact.

It was the skull of a rather small adult but it was made entirely of quartz crystal with a most peculiar lavender hue. And it was flawless, both anatomically correct and in the exquisite workmanship it displayed. Almost totally transparent, the skull's interior had a way of catching light and reflecting it back in a myriad of colors and patterns that provoked strange feelings in those who viewed it.

Miguel and the guides were obviously uneasy around the skull. They generally shunned it, claiming it had great power for both good and evil. The trio of archeologists had collected legends and beliefs concerning the skull from both the guides and local natives. They were still collating them when Giselle had departed for the States.

By then they had learned that the skull was reputed to enhance the psychic powers of whoever controlled it, even the power to influence the entire world depending on the knowledge of its possessor. Both she and Jim had laughed privately at such beliefs, but Peter had showed keen interest.

The laughter had quickly subsided when they found that the skull generated strange dreams and visions within them. Night after night, the powerful talisman had somehow affected all of them, producing a strange and delirious lethargy during the day and hallucinatory dreams at night.

Giselle could still recall the vivid impressions of strange and ancient cities built of stone with tall spires and monolithic temples. People in peculiar dress filled the streets and participated in outlandish rites honoring deities unheard of in modern times. Despite her education and skepticism and after experiencing such dream visions, Giselle had begun to take more seriously the stories of the natives.

The natives called it the Skull of Fate and claimed it was more than 100,000 years old and could confer enormous power on whoever possessed it. Early on, Giselle was skeptical of these accounts, particularly since the skull evinced a craftsmanship that would have been impossible for a Stone Age people. But her skepticism wavered following the series of strange and vivid dreams.

The skull was truly the most amazing object Giselle had ever seen. She began to sense that the object indeed carried some strange force within it. She knew from her research that at least two other such skulls existed in the world, but she had never seen them or paid close attention to their attendant stories.

Her thoughts were suddenly cut short by a shot. It came from in front of her, in the direction of the camp. She stopped. Crouching, she quickly scanned the jungle about her.

With every fiber of her body on alert and the revolver at the ready, Giselle crept forward until she could make out the canvas tents in front of her. The firing had ended and all she could hear were the screaming of startled monkeys and birds and an occasional shot from the direction of the truck. Miguel and his men must still be holding their position, she thought.

Creeping up to the back of the supply tent, she listened intently for any sign of human activity. Not hearing any, she began to move cautiously around the side of the walled tent, when she stumbled across a large bulky form on the ground.

Looking down, Giselle was horrified to see the body of one of Miguel's guides. She recognized the man's sharp Indian features. She also recognized the exit wound of a large-caliber bullet on the side of his head.

Gagging, she cautiously stepped over the body and made her way to the tent she and Jim had shared. It was empty. She looked around the camp that had been their home since arriving in the Honduran jungle. It was a shambles. Most of the tents were down and the lab tent was still smoldering from a fire that had destroyed most of its contents.

"Oh, shit!" hissed Giselle surveying the destruction. All that equipment so laboriously manhandled into the jungle, all those specimens and artifacts. What a waste, she thought, anger welling up inside her.

Moving on, she came across two more bodies sprawled on the ground. With a churning stomach, she made a quick examination. She did not recognize either one. Their dark, scarred features coupled with their Western clothing told Giselle they were *banditos*, hirelings who would commit any crime for money.

She was relieved to find they were not her men and surprised to find a dark rage surfacing. "I hope they rot in hell," she muttered and instantly was horrified at her thought.

She glanced about at the ruin and loss and felt a new horror growing within her. The temple. My God! Jim must be in the temple.

Throwing caution aside, she ran along the path leading to the immense hidden pyramid but there was no one waiting in ambush. Quickly, she found herself at the opening that had been cleared through the moss and vines.

She paused and listened intently but heard no sounds out of the ordinary. Even the distant gunfire from the direction of the truck had died away. All was quiet save for the usual chattering of monkeys and the screams of parrots in the trees.

She stepped back and studied the overgrowth before her. No one but a trained archeologist like herself could possibly have seen this great pile of vine and moss-covered rock for what it was: a giant Mayan temple that had been reclaimed by the jungle. She was convinced that no human foot had stepped into the great structure for hundreds of years. It had remained hidden, lost within a green blanket of foliage and vines, harboring its secrets and treasure until Giselle, Jim, Peter and Katrina had disturbed its centuries-long tranquility.

And now despoilers had raided her camp and killed her workers, obviously seeking the temple's treasure for themselves. Her rage returned. Cocking the revolver, Giselle stepped cautiously into the opening.

She passed along the dark and dank interior corridor of the giant stair-stepped pyramid as silently as possible, still awed by the antiquity of the place. She knew only too well the ancient rites and repugnant rituals that had taken place here in the distant past. Her hair was becoming matted to her face in the humid heat.

She stopped suddenly, ears straining. She heard a low murmuring sound. Listening intently, she realized it was the sound of voices. There was light up ahead.

Giselle crept forward and peered into the large chamber at the center of the pyramidal temple. Torches flickered, casting giant and grotesque shadows on the lighted walls as well as the room's occupants.

They were all there. She could see Jim standing against one wall while Katrina cowered on some steps leading to a raised dais. Standing in the center of the stone room was Peter. In one hand was the Skull of Fate, its eyes glowing red and menacing in the light from the torches. In his other hand was a lethal-looking Luger pistol. It was pointed at Jim.

Giselle stared for long moments, befuddled, confused at the meaning of the scene in front of her. Why had Peter reclaimed the Luger he had given her to carry on their long jungle adventure? And why was he pointing it at Jim?

Giselle was both relieved at the sight of her lover and horrified at his predicament. Jim had always had a predilection for unkemptness but now he looked unusually haggard and worn. I should never have left him alone, she thought. She realized that Miguel was right. There was indeed big trouble here and for the first time, she began to truly believe that Peter had turned against them. Her eyes narrowed in anger over such betrayal. She thought furiously how she might gain the advantage over this surprising development.

"Peter, Peter, you must not do this. Please, Peter," Katrina was pleading, her eyes brimming with tears and fear. Giselle had always felt sorry for Katrina. The young German student had been studying in Mexico City at the famous *Universidad Nacional Autónoma de México* when she fell under the thrall of Peter's suave European manners. Peter had shown his uncaring, aristocratic upbringing by insisting that Katrina accompany them on their expedition to the Yucatan despite her pregnancy. Young and deeply devoted to Peter, Katrina was never comfortable in the jungle and giving birth in a primitive native village had been an added insult. Though she rarely complained, Giselle knew the young woman was thoroughly miserable the entire time, especially at the necessity of leaving her newborn child with Indian caretakers.

Jim was grim faced, his teeth clenched, "You rotten son of a bitch," he hissed, never turning his eyes away from the pointed automatic. "You can't get away with the treasure. There's not enough time before Giselle gets here and you haven't enough men. Besides, we'll follow you no matter where you go."

"You'll follow no one, you pathetic sot," snarled Peter in a deadly tone, leveling the Luger at Jim's head.

Giselle realized the time for deliberation was over. Jim's life was within seconds of being over. Katrina cried out and brought one hand to her mouth in horror.

Giselle's body was coiled and ready to leap into the room when she felt two arms embrace her shoulders. They were thick and covered with coarse black hair and were unbearably strong. Struggling violently, she was jerked into the room. The circulation to her arms cut off, the revolver fell from her numb hand to the stone floor with a loud clatter. Everyone turned at the commotion.

For what seemed an eternity, no one spoke. Giselle was forced to her knees. Her arms were pulled up behind her back until she felt they would break. Unwillingly, she made a groaning sound. Peter's angular features broke into a smile, a smile devoid of any warmth or humor.

Jim started to move toward her but Peter swiftly pointed the Luger in his face, forcing him to reluctantly resume his position against the wall.

His eyes never leaving Jim, Peter spoke over his shoulder. "So the prodigal daughter has returned. I knew I should have moved sooner, but no matter now. Nice work, Gomez."

Giselle was able to turn her head and catch a glimpse of the burly Gomez who had her arms in a vice-like grip. His rancid breath was on her neck and she almost gagged at the odor of stale sweat. How stupid of me not to check the side corridors, she thought absently. Her mind whirled in a mixture of fear and confusion; fear over her fate and Jim's and confusion over how she could have so misplaced her trust in Peter. Yet even in her befuddled mental state, a small distant corner of her mind was already coolly appraising her options, although unfortunately they seemed entirely too few.

Obviously feeling in complete control of the situation, Peter appeared to relax. Tucking the crystal skull under his left arm, he said quietly, "I realize that none of you can understand why I must do what comes next. When Katrina and I leave here…," he held up the skull, "… along with our little friend here, you two will be dead."

"Peter, don't do this!" cried Katrina, her face streaked with tears mixed with grime and dust.

Peter turned on her and shouted, "Quiet, woman. You have no

concept of what is at stake here. There is so much more to this place than just gold and gems." His blue eyes took on a faraway look. "So much more," he murmured. He was no longer the cold and calculating man that Giselle had known during the long jungle adventure. She could clearly see the intense light of fanaticism in his unfocused eyes.

"How can you do this, Peter," Giselle gasped through her pain, "after all we've been through?"

A sad expression passed across Peter's face and with a tone of sincerity he said, "It is true that I hesitated to take these drastic steps against the friends who have shared such difficulties with me." Then his mouth became grim and set. His eyes flashed. "But I know my duty."

"What duty?" growled Jim, obviously stalling for time as his eyes quickly scanned the room for any possible advantage.

"I will help you to understand," said Peter with a slight smirk. His craggy features relaxed. "Today I have found my true destiny."

Holding the crystal skull in the air, Peter said in a rising voice, "The power of this skull is unimaginable. I found the inscriptions that showed me the way to use this power. Nothing is now beyond my reach."

"What are you talking about?" asked Jim glancing about with a deep scowl. He was still playing for time as he sought some means of escape.

With a look of cunning, Peter leered at his former colleague. "You, with your Yankee college boy education, you think you know everything. But there are things in this world that you will never know. You see, my father was a ranking member of the party…"

"What party?" Jim interrupted. His tone indicated no real interest in an answer and Giselle realized he was stalling, hoping to distract Peter.

"The National Socialist Party, of course," sneered Peter. "The party of our *Führer*!"

"The Nazi Party!" Giselle exclaimed. "You never mentioned that you were a Nazi, Peter."

Peter's condescending smirk had returned as he said, "You never asked. I believe we agreed not to discuss political matters on our trek. It makes things much more pleasant in the jungle."

Giselle nodded slowly, still trying to grasp the situation. "But I don't understand…" Her voice trailed away.

"You, all of you, understand nothing," interrupted Peter. "You do not understand our *Führer* or his plans … or the secret society behind him. It is called the *Thule Gesellschaft*," he said. Lowering his voice, he added in a conspiratorial tone, "It is a very old society with antediluvian secrets you could never understand. My father was a member. He inducted me into this circle not long before I was dismissed from university."

Pulling himself to full height, Peter's voice rose in emotion. "There is an ancient prophecy handed down from the lost land of Thule and known only to a few select members of the Society which states, 'One shall arise who, by means of forbidden knowledge, will unite the world and prepare the way for the olden ones.' I now understand this prophecy and my role in it."

Giselle was in shock. The Nazi Party? A secret society? Peter, the man she had shared hardship and triumph with over the past months, was connected to those goose-stepping goons who had gobbled up most of Eastern Europe.

"You're mad," declared Jim with disgust. "Do you really believe you will rule the world?"

Angered flashed in Peter's eyes briefly but was quickly replaced with a smug and calculating expression on his face. "Of course not, my dear Jim. Not I. But it will not matter to you as you will be dead." He slowly raised the Luger toward Jim and squeezed the trigger.

"Peter, no, you can't!" cried Katrina, rushing forward to thrust herself between the two men just as the deafening roar of the automatic filled the stone chamber.

Giselle's eyes widened with horror as she saw Katrina slump soundlessly to the rock floor. Peter stood still, shocked to see that his wife had become his victim. He started to move to her, but saw that she did not move. He stopped and turned to Jim.

Hatred and anger twisted his features as he screamed at Jim, "See what you have done! You swine!" he pointed the still-smoking Luger at Jim's head and pulled the trigger.

"No!" screamed Giselle as the gun flashed. Again the room was filled with the crack and reverberation of a gunshot. She saw Jim's face, the face that had touched hers on so many love-filled nights, shatter into an exploding red mist. His body crumpled lifelessly to the dank floor of the chamber.

An unthinking rage filled her entire being. "You bastard!" she hissed, struggling in Gomez's grip.

"Ah, the little ballerina wants to be a spitfire," responded Peter with a sneer.

The fear and confusion dropped away as Giselle felt a rage she had never experienced before swell up within her. With a strength she would not have thought possible, she twisted in Gomez's arms and lashed out with her right foot. Her heavy jungle boot crashed into the big man's shinbone. With a sharp cry of pain, he momentarily loosened his hold. Giselle broke loose from Gomez's grip and lunged at Peter.

But he was not to be caught off guard. Again the Luger roared within the chamber and Giselle felt something hot and burning punch deep into her left shoulder, knocking her violently backwards. The force of the bullet as well as the shock of hitting the stone floor left her unable to breathe or cry out. She could feel a warm wetness soaking her blouse. She lay stunned, barely conscious of her surroundings due to the pain and shock. Raising her head she saw a dark alcove ahead and began frantically pulling herself toward the welcomed darkness.

Glancing back, she saw the hulking Gomez was moving after her, drawing a long and ugly machete from his belt. She tried to move faster but her body wouldn't respond. She collapsed on the cool stone floor of the pyramid.

"Leave her," she heard Peter say. He seemed genuinely shocked and even a bit chagrined at the carnage within the blood-splattered chamber. "She won't last until morning without medical attention."

Giselle's thoughts were spiraling toward unconsciousness. Jim and Katrina were dead and her colleague Peter was a thieving Nazi, taking a priceless treasure that rightfully belonged to her and the world. Through searing pain, Giselle's last thoughts were of vengeance as her awareness faded into an uncomprehending darkness.

Her last sensation was the sound of Peter's voice rising to a fanatical shrillness as he shouted, seemingly more for himself than any apparent audience, "My work here is now finished and my true destiny awaits. I will return home and present this skull and the power it represents to *mein Führer*, Adolf Hitler!"

CHAPTER 2

France
September, 1940

GISELLE'S SCREAM ALMOST PERFECTLY MATCHED the shrill whistle of the steam engine as it signaled its approach to the train station in Limoges, France.

Another scream began forming in her throat but was choked off as she sat bolt upright and realized that she was in the sleeping compartment of the northbound *Paris Express*.

She had been dreaming of the Yucatan again. The nightmares over her Central American experience had diminished lately but they still continued. It was as though she was strapped into a seat in some third-rate movie house and forced to watch the same B-grade horror film over and over again.

There was the villainous Peter, his finely chiseled Nordic face twisted by zealous excitement, holding the smoking Luger while hoisting the crystal skull in his other hand. Unlike the Saturday morning matinees, there were no heroes, just the still forms of Katrina and Jim lying dead on the cold stone floor of the lost Mayan temple. She feared she would relive the horror of the temple for the remainder of her life.

Superimposed were scenes from the current newsreels she had seen since arriving in Europe. Jackbooted Nazi soldiers marching through Paris in long uniform lines of field gray. Martial bands blaring loud and repetitious marches emphasized by a thundering drum corps. Red *swastika*-embossed banners fluttering along the near empty boulevards.

Giselle closed her eyes and mopped the night sweat from her forehead with the linen sheet. The entire nightmare—from the deaths in the lost temple to the conquering Nazi storm troopers—was so hideous because it was all too real.

The shriek of the steam whistle sounded again and brought her to full wakefulness. She unconsciously rubbed her left shoulder. The wound was nearly healed but there was still considerable tenderness.

She knew she was lucky to be alive. Giselle still recalled how she had initially believed the faithful Miguel to be a specter sent from hell when he entered the inner chamber and lifted her from the bloody floor of the temple.

Miguel and the two hired men, one nursing a slight head wound, had slipped into the jungle when their ammunition ran low. Cleverly, they had left an obvious trail leading away from the abandoned truck deceiving their attackers into thinking they had fled for home. But quietly they had circled around and watched from cover as Peter and his hirelings had gathered up both treasure and what usable supplies remained and departed.

Only after making certain that they had left that part of the jungle did Miguel and his *compadres* emerge from hiding and enter the devastated camp. While the two riflemen searched the wreckage, Miguel had entered the temple and found Giselle.

His first aid had been primitive but effective. He had applied a compress with a bandanna and poured the last of his tequila on her wound to prevent infection.

The long ride back to Belize City in the bullet-riddled Ford truck had seemed interminable. A bullet had pierced the radiator forcing frequent stops to add water. Once at the city's hospital, nurses in clean white uniforms had hovered about her metal-frame bed for more than a week, gently tending her shoulder wound and restoring her vitality.

While Giselle's health, both physical and mental, steadily improved, she never stopped thinking of revenge against Peter.

She had pieced together the man's life from letters Miguel had recovered in the ruined campsite as well as comments in Jim's diary, which was found in the well-worn rucksack still strapped to his body.

To begin with, the man was not even Peter Mantel. His real name was Peter Freiherr von Manteuffel. From her travels, Giselle knew this was a proud and aristocratic Prussian family. Peter was a distant relation of the noted Field Marshal Edwin Freiherr von Manteuffel. After a promising start in medical school, Peter had been dismissed following charges of practicing cruel and inhumane experimentation. He had been disowned by his family and had left Europe for Central America as an archeological assistant.

When he had joined Giselle's expedition in the fall of 1939, she quickly became aware of Peter's distant and cool demeanor. But she never conceived that he would be capable of taking life despite the fact that he carried a Luger pistol every day. It was this gun that Peter had given to her as a sign of his trust and protection. How ironic that it was the same pistol he used to kill Jim and nearly kill her.

Lying in the hospital bed, Giselle had time to evaluate her relationship with Jim. She had loved Jim but she now realized it was more as a comrade than as a life partner.

She recalled how the tedium of her work as an assistant had driven her from the hot archeological dig at Teotihuacan's Temples of the Sun and Moon to the cool mountain village of San Miguel. It was there she had met Jim in one of the many cantinas.

They were both young and filled with the spirit of adventure. And they made an excellent team. From Jim, she had learned courage and forcefulness while he had profited from Giselle's knowledge of archeology and incisive thinking. Giselle's interest was further aroused by Jim's hints that he knew the way to undiscovered Mayan ruins. Their days of arduous jungle treks and their nights of drinking and lovemaking had bonded them together in a special way.

Yet she now realized that she had never really thought of him as a soul mate. She knew too well his drinking and his love of travel and discovery would never allow him to settle in one place.

Her tender memories of Jim slowly faded as she more and more thought of retribution against Peter and the evil he represented. Not only had he killed Jim, he had bested her and taken the fruits of her hard work. A perfectionist at heart, Giselle had never allowed herself second place in anything. Whether academic studies or dancing, she always had to be the best, number one. It was a questionable attribute, one that had cost her more than one friend.

She could not yet think of how she would find Peter and regain the Skull of Fate, but she knew that she would never stop until she had righted the wrong against both her and Jim. She could not shake the feeling that she also owed the world a debt. With the powerful skull, Hitler might indeed achieve his goal of world conquest. He had to be stopped.

Several weeks had been spent convalescing in Miguel's modest but comfortable home. The small two-room stucco hut was nestled in a grove of mango trees on the outskirts of Belize City. Surrounded by the towering trees and gorgeous jungle flowers, she would have thought the place a paradise if not for the never-ending impatience to pursue Peter and the skull.

She had lived on a diet composed primarily of mangoes and coconuts and her health steadily improved, as did her desire for action. With the summer of 1940 drawing to an end, Giselle's patience ended. She knew she could wait no longer. During her three-month convalescence, her beloved France had fallen to Hitler and the British were engaged in an aerial death struggle over their island home.

Although proud of her American citizenship, Giselle had developed a deep affection for *la belle* France during her frequent stays with the Paris Ballet.

Over the strenuous objections of both Miguel and the British doctor at the hospital, Giselle had declared herself well enough to travel and began making preparations for her journey to Europe.

Although she well knew that her health was not fully restored, she considered it a waste of time to lie useless in Miguel's home when she knew that serious and immediate work needed to be done. She had hoped to stop Peter and his maniacal plans to take the power of the Skull of Fate back to Germany. But with the unexpected and spectacular successes of the Nazi war machine during the past weeks, she knew she was too late. She did not know how the crystal skull worked but she had no doubt that its power had contributed to Germany's successes. The many strange dreams and potent visions she experienced since finding the artifact had convinced her of its influence.

While she lay recuperating and planning her vengeance, the faithful Miguel had brought her news of the war's progress. It had begun with Hitler's invasion of Poland in September, 1939. This was just after she, Jim, Katrina and Peter had begun their trek into the Yucatan jungles. It was incredible how the world had changed in less than a single year.

Usually an ardent follower of the news, Giselle had paid little attention to the man with the Charlie Chaplin moustache who had rebuilt Germany during the 1930s. He had seemed like a comical caricature although many of her father's business associates had voiced admiration and support for Hitler and his policies along with many prominent Americans such as Henry Ford, Charles Lindbergh, Joseph P. Kennedy and Prescott Bush.

As usual, there was a provocation for the attack on Poland. Hitler claimed that Polish troops had attacked a border radio station. From her vantage point half a world away and with her knowledge of world politics gleaned through her many high-level friends and associates, Giselle suspected that the attack, if it happened at all, was orchestrated by Hitler himself. One thing was clear: no one in Europe was snickering at the strutting little Austrian corporal any longer.

Poland had fallen in a mere four weeks. Its allies, Britain and France, declared war but could only watch helplessly from afar as the German *Wehrmacht* slashed through the countryside using a knockout combination of air and armored power quickly named the *Blitzkrieg*.

Giselle had noted that the victorious Germans had been joined toward the end by the Russians who, momentarily free from worry over a German advance into their own country thanks to a Nazi-Soviet non-aggression pact signed on August 23, 1939, took their own share of eastern Poland as well as the previously independent Baltic states of Latvia, Estonia and Lithuania and the Bessarabia section of Romania.

Then began the *Sitzkrieg*, or sitting war, as some of the more jocose commentators dubbed it. It was a strange and pregnant war in which none of the combatants moved against the other. This inaction had lasted until May 9, 1940, when Hitler's *Wehrmacht*, reconsolidated and flushed with its victory over the Poles, launched Operation *Fall Gelb*, the invasion of France. Giselle had learned of the tragic invasion of her beloved France as she traveled to the United States from the Yucatan.

During her return trip to British Honduras, she had kept a watchful eye on the events that followed. There was no good news. Instead of bulldozing through Holland and Belgium as expected by the hidebound Allied strategists, Hitler had followed the suggestion of the brilliant *Generalleutnant* Erich von Manstein and split his forces.

Army Group B had indeed marched through Holland into central Belgium drawing the French and British up to meet them. Meanwhile, Army Group A, with seven of the 10 available *panzer* divisions audaciously bypassed the Maginot Line defensive emplacements on the French border, snaked through the heavily wooded hills of the Ardennes Forest and crossed the Meuse River at Sedan. The allied forces were split apart. Giselle could only imagine the demoralization that ensued.

While the British Expeditionary Force frantically sought to evacuate for home from the beaches at Dunkirk, the defense of France was left solely to the French. Despite isolated incidents of daring and heroism, many Frenchmen showed little desire to fight. Giselle was aghast to read that entire columns of French soldiers were sent off to German POW camps without the need for guards.

As she lay in Miguel's home recuperating, she had been deeply saddened on June 11th to learn her beloved Paris had been declared an open city. Just three days later, the footsore but jubilant *Landsers* of *Oberstleutnant* Dr. Hans Speidel entered the city without firing a shot. She shuddered to think of the gracious *Champs-Elysees* echoing with the thud of German hobnailed jackboots.

Her sorrow deepened at the end of the month when she read accounts of the armistice that ended the fighting. On Hitler's orders, a dreadful peace based upon occupation was signed in the same railroad car where 20 years previously the Germans had been forced to sign the armistice that ended World War I.

This nose rubbing had only heightened Giselle's fury and determination to stop the German *Führer* at any cost. She felt her life up to that point had conditioned her for the task. A child prodigy, early on she was given the finest education and an appreciation of the better things in life, thanks to her wealthy parents. Her mother was French and sophisticated in the ways of the world. Her father was a Jewish immigrant from Russia, who had changed his name upon arrival in the United States to conceal his immigrant status. Far from poor, he was well educated and well connected to the world of business and finance. Giselle had learned from her aunt that he also was a member of a mysterious and powerful group known only as the Committee of 300. It was through this connection that her father had seen the coming collapse of the Romanov monarchy and fled with his family to America.

Growing up on a sprawling estate in upstate New York, Giselle had never lacked for anything material. Yet she had excelled in everything. An obstinate and competitive spirit caused her to excel despite any hurdle. Physically and mentally, she was superior to all of her peers. By age 14, she had become an accomplished and celebrated ballerina touring the capitals of Europe with her mother's sister, Aunt Gez.

Aunt Gez was also a Giselle. The name Gez had stuck when Giselle was barely a toddler to avoid confusion between the two. Giselle's mother and Aunt Gez were born of French Catholic immigrants.

A stylish woman with a tendency toward middle-age spread, Aunt Gez was a jovial and wealthy socialite who appeared to be intrigued by virtually everything in the world. She had gladly agreed to accompany Giselle on tour. The impressionable Giselle had been inspired by her aunt's enthusiasm for life and the ease with which she moved within the highest of social circles.

Her lengthy convalescence had given Giselle time to look back over her young life and consider her options. Confidant in her abilities but plagued with regret over the strange but awesome power she had unwittingly unleashed on the world, Giselle grew more and more determined to somehow retrieve the Skull of Fate. She knew that she could never live with herself if she didn't at least make the effort to recover the skull and to liberate France from the Nazis.

Declaring herself fit for travel in the late summer of 1940, Giselle had purchased passage on a freighter with money wired from her Aunt Gez. She had asked her aunt to advance the money without informing any other relatives or friends. Giselle was not certain of her plans but she knew that they might well include the need for secrecy and anonymity.

She had lavishly repaid Miguel for his kindness and loyalty and after a tearful good-bye to his entire family, she sailed from Belize City.

Her crossing of the Atlantic had been uneventful, although the crew talked constantly about the danger of German U-boats. They also gave their beautiful blonde passenger thinly concealed looks of admiration. To avoid any unpleasantness, Giselle had spent the long hours of the voyage in her small compartment or in the ship's radio room. She befriended the ship's radio operator and kept up with the news broadcast by the BBC over shortwave frequencies. With great concern, she listened daily to the accounts of the unprecedented air battle being fought in the skies over London and southeast England.

Against the odds, the British RAF continued to defy the German war machine. As the days stretched into weeks, the feared German invasion of England failed to materialize. She could read between the lines of Radio Berlin's boastful announcements of successes in the air. It was obvious that the Germans had failed to deliver a knockout blow and the initial fear of a German invasion seemed to be fading.

She arrived at Lisbon, Portugal, in mid-September. Her leisurely and uneventful voyage coupled with the air of normalcy in the bustling port caused her momentarily to question if there was really a war on.

But after a few days of clearing her papers with the authorities and arranging passage to Paris, Giselle began to see a darker undercurrent to life in the Portuguese capital.

The city was overrun with refugees, from France, Germany and England. Many were wealthy Jews who had managed to escape the Nazi onslaught. With America and Britain making it difficult to emigrate, most were resigned to riding out the war in Lisbon.

With the German invasion of France, more refugees had poured across the Spanish border, some 100,000 making their way to Lisbon hoping to travel on to America. But the flights to England were erratic and always fully booked. Passage by sea to America was at a premium and accommodations in the crowded city were almost nonexistent. Fortunately, her considerable resources as well as the recollection of her celebrity status as a ballerina gained her a well-appointed suite in one of the city's newer, more luxurious hotels.

It had taken the better part of two weeks to arrange for the sleeping compartment on the *Paris Express*. Everything moved at a snail's pace, as though the war had caused everyone to become lethargic and hesitant. After taking a train to the Spanish capital of Madrid, Giselle's spirits were further dampened.

Viewing the city over the wide sweeping fenders of a decrepit taxi, Giselle compared Madrid with Lisbon. The difference was dramatic. Where Lisbon had been a bustling crossroads for refugees and world travelers, Madrid was a dull and bleak metropolis. Bullet-scarred and bombed out buildings were constant reminders of the recently ended Spanish Civil War. The soldiers of General Francisco Franco, the *caudillo* of Fascist Spain, were prominent in the streets, demanding identity papers and occasionally detaining those whose documents failed to satisfy them.

Madrid was also suffering from overcrowding and scarcity but with none of the energetic commerce evident in Lisbon. The population obviously had not recovered from the privations of the civil war. There were long lines outside food stores and the poor were dressed in little better than rags. An air of want and hopelessness permeated the city.

Then there had been delays in having her travel documents approved. The resolution of this problem required almost daily trips to both the French and American consulates before Giselle was able to travel on to Barcelona. She had been more than happy to leave depressing Madrid.

There had been the interminable wait at the Spanish border north of Figueras. As the Spanish railroad used a wider gauge track than the rest of Europe, Giselle and the other passengers were forced to disembark and wait in a large and drafty waiting room for the whole night as rail cars were exchanged.

Through that long and largely sleepless night, Spanish soldiers roamed through the crowd. They questioned the passengers and searched those suspected of currency smuggling. They had been deferential to Giselle in view of her obvious social standing and American passport. She had hoped for a decent meal once she reached the French frontier but had to content herself with a few hard rolls, an orange she bought from a pushcart vendor and some watery coffee.

By late morning, Giselle was again on her way to Paris, ensconced in the small but comfortable sleeping compartment. She had grown sleepy as the train rolled on to Narbonne, then turned west through Carcassonne to Toulouse. Moving northward toward Limoges, she decided to regain the sleep lost at the border crossing.

But the dreams came and it was the Yucatan nightmare all over again. She hoped that her screaming had not disturbed the other passengers. She wrapped a cloth robe about her and waited anxiously to see if the porter would knock on her door to enquire if everything was all right.

When no one came, she relaxed and began laying out her dress clothing on the small fold-down bed. Giselle told herself it was time to prepare for her arrival in Paris but deep down she knew that she dreaded the thought of going back to sleep, fearful of a return of the recurring dreams of terror and death.

Selecting a demure cotton dress and holding it up to her body, she looked at herself in the long vertical mirror on the back of the compartment door. At age 23, she still had the look of a young and trim ballet dancer. Her skin was clear and a healthy bronze from the long afternoons in the sun during her convalescence. Her blonde hair was full and luxurious, her neck long and slender and her body the object of desire by every red-blooded man. Her breasts were slightly larger than would have been normal for her height but this was offset by the long curving legs of a dancer.

She smiled to herself thinking of how older men had thrown themselves at her feet during the years of her ballet career. She had quickly learned the art of gracefully applying her womanly charms to gain advantage with men.

Pulling the dress over her head, Giselle preened in front of the mirror and began making plans for her arrival in Paris.

She had wired ahead to notify the Paris Opéra Ballet of her arrival. She knew they would have someone meet her at the station. After all, just a few years previously, she had been the toast of the town following her triumphant starring role in their production of *Swan Lake*.

Giselle still had no idea how she would regain the Skull of Fate but she had decided to make her start in Paris where she had many friends and contacts from her dance tours of the early 1930s.

It had been a wonderful time. The applause and solicitation of her many admirers had been a heady tonic for a New York girl in her teens. With Aunt Gez on hand to keep her from serious trouble, Giselle had reveled in her celebrity status. It was like a visit to Wonderland, a constant swirl of parties, receptions and soirées interrupted only by rehearsals and productions of the ballet she loved so much.

Why had she given all that up? She scowled and sank down on the small bed as she recalled the constant strain of her public life. It had become like a straightjacket. Propping herself on one elbow, she looked out the window and once again remembered the feelings of suffocation and restraint. A famous young ballerina, after all, was expected to be beautiful and talented, but not smart and savvy. Not one of her male admirers had cared one whit about her views of the world, politics or philosophy.

She could still recall the eagerness she felt after enrolling in Rochester College as a student of archeology in 1935. Her passion for history, ancient artifacts and exotic precious gems had soon rivaled that for dancing.

She also discovered that much of what she believed about the history of the world and the origins of man could be called into question.

The archives at Rochester, as well as most colleges and museums, were filled with items that could only be classified as "anomalies," a fancy scientific word for anything that did not fit into the neat and tidy conventional theories of history.

From the giant perfectly symmetrical round balls of Guatemala to the ancient and eerie winged animals being discovered in Mesopotamia, the world was full of artifacts that affronted accepted knowledge. Giselle's insatiable thirst for learning, encouraged by Aunt Gez's fascination with the unconventional, drew her to such things and soon she had become a thorn in the side of her professors. They were always happy to send her off on some dig or another, just to get her out of their hair for a time.

Her college days had been perhaps the happiest time of her life. They were not as thrilling as touring the capitals of Europe and America as a young and precocious ballerina, but they also carried none of the pressure of stardom. They had afforded Giselle time to mature at a slower pace and to build up her intellectual muscles.

Gazing out of the compartment's large window without truly seeing the passing French vineyards, Giselle thought of the boys she had met during her college years. They were not yet like the sophisticated men she had met on her travels. They were insecure but open and searching. They were fun. There had been several brief flings but none had held her attention for long.

She blamed that on Michel, beautiful, tender Michel, her first real lover. She had met him when she first traveled to Paris for a European dance tour. She had succumbed to his boyish charms as they practiced together for the ballet stage.

Michel Devereaux was dark and moody, the antithesis of Giselle with her striking blonde hair, fair skin and buoyant personality. They immediately became fast friends and, despite her tender age and the watchful eye of Aunt Gez, they were soon lovers.

Michel had taken it upon himself to teach her the ways of love in chivalrous Gallic style. In the ecstasy of her sexual awakening, Giselle had quickly abandoned her strict but spotty Catholic upbringing. The life of a sexually-active international celebrity left little room for repressive piety.

Her expression became pensive as she braced her head in both hands and gazed at the passing countryside. She realized that her love for Jim had been immediate and tempestuous, a thing of shared sexuality and common interests. With Michel, the relationship had grown slowly, based on genuine concern and admiration for each other. She recalled the slow breakup with Michel and wondered as she had so many times before what had become of her first love.

They had written to each other often but cool paper could not take the place of a warm body. With Giselle's return to the United States and Michel's ongoing interest in forming his own dance company, their worlds had slowly drifted apart.

Once, Giselle had heard that Michel, discouraged over the lack of financing available for a dance troop, had obtained a political office in his hometown of Chartres. Often, over the years, she thought of Michel and wondered what had become of him.

She was somewhat surprised at the feelings that welled up within her at the thought of her former young love. She wondered if she should look him up during her stay in France.

Giselle lay back on the compartment's bed and idly thought of the great times with Michel. She remembered how he would tease her about her naiveté in matters of lovemaking and the rose-shaped birthmark on her upper thigh during those delightful stolen moments when they were able to slip away together. They were young, physically fit and in love. There were quick, but passionate, trysts in parks and movie theaters.

She thought of all those times they had secretly kissed and fondled each other while waiting backstage for an entrance cue. They were always careful to fold themselves into the black stage curtains to prevent prying eyes from discovering their deliciously dangerous games. The rules were quite explicit regarding relationships between students: There were to be none. And Aunt Gez seemed to be everywhere, although more than once Giselle had the impression that nothing was truly escaping her aunt's notice. She had been so thankful that Aunt Gez had become more like a sister than a chaperone.

In the warm glow of such fond memories, Giselle soon fell into a welcomed dreamless sleep.

Some hours later she was awakened by the conductor knocking on the door.

"*Prochain arrêt Paris!*" came the droning call from the corridor. Giselle splashed water on her face from a small basin in one corner of the compartment and began gathering her belongings.

Her feelings were decidedly mixed. On the one hand, she was back in the City of Lights, her most favorite city in the world, the scene of so many past triumphs.

But on the other hand, it was now a city in wartime, occupied by a foreign army and under the heel of a despot. It was almost too painful to contemplate.

Her eyes sparkled with a burning intensity. She would do something about this situation. It would surely change before she was finished. She had never known defeat in any area of her life before and she was not about to accept it now.

It was late afternoon as the steam engine huffed to a jerky stop in the *Gare d'Austerlitz*. Giselle stood in the doorway of her car, baggage in hand, her thoughts a mixture of apprehension and anticipation. Although she had wired ahead to the *Ballet de l'Opéra* concerning her arrival, she had no idea of who would greet her. After all, it had been more than six years since she had last been in Europe and much had changed.

As a porter helped offload her considerable amount of luggage, Giselle gazed about the crowded station. Everywhere she looked there were Germans. Many were officers in dress uniform arriving with their wives to taste the delights of the city. Enlisted men, some in full combat gear, were being transferred back to the Fatherland while others in their walking out uniform were arriving on leave for some time on the town.

The many civilians did not seem to pay attention to the occupying troops. They went about their business with a complacent attitude.

"Giselle?"

She just barely heard her name called above the din of the station. Turning, she sought the source. But everyone about her seemed intent on either entering or exiting the steam-enshrouded train platform. She felt trapped in the surging crowd.

"Giselle, you've made it." This time the voice was much nearer. Turning, Giselle saw a man in a dark coat and hat approaching. There was something familiar about the voice.

"Oh, my God!" she shrieked in sudden recognition. It was Michel. In spite of her concerns over the fate of France and the crystal skull, her heart leapt at the sight of her former lover.

They stood staring at each other for long moments, then embraced on the loading platform oblivious of the swirling crowd of travelers, soldiers and vendors. She felt the familiar shape of his body and, after the long and arduous journey from Central America, she gave herself totally to the experience.

"Michel, my dear, I can't believe it's you," said Giselle, at last pulling herself away from him. She studied his face intently. He was older, of course, but also seemed more careworn. His flowing black hair seemed thinner and there were distinct lines about his eyes and mouth. The poor thing, she thought; it must be hard living in an occupied land.

He smiled at her and from the look in his eyes it was obvious that his affection for her had not diminished over the years. "I learned you were coming from some of the dance troupe and I just had to be here to greet you," he explained, looking away with just a touch of embarrassment.

"Oh, Michel, I'm so glad you did. I didn't know whom to expect. I thought the theater would send someone. But you, I can't believe it."

She could feel the old familiar urges welling up inside her at the sight and touch of Michel, the man who first introduced her to the delectable pleasures of caring sex. It was as if the years since their parting had fallen away. She was filled with a sudden and inexplicable yearning to lose herself in Michel, so as to forget her recent pain-filled past.

On a sudden impulse, Giselle pulled him close and whispered, "Take me to my hotel, *mon cher*." She gave him a lascivious and inviting smile. Longings she thought had died with Jim were coming to life within her. "Perhaps we can make up for lost time."

Pulling away from her embrace with a sad expression, Michel glanced about and said quietly, "I will take you to your hotel. But there is serious business to be done. We must talk, but not here."

Dumbfounded at what she considered a rebuff, Giselle took a few steps backward and surveyed the man standing in front of her. For the first time, she noticed the white collar he wore and realized that he wore a frock under the black wool overcoat.

As Michel took her by the arm and led her from the station, she followed, numb with shock. As they reached the street she finally found her voice and blurted out with astonishment, "My God, you're a priest!"

CHAPTER 3

Paderborn, Germany
September, 1940

As Peter Freiherr von Manteuffel gazed out the side window of the large Horch staff car, he was entranced with the fairytale quality of the passing landscape.

The summer of 1940 had been good to the Alme River Valley, located near Paderborn in Central Germany. Heavy rainfall had drained from the towering *Eggegebirge* and seeped into the ground filling the more than 200 springs in the area.

Now in early September, the foliage was still lush and verdant, with only a scattering of brown interspersed among the tall poplar and pine trees. The Paderborn Town Hall with its three distinct gables, the twin-towered *Abdingshofkirche* and the cluster of medieval-looking houses added to the storybook appearance of the well-ordered countryside. The weather was warm and Peter wished the canvas top of the Horch had been put down.

Peter had every reason to believe himself a participant in some fairy tale. His life had taken on new meaning and relevance. Far from being the poor and disdained archeological student forced to work outside his Fatherland, Peter now had significant social standing and authority.

He glanced down at the silver lightning runes on the black wool collar of his new uniform and felt a smug sense of satisfaction. The lightning flashes identified Peter as a member of the *Schutzstaffel* or SS, Hitler's black-clad elite troops. Now people would show him the respect he deserved. He thumped the door panel with his fist as the ungainly command car ground its way along the tree-lined road.

Peter could make out his destination ahead. Perched atop a high hill and dominating the surrounding area was the imposing 17th century fortress of Wewelsburg, now the center of *Reichsführer-SS* Heinrich Himmler's private empire. With its huge North Tower and opposing twin south turrets, it was the only triangular shaped castle in Germany. Even with the use of free concentration camp labor, restoration of the castle in the mid-1930s had cost more than three million American dollars. Newly completed, it was considered the spiritual "Camelot" of Germany's National Socialist state.

Millions inside the new German *Reich* viewed Himmler with fear and dread. But Peter saw him as a kindred spirit. After all, like himself, Himmler had once been an obscure man, poor both in health and in pocketbook. But circumstances had turned and now, with *Reichsmarschall* Hermann Göring's failure to subdue England from the air, Himmler was unquestionably the second most powerful man in Germany. Peter had taken some pains to learn what he could about this powerful man.

Although Himmler's parents had been typical middle-class Germans living in Munich, his schoolteacher father had briefly tutored Bavaria's Prince Heinrich. The prince had agreed to become young Heinrich's godfather. This connection to the social elite coupled with a dogged tenacity at sports despite chronic respiratory problems had earned the young Himmler a berth as an officer candidate during the Great War of 1914–1918. But the war ended before he could see action.

Himmler, carefully schooled in taking advantage of both the German economy and aristocracy, found himself adrift following the collapse of both after the war. He eventually took up the cause of National Socialism becoming one of the initial party members in 1923. Following the abortive Beer Hall Putsch that November, Himmler had fled Munich but continued to work for the Nazis as their business manager as well as delivering speeches with titles such as "The Enslavement of the Workers by Stock Exchange Capitalists."

After an unsuccessful attempt at poultry farming near Munich, in early 1929 Himmler was appointed by Hitler to head his personal bodyguards, the Black Guard, which soon became the *Schutzstaffel*, the dreaded *SS*.

Now in charge of all concentration camps as well as a unified police system, Himmler was chief of all *Vaterland* security and undeniably the most feared man in Germany.

And he had asked to meet with Peter.

Full of pride and anticipation, Peter sat back on the rear canvas seat of the Horch as the big vehicle rolled over a stone bridge and turned left down a road lined with tall poplar trees along the river on the left side and a tall slope up to Wewelsburg on the right.

As its big 8-cyclinder engine pulled the Horch up the steep incline to the castle's entrance, Peter reflected on his own good fortune.

The sale of a few gold trinkets from the lost Mayan temple had provided him with enough funds to pay off his native hires and book passage to Italy. Following a long train ride into Germany, he had arrived in Munich in late May. Immediately, he had contacted Himmler's office in Berlin.

Knowing of the *SS* chief's avid interest in the occult, Peter had thought there would be an instantaneous response to his report concerning the Skull of Fate.

But in practice, things moved quite slowly at first. There were several unproductive conversations with underlings, but once they reported Peter's find to their chief, Himmler had agreed to a meeting.

It was June 4th before the meeting was arranged in the Berlin Chancellery of Adolf Hitler. Peter had acquired a brand-new pinstriped suit and looked quite the gallant as he was escorted through the massive hallways by black-clad *SS* guards. He clutched the leather satchel containing his gift to the *Führer* tightly against his chest.

He clutched it so tightly that one suspicious *SS* sergeant had demanded an inspection of the case. One glance inside and the thick-faced guard had blanched, his eyes growing wide in astonishment. A nearly imperceptible shudder coursed through the man's shoulders as he hurriedly closed the satchel's cover flap over its remarkable contents and waved Peter on.

Peter had been so awestruck at the magnificence of the ornate and *swastika*-festooned rooms of the Chancellery that he was actually disappointed to find himself being escorted outside into a courtyard. In the center, a group of men stood talking around a sleek silver metallic sports car.

As he approached, a slender man also dressed in *SS* black turned to greet him. Piercing blue-gray eyes peered at him through small pince-nez glasses perched on a thin pointed nose.

"Ah, *Herr* Manteuffel, so good you could join us," the man said in an amiable but impersonal tone.

"The pleasure is all mine, *Herr Reichsführer* Himmler," replied Peter with a slight bow of his head and click of his heels.

A smile came over the tight face of Himmler. He pulled a small handkerchief from his pants pocket and stood cleaning his eyeglasses, all the while making a survey of Peter.

"I see you recognize me. Most people do these days. I sometimes think Propaganda Minister Goebbels may have overdone things." his small mustache curled upward with his smile. Replacing his glasses, he said in a business-like tone, "I understand that you have something of interest for me." His eyes shifted to Peter's leather case.

"Actually, *Herr Reichsführer,* I have something for our *Führer,* "said Peter in a respectful, yet resolute, tone. He was well aware of the competitive relationship between Himmler and Hitler, especially when it came to esoteric matters.

Obviously, somewhat taken aback, Himmler huffed, "Yes, well, let me introduce you to these gentlemen."

The *SS* chief began rattling off the names of the group of men by the sleek racing car and Peter shook each hand in turn. But their names went in one ear and out the other. He was more interested in the object of their attention.

A small one-seater with a long bullet-shaped body, the racer sat close to the ground. Its pointed hood was set off by a large Mercedes emblem and perforated with air vents. With its wire wheels and un-adorned aluminum body, it was the epitome of a speed racer. One bystander laughingly remarked that its lack of paint and varnish actually increased its speed.

But Peter was even more interested in the slightly built figure bending over the open hood of the car and peering intently at the 1.5-litre V8 engine.

It was his *Führer,* Adolf Hitler, arguably the most powerful man in the entire world. In his wildest dreams, Peter had never thought he might meet this great man face to face. His knees were weak and it was all he could do to keep his lips from trembling.

Seemingly unaware of the conversations about him, Hitler raised his head and said to no one in particular, "This is German creativeness at its finest." Peter saw that he was dressed simply in a brown double-breasted tunic. Its only adornments were the ubiquitous *swastika* arm-band, his Nazi Party pin and the Iron Cross and Wound Badge Hitler wore with pride from his service in the last war.

Hitler stood staring into space, lost in thought and talking to him-self. Peter edged closer to catch his words.

"Just imagine," Hitler said with awe in his voice, "a motor car that can reach speeds of more than 200 miles per hour. It's just too perfect. It's exactly what is needed in the New Order. Modern man with mod-ern machines." He shook his head in sudden appreciation.

Several of the men had stopped talking and were listening intently to their *Führer*'s words.

"At speeds such as this, a man does not have time to think, but only to react. His basic Aryan instincts take control. It is the perfect example of the type of modern man that National Socialism hopes to achieve. He survives by the sheer power of his will and innate abilities. A man whose base emotions, rather than any puny and convoluted intellectual application, will bring him triumph in all areas of life. This is the type of man that we will fashion in the coming years. This is the kind of person that will populate the greater *Reich*. A person born of new technology, freed from the restraints of past ignorance and superstition, a man who will react intelligently to orders and never bother to think for himself."

Hitler's voice was rising and one of his aides, Peter believed it to be his Chief of Staff Martin Bormann, moved to distract his *Führer*. It was still morning and no one present was in the mood for one of the *Führer*'s lengthy philosophical tirades.

"Gentlemen," the man believed to be Bormann said in a loud voice, "I think we can all agree that this car, the Mercedes W165, will once again show the world the perfection of German engineering."

"Hear, hear," the cry arose. Even Hitler was caught up in the pride of the moment. He stood beaming in the midst of the applause.

A small man in a double-breasted suit whom Peter vaguely recalled worked for the huge Mercedes plant in Stuttgart shouted with enthu-siasm, "Our Mercedes Silver Arrow series has dominated the tracks at Tripoli, Monte Carlo and the Grand Prix since 1934. With our own

Hans Stuck at the wheel, we will continue to dominate the racing scene for many years to come."

"*Ja!*" exclaimed one beefy man in the uniform of the NSKK, the National Socialist Motor Corps. "Just after we bring down the curtain on that liar Churchill and his pathetic army of home guards!" A chorus of appreciative laughter rose from the small knot of men.

Still laughing, the group moved through large French doors into the Chancellery. Peter found himself taken by the arm and ushered into a large conference room as the rest of the entourage moved down a giant marble-floored corridor festooned with *swastika* banners and flags. His attendant was none other than Himmler and Peter was suddenly anxious about his remark concerning his gift being for Hitler alone.

But Himmler was quite cordial and even made glowing remarks about Peter's illustrious family. It was apparent that the man had not lost his respect for the aristocracy despite the National Socialist revolution.

As Peter was taking note of the elaborate candelabras lining the walls and the plush high-backed chairs, each emblazoned with an eagle clutching a *swastika*, a tall door opened and Hitler entered.

Walking purposefully to Peter, his eyes bright with anticipation, he seemed hardly the demon portrayed by the Western press. As he peered intently at Peter's satchel resting on the immense conference table, the man looked for all the world like a prim college professor who had just discovered a priceless artifact among some ancient debris.

"Well, *mein sohn*, I have heard glowing reports concerning you and what you found in the Yucatan. Might I have a look?" said Hitler in a soft but somewhat raspy voice.

"Most certainly, *mein Führer!*" replied Peter, straightening himself abruptly. He bent, opened the satchel and withdrew the object inside.

Both Hitler and Himmler leaned forward, their eyes bright with awe and appreciation as Peter lifted the Skull of Fate out with both hands and placed it on the conference table.

Perhaps it was a trick of the morning light streaming in through the tall windows, but Peter thought a strange yellowish glow played across the faces of the two observers. No one spoke for some time as the energy of the skull seemed to spread out into the room bringing each man's senses into razor-sharp clarity. A palpable aura of energy flooded the room.

Even Peter, who had sat and admired the skull nearly every night since leaving Central America, felt a strange, awesome power emanating from the artifact as it sat in the midst of this large room covered with Nazi symbolism. It was the same energy he had first experienced upon viewing the skull in its pyramidal resting place in the Yucatan.

Peter had served his Fatherland well thus far in spite of the meddling of his American companions. He thought of Jim and Giselle, but only briefly. They were of no consequence in the grand scheme of things. Now was the time for him to benefit from the skull's power. He noticed Hitler's total fixation on the artifact and guessed that his *Führer* could also perceive the energy emanating from it. It was as though the powerful skull was prepared to aid whoever provided its deliverance.

"This will nearly complete my collection," Hitler muttered, placing his hands on the skull. "When this skull is combined with the Holy Lance and the Grail Cup, nothing can stop the New Order." He turned and looked at Peter, a look of absolute gratefulness in his piercing eyes. Placing one hand on Peter's shoulder, he said seriously, "*Mein sohn*, you have no concept of how your accomplishment will aid your Fatherland in fulfilling its destiny."

Peter stood silently, stunned by what he suddenly saw as his rightful place in the world, in the grand scheme of things. He had made history. The door to his true destiny had finally opened.

"Perhaps, *mein Führer*, we should keep this stored with the other artifacts at Wewelsburg," interjected Himmler. There was an almost pleading note in his voice. His eyes were wide and round behind his small glasses and it was obvious that he too coveted the mystical skull.

"No!" Hitler snapped, turning on Himmler. "We will not go through all this again, Heinrich. I am well aware of your interests and concerns. But the skull will remain with me in Berchtesgaden. I allowed you to keep the Holy Lance for a time so you could make a copy to display at your castle. That should satisfy you."

He made a snorting sound and smiled, "I doubt very seriously if even our most skilled forgers could duplicate this." He took the skull and held it close to his face, which appeared to glow in the reflected light. He stood there for several minutes as though entranced.

Himmler finally motioned to Peter and they both withdrew from the room leaving the German dictator alone with what Peter felt was one of the most powerful objects in the world.

Following Hitler's receipt of the Skull of Fate, progress in the war seemed to speed up exponentially.

Within days, the French defenses along a hastily prepared defensive position south of the Somme known as the Weygand Line had crumbled. Despite heroic and desperate fighting by the French *poilus*, the German *panzers* broke into open country and fanned out through the French countryside. The rapidity of the French collapse cemented Peter's belief in the power of the skull.

Following the surrender in late June, the upper half of France was placed under a German-controlled government headed by Marshal Henri Pétain, seated at the famed mineral water producing city of Vichy.

It was during this time that Peter had been rewarded with a commission in the *SS* and attached to a branch known as the *Ahnenerbe*. Created in the mid-1930s, the *Ahnenerbe-SS* was tasked with providing the scientific, archeological and anthropological evidence to support the theories of the Nazi leadership and its hidden mentors within the Thule Society. He was even presented with one of the enigmatic rings of sapphire set inside a ruby with diamond points and emblazoned with a Germanic rune which identified *Ahnenerbe* members to each other. The gold ring itself was covered with various esoteric symbols, many similar to those found in certain Masonic orders.

Then in late September, despite no clear victory over the British, Peter and others within the *SS* saw further proof of Hitler's unconquerable power granted by the mystical artifacts he possessed.

On September 23rd, Radio Berlin announced that French General Charles De Gaulle and a fleet of troop transports escorted by British warships had arrived at the West African port of Dakar. Apparently, de Gaulle had expected to be warmly welcomed by the French forces there and must have been greatly chagrined when the officer he sent ashore to deal with Vichy officials was shot and wounded. Despite a bombardment that lasted until ammunition stores ran out, De Gaulle and the British were forced to withdraw having accomplished nothing except providing the Germans with a propaganda coup and further animosity between Britain and Vichy France.

Peter had entered this new stage of his life with a buoyant feeling of anticipation and pride. Now he could apply his education and expertise to the greater good of the Fatherland. He was in constant attendance at the diplomatic soirées and party dress balls in Berlin. He reveled in his newfound popularity and authority and was rarely seen without a beautiful woman on his arm.

And this day, he had been asked to visit Himmler, his commander, at the Wewelsburg castle. He knew that the *SS* chief was genuinely grateful and impressed by his discovery and delivery of the Skull of Fate, so there was no concern that this summons was anything but even greater opportunity. Still, Peter couldn't imagine why Himmler would ask for him personally.

The question continued to puzzle him as the *Horch* ground to a halt in the courtyard entrance to Wewelsburg. "I guess I'll know soon enough," thought Peter as he watched an entourage of *SS* troopers and aides rushing out to greet his arrival.

As Peter entered the large wooden doors of the castle, he was met by Himmler himself. Dressed immaculately in his stylish black wool *SS* uniform with its silver piping, the *Reichsführer* was in a gregarious mood as he led Peter along a lengthy corridor flanked on both sides by a phalanx of *swastika*-laden flags mixed with ancient banners and rune-covered tapestries.

Waving one hand expansively, Himmler said, "This was all in ruins when I first came here in 1934. It cost a small fortune to restore its greatness, let me tell you. But I was able to cut costs by using concentration camp labor. Of course, you have to watch them like a hawk. Those people have no sense of pride in their work.

"But, look at it now, a monument to both the heritage and the future of the New Order. A National Socialist temple and shrine for the study and reverence of the bloodline and the ethics of honor. It contains a library with more than 12,000 volumes on Aryan lore and history. The dining room alone is more than 1,000 feet long."

"I have heard," interjected Peter, contributing a bit of common gossip, "that this dining room contains a round table similar to the one used by the legendary King Arthur."

Himmler gave out a short laugh. "Yes, it's true. I have patterned the rebirth of the Teutonic Knights after Arthur's Knights of the Round Table. And don't believe the ignorant skeptics. King Arthur was no legend. Just as the story of Excalibur is no mere myth. Come, I will show you."

The two men came to a stone stairway that spiraled downward inside the gigantic multi-tiered North Tower to a huge subterranean chamber. Although shaded lamps cast illumination at intervals all along the walls, light in the great hall remained dim due to its immensity. Large fluted windows slanting upward well past ground level allowed further light but failed to brighten the vast circular hall appreciably. Overhead, the domed gray brick ceiling arched toward a large *swastika* inlaid in the masonry. The grand and cyclopean proportions of the place awed Peter.

In the center was a large circular area made of dark green marble sunk into the rock floor. Surrounding the circle and placed against the stone walls were 12 round pedestals.

"This is the final resting place for heroes. I call it the Supreme Leaders' Hall," Himmler said with great reverence in his voice.

"You mean our *Führer*," gasped Peter, astonished that Himmler would have a final resting place for Hitler already prepared.

Himmler gave out a thin, high-pitched giggle. "No, no, my young friend. The *Führer* is just fine. This is the hall of leaders, plural, the cream of our Black Order.

"You see these 12 pedestals here. When a ranking *SS* leader dies, he is cremated in the pit and his ashes are placed in an urn which then rests on one of the pedestals."

"Of course, I see," stammered Peter with some embarrassment.

Himmler seemed unaware of Peter's discomfort as he continued to rhapsodize about the rituals of his Order of the Death's Head.

"After the successful conclusion of this war, we will continue to build up our Order. We *Alte Kameraden*, the old veterans, will see that it remains youthful, strong and revolutionary as we march into the future. It will provide the leadership elite that will unite our people and, in fact, a union of all Europe."

Himmler's eyes had taken on a dreamlike stare, as if his inner being was looking directly into that future of which he spoke. Shaking himself into the consciousness of the moment, he turned to Peter.

"Peter, my young friend, you have much to learn. Our Order stems from that of the Teutonic Knights, a powerful and wealthy organization founded by the legendary Knights Templar many centuries ago. We are the inheritors of their secret knowledge, knowledge that will make Germany the master of the world.

"Come, I have something to show you."

The *Reichsführer* took Peter by the shoulder and guided him to a nearby alcove, so cleverly concealed that he had not noticed it when they first entered the chamber.

With the flip of a switch, a small light came on revealing a large broadsword resting upright with its tip held firmly in a wooden block.

"Excalibur!" said Himmler triumphantly, with a flourish of his right hand.

Peter was astonished. "Do you mean this is the actual sword, *Herr Reichsführer*? It is not just a myth?"

Himmler was beaming. "*Ja, ja*, my young friend. It is as real as you or I. Its reputation is one of possessing great strength while at the same time defying gravity. We concluded this legend was based on it incredibly light weight. Our experts believe it is made from titanium although they cannot explain how such a sword could have been made more than a thousand years before this metal was discovered. But come, you haven't seen anything yet."

The SS chief was obviously enjoying presenting his collection to a new admirer. He ushered Peter to another nearby alcove.

There in a long, upright and elaborately carved case was what appeared to be an ancient spear. Himmler turned a switch and two small spotlights illuminated the case bringing out every detail of the relic.

It was a spear point more than a foot long, the blade and the shaft held together by a silver sheath. Peter noticed a sliver of metal in the center of the blade and recalled that according to legend a nail from the crucifixion of Christ had been inserted sometime in the distant past. It was fastened by gold, silver and copper threads. The entire spearhead was fixed to the shaft by threads passing through holes in the blade. The base was embossed with gold crosses.

Peter was dumbfounded. "*Mein Gott*! Is this the…" he began.

Swelling with pride, Himmler interrupted, "*Ja*, but of course. This is the *Heilige Lance*, the Spear of the Roman centurion Longinus, the fabled Spear of Destiny."

Without taking his eyes from the relic, Peter intoned the words of the famous prophecy about the spear, "Whoever possesses this Holy Lance and understands the power it serves, holds in his hand the destiny of the world for good or evil."

"I see you really do know your history," said Himmler. He was clearly appreciative of Peter's knowledge.

"But just a moment," said Peter halting in his move toward the other alcoves. "*Herr Reichsführer*, I thought the Spear of Destiny, along with the Imperial Austrian treasures, the *Reichkleinodien*, was in the Treasure House of the Hofburg Museum in Vienna."

Himmler sniggered. He said with a smirk, "They were and now they are here."

"But, *Herr Reichsführer*," Peter continued, "I recall the *Führer* said that you had a replica. Is this the replica?"

Himmler's eyes flashed with irritation. "Yes, yes, it is the replica. The *Führer* wanted the Lance for himself. But it really doesn't matter, does it? What is good for the *Führer* is good for Germany, isn't it?"

"*Jawohl, Herr Reichsführer*," Peter almost shouted as he snapped to attention. He realized that his question had annoyed the one man who had done so much for him.

Changing the subject, Himmler motioned Peter to another corner of the round chamber.

"Now, I would like to show you these." He indicated more partially hidden alcoves in the huge chamber.

Peering into the gloom, Peter noted, "But they are empty."

Again smiling, Himmler put an arm around Peter's shoulders and replied, "That's right. And do you know what will be displayed there soon?"

"No, *Herr Reichsführer*," responded Peter with unconcealed puzzlement.

His voice approaching a whisper, Himmler pointed to each alcove in turn. "There will rest the Emerald Grail cup and there the Ark of the Covenant. Here will be Moses' Tablets of Testimony. Over there will repose the Sword and Harp of King David, there the Sacred Candelabra and the Urn of the Manna along with many other ancient and sacred objects."

Peter's mind was swirling. "But, those items have been lost for centuries. No one knows where they might be or even if they still exist," he blurted.

The slight smile never left Himmler's face. Squeezing Peter's shoulder, he said in a low tone, "That's where you come in, my young friend. With information that I have collected coupled with your demonstrable expertise in locating and securing such prizes, I have decided that you, Peter Freiherr von Manteuffel, can best serve the *Reich* by obtaining the fabled lost Treasure of King Solomon."

Peter stood speechless. Himmler merely smiled and confided, "You see, my young friend, this is the greatest treasure in the history of the world. With such wealth in our hands, the *Reich* will be unstoppable, our destiny assured."

Peter could think of nothing to say as the *SS* chief walked him back toward the spiral stairway.

The remainder of the Wewelsburg castle tour, the subsequent elaborate dinner and the continued conversation concerning holy relics and lost manuscripts were later just a blur to Peter, who remained in a state of shock following his commander's fantastic mandate.

How was he to locate a treasure that so many others had failed to find? Did it even really exist? And what terrible consequences would follow if he failed?

CHAPTER 4

GISELLE LAY IN THE TOUSLED sheets and played with the priest collar while occasionally glancing lovingly at the sleeping form of Michel beside her.

She rolled toward him slightly, pulling the white sheet up in the process to reveal the small reddish rose-shaped birthmark on her right thigh. She smiled recalling how Michel had mentioned the mark shortly after they made love, evidence that he had not forgotten any aspect of her body in the long years they were separated.

His long, dark wavy hair, slight build and smooth, white untanned skin were exactly as she remembered. Although Michel did not have an obvious athletic build, Giselle knew from their dance experience that he had a strength and agility far surpassing most men.

Flicking the collar aside, she leisurely reached to the nightstand for the small green pack of Lucky Strike cigarettes. Lighting one, she pulled herself up onto the large down pillow and inhaled deeply. She thought how she could now return to the small and slender *Gitanes* French cigarettes that she favored. She had carried a few cartons to British Honduras but they were long gone. She had purchased several cartons of Luckies before embarking for Europe, knowing full well that quality tobacco in wartime Europe would become increasingly scarce and would make for a valuable trade commodity.

It was amazing how being with Michel had caused the past six years to fade from view. It was as if those years, filled with college study, superficial men, archeological adventure and the horror of her return to the Yucatan, had only been some strange dream.

She slowly and languidly exhaled. How incredibly marvelous that so many miles away from the horrors of the Mayan temple she should find comfort in the arms of a past lover. While thoughts of Jim and revenge for his death had not diminished, intellectually she knew that life must go on. She and Jim had had an honest and open relationship and she knew that he would have approved of her sojourn with Michel.

She also now suspected that Michel just might be the very person to help her in her crusade against Hitler and his Nazi fanatics currently overrunning Europe.

Giselle crushed out the butt of her cigarette in an ashtray on the nightstand and rolled over onto Michel's prone form. He grunted slightly as her weight pressed down on him. She stretched herself out until their noses were almost touching.

"Are you asleep?" she whispered. Michel slowly raised his eyelids.

"I was until you woke me," he said with a grin that belied the mock irritation in his voice.

"But it's daylight," whimpered Giselle. She pursed her lips into a little girl's pout.

"Is there something that I must do?" muttered Michel, still groggy with sleep.

"Of course there is, silly. Me!" She laughed aloud with sheer joy. It was marvelous to finally rediscover joy and laughter within herself.

They clasped each other and rocked together in the over-large hotel bed. Michel propped himself on one hand. Looking down, he commented, "I see you still have that flower on your hip."

"Well it *is* a birthmark, you witless Frenchman," she replied in mock exasperation. Giggling, she added. "Would you like to rub it for good luck? I'll rub you."

Still giggling, she reached down into the sheets, probing for his manhood.

"Hey," he laughed, "can't we at least get some breakfast first?"

"Later." she chirped. "Just think of it as your day of fasting, father. From food anyway. *Viens ici, mon amour.*"

They both roared with the laughter that had begun the night before. They had only just arrived in Giselle's hotel room when Michel had confessed that the priest's frock was merely a disguise to prevent any serious interrogation by the Germans. This frank admission had swept away any hesitancy on her part and ushered in a night of intimacy.

Later, over a breakfast of eggs, a thin slice of bacon, croissants and coffee, Michel and Giselle compared notes on their lives since they parted more than six years before.

They talked of how Giselle had grown tired of the constant glare of publicity over her dance career and, despite the pleading of her Aunt Gez, had eventually returned to the United States to enter college.

"My interest in archeology and physical fitness quickly drew me to field expeditions," she said, after savoring the hot fresh coffee. "This led to an expedition in Central America where we made some amazing finds."

She glossed over the relationship she had with Jim during those adventures. She also hesitated to tell Michel about the Skull of Fate and her agenda against the Nazis. Although she knew Michel was a kindred spirit and would never side with the Fascists, she decided to hold back until she knew his situation better notwithstanding the fact that his priest disguise indicated he was already part of the struggle against the Nazi occupation. After all, these were troubled times and people all over the world were being forced to choose sides. Nations, cities, communities, even families were being torn apart.

"But enough about me," said Giselle as she replaced her demitasse in its saucer. "I want to hear about your life, every detail." She looked at him with adorning eyes. She was still luxuriating in the glow of their night together and her newfound love of life. Even her shoulder wound had not pained her much during their lovemaking.

Michel looked at her with sadness in his face. "This is such a terrible time for you to be here," he said seriously. "France is on her knees. Many people don't know which way to turn. If we support the British, the war could last for years and we will have to suffer under the Germans. If we side with the Germans, at least the war might be over sooner."

Giselle bristled at what she took for appeasement sentiments. Michel, noticing her scowl, quickly added, "Of course, all of us who value freedom are committed to fighting the invaders. I was only remarking on what certain people are saying."

Taking his hands in hers, Giselle looked deeply into his eyes. "Oh,

I hope so, Michel, for I too have committed myself to the fight for true freedom. I feel some responsibility for what is happening."

Michel was puzzled. "What on earth do you mean? You can't be responsible for Hitler and his aggression," he said, scoffing.

Giselle smiled. "I'm not sure you would understand. I'll tell you about it later. Right now I want to hear about you. You can tell me all about it as we take a morning stroll."

Paris in late September was beautiful. The weather had turned cool but the usual cold dampness of winter had not yet arrived. The trees were changing color and, despite the recent occupation, the city appeared normal to Giselle as she and Michel strolled among the large block-long gray buildings of the central city. Soft music drifted from the cafes along the boulevards.

Only a few telltale signs of war had intruded on the bustling city. There was, of course, the omnipresence of the Germans. Both officers and enlisted men wandered the city streets gawking at the department stores, fine restaurants and cinemas.

Most appeared to be smooth-faced young men who seemed more like farm boys on their first visit to the city than avaricious soldiers of a conquering army.

Many officers had a woman on their arm, some had sent for their wives, taking advantage of the chance for a romantic visit to Paris. Others were Parisian women eager to make friends with the new authorities or simply content to be with a man.

The propaganda from the last war had instilled much apprehension in the French public. They still feared that the Germans would loot the city, rape the women and kill innocent babies. When none of this occurred and the initial fear of the *Boche* subsided, life in the great city had returned to a semblance of normalcy in a surprisingly short time. However, the avenues were not as crowded as in the past. Many Parisians were staying close to their homes, taking a wait-and-see attitude.

Michel said that for a time, many people thought the French Army might rally and mount a counterattack on their enemies. But as the days stretched into weeks and numbers of soldiers, those who had escaped the prisoner of war camps, straggled into the city, it became obvious that, as far as the French were concerned, the war was lost.

The pair strolled slowly south along the *Rue Royale* toward the

Seine but turned left on the *Rue de Rivoli*, avoiding the *Place de la Concorde*, which was teeming with Germans.

Reaching a point where the Seine flowed along the *Quai de la Megisserie*, Michel purchased a bottle of sparkling water and joined Giselle on a wrought iron bench under a stand of trees. The sun was warm and it was hard to believe that this was a conquered city during wartime.

Looking deeply into her eyes, Michel said, "I'm glad we have this chance to talk alone. There is something very important I have to tell you.

"While I still have many friends and connections with the ballet, I no longer dance. When I failed to find the backing for my dance troupe, I returned to Chartres and managed to secure a position in the *préfet*'s office," explained Michel.

He smiled. "You know how my father was always trying to get me to follow him into civil service."

"Yes, although he never said so, I think he felt that ballet was no career for his son," said Giselle. "So you have made him a happy man."

"I hope so," replied Michel. He looked away. "He passed on two years ago."

"Oh, Michel, I am so sorry."

"No, it's all right. It is for the best. He had been in ill health and I don't think he could have lived working for the Germans.

"After he was gone, I grew restless and that is when I took a second job."

"Oh? And what is it you do now? A chicken farmer perhaps?" Giselle laughed, still slightly giddy from the marvelous night.

Michel smiled briefly at her exuberance but said quite seriously, "Giselle, listen to me. I am not wearing these priest's robes for some part on the stage. This is serious business. I am, or was, a member of the *Deuxième Bureau*."

Giselle gasped. "The Secret Police?"

"*Oui, ma chère,* the Secret Police. But I was not a usual policeman. I was more of an undercover agent, keeping tabs on enemies of the state. I would attend various meetings and file reports."

"It sounds dull," quipped Giselle. She was still trying to cope with the idea that her former dance partner was some kind of spy.

"Oh, no, *ma chère*, compared to my daily work as a city administrator, it was quite adventurous. And I always maintained contact with the society members close to the theater.

I've been working for them for almost two years now." He stopped and frowned. "Or perhaps I should say I was working for them. I was ordered to report to headquarters in Rouen on June 10th but I was just in time to help evacuate the offices. The city was burning and the Germans were all around. I was lucky to make it back to Paris without being taken prisoner.

"I don't know what to think now. I don't know who to trust. Many of the officers have gone over to the Germans. They think it is best for the future of France. After all, our so-called Allies are now all gone. Norway, Holland, Belgium, all conquered. And Britain looks like it will be next, even though they're not quitting. One has to admit, the situation appears grim."

Giselle was quite serious now. Her mind was racing with thoughts of what should be done.

Taking Michel's hands in hers, she said earnestly, "Oh, Michel, you know you can trust me. And more than that, you can help me. Or perhaps I should say I can help you and your cause. I think it is time for me to be totally honest with you. I know that you love France very much and would do anything for her."

"This is true, *ma petite*, I will never stop fighting until *la belle* France is free once again."

Michel, her dear Michel, was a member of the Secret Police and a patriotic Frenchman. How could she have thought otherwise? She gazed deeply into his soft dark eyes and a conviction grew within her.

"I must tell you something," she said. "Then you will understand. I need your help."

She smiled faintly at his look of puzzlement.

As they held hands, Giselle told Michel of her expedition to Mexico and British Honduras and of the extraordinary finds in the hidden Mayan temple. Her voice choked with emotion as she recounted the gun battle with Peter's henchmen, the death of Jim and Katrina and the theft of the Skull of Fate.

Michel's eyes grew wide at her account of jungle adventures, murder and stolen ancient treasures.

Burying her face in her hands, Giselle sobbed, "Oh, Michel, what am I to do? I feel responsible for all this misery. Hitler has the skull. I just know he does. And look what this power has given him. France, the very heart of civilization, has fallen in a matter of weeks. General de Gaulle tried to rally the French forces outside the country and his emissary is fired upon by his own people. Britain is almost on her knees. What have I done?"

Michel placed his arm around her shoulder and pulled her close saying, "*Ma chérie*, you must not blame yourself for all this. I have no idea if this talisman carries the power you say it does, but the fault is not yours. That is too much responsibility for any person. The world has gone mad and we simply must find our place in it."

"Thank you, Michel, thank you," she sobbed, kissing his hand over and over. One part of her knew that he was speaking the truth, yet another still held the terrible fear that in some way she and the skull were responsible for the horror loosed on the world. She wished she could totally reject the notion that the skull carried that much power. But it was difficult considering the strange dreams and sensations she experienced after its discovery.

She dabbed at her eyes with a handkerchief and looked squarely at Michel.

Her eyes now dry, Giselle said in a matter-of-fact manner, "I intend to retrieve the Skull of Fate and stop Hitler's monstrous plans."

For a moment, Michel felt like laughing at her audacity but one look at the grim determination in her eyes gave him pause. He knew Giselle well enough to know that once she set her mind to something, there would be no stopping her.

"Very well," said Michel in a serious tone as he grabbed her shoulders in both hands and held her upright before him. He was silent for several long moments as his mind worked to find a place for Giselle in his plans.

Michel appeared to make a decision. "Let's pull ourselves together and go for an aperitif. I have an important meeting scheduled soon and I want you to come with me," he said finally, rising to his feet. "I have no idea if what you have told me about the power of this stolen artifact is the truth but I have no doubts as to the sincerity of your conviction to fight the Germans."

The sun sank lower, casting long shadows over the houseboats and barges on the Seine and plunging *Notre Dame* into shadow. There was accordion music off in the distance as Michel, having cast off the priest disguise, strolled arm-in-arm with Giselle past the *Louvre* toward the garden of the *Tuileries*.

As they watched the last of the sun's rays disappear behind the

Paris skyline, Michel leaned close and whispered in a conspiratorial tone, "My darling, tonight I am to meet with my boss, the *préfet*. He is a true Frenchman. I can't wait to introduce you. In fact, we'd better get going. It's a long drive and we may have difficulty in obtaining a taxi.

"I believe he is a man that can help all of us."

Despite Michel's concern, there was no problem in finding a taxi and they arrived in Chartres in good order after a long, dark drive from Paris. The ancient gothic cathedral was visible in the gloom towering over the town, which sprawled along the hillside below.

Walking past the city hall, *La Mairie*, Michel guided them to a tall apartment building. Giselle was glad to see that it contained an antique lift that carried them to a third floor landing. Most people in Paris lived above the shops and offices on the street level and most had to climb stairs as few apartment buildings had elevators.

"This doesn't seem a very fashionable building for a *préfet*," commented Giselle, glancing at the fallen plaster and faded wallpaper in the lobby.

"Oh, he doesn't live here. This is merely a secure meeting place. *Préfets* know all the hidden away places in their city," said Michel. He touched his nose with one finger and winked.

As the aging elevator clanked its way upward, Michel spoke about his boss.

"Jean is a great fellow," Michel said. "He studied law at Montpellier and he's an excellent skier. We've made lots of ski trips together. But now he is an important figure. He became *sous préfet* of a government department back in 1925, the youngest person of that rank in French history.

"His political activities may be leftist but he is not a communist. He was a leader of the Popular Front and helped organize covert assistance to the Spanish Republicans during their struggle against Franco."

"Yes, I saw the effects of that struggle during my recent stay in Madrid," commented Giselle dryly.

Michel was warming to his subject. "I met Jean in 1937 when he became the chief administrator of the Eure-et-Loir Department, the youngest full *préfet* in the nation."

"Doesn't that department include Chartres?" asked Giselle with interest.

"But of course."

"My Aunt Gez has a château very near here," she effused. "That is where I am planning to stay once I have my papers in order."

A calculating look came over Michel's countenance. "This might work out well for all of us," he said with an enigmatic smile.

Returning to the subject at hand, he said, "But I really must tell you the rest of the story before we meet. He would be embarrassed at my telling it in front of him. During the *Sitzkrieg*, Jean joined Battalion 117 of the Air Force but was ordered to return to his political post after only two weeks. It was decided he was too valuable to waste in the military.

"He stayed at his post even after the *Boche* finished off our army. What a man he is, *ma chère*. I was there in mid-June when the German commandant came to our office and demanded that Jean sign a document stating that civilians had been murdered by our Senegalese troops. It was a preposterous charge and Jean refused to sign."

The creaking lift came to a halt and Michel pulled open the metal grill door. As the couple stepped out onto the landing, he stopped Giselle with a hand on her arm and turned her to face him. His eyes were moist and sparkling with the intensity of his emotion. It was clear that Michel was fully devoted to his chief.

"Giselle, *ma petite*, Jean was *très magnifique*. And what a terrible price he paid. A short time later a squad of *Boche* soldiers showed up at the office and beat him unmercifully. They offered to stop if he would sign the document, but still he refused. I feared they would kill him right then and there and was about to intercede when he took a knife and tried to cut his own throat."

Giselle cringed. "My God, *c'est horrible!*"

"Yes, but it worked. After some further beating, the Germans left him for dead. I hid him in my apartment for several days. Then guess what?"

Giselle was wide eyed at this description of such brutality. "What?" she mouthed quietly.

"He returned to the office and has continued his duties as *préfet*. He told me he would continue to try and protect the citizens against these swine."

"My God, what bravery. Have they come for him again?"

"Not yet, but I fear it's only a matter of time. I think this is the purpose of our secret meeting tonight. Here's the apartment."

Michel stopped in front of a large door, distinctive only for its peeling olive paint, and rapped three times in quick succession.

the $istec$ood of the $ose

The door opened immediately as if the person behind it had anticipated Michel's knock. Stepping into an aging and threadbare apartment furnished only with a small writing desk and two antique chairs, Giselle took stock of the man closing the door behind them.

He was of slight build but was dressed quite nattily in a double-breasted suit with wide pin stripes. His solid black necktie was immaculately bound into a single Windsor knot. His dark hair was slicked back with the pomade that was the current fashion. His face was round and ordinary but his large dark round eyes reflected intelligence and even humor.

Despite traces of bruises still on his face, the man was smiling and appeared to be in high spirits.

"*Monsieur Préfet*, may I present an old friend, *Mademoiselle* Giselle Tchaikovsky. We danced together in the ballet years ago," announced Michel with an elegant sweep of his hand. "Giselle, this is my employer and my friend, the honorable Jean Moulin."

"But of course, of course," cried Jean exuberantly. "I watched you on the stage of *l'Opera*. Who could forget such grace and beauty?"

"You are too kind, *Monsieur Préfet*," replied Giselle graciously.

"Not at all, not at all, *ma chère*. And please just call me Jean." Turning to Michel, he said in mock chastisement, "Michel, you never mentioned that you knew a famous *danceuse*. You have been holding out on me."

Michel was embarrassed. "Well, sir, the truth is that I have not spoken much about the past. Some things are best kept to one's self."

He looked at Giselle with a contrite expression. She returned it with a slight smile of understanding. Her past affection for Michel was now fully awakened after their afternoon of bearing souls to each other.

Sensing that there was something deep and private between the two, Jean quickly changed the subject. "I apologize, but I have only the two chairs. I was not expecting company. Please be seated. I will stand."

Knowing that it was pointless to argue with such politeness, Giselle sat in one of the chairs while Michel took the other.

Jean moved to the small writing stand which was illuminated by a solitary old corkscrew metal lamp with its shade askew, he snatched up a piece of paper and proudly showed it to Michel.

"See here, Michel, my latest creation. I think I will try to get it published."

Michel looked at the paper while Giselle leaned toward him and peered over his shoulder.

It was a cartoon depicting the aging Marshal Pétain as a puppet dancing at the end of strings being pulled by an outlandish caricature of Hitler. A caption read, "Pétain's jig of victory." It was an obvious reference to Allied propaganda showing a jubilant Hitler dancing a jig at the signing of the French armistice at Compiègne.

Giselle remembered how she had taken the newsreel footage at face value until a well-connected friend had informed her that the effect was achieved long after the fact in a film studio by repeating a single stamp of the *Führer*'s foot over and over.

She complimented the *préfet* on his artistic talent, but it was Michel who voiced the irritating question.

"And just who would publish such a thing?" he asked.

Jean scowled and shrugged. "I don't know, perhaps the communists?"

"Don't you think you have caused enough trouble, sir? Your wounds are barely healed. You must think of yourself," said Michel with solicitude. He paused and added, "And the future."

Jean Moulin's handsome face darkened. "Actually, Michel, I am thinking of the future. I don't know how much longer I can remain here in France. My conscience won't allow me to work with the Germans and you see what happened when I resisted their orders. I've been thinking of going to England and offering my services to Charles de Gaulle."

"Charles de Gaulle?" Michel was taken aback. "But de Gaulle's politics are not your politics. You know that the international financiers have his ear."

"I know that, Michel," Jean said in a placating tone. "But de Gaulle is willing to fight and right now, France desperately needs men like him. I would even follow Maurice de Rothschild if it meant freeing my beloved France."

"Rothschild? What's he got to do with it?" asked Giselle. She was only vaguely aware that the Rothschild banking family had been the power behind several European thrones for many years.

"But, of course, you don't know, do you my dear," answered Jean. "Few people know this but according to my sources, just after the Germans invaded in May, Maurice de Rothschild, the son of Edmond, arranged a secret meeting at the Ritz Hotel in Paris.

"It involved Prime Minister Paul Reynaud and Minister of War

Georges Mandel, whose real name is Rothschild though the claim is that there was no relation to the banking family. They met with Churchill and Anthony Eden to determine the future of France.

"I might add that de Gaulle was also present and within a month had organized the French government-in-exile in London, obviously with the blessing of the power brokers."

Giselle was astonished. "My God, you make it sound like some kind of brokered business deal."

Jean Moulin only smiled and shrugged his shoulders. "Wars come and go but business goes on," he replied. "I may be a republican and somewhat of a radical, but I am also a realist. I shall commit myself to whoever can free my beloved France."

"But how do you propose to get to England?" asked Michel, obviously concerned about the fate of his friend and mentor. "As you well know, I have been pulling double duty, working for the Secret Police on the side. I think I can arrange passage to England but it will take a substantial amount of money. I have none and you have none and the Germans have impounded the treasury. It will be months before they sort things out and we are able to put our hands on government funds."

"This is indeed the problem, *mon ami*, where can we find the money?" muttered Jean. "Few boat captains are willing to risk running into German E-boats in the English Channel just out of the goodness of their heart."

"I have money," said Giselle quietly. Again, Michel saw in her eyes a look of determination that was not to be swayed by argument.

Giselle inwardly was jubilant. For the first time, she saw how she could contribute to the struggle against the Nazis.

Both men turned to look at her, Jean with renewed respect.

"No, *ma chérie*," said Michel quickly. He rose to his feet. "I cannot ask you to get involved in this. It is too dangerous, even for someone on an American passport."

"He's right, my dear, I appreciate your thought but this is something that we must work out for ourselves," said Jean in a patronizing tone.

Giselle stepped back and glared at both men. "Look here, you heroes, did Hitler concern himself with nationalities, gender or station in life when he launched his invasions?

"I have performed in Europe's capitals, traveled the world, survived tropical jungles and you want to talk to me about danger? I came here to perform a mission and you have shown me where to start. I have money, my aunt has money and my family has money. Money is the easiest way I know to launch my crusade against Hitler.

"And I will not be aiding you for nothing, *Monsieur* Moulin," she added with a shrewd look on her face. "I expect you to help me in my quest for a Nazi who has something that belongs to me."

"Just any Nazi?" asked Jean. Sarcasm was thick in his words.

"No," replied Giselle calmly, "It is a very special one, one who has brought a powerful talisman to Hitler. It may well be responsible for the defeat of this country."

Jean stared at her dumbfounded as though he could not believe the woman was serious.

"Do you really expect me to locate a man who must be close to the German *Führer*?"

Giselle smiled. "No, Jean, I don't suppose I could ask that. But I do need to meet someone with a working knowledge of occult matters, for it is in that area that I think I will find the person I seek."

Jean smiled broadly. "Ah, then I think I have just the man for you. He teaches at the Sorbonne."

Summoning her most businesslike tone, Giselle said, "There, it's all settled. You connect me with this man and make the necessary contacts for transportation to England and I will provide the money. And if need be, I can hide Jean at Aunt Gez's château until it is all arranged."

Both men looked at each other in stunned silence then burst out laughing. Giselle felt anger boiling up within her.

It must have shown in her face for Michel quickly explained, "*Ma chérie*, do not take offense. We both realize that you are quite a determined woman and, frankly, we can use your help, perhaps in more ways than money."

"Yes, *mon amie*," agreed Jean, "we only laughed at your obstinacy, not your intent. We Frenchmen know that when a woman has her mind made up, it is useless to argue. We accept your generous offer with all due gratefulness." He made a slight bow.

Giselle smiled in spite of herself at this demonstration of gentlemanly concession.

"Now," said Jean in a more serious tone, "Most people think Britain is finished. But according to information I have received, this is far from the truth. Damage has been extensive, particularly in central London.

But the Germans have made a fatal error.

"At the beginning of the air battle in July, *Luftwaffe* bombing raids had almost crippled British defenses. But then those idiots in Berlin decided that indiscriminate bombing of population centers would destroy the English will to fight. Instead, the incensed English are more united under Churchill than ever before. Better yet, these uncoordinated attacks on London and other areas have left England's war production facilities largely intact. I understand that more than 95 percent of the factories necessary for the war effort have survived the *Blitz*."

"But if Britain survives and continues to fight, the war could drag on for years," bemoaned Michel.

"That's right and this is what has divided our people. At least half the population views a German victory as the only hope for peace for many years.

"Others, like myself, are willing to aid the British in any way possible. We know that true peace can never come about as long as one German soldier remains within our borders. It is time we all make our choice." Jean began pacing.

"My choice is made," he said in a voice full of conviction. "I have been thinking it over and I realize that mere lack of cooperation with the Germans is not enough. We must form secret fighting units to actively combat the occupation forces. And even that is not enough. To be truly effective, we must coordinate our efforts with our British allies. We must begin devising plans to mount a meaningful resistance to this beastly occupation."

Giselle's eyes shone with inspiration. Her mouth and jaw set in firm resolution. "Resistance. Yes, that's it," she muttered, thinking that a resistance could be also useful in learning the whereabouts of Peter and the skull.

"Yes, I think I have found my role," she said with determination. "I will help you mount an internal resistance to *Herr* Hitler's plans for a New World Order."

Both Jean and Michel looked at each other in mock alarm. After a long moment of silence with both men staring solemnly at Giselle, Jean Moulin smiled and spoke to Michel, "I think *Herr* Hitler is in big trouble."

CHAPTER 5

Paris,
October, 1940

WHILE FRANCE LAY A DEFEATED and divided nation, in the days following their reunion, events moved rapidly in the war and for Giselle and Michel.

Although Radio Berlin would never admit it, the Battle of Britain had been lost. Proud England still stood defiantly in Hitler's path to world conquest, bloodied but unbowed, while thousands of German aircraft and crews lay in wreckage strewn from London to their airfields in France.

Giselle and Michel regularly listened to the BBC and were thrilled by the heroic defense of England by a mere handful of British airmen together with Poles, Frenchmen and even a few Americans. But they had to keep their feelings carefully concealed in public as listening to British radio had been outlawed by the authorities.

The German Army stood impotently on the French beaches, its grand plan for an invasion of England, Operation *Sealion*, quietly and indefinitely postponed by Hitler in mid-September following the humiliating defeat of his much vaunted *Luftwaffe*.

Near the end of September, it was announced that Japan had joined the Rome-Berlin Axis, a military pact forged between Hitler and Mussolini in 1939. Seeing the handwriting on the wall, the smaller nations of Hungary, Bulgaria, Romania, Slovakia and Croatia reluctantly

the Sisterhood of the Rose

joined, becoming mere satellites to the *Reich*. Giselle and Michel were appalled as Germany divided Romania with Hungary and thereby gained control over the vital Ploesti oil fields.

Even Giselle's homeland of America was edging closer to the conflict. On October 16th, more than 16 million men were registered for the first draft instituted since a balky Congress had grudgingly agreed to national conscription in 1917.

Preparations to reopen her Aunt Gez's country estate, *Château les Fleurs*, were nearly completed and Giselle prepared to move out of her hotel suite to the comfortable accommodations near Chartres.

Revisiting the old estate had brought back memories of the wonderful parties and weekend guests. But most of all, the château was a constant reminder of Aunt Gez. Giselle wished she had daily access to her aunt, with her knowledge concerning social etiquette and diplomacy.

Her aunt had married into the old and prestigious French St. Clair family just after the turn of the century. The death of her husband, Henri St. Clair, had left her self-sufficient and well connected. She also was left the *Château les Fleurs*. She had not visited the château since the early 1930s when she and Giselle had used the estate as home base during the dance tours.

The château was located down a long country lane just off the highway to Paris. It had been built by an André St. Clair in 1698 on the site of a much earlier structure said to be a religious center of the Canutes, a Celtic tribe dedicated to the worship of the Mother Goddess.

Located near the Eure River, the sprawling two-story estate was surrounded by an elaborate system of parks, which in the spring produced a colorful kaleidoscope of flowers, vines and hedges. From this annual array of beautiful and bountiful flora came its name, Château of the Flowers.

A long narrow driveway branched off the country lane and led to a large circular drive in front of the château, which encompassed two large wings flanking the main structure to form an inverted "U" shape. In the center of the drive's circle was a large round pool almost totally covered with lily pads. The tall, slanting blue roof was studded with brick chimneys and gabled windows flanked by white painted shutters. Large French doors set between tall columns served as the front entrance and opened directly onto the gravel drive.

Inside were numerous rooms, most long closed to conserve both heat and maintenance. Giselle had decided to make her living quarters in the east wing, so as to better catch the warmth of the morning sun. Two large windows looked out onto the well-landscaped garden stretching away for several acres from the house. It was a magnificent view.

She had spared no expense in having the spacious grounds well attended, a gesture which also was designed to ingratiate her to the locals. Since the arrival of the Germans, work was scarce and money hard to come by.

Giselle recalled with great fondness the idyllic days she and Aunt Gez had spent there in the early 1930s during her dance career. She remembered the days boating on the Eure, idly reading under large leafy trees and the exciting afternoons listening to her aunt tell of her fabulous adventures as they strolled through the manicured gardens.

Although born American, Aunt Gez had a thoroughly European outlook, thanks to her total devotion to her late husband, Henri St. Clair. Having lived on the Continent for many years, she always had the right answer to Giselle's questions regarding etiquette, manners and social responsibilities. In light of the German occupation, she was thankful that Aunt Gez had not married into a Jewish family as her sister, Giselle's mother, had.

After her years of study and archeological adventures, Giselle was looking forward to wintering at the large and hospitable château.

But one night over dinner in Giselle's hotel suite, Michel reminded her of one very large problem lying in her path. Such meals had become a safety precaution to avoid problems with the German authorities and their nightly curfew. The hotel suite was littered with her clothes and luggage in preparation for the move to the château.

Michel had been telling her how the pressure to conform to the new regime and its edicts was increasing within the *préfet*'s office. Both he and Jean Moulin were spending less time there and more time planning an organized resistance to the occupation.

"Yes," said Giselle with a sigh, "The world is rapidly choosing sides in this struggle between the free nations and the Axis partners. I have no doubts about which side Americans will choose. My countrymen might be neutrals at the moment but if push comes to shove, we'll side with Britain, no question about it."

"*Oui, ma chère*," Michel agreed gently, but added, "Therein lies the problem. What shall we do with you should America enter the war. You will become an enemy citizen. You will be on every German detainment list."

Giselle sat silently for a time. Michel was, of course, correct. In her haste to journey to France in hopes of somehow preventing Peter from delivering the Skull of Fate to Hitler, she had failed to consider this issue. While she had easily entered France as Giselle Tchaikovsky on her American passport, she knew that soon this might prove a problem. How could she protect herself should war come between the United States and the German *Reich*? Furthermore, how could she prevent the authorities from quickly identifying her once she became active against the regime?

Suddenly, she was inspired. "Michel, I have it," she said with excitement. "My aunt's name is also Giselle and neither of us has been here for more than six years. As a member of an old and well-known French family, she for some time has carried a dual citizenship, one in the States and one here. Why couldn't I simply become my aunt? I could be the wealthy Lady Giselle St. Clair. I could hire all new house servants, stay reclusive and no one would be the wiser. If need be, I can always add some makeup and perhaps a little padding."

"But, your citizenship papers and your passport…" Michel began to object.

With a knowing grin and eyes that reflected both adoration and slyness, Giselle leaned across the small lace-covered dining table and murmured, "Surely the *préfet*'s office could take care of such details?"

Michel was momentarily taken aback but quickly broke into a broad grin. He was now following her thought. "But of course, *ma chère*, I think that might be arranged." He too leaned forward and in a conspiratorial tone whispered, "I have friends in high places."

The couple laughed loudly and raised their champagne glasses in a toast.

"I have another brilliant idea too," said Giselle as they resumed their meal. "In the event that circumstances force you from your current position."

"Oh?" asked Michel as he tucked into a meal seemingly prepared with as much flavor and quality as any he'd had before the occupation, despite the Germans rationing supplies. "And what might that be?"

"You'll be my chauffeur!" she announced proudly.

Michel almost choked on his chicken. "A chauffeur? Never!" he finally managed to exclaim, the wound to his pride clearly expressed on his scowling face.

"Calm yourself, darling," replied Giselle placing one hand on his. "It would be perfect. We could change your name and the Germans would never think of looking for you as the driver of a country *dame*."

Squeezing his hand, Giselle stood and leaned across the small table placing a tender kiss on Michel's forehead. "And just think, *mon cher*, it would provide the perfect excuse for you to be constantly by my side."

Michel sat musing. Finally he gave a short laugh, "I don't know about the constantly being with you part," he said, adding in a more reflective tone, "but it would allow me freedom of movement, an attribute that might prove most beneficial if we are to create a resistance movement."

He smiled up at Giselle and said quietly, "I will think about it, *ma chère*." They completed their dinner with a digestif of Chartreuse, a pale-yellow brandy laced with aromatic herbs.

The gossip spread rapidly throughout Chartres. The Lady St. Clair had decided to return to her late husband's ancestral château until the current hostilities had ended. No one had seen the lady for years, not since she had lived there with her young American niece, the ballet prima donna. And even then, neither was in residence for long periods as they frequently were on tour.

The entire town was abuzz for several weeks as local craftsmen and groundskeepers were hired to renovate the château in preparation for her arrival. Maids, cooks and other servants were engaged. No one noticed that each was specifically asked if they had ever seen Lady St. Clair. Only one elderly woman claimed to have met *Madame*. Her application was declined.

By late October word circulated in the town that the lady had taken up residence in the château. It was also whispered that Lady St. Clair had become somewhat of a recluse. Hopes for social gatherings at the renovated château or a glimpse of the new resident dimmed and soon the townsfolk turned to other topics of gossip.

Giselle and Michel began laying the groundwork for a resistance organization against the German occupation. Modern short-wave radio equipment was secretly installed in the château along with a small cache of arms provided by some of Michel's Secret Service friends who were loyal to the De Gaulle government-in-exile.

All of this was placed in a sub-basement of the château. The entrance was cleverly concealed with a false wall that could slide open.

Late in the month, Giselle received a telephone call from Paris. Michel asked if she could meet with him and Jean Moulin at the *Vieux Logis*, a restaurant at the top of a steep hill near *Le Sacré Coeur*. Giselle recalled that it was well known for its Alsatian cuisine. Happy to have an excuse to leave the château after weeks of confinement, she arranged for a taxi.

Upon reaching the restaurant, Giselle found it a charming barn-like place decorated in a rural and rustic style. She also quickly noticed a table of German officers in a far corner loudly talking and lifting huge beer steins. Hurrying to the opposite side of the room, she found Jean Moulin waiting for her at a rear table. His back was against a wall nearly covered with a giant, but aging, poster of a glamorous dancer with a white cat holding a bottle and glass of the aperitif Quinquina Dubonnet. He was glancing about nervously. He stood as Giselle seated herself. "It's not like Michel to be late," he muttered, as much to himself as to Giselle.

For several minutes she and Jean discussed her move to the château near Chartres and possible avenues for recruiting additional members to their cause.

Over glasses of an excellent 1923 *Chambertin*, Jean warmed to his subject all the while glancing anxiously toward the restaurant's door for any sign of Michel.

"You realize that Michel has been ordered to remain in Paris and mount whatever resistance to the Germans that seems practical, *non?*" he said in a conversational manner. He did not notice the look of concern that crossed Giselle's features over the thought of her dear Michel putting himself at risk. But she had quickly recovered, feeling a momentary pang of guilt at placing her personal concerns above the good of the world.

Lowering her voice, she leaned toward Jean and said with great emotion, "I am prepared to help both you and Michel in any way possible to rid the earth of the Nazi vermin." Looking past Jean to some unseen vista, she added with vehemence, "Especially one certain piece of slime."

Jean, who had already caught the brunt of Nazi brutality himself, nodded in silent agreement, then spoke, "As terrible as it may seem, I am very happy to hear you say this. Now is not the time for consideration or correctness. Those of us who can see the situation clearly must begin working to free not only our beloved France but all the occupied countries.

"But we must be extremely careful. We can do no one any good if we are dead or locked away in a concentration camp. We must quickly identify those whom we can trust and those whom we cannot. We must pay careful attention to every detail of our plans and work closely with our allies."

Giselle was electrified by both his words and determination. She knew without any doubt that this was her true calling, her very reason for being who she was and where she was at that very moment. It was an inner knowledge born of intuition and certainty that no amount of intellectual contemplation could have mustered. She also sensed that this path would lead to Peter and the skull.

She was startled by a sudden movement as Michel sank into the chair beside her. He looked tired and harried.

"*Pardonnez-moi, mes amis*," he said quickly, "Sorry I'm late, but I thought I was being followed."

"You were followed," murmured Jean, his eyes narrowing as he stared past Giselle at a small man who had just entered the restaurant and was staring directly at the threesome.

She started to turn and look but stopped as Jean whispered urgently, "Do not turn around. Act as though nothing has happened."

Michel leaned forward and whispered quietly, "I only got a glimpse of the man, but I am afraid it is one of the detectives from the *Deuxième Bureau*."

"But then he is a Frenchman. Why would he follow you?" whispered Giselle with genuine puzzlement.

Michel took her hand in his and smiled. "Ah, *ma petite chou*, you are so fortunate to come from a country where there is no Secret Police. Many of my coworkers are simply skilled bureaucrats. They care not for whom they work as long as the pay and benefits are good. There are too many good detectives now working for the Germans. He may know, or at least suspect, that I am not a good collaborator.

"After all, they know I still work for you, Jean," he added, with a knowing glance at his boss.

"Well, what shall we do?" asked Giselle. She was becoming a bit frightened.

"Calm down," said Michel in a low voice. "Let's be certain what this is about."

Jean picked up his napkin and used it to cover his mouth. "He is at a table directly behind us. Pretend you are powdering your nose and describe him," he whispered through the cloth.

Slowly, Giselle retrieved a compact from the purse on the floor beside her and elaborately began to dab face powder on her nose and cheeks.

Glancing up from time to time, she whispered calmly, "He is a small man with dark hair parted in the middle. He has a rather small mustache and is wearing a blue serge suit that looks a size too small for him."

"Does he have a mole on the right cheek near his nose?" asked Michel.

"Yes," whispered Giselle.

Michel groaned, "*Mon Dieu*! It is exactly as I feared. This man knows no allegiance but to himself. What is he doing now?"

Giselle, who had been paying attention to Michel, looked up from her compact. "Oh no!" she cried softly. Glancing swiftly about she exclaimed, "He's gone. Oh, there! He is at the telephone box near the door. He's dialing a number."

"Calling the *Gestapo*, no doubt," said Jean through gritted teeth. "What are we to do, Michel? I'm already in enough trouble and I suspect that you have been placed on a watch list. And now we have dragged poor Giselle into this."

"If the *Gestapo* arrives, we will be arrested for sure and they will find this," said Michel. He slowly withdrew his right hand from his coat pocket and opened it just enough to reveal a small automatic pistol with the marking "Modele 1935 S" stamped on the receiver.

"Michel!" gasped Giselle. "You can't make trouble here." She nodded her head toward the nearby table of German officers.

Michel took her arm and whispered adamantly, "*Ma chérie*, this man does not know you and I doubt that he has reported anything more than he has some suspects. If I move quickly now, I may be able to save all of us."

To both Giselle and Jean, he hissed through clenched teeth, "You don't know me. We've never met. I bothered you at your dinner and you ordered me to leave."

Without waiting for a reply, Michel rammed his hand back into his coat pocket, stood up and said loudly, "You can say what you like, I tell you the *Boche* are swine, evil parasites that will eventually suck the life's blood from our homeland. I don't know why I bothered speaking to you. You are not true citizens of France."

Before Giselle or Jean could begin to react, he reached over the table and slapped Jean hard in the face. He quickly moved away from the table, taking no notice of the Germans who were turning to see what the disturbance was all about. Rushing to the small man in the blue serge suit, Michel wrestled the telephone from his hand and smashed it down into its cradle breaking the connection. "I know you!" shouted the man. "You're under arrest!"

The pair struggled for several seconds with each man trying to gain the advantage over the other.

However, the small detective was no match for the larger and stronger Michel. Desperately, he called to the group of German soldiers who sat staring blankly at the struggle taking place before them. "Help me!" he cried. The words spilled out as a nearly unintelligible garble as Michel kept forcing his face into his coat, muffling his voice. "This man is an enemy of the state. I am with the *Gestapo*. Help me!"

The officers began to rise from their table when a muffled boom echoed through the restaurant. An elderly woman patron screamed and the pungent smell of burnt gunpowder filled the room.

The *Gestapo* agent went rigid and slumped to the floor where a pool of bright-red blood began to seep from under his coat. Michel was left standing alone with the automatic still smoking in his hand.

Pandemonium broke out as the restaurant's customers either ran for an exit or dived for cover.

As Michel jerked open the front door, Giselle was dismayed to see one of the German officers run past her, then stop and plant his feet taking careful aim at her lover with his service pistol. The man was too far away for her to reach, but she noticed his companion was rushing to join him.

With only a slight, almost imperceptible, movement of her foot she was able to trip the running man, who crashed heavily into the first just as he fired. The shot went high, blasting apart an ornate ceramic bowl on a display board near the ceiling. Cursing loudly, both men landed on the floor in a tangle of arms and legs.

Their slower reacting companions gathered above them, service pistols aimed at the door, but no target presented itself. Michel had escaped into the darkness.

The officers crowded about the felled *Gestapo* agent who was lying still on the floor. One rushed to the telephone and hurriedly dialed for assistance, while another peered through the doorway, trying to catch sight of the assailant. He turned back with a hopeless shrug.

The man who fell over Giselle's foot, a big brawny captain, stalked back to her. "You tripped me!" he accused angrily, pointing a beefy finger in her face.

With a calmness she did not feel, Giselle rose to her feet and stared back at the man. She batted her long eyelashes and purred in perfect French, "But, *non, Monsieur*, you are mistaken. I did no such thing. You hit my chair leg with your boot. I would never dare interfere with the victorious German Army."

The man stared sullenly at the beautiful blonde before him, their eyes locked. It was a contest of wills and Giselle knew that no man had ever bested her.

"That is correct, *mon capitaine*," said Jean, rising beside her. "I am *Préfet* Jean Moulin and I witnessed the entire incident. I had just ordered that poor stranger away from our table when he went berserk. I think he has some sort of mental problem."

The burly captain still glowered at the pair, but a look of uncertainty began to cross his features. In the distance the rising and falling wail of a police siren could be heard.

Another of the German officers, a large grim-faced man with angry eyes, stood in the middle of the room waving a Luger pistol. "I am placing everyone under arrest. No one leaves until the proper authorities arrive to sort this out!" he shouted in a hoarse voice.

Giselle and Jean looked at each other apprehensively. Were their plans to fight the German occupation going to end even before they began?

CHAPTER 6

THE FRENCH GENDARMES WHO FIRST arrived on the scene had not seemed overly concerned with what happened to the German agent although they went through the proper motions of making reports and questioning the guests.

The two *Gestapo* men who arrived some time later were of a different stripe. One of these, a thin cadaverous man in a long black wool overcoat and slouch hat, kept needling Jean with both questions and insults.

"You say you never saw the man before," he asked Jean for the fifth time, peering closely into his face.

"I have already told you that," Jean replied quietly.

"Look, Moulin, we know you. You are just the sort of swine to get mixed up in some nasty business like this. I have a mind to haul you down to headquarters. There are people there who would get the truth out of you in no time."

"But I have already told you the truth, sir," responded Jean in a respectful tone. "I never saw that man before he accosted me tonight."

Turning to the German captain who was hoisting a large beer stein to his mouth, the *Gestapo* man said loudly, "And you say Moulin's companion tripped you as you were attempting to aid the deceased?"

Wiping foam from his mouth with a beefy hand, the captain

looked hard at Giselle, who returned his look with the most innocent expression she could muster. The man's certainty faltered.

"Well, everything happened so fast. I'm not entirely certain what I struck with my boot," grumbled the captain. Giselle gave him a slight smile of gratitude and the captain brightened in return. "All I know is that the man who escaped shot your man before disappearing into the night," he added with a tone of certainty.

The plainclothesmen again checked identity papers and were particularly interested in Giselle's American passport. As they had received orders to be respectful of such neutrals, they declined to move their questioning to *Gestapo* headquarters. After a few more insults and threats, Giselle and Jean were finally allowed to leave after signing written accounts of the incident.

As they walked down the steep street away from the *Vieux Logis*, Jean took her arm and spoke to her earnestly, "That was entirely too close for comfort, *ma chère*. Do you see now that we are playing a most dangerous game? Whatever protection I might offer as *préfet* is rapidly diminishing. I will get to work on securing your French citizenship papers in the name of your aunt today. You return home and get what sleep you can. God help poor Michel, wherever he may be."

It was morning before Giselle reached *Château les Fleurs*. During the long cab ride, her concern for Michel plumbed new lows. She pictured him slipping through the dark streets of Paris, like some hunted animal.

After paying the cab fare, Giselle hurried into the château only to find Michel had arrived before her. He was fast asleep in her bed. Her whole being was relieved and exhilarated that Michel had returned to her safely.

Giselle looked down at his sleeping form and felt a wave of affection wash through her. Her desire to avenge Jim remained strong but her feelings toward him were dulled by the rekindled emotions she felt for Michel.

She looked down at his face, now peaceful in sleep, and decided not to wake him although she was dying to ask how he had escaped. Instead, she curled up beside him to gain some much-needed sleep for herself. Michel stirred but did not awaken.

Several hours later she awoke and made her way to the château's kitchen. After assembling a light breakfast, she gently awakened Michel with steaming hot coffee and buttered croissants.

During breakfast, Michel explained that he had made his way to a trusted police friend that owned a car. The man had driven him to the château. There was no fear of trouble from the authorities.

Giselle described the events in the restaurant following his escape.

"Your shot was most effective. That *Gestapo* agent will never tell anyone anything again. The witnesses in the restaurant were confused and uncertain about exactly what had occurred. The *Gestapo* officers were almost polite in the face of my American passport," she said.

Both Giselle and Michel agreed that the events of the night had clearly demonstrated the need for caution in the new and dangerous game they were playing.

"I suppose I will have to stay with you for some time," said Michel, finishing off his croissant. He looked morose, undoubtedly feeling trapped now that the authorities would be actively looking for him.

"Well, I have just the thing for you," said Giselle brightly. She walked to her wardrobe and withdrew a hanger. Smiling with pleasure, she held up a smart gray chauffeur's uniform. "I told you I could keep you undercover. I've had this ready for you for some time."

Michel groaned loudly but thrust out his hand to take the clothing.

Minutes later, he turned from the large free-standing dressing mirror in Giselle's bedroom and asked grumpily, "Well, how do I look?"

Giselle put a hand to her mouth to stifle a giggle as she took in the sight of her beloved Michel dressed in a chauffeur's uniform, complete with black visor cap, tunic, riding breeches and shiny high boots.

"*Mon chéri*, you look positively divine," she replied as seriously as she could. She knew her lover and former dance partner found his new role as a lowly chauffeur difficult to accept, but she also realized the importance of keeping him unnoticed by the Germans.

She also was conscious that her emotions toward Michel were growing deeper. As the days together passed, Giselle saw that her love for the dark Frenchman was now fully rekindled and was proving to be much more than a youthful fling.

In a serious tone, she said, "Michel, my dear, I want you to stay with me as long as you like. You may take one of the smaller guest bedrooms on the second floor."

Michel turned from the mirror and looked at her quizzically. Her broad smile reassured him of a different reality. They both understood that he would spend his nights in Giselle's spacious master bedroom, with its high ceiling, tall curtained, mullioned windows and canopied bed.

Giselle slipped up behind him as he turned to look dubiously at himself in her dressing mirror once more. Throwing her arms around his neck, she murmured, "Today I feel like a dalliance with the servants. You may take the day off." She began pulling him toward her large double bed but Michel resisted.

"I can think of nothing I would like better, *ma chère*," he said with a loving smile. "But today we both have serious business to address."

"Ahh, *chéri*, what could possibly be more important than you and I … and that bed," she pouted, with a longing look at the disheveled bed where they had slept away the early morning hours.

"What if I told you we have the opportunity to present the English with a machine that could change the course of the war?" Michel's eyes were bright with the excitement of his secret knowledge.

Giselle was stunned. She sat on the edge of the bed and asked, "Michel, is this true?"

Michel, resplendent in his new gray uniform, drew himself to full height and replied with excitement, "It is, *ma petite*, this is what I was going to tell you and Jean last night before we were so rudely interrupted.

"My opposite number in the Polish Secret Service has smuggled some people into Paris who are familiar with a certain machine critical to the German war effort. It could be of immense value to the Allies. It might even win the war for them."

"Then what are we waiting for," said Giselle, rushing to her wardrobe in search of something to wear. "I must bathe and get ready."

Some time later, she hurried downstairs to find Michel in the circular drive in front of the château. He was standing beside a tall man in grease-covered overalls who was tinkering with the vintage Nash Landau sedan her aunt had imported from America in early 1929. With the crash of the U.S. stock market later that year and the subsequent travels with Giselle on her European tours, the big 1928 Model 328 six-cylinder sedan had mostly sat idle in the château's carriage house.

"I discovered this beauty and thought it would be a good idea to have a mechanic get it into working order. I was referred by the staff to *Monsieur* Claude," commented Michel as he continued to examine the car's spark plug wires for wear. The tall man tipped his cap and said, "I think with just a little work, I will have her running well in no time."

Giselle was greatly impressed that Michel, over and beyond his talents in dance and the bed, knew how to locate a competent shade-tree mechanic. She also was impressed that he had a plan that might actually greatly aid the Allied war effort. Her estimation of the man continued to rise.

Michel was as good as his word. Within an hour's time, he told her Claude had pronounced the old Nash ready for the long drive to Paris. On the way, he explained that Claude had plans to convert the gasoline engine to one that would run on wood gas.

"According to Claude, it's really quite a simple process," Michel explained. "Thanks to the Imbert generator developed in Cologne, there have been vehicles running on wood gas since at least 1933."

"But I didn't know cars could run on anything but gasoline," interjected Giselle with some amazement.

"Oh, yes, my sweet, they can run on all kinds of things, including butane and propane gas. Wood gas is derived from burning dried wood, in our case, pine from the trees around the château. The generator is quite large, so I may have to take away part of the trunk. With the generator, connecting pipes and sacks of wood, this old Nash won't look very sleek but it should get us where we need to go."

"But how does it work?" asked Giselle, still slightly bemused that an automobile might run on anything but gasoline.

"The wood is burned and the resulting gas is cleaned and cooled to separate the water vapor. The gas, mixed with air, can be burned in the engine, although it will take a small amount of gasoline to start the process," he explained. "You do realize that gasoline will become increasingly hard to come by as this war progresses?"

Giselle merely nodded as she watched the French farmland pass by her window. She well knew that many items, especially gasoline, would soon be in terribly short supply. But she was more preoccupied wondering how only two people and an old car could help the British war effort.

The answer came as Michel drove the large Nash sedan into one of the seedier sections of Paris on the west bank of the Seine. It was full of warehouses and small manufacturing concerns and almost devoid of people. Splashing through puddles left from recent rains, he pulled up behind one of the warehouses. It appeared to be empty and untended.

"It looks abandoned," grumbled Giselle. Her idea of intrigue had heretofore largely centered upon visions of obtaining vital information from handsome German officers at well-appointed soirées. "What's at this place that could possibly be of interest to us?"

Her puzzled thought was interrupted by Michel's quiet laughter as he switched off the engine. Resplendent in his smart chauffeur's uniform, he rushed around the Nash and elaborately opened her door. As she exited, he made a slight bow and replied with eyes sparkling with excitement, "Only the one thing that might win the war for the English."

Brimming with curiosity, Giselle held her questions as Michel led her to a small door, which opened into a cavernous assembly shop. Whatever had been there originally had long since been taken away and the whole gigantic area was empty but for trash and discarded unidentifiable bits of equipment. Their leather-soled shoes echoed loudly as they traversed the empty plant, finally coming to another door partially hidden behind some lumber, which appeared to have been carelessly stacked in front of it.

After Michel knocked once, paused and knocked again two more times in quick succession, the door opened to reveal a petite, dark-haired girl with large, apprehensive eyes. As Giselle and Michel entered, the look of apprehension vanished, replaced with recognition and joy.

"Michel! How marvelous to see you finally. We wondered when you would come," effused the young woman, throwing her arms around Michel's neck and quickly kissing both cheeks. Giselle felt a brief stir of jealousy and was surprised at how quickly she had developed feelings of possessiveness toward Michel. She knew she would have to learn to reconcile her female emotions with her calculating mind if she were to become truly effective in this new world of war.

"Giselle, I would like you to meet Irena Rozychi. Irena is an unusual combination, both a lovely young lady and a most competent mathematician," said Michel with a smile. He added, "Irena, this is Giselle Tchai … uh, perhaps we'd better just go with first names for the moment. It might be safer that way. One cannot be made to tell what one doesn't know. Irena, Giselle may be the answer to our problem."

"And what problem is that?" asked Giselle with some slight irritation. She could not have truthfully said if her irritation stemmed from her lack of understanding of the situation or the warm greeting the woman had given Michel.

Michel held both hands up in front of her. "Patience, *ma petite*, patience," he said with a large smile. "All will be explained in good time. Come, you must see for yourself."

The object of his attention turned out to be a large, wooden, rectangular box-like affair that looked for all the world to Giselle like a homemade upright piano. It was standing in one corner of the room. Hovering around it was an older man in his shirtsleeves operating a large electrical sanding machine.

Sitting on a tall stool at a nearby workbench was a younger man. He was small and slight of build and wore large horn-rimmed glasses that made his eyes appear twice their normal size. With the noise of the sander and his attention so focused on the work before him, he had not noticed Giselle and Michel's entrance.

"Marian!" shouted Irena over the din of the sanding machine. "Marian, we have company."

Glancing up at his visitors, the man tossed a small paperclip at his companion. Looking up, the man called, "Hello." The older man switched off the sander and pulled the goggles from his face.

"Michel! Hello," said the man climbing off the stool with a smile. "I have been expecting you for days. What kept you?"

Michel put his arm around Giselle's waist and gently pushed her forward. "Oh, I had some old, unfinished business to care for," said Michel giving Giselle a knowing grin.

Somewhat flustered at meeting unexpected company, Giselle smoothed her skirt, glanced over her shoulder at her silk hose and whispered to Michel, "Are my seams straight?" Still grinning, Michel gave a brief nod.

Emboldened, Giselle smiled and stepped forward extending her hand, "I'm Giselle. I'm afraid I'm the 'old business' of which he is speaking."

"It is a pleasure to meet you," said the man warmly pumping her hand. He motioned to the man with the sanding machine. "That man there is Henryk. I am Marian Rejewski, a man very much out of my element."

"Apparently," said Giselle sympathetically. "Michel said you are from Poland."

His smile fading, the man turned and surveyed the cluttered workbench. Giselle suddenly realized he looked tired and careworn.

"Yes and a little more than a year ago I was happily working away at breaking German codes at the Cipher Bureau in Warsaw. I had been working at this since 1932 and I don't mind saying that my friends and I had become pretty good at it.

"We knew from message traffic that the Germans were laying plans for an invasion but no one would listen. The stupid politicians thought they could talk Hitler out of it. Then, last September they came. Warsaw was destroyed. I barely got out myself. Since then it has been nothing but being shuffled from one place to the next. I'm beginning to wonder if I shall ever see my homeland again."

"Cheer up," said Michel, placing his hand on the man's shoulder. "When the last German has been sent packing, we'll all return home and take up our lives again." He spoke with a confidence that Giselle knew he didn't really feel. Following the incident in the restaurant, Michel knew better than return to work in Moulin's office. He had been fretful at the idea of being restricted to the château. She was pleased to note his attempt to boost the morale of the refugees.

Michel quickly turned to Giselle. "And with Marian's work, the day of liberation may come much sooner."

Walking to the box-like affair sitting in the center of the room, Michel gestured expansively. "Marian, would you explain to Giselle what we have here."

Diverted from his personal concerns, Marian quickly moved to the large wooden box. "This is my large-scale mockup of the German M3 Enigma decoding machine. I was able to build this thanks to some fellow Poles who managed to smuggle out both parts and designs from a manufacturing plant in eastern Germany."

"That will teach the *Boche* to force us to work for their war effort," snorted Irena with a humorless laugh. Noting a glare from Marian, she stepped back quietly.

"As I was saying," continued Marian, "the Germans developed this machine in the 1920s and by the early 1930s, myself and some other students from the Institute of Mathematics at the university in Poznan had determined its workings. But there is still much to be done to fully deconstruct the Germans' codes.

"Following the fall of Poland, we have been working with the French *Deuxième Bureau*."

"*Oui!*" agreed Michel. "We managed to bring Marian here and set him up with this workshop. Only a few of us in the bureau knew of this place. When France fell, it was chaos. But I think it is safe here now. One of my trusted agents is outside keeping watch."

"I didn't see anyone outside," Giselle said.

Michel winked. "He is very good at his job."

He turned and stalked a few paces, then turned abruptly. "We have been working for weeks now in an effort to get one of these newer machines to England."

"Yes," spoke up Marian. "They already have some of the older three-wheel machines, but the Germans have now developed ones with four and even five rotors."

"Rotors?" asked Giselle. She was still trying to understand how the big mockup box could decipher coded messages.

"Yes, these rotors here control the permutations of the alphanumerical code," responded Marian with great enthusiasm. Giselle's blank expression remained unchanged.

Realizing that her befuddlement came from looking at the giant box-like affair, Marian took her arm and led to a nearby workbench. Sitting on the bench was a wooden box not much more than 12-inches long and about five inches high.

"This is the genuine article," he said in a serious tone. "The big box is not to scale. We made it large so that we could study the inner workings more closely."

Proudly, Marian pointed to the smaller box on the bench and proclaimed, "Here, my dear, is a fully functional Enigma machine."

Still somewhat puzzled, Giselle muttered, "It just looks like a wooden box."

"Ah, but it is so much more," laughed Marian. "Here, let me demonstrate."

Unlatching the wooden top cover, he drew back the lid to reveal what appeared to be a small typewriter keyboard with three rows of tiny lights above it. Above this were four notched wheels.

"These wheels are interchangeable," he explained, demonstrating as he talked. "You free the wheels with this release lever here and then the operator can change the configuration of the wheels."

"And?" asked Giselle, her curiosity now finally aroused by the innocuous looking machine.

"And, by doing so, the operator is able to scramble each letter or number typed into the keyboard. Even the old M3 machine had a potential of 150 million trillion possible settings. Without knowledge of the machine and the proper code, it would take a roomful of the world's most expert cryptographers years to decipher its code.

"And down here is what makes the machine so important for military application," Marian said, unsnapping and lowering a bottom panel on the box to reveal nine connectors set within a maze of wiring.

"This is the *Steckerverbindung*, the *stecker* or plugboard. It changes the swapping of the letters so that field commanders can both read and respond to coded messages."

"And this is good?" queried Giselle, staring in fascination at the contraption before her.

"But, of course, *ma chérie*," interjected Michel. "Don't you see? If the *Boche* can decipher and read each others' messages, then so can we."

"But this wiring also means that no letter can ever be enciphered to itself, which is a critical flaw in the design," said Marian. "Working though the permutations mathematically, we were able to break their codes, but it continues to change and this latest design will enable the British code breakers to move much more quickly.

"And time is of the essence. So far, the German code has been primarily used by their U-boat service. It is called *Heimische Gewasser* and is already known to the British as the Dolphin cipher. But now they are expanding the use of this machine to all branches of service. Already, decoding has proven essential in the Battle of Britain. And the technology is ever changing, not only by the wheel order but also in the rotor and ground settings and *stecker* connections."

"You've lost me," muttered Giselle. "The only thing I truly understand is that it is imperative for this piece of equipment to reach British hands as soon as possible."

Michel, Marian and Irena all stood looking at her, solemnly nodding their heads.

Looking at their expectant faces, Giselle felt her confidence returning, the same confidence she had felt on the stage and during the start of her adventures in Central America. It was confidence gained from wealth, privilege and an ego that had never experienced defeat until recently.

She knew her primary mission was to find Peter and recover the Skull of Fate. But she was going to need all the help she could find and here was an opportunity for her to help the war effort.

Looking from face to face, she realized the trio expected her to find a solution to their problem. Michel was now cut off from the power of the *préfet*'s office and the two Poles were far from their homeland. Giselle knew that if the Enigma machine was to reach England, she would have to take the initiative.

"Michel, you've said that with your secret service connections, you can find someone with a boat who will risk crossing the channel, yes?"

Michel nodded slowly, wondering what she had in mind.

"And it will only take money to buy the allegiance of the people involved?"

Again he nodded.

"Well, I have money and I have already determined to stop the Nazis by somehow recovering the Skull of Fate. Since I must start somewhere and I have no idea where the skull might be, this mission will be the beginning. Can we leave tonight?"

Everyone laughed at her naiveté but there was no mockery. The group was stirred by the American's infectious enthusiasm.

CHAPTER 7

Paris
November, 1940

"IT IS BEING ARRANGED AS we speak," whispered Michel as he slid onto the smooth leather seat of an adjoining booth in the rear of Paris' largest brasserie.

Giselle gave him the slightest of nods while noting with approval that his new mustache was coming along nicely. He was sitting in the booth next to Giselle in deference to his new station in life as a chauffeur.

After all, *La Coupole* was one of the most chic restaurants in Paris and in such a place no one of any breeding would be caught fraternizing with their chauffeur.

La Coupole had become Giselle's operations center while in Paris. Here she held court to friends and admirers as well as members of the fledgling Resistance. Since mid-October she had spent every weekend and some weekdays in a rear booth of the avant-garde eatery, hosting a constant parade of visitors. Something about the gold geometric designs on the restaurant's tile floor seemed to give her added energy and vitality. She could not understand what it was but the patterns seemed to stimulate her on a subconscious level. Once the word had spread among the artists and intelligentsia of the Left Bank that the young dance star of the *Ballet l'Opéra* was again visiting the city, visitors flocked to her booth.

La Coupole was on the *Boulevard du Montparnasse*, a pleasant walk south from the Sorbonne. The Sorbonne, that famed medieval theological center founded by Robert de Sorbon and later rebuilt by Cardinal Richelieu, had been incorporated into the University of Paris not long after it was reestablished following the French Revolution. The university, particularly the independent minded members of the *College de France*, had proven to be fertile ground for the recruitment of young men and women willing to resist the German occupation. Both Giselle and Michel had been successful in enlisting a number of student radicals to their cause.

The full weight of the occupation was now being felt throughout the city. Early curfews and dwindling supplies in the stores had curtailed much of the city's gaiety. Prices were soaring and most luxuries hard to obtain except through the black market.

At the first opportunity, Giselle took a sip of wine and stole a glance at Michel. He seemed even more preoccupied and careworn than usual as he sat leafing through a magazine.

She knew that the arrangements Michel mentioned upon his arrival referred to the transfer of Marian Rejewski, Irena and the Enigma machine to England. They had been working on a plan for weeks. With the help of her aunt in America, Giselle had transferred considerable funds to the Swiss bank account Aunt Gez had opened many years before, so money presented no problem. The biggest problem was the uncertainty and fear still rampant in France. No one knew who was to be trusted and who would turn them in for a few francs.

Giselle finished her wine and Michel got to his feet. "I shall bring the car," he said, formally reprising his chauffeur's role.

Holding up a hand, Giselle said quietly, "Not just yet; I hope to meet someone here before we leave tonight." Lowering her voice even more, she added, "I asked Jean to find someone who is both conversant in French politics and history as well as matters of the occult. I've been in Paris for weeks now and I must find a way to locate Peter."

Returning to his seat, Michel gave her an encouraging smile and said, "I understand, *ma chère*."

After ordering a small aperitif, Giselle looked from the retreating waiter to see a tall, imposing older man, accompanied by a young man and girl, approaching her table.

"Do I have the pleasure of addressing *Mademoiselle* Giselle Tchaikovsky, the ballet star?" said the man. He was slightly more than six feet tall with a thick shock of silver hair combed back over rather large ears. He was gaunt, with high cheekbones that accentuated his long, aquiline nose. His striped suit was fashionably cut but of inferior material, indicating a person with breeding but low finances.

"You have, *Monsieur*...?" replied Giselle.

"*Monsieur* Charles Richer," said the man with a slight bow. Straightening, he added, "I teach history at the Sorbonne and this is one of my students, Gabriella Duprey, and her friend, Jean Paul. May we join you?"

Giselle hesitated.

"Do I know you, *Monsieur*?" she asked in a formal tone.

Bending toward her, the man replied quietly with a small smile, "No, but I believe we have a mutual friend, a man of some prominence in Chartres."

Giselle relaxed as she realized that this was the man sent by Jean Moulin.

"But of course, my dear professor, please sit down." Giselle smiled motioning with her hand. She turned and imperially called to the approaching waiter, "Never mind the aperitif. Please bring another bottle of *Beaujolais* with three additional glasses."

As the waiter departed, Giselle leaned back and whispered to Michel in the adjoining booth, "This is the man I spoke to you about."

She looked up to find the professor looking straight into her eyes. She returned the look and each took the measure of the other.

She had indeed heard about this man. According to Jean, Professor Charles Richer had reached tenure at an early age at the Sorbonne. He was worshipped as a god by his students and had gained a small reputation as an anti-Nazi. But that had been before the collapse of the French Army.

Taking the initiative, Giselle slid her hand across the table and placed it over his. Smiling warmly, she said, "Professor Richer, I am truly honored to meet you. I know that you are a true friend of France."

"I have heard of you also, my dear," replied Charles, glancing at Michel, who quickly looked away. In the late afternoon, only a handful of guests remained. The staff was busily preparing for the dinner crowd.

Giselle caught the professor's glance. "And what about your little friend here?" asked Giselle sociably.

"I am not a little friend!" said the young girl loudly, anger in her voice. "I am a true patriot too."

Michel turned and glared a warning as Giselle quickly hushed the girl. With a hard stare, Giselle said evenly but quietly, "Of course you are, my dear, but we must make sure then no one in this place gets the wrong idea about our activities."

Sensing the mood and realizing her gaffe, the girl lowered her voice, "I am sorry, *Mademoiselle*, but I am not that much younger than yourself and I offer myself freely in the defense of my country."

"And we all welcome your offer with great gladness and respect," said Giselle with a broad smile. She looked closely at Gabriella's short-cropped blonde hair and impish clean-scrubbed face. Her short skirt with high stockings and fashionable heavy jacket gave her a definite schoolgirl look. But one look at the determination in the young girl's eyes and Giselle knew that this Gabriella was a person to be reckoned with. She immediately sensed that they would become great friends. "It's just that we must keep our voices down so as to not attract attention."

Somewhat cowed, Gabriella meekly said, "*Oui*, of course you are right. I'm sorry, *Mademoiselle*."

"Please, Gabriella, call me Giselle."

The girl brightened and said with a giggle, "And you may call me Gabby. That's what my American friends call me. I think it's because I talk a lot." Giselle joined in her laughter.

Turning an appraising eye toward the serious-looking young man sitting beside Gabby, Giselle asked, "And you are?"

"I am just a little boy who knows nothing," the man replied. He was somewhat short but muscular and well-groomed. Thick brown hair was greased back along his head and an intelligent sparkle in his eyes betrayed his self-deprecating words. "But since people insist on having a name to call me by, I am known simply as Jean Paul."

Giselle smiled. "And you are with Gabby?"

Gabby scowled as the man answered, "Oh, no, *Mademoiselle*. Alas, dear Gabby has an affinity for older men at this point in her life. I'm afraid I am more like a brother to her at the moment." His tone suggested he desired more from their relationship but Giselle decided not to press the issue.

"Well, Jean Paul, I am certain there are many women in this city who would be more than happy to provide companionship," she said with a mischievous smile.

Jean Paul turned to meet Gabby's gaze and smirked. "I have no complaints, *Mademoiselle*."

Breaking the tension between the young couple, Giselle announced loudly, "Well, I have one." When both turned to look at her, she added playfully, "Please call me Giselle or we shall never develop our own proper relationship."

The remark prompted smiles all around and a sharp quizzical glance from Michel listening intently in the adjoining booth. Giselle was gratified to sense some jealousy in her lover and impishly scooted her chair a bit closer to Jean Paul.

After the waiter arrived with more wine, the professor turned to Giselle. "Jean mentioned that you wanted information on the occult and how it might be used by the Germans."

"This is true," replied Giselle. "It's vital that I locate a certain man who has presented Hitler with an object of terrible power. It was stolen from me. I believe the only way to locate him may be through occultists in Germany."

"I will gladly help in any way possible, but I want your help in return. Gabby and many of her friends desire to work against the occupation. I believe that you and your friends can be of assistance."

"I'm sure we can," responded Giselle. Lifting her glass, she announced quietly, "Here's a toast to a successful conclusion to this terrible war and may all our desires come true."

Smiling at the double meaning of the toast, everyone touched their glasses and sipped the fine *Beaujolais*.

With Michel looking on from the next booth, somewhat irritated by his exile, Giselle, the professor, Gabby and Jean Paul spent the evening hours discussing how to organize the students into effective Resistance units.

During the following days, the foursome became close friends.

Gabby, it turned out, was quite popular with her fellow students and provided many good references for those students ready to join the ranks of the Resistance. She also was well informed on those of questionable loyalties who were to be avoided.

Jean Paul also was quite helpful in recruiting university students for their cause but Giselle sensed a deeper side to the man and decided she would keep a close eye on him.

On November 11th, under Giselle's direction, Gabby, Jean Paul and several friends organized a student protest. Carrying the Cross of Lorraine, the symbol of a free France, they paraded down the *Champs-Elysees* under the watchful eyes of both Vichy and German authorities.

Standing along the route, Giselle and Michel were greatly gratified to notice that most of the gathered crowd seemed to be in sympathy with the protesters.

The march was followed by further agitation among Parisian students. Leaflets were covertly printed and handed out on several campuses. Various "study groups" were formed in which the talk often turned to resistance and sabotage.

Gabby's vitality and high spirits continued to impress Giselle, who began to think for the first time about the role of women in the struggle to free the world of Hitler's tyranny. Until then, she had only considered her personal interest in regaining the Skull of Fate and avenging the death of her friend Jim. She noted with interest that since Michel had joined her, she more and more thought of Jim as a close friend and not as a soul mate.

Such thoughts regarding the role of women were hastened one evening in mid-December when Giselle stayed late in Paris to visit Professor Richer's apartment. She had informed him that she wanted to pick his brain for ideas on how to locate Peter. He had not felt comfortable speaking openly at the restaurant.

Gabby, accompanied by Jean Paul, had escorted her on foot from *La Coupole* through the darkening streets to *Rue de Rennes*. Although she had invited Michel to join them at the professor's apartment, he had begged off with the excuse that he was to meet with Jean Moulin.

Charles Richer lived in a third-floor apartment in a large building that managed to seem both well heeled and somewhat threadbare at the same time. Climbing the wide staircase to his apartment, Giselle was again reminded of the splendor that once was Paris, before the effects of war and depression took their toll. A large and ornate chandelier hung from the ceiling five floors above down through the center of the staircase, but it was unlit. Light bulbs were becoming prohibitively expensive and hard to obtain and everyone was conserving electricity.

The apartment proved to be spacious and filled with books, periodicals and historical artifacts. A rather tiny and spindly tree, more like a small shrub, decorated with a few ornaments was centered on a round table and appeared to be his only acknowledgment of the Christmas season.

Giselle noticed there was an ornate urn from ancient Greece, pre-Colombian pottery from Central America, figurines and brush paintings from the Orient and even tablets covered with Egyptian hieroglyphics.

Giselle peered at one of the tablets. It was obviously genuine.

"Do you like that one? It's from Egypt," said Charles in a tone that Giselle found condescending.

"From the Fifth Dynasty," came Giselle's rather too rapid reply. Her blunt but precise statement caught Charles off guard and he realized that Giselle was not one of his students, but quite knowledgeable in her own right.

Noting her irritation, Charles laughed in a good-natured way and asked, "I see you know your Egyptian history and I expect you are wondering how someone on a poor professor's pay could afford such treasures?"

Before Giselle could reply, he continued, "The secret, my dear, is that I didn't buy these in regular markets. I picked them up on my many travels. That stone tablet, for example, I purchased for only a few francs during a visit to Cairo in 1923. The poor trader had no idea of its true value."

Giselle smiled in appreciation of his luck and sighed absently, "I have always wanted to travel to Egypt but my career took me elsewhere."

"Well, you'd have a hard time going there today," Gabby chimed in. "What with the British and the Italians fighting for control of North Africa."

"Yes, I understand that Cairo is a hotbed of intelligence activity," agreed Charles. "Despite the British success at Sidi Barrani against the Italians earlier this month, I don't expect the Axis to give up Africa that easily. Mussolini may be a joke to many people but now that he's bogged down in Greece and on the run in North Africa, Hitler will be forced to stand by him. I expect Hitler to send troops to the Western Desert if the British continue to gain ground."

"But that would be good, right?" Gabby interjected. "Yes," added Jean Paul. "It will drain their resources from Europe."

"True," replied Charles, who added with a sigh, "But this will also widen the war. Sometimes I think this war will spread all across the world."

"I have thought that myself," muttered Giselle. The mood in the room turned somber. Giselle pulled a volume from a bookshelf and absently toyed with it, staring past the people in the room. "Why does every little difference we humans create between ourselves seem to end in a war? And what does war accomplish anyway? Oh, I know some national boundaries are redrawn and some new rulers take charge. But in the end, there's always another war."

Gabby had been listening raptly. She snorted with disgust. "It is the men. The only way they seem to know how to settle disagreements is to fight. Maybe things would be better if women were in charge of things."

"But then, maybe not," said Charles quietly. He was sitting in a large, overstuffed chair, which made it difficult for the tall patrician to sit erect. Nevertheless, he was not slouching. "Haven't you heard of the Amazons?"

"Of course," said Gabby with enthusiasm. "They were warrior women in South America. The Amazon River is named after them."

"Oh, dear, I'm afraid your education is not yet complete," said Giselle with a laugh that carried slight tones of superiority. She placed the book back on the shelf. Jean Paul eyed her sharply obviously playing close attention to the conversation.

"I'm afraid she's right," agreed Charles. "While some people believe that the Amazon was named after fighting women encountered by the Spanish explorer Francisco de Orellana in what was then known as the Maranon, the name originally came from Greek mythology. According to the Greeks, the Amazons were a race of women who had lived in northern Mesopotamia near the Black Sea. Their name came from the Greek meaning 'breastless.'"

Gabby sat at Charles' desk, her mouth agape. "Do you mean they had no breasts?"

Charles smiled somewhat patronizingly. "No, according to legend, they surgically removed their right breast so as to improve their proficiency with the bow and arrow." Gabby winced at the thought.

"In Greek mythology, Hercules, as one of his twelve labors, was ordered to obtain the ceremonial sash of the Amazon Queen Hippolyta," added Giselle, recalling her mythology course at college. "The queen took a fancy to Hercules and freely offered him the sash but this gift angered her Amazon followers. When they tried to storm his ship, Hercules felt threatened and betrayed. So he killed Hippolyta and sailed away with her sash."

"That sounds just like a man," said Gabby with an angry shake of her head. The bemused looks on the faces of Giselle and Charles only intensified her ire. She stood and glared from one to the other.

Giselle was shocked to realize that she must have sounded exactly like one of her old college professors, the ones she disliked so much because they were pompous and condescending to the untutored.

Facing Gabby, she said quietly, "Gabby, I'm sorry, I didn't mean to upset you. You made a very good point. Women do seem to get along better than men and the imbalance of sexual power in the world today has not always been the way of the world."

"Really?" Gabby sat back in her chair. Jean Paul was nodding in agreement and Giselle began to wonder what knowledge the young man might keep within his quiet demeanor.

"Yes, and even the ferocious Amazons were said to be connected to Athena, the goddess of reason, handicrafts and war," interjected Charles. Turning to Giselle, he said, "Giselle, you impress me with your knowledge of ancient mythology. You obviously were a good student."

"Well, I do have a degree in archeology, my dear professor."

"Yes, but do you know that Athena originally represented a matriarchal system which can be traced back through the goddess Isis to human pre-history?"

Giselle looked uncertain while Gabby delighted in her confusion. She was intrigued to find there was something her idol did not know.

"As you know, Athens was named for Athena," Charles continued. "According to the story, she won rulership by a mere one vote from the citizens of the city following a dispute with Poseidon, the god of the sea."

"That wasn't a landslide vote, then, was it?" said Gabby with a snicker.

With a look of disdain at being interrupted with such levity, Charles said, "No, the women had one more eligible voter than the men. And this is when the trouble began, according to legend. The men of Athens grudgingly agreed to Athena's leadership but only on the condition that the women could no longer be called citizens, lost their voting rights and that all children would take the name of their father not their mother." Gabby grew sullen, her anger returning.

"But surely you don't believe that the matriarchal system was overthrown as recently as ancient Greece, do you?" asked Giselle, brushing a lock of blonde hair from her face. "That took place long before the Greeks rose to prominence."

Charles smiled. "This is mythology after all, *ma chère*. Obviously it was a story to explain to the people of that time why males dominated their society. Very much like the little-known story of Athena accepting a half-reptilian boy named Erichthonius as her son. This story, coupled with her association with the serpent-headed Medusa and the giant snake by her statue in the Parthenon, engendered the belief that Athena was somehow directly connected to the Serpent Kings thought to have ruled the Earth in pre-historical times. Perhaps it was intended that she would be connected to the serpent in the Garden of Eden. I have reason to believe that Athena was merely a manifestation of the older goddess Isis who, in turn, represented the same Mother Goddess spirit as the Babylonian Ishtar and the Sumerian Inanna."

"These are just stories," scoffed Giselle. But her tone was hesitant and unsure. She had been schooled in only the hard facts of history, not its philosophic origins.

"Yes, but most stories have a basis of truth in them," countered Jean Paul.

Charles said quietly, "Shall I tell you a story about how we came to live in a patriarchal society?"

"Oh, please do," said Gabby quickly. She sat straight up in her chair, focusing her full attention on Charles. Giselle shrugged indifferently and turned back to the bookcase. As she drew a book from its shelf, she glanced back at the professor. It was clear she took keen interest in what Charles had to say but did not want to give him the satisfaction of admitting it.

Charles leaned forward in the big chair and addressed the women somberly. "I teach history but I have also studied in a great many fields including the occult."

Gabby gasped while Jean Paul smiled cryptically. Giselle raised an eyebrow and focused her attention. Perhaps she might gain some information to help locate Peter and the skull after all.

Seeing Gabby's reaction, Charles explained, "Please understand, the word occult comes from the Latin *occulere*, simply meaning something hidden or unseen. This is the origin of the English word 'ocular' meaning to see. It was only the Roman Church through its Inquisition that twisted the word into something implying evil and devil worship. The Inquisitors did not want anyone learning the truths hidden by the Church.

"Now, if I may continue," he added. Charles looked around but no one moved or spoke. "There are beliefs that in the days before recorded history, a great civilization flourished on our world. This civilization, which some call Atlantis, was guided by a group known as the 'Eternal Beloveds' composed of a male and female with 12 followers each of the same sex. They represented mirror reflections of the perfect human being, being a healthy balance of the masculine and feminine aspects of humanity.

"This balanced combination was extremely powerful, though they failed to prevent the cataclysm that destroyed their civilization.

"Also lost at that time were some blue stones referred to in alchemical symbols as 'Blue Apples,' said to be connected to the Apple of Knowledge in the Garden of Eden and the 'science' of immortality. These were stones of immense power. Unfortunately, there has been no mention of them since the time of the great Library at Alexandria. They reportedly could not be used except by one who had conquered his ego, which is why only the priest class was permitted access to them."

Charles began pacing, ignoring Giselle and Gabby as his thoughts moved deeper into his subject. "But the twelve men and twelve women of the Eternal Beloveds are what fascinate me. It was a most interesting arrangement. The women were considered equal to the men. There were equal numbers on both sides with one additional leader for the men and one for the women, making a total of 26.

"According to legend, these 26 perfected beings were later reincarnated in ancient Egypt and again attempted to create a balance in life, a balance between the sexes and a balance between humans and nature."

Giselle waved a hand in the air as a queen might imperiously wave away her attendants. In spite of her dream experiences in the Yucatan, her scientific dander was aroused by such metaphysical talk. "Charles, you don't really believe in that nonsense about reincarnation, do you? I thought that was just for spiritualists, mediums and their gullible patrons. Surely, you, as a sophisticated and educated man wouldn't..."

"I'm sorry, my dear, but at the risk of talking down to you just as you did to Gabby, I must inform you that your education has been incomplete. Just because you don't know about something, does not mean that thing does not exist. I can assure you that at the highest levels of control on this world, the Rothschilds, the Rockefellers in America and even Hitler and his top henchmen, they pay serious attention to such matters. I have learned through some associates in Germany that Hitler even now continues to acquire knowledge and holy relics in an effort to gain total power over this world.

"Furthermore, it is still believed today that there were 26 immortal beings who came together in the time of Jesus, who led 12 apostles. Legend has it that Mary Magdelene led a group of 12 women. Through reincarnation, the Eternal Beloveds were once again together and working for equality and completeness in humanity.

"But there was always opposition from some of the male disciples who could not shake off their patriarchal conditioning. The disciple Peter was in conflict with Simon the Magus, the most trusted of Jesus' followers. Peter broke from the path to equality by preaching the merits of the patriarchal system and supported his view by borrowing some theology from Judaism."

Giselle stood quietly, staring at Charles. It all came rushing back to her—the hidden Mayan temple, Peter's dastardly plan, the crystal skull, the dreams, visions and death it had caused. In her heart she knew that Charles was speaking truth. She felt it, just as she had felt the power of the skull. She could only deny such matters by denying her own experiences.

"What about a crystal skull? Do you know anything about this?" Giselle's tone was sharp and her eyes hard as she tried to penetrate Charles' knowledge.

Charles only looked puzzled. "Do you mean the crystal skull in the British Museum? I believe it was found in British Honduras by a woman named Anna Mitchell-Hedges."

"Yes, yes, I know all about that one," replied Giselle, surprised by her own impatience. "I am referring to another skull that may have found its way to the Nazis."

Charles was still confused. "I'm sorry, Giselle, but I have no knowledge of this."

Dejectedly, Giselle took a chair and said quietly, "I'm sorry. Perhaps later you can query some of your contacts in Germany. Please continue."

Charles looked at the floor, deep in thought for some moments before continuing. Looking up, he said, "Before the time of King Solomon, religion included both sexes. It was only under Jehovah that women were excluded. Prior to that time, the female aspect in spiritual thought was predominant. Most of the religions of the world focused on the concept of an Earth Mother or goddess who was responsible for the renewal of life.

"With the death of Queen Cleopatra and the destruction of the Library at Alexandria, this history was lost. But the attempt to bring balance to the world continued through the ages. Although later down-played by Church dogma, the disciples of Jesus had wives and female friends. They all carried on the work of the Eternal Beloveds. After the crucifixion, the power of this effort shifted to southern France where many ancient texts, scrolls and holy relics were hidden away, first by the Goths who sacked Rome and later by the powerful Knights Templar."

"This is profound," muttered Giselle, her eyes taking on a far-away look.

Jean Paul spoke softly but clearly, "Perhaps more profound than you realize."

Giselle glanced at Jean Paul, "What do you mean?"

Jean Paul glanced at the professor. He felt awkward in sharing information that might be beyond the professor's scope of knowledge.

"There are legends in certain circles, as I am sure the professor knows, of a Sisterhood that has incarnated throughout the ages, some-times coming together as a group as in the time of Jesus and at other times working alone," said Jean Paul quietly. "Clues to the existence of such a Sisterhood can be found down through history, from the temples of Atlantis to the temples of Isis, in Celtic wisdom and on to the original Delphi oracles and to certain spiritualists of today."

Jean Paul stared solemnly at Giselle. "Perhaps, it is no accident, *Mademoiselle*, that you are here now, in this place and time, a time of great evil and danger to this world. And you are once again assembling the Sisterhood."

There was a long silence in the room.

"Perhaps we should call you, 'Giselle, the *Magdala*,'" he added quietly.

Giselle felt the shock of his statement and the incredible impact of his words. She seemed to be trapped between worlds. At one level, her soul was moved to tears at the overreaching concept while on an-other she felt burdened by the thought of such responsibility. Before this evening, she had never given serious consideration to the concept of reincarnation.

As the internal conflict raged within her, Giselle suddenly noticed the small smirk on Jean Paul's face. At once angered by his humor and relieved that it might all be some jest, she tried to regain her composure by saying loftily, "Well, I have no idea if I am this Magdala you are ranting about, but I can assure you that I am one Sister who plans on giving that goose-stepping tyrant in Berlin his comeuppance."

Charles stared at Jean Paul. He did not appear amused by Jean Paul's jest at the expense of this kind and generous American woman. He also did not care to be upstaged by a young upstart.

Giselle sat entranced, her mind contemplative. She was beginning to grasp a larger picture, a pattern to what had until now seemed like random and unconnected events. She had known about the intriguing similarities between the civilizations in Central and South America and ancient Egypt. But she had never given them much thought since the issue was never addressed in her archeology classes.

She now began to consider the possibility that elemental forces were at work in the world, manipulating events behind the scenes of war, invasion and occupation. And she realized that her effort to regain the skull had broadened into a war to stop the Nazis. And now this effort had broadened into yet something else.

Sensing Giselle's awakening vision, Charles left her alone as he opened a new bottle of *Bordeaux* and filled their glasses. Regaining a seat, he said softly, "So, *ma chère*, I think you are beginning to see that there is much more at stake than that paperhanger's plan to take Europe by force."

"Yes, there is a broader historical picture in all this," said Giselle nodding her head. "And I will dedicate myself to doing much more than simply ridding France of the Nazis. I will work to reestablish humanity's equilibrium that was lost centuries ago.

"And I will do it by using the suppressed power of the feminine aspect," she added with just the right mix of sincerity and jocularity.

Her eyes were bright with excitement and inspiration. She now knew that her destiny involved much more than simple revenge for Jim's death or even regaining the powerful Skull of Fate.

"Jean Paul, maybe you were joking but nonetheless I see the path before me clearly." Giselle's voice was filled with sudden conviction. "It is time that women work together to restore peace and balance to the world. I shall form a Sisterhood to that end."

Gabby, who had sat quietly soaking in the deep conversation between the three people in her life that she most venerated, jumped to
her feet. "Count me in, I want to work for peace and balance in the
world too."

The young girl looked at Giselle with eyes full of youthful idealism.
"Giselle, tell me what must be done and I will do it," Gabby declared.

Giselle, her mind still reeling with the scope of her vision, sat
dumbfounded. She could only stare at the young woman pledging herself to Giselle's will.

With a gentle and understanding smile, Charles rose to his feet,
lifted his wine glass toward Giselle and said, "Well, it seems as though
you have recruited the first member of your Sisterhood."

Since the nightly curfew was well underway, it was decided that
the visitors would spend the night. Charles graciously took his living
room sofa, offering his one large bed to the women and an unused
bedroom to Jean Paul. But no one went to sleep for some time. The
foursome talked well into the early morning hours laying plans for the
formation of Giselle's Sisterhood and its first major mission—conveying
both the Enigma decoding machine and Jean Moulin to England.

* * *

Christmas, 1940, came in the middle of the week and was a quiet
affair. Giselle and Michel had been joined by Gabby and Charles at
the château where they all toasted the holiday and exchanged small
gifts.

Three days later, Giselle was sitting in her usual back booth at *La
Coupole*. Even in wartime, on Saturday nights the restaurant was full
and noisy. Shortly after 9 p.m. Jean Moulin arrived as scheduled.

Using the communication network that had grown rapidly once
word had spread among the university students, Giselle had sent word
to Jean that arrangements had been made to take him out of France.

Jean dropped his overcoat and fedora on the seat cushion beside
him and sat down next to Michel in the booth Giselle had reserved
next to her own.

He did not turn to look at her, well aware that they might be under
observation. But he felt confident that he could not be heard over the
din of the restaurant. Addressing himself to Giselle while appearing to

speak to Michel, he said in a hushed tone, "Excellent work, *mes amis*. How soon can we start for England?"

"On Tuesday night, weather permitting," responded Giselle under her breath, while trying to appear to be in nonchalant conversation with Gabby. "And you will have a companion," she added.

"I said I wanted no companions," Jean whispered harshly in reply. "There must be no slip-ups. It is vital that I reach England and De Gaulle. I may be the only one who can bring the various Resistance groups to the same table."

Placing his elbows on the table, Jean put his head in his hands. He appeared tired. In early November, the proud *préfet* had been stripped of his office, credentials and declared *persona non grata* by the Vichy government with the full approval of the German authorities. He had stayed with Giselle and Michel at the *Château les Fleurs* for a time but then traveled to southern France to meet with some of the Resistance groups forming there, such as *Libération, Liberté* and the *Mouvement de Libération Nationale*.

He turned his head and whispered back to Giselle, "All I found down south was squabbling and petty bickering." He quickly gulped a glass of *Bordeaux* that Michel had thoughtfully ordered for him. "Everyone wanted to be the leader but no one wanted the responsibility for being one. *Mon Dieu*! And then I also had to contend with the communists. I very much sympathize with them, but they can be absolutely intractable in their views. No one seems to have ever heard of working together on anything. It's maddening."

Giselle let the man vent his frustrations, then responded, "But this is not a person, Jean."

Jean looked up with a puzzled expression. "Not a person? But what...?"

Dropping her knife accidentally on purpose, Giselle leaned down to retrieve it and quickly whispered to Jean, "You will be accompanied by one of the latest German decoding machines."

Jean's eyes widened and his mouth flew open, but no sound came out. Regaining his composure, Jean could only sit and stare.

"But how?" he finally said in a soft voice. "We've tried to get one of the newer machines over the channel for almost a year. We almost had it arranged when the *Boche* invaded and threw all our plans into disarray. Communication with London has been hit and miss since then." He looked at Michel, who only smiled and shrugged as if to say that Giselle was in charge of the operation.

"I think we have the situation well in hand," replied Giselle, glancing around quickly to make certain they were not being overheard. She daintily sipped her wine.

"But I want details," insisted Jean. His years as a notable civic official had left him unused to being dependent on the decisions of others. "Are we going by sea or air?"

"Now, my dear Jean, don't get impatient," said Giselle in a tone like that of a schoolteacher lecturing an unruly student. "There is really nothing to discuss. Come to the château tomorrow and all will be explained before we leave for the coast. With any luck, you will celebrate the New Year in London."

Still scowling over the lack of information, Jean looked over at Michel who smiled and said quietly, "Bring a warm jacket. The channel is cold this time of year."

As Jean stood and pulled on his coat, he flashed a knowing smile indicating he both understood and approved. With a quick nod of his head, Jean pulled his hat down to partly conceal his face and walked toward the exit.

CHAPTER 8

Dachau, Germany
January, 1941

DESPITE THE PRESENCE OF A canteen and a full-time orchestra, Dachau concentration camp was a dire place in which to find oneself.

As he slowly sauntered along the tree-lined *Langerstrasse*, the long road that bisected the camp, Otto Rahn mused over the great fall his life had taken over the past months. He pulled his threadbare, hand-me-down coat closer around him in a vain attempt to stop the January dampness from penetrating his chilled body.

He was a slender, intense man with prominent cheekbones and dark hair combed straight back from his high forehead. He looked much older than his 36 years, but then more than a year and a half in a concentration camp would age anyone.

Otto was thankful that none of the *Kapos*, the inmate trusties, seemed to be taking notice of him. They often were more heartless than the guards. He made his way slowly along the tall poplar trees that had been planted back in 1933 when the camp was first built on the grounds of an old ammunition factory. He fervently hoped that the *Kapos* would not recognize him from his tour of duty at the camp. If they did, things would go very hard on him.

But Otto had every hope that his background would never become known. In his work for the *Ahnenerbe-SS*, Otto had primarily worked

the Sisterhood of the Rose

with the racial doctors in the experimentation laboratories. He rarely had had contact with the guards or *Kapos* who worked the compound.

As he walked, Otto shivered uncontrollably in the January cold. He thought back to his *SS* training when he first learned of the three original facilities of the *Reich*'s concentration camp system—Dachau in the south, Sachsenhausen in the north and Buchenwald in central Germany. He had no inkling at the time that one day he himself would become an inmate.

Now he was shuffling along in the numbing winter air, moving toward the camp's marketplace in hopes of finding something to augment his daily ration of food, which consisted of a thumb-size piece of black bread smeared with some margarine and a few spoonfuls of stew. He was also hoping to meet his new friend, Peter Hofsinger.

Peter was a new arrival in the camp. Otto had been immediately drawn to his quiet, reserved manner, which masked a pair of quick and intelligent blue eyes. He knew from conversations during the past few weeks that Peter was a man of breeding and education like himself. He also knew he would need every friend he could find if he was to survive this place.

Arriving at the marketplace, which was located at the camp produce garden, he saw several inmates digging up beets. Otto was furtively rummaging through the baskets of beets when he heard Peter's voice behind him.

"Otto, don't you realize that overeating is bad for your health?"

Otto smiled at the joke and turned to greet his friend. Suddenly, there was a shout from a nearby guard tower and all heads turned toward the distraction.

If a prisoner was discovered inside the 27-foot grassy strip that was no-man's land between the camp and the fence, he was liable to be fired upon by the guards in the watchtowers that anchored each corner of the large compound. Someone may have gotten too close to the strip and a guard had shouted a warning. During the momentary distraction, Otto quickly slipped a large beet into his coat pocket. He noticed Peter was watching him.

With a thin smile, Otto murmured, "Would you care to join me for lunch?"

Peter smiled, nodded and allowed Otto to lead the way as the pair trudged toward their bunks in the *Wohnbaracken*, or barracks, building 11.

The camp was built within a large rectangle of wire near the small town of Dachau, about seven kilometers north of Munich. On one end was the camp's prison, the *Lagerarrest*, and the *Wirtschaftsgebäude*, which housed the kitchen, laundry, storage rooms and the showers where guards would often flog and hang prisoners.

Just south of these buildings was the camp's only entrance. Known as the *Jourhaus*, this two-story structure served as administrative offices and SS guard rooms. Across the entrance were the words "*Arbeit macht frei.*" ("Work will make you free.") Otto had always cringed at these words, knowing as he did that the only true freedom in this hellish place was death.

At the other end of the camp were the marketplace, garden and a disinfection barrack. Sandwiched in between were 15 barracks housing prisoners, two hospital barracks, a canteen and a workshop. The barracks were divided into four *Stuben*, which included a living area and dormitory. Each two *Stuben* shared a washroom and lavatory.

The barracks, or *Wohnbaracken*, were designed to accommodate 208 prisoners. By the time Otto Rahn arrived, there were as many as 1,600 prisoners in a barrack. This overcrowding contributed significantly to the annual death toll from malnutrition and disease.

Otto was always hungry, even after the daily meal. So as he approached his barracks, his pace quickened. Peter, the taller of the pair, hurried to keep up as they walked up the narrow wooden steps to the barrack door.

"You must want a seat by the fire." said Peter in a light tone.

"Very funny," Otto said with a snort as he hunkered down on the floor beside his bunk. The barracks were empty. Many of the prisoners were off on work details and the remainder took every opportunity to leave the indescribable stench caused by the overcrowded conditions. But for Otto, during the day it was one of the few places where one could find some modicum of privacy from the watchful gaze of the guards and *Kapos*.

Peter held out his hand for the beet and Otto hesitantly handed it to him. Otto then watched in fascination as Peter withdrew a small pocketknife from his pants pocket and began to carefully section the vegetable into equal shares.

Otto stared intently at the knife, noticing the SS runes clearly engraved on its handle. "You know you could get into trouble if they found that knife?" he said in a quiet voice.

Without looking up from his carving, Peter replied, "Yes, I know. I hid this in my sock when I arrived." He held it up with pride. "I still have it."

"And the lightning flashes on it?" inquired Otto. He was casual with the question, as he did not want to appear too inquisitive.

With seemingly no concern, Peter stated, "I was once wearing those lightning bolts."

"You were a member of the *SS*?" Otto was flabbergasted.

He searched Peter's eyes for any sign of betrayal but the man's countenance was calm and friendly.

"Until recently, I too was an officer in the *Schutzstaffel*. In fact, three years ago I was assigned here to Dachau. Funny, no?" muttered Otto. His eyes showed he found nothing funny about it.

"What happened, my friend?" asked Peter in a sympathetic tone. "You can trust a fellow *SS* man. I still have a few connections in the Order. Obviously, a terrible mistake has been made. Perhaps I can help pass the word to someone who can help get you out of this awful place."

"You would do that for me?"

"Certainly, it is obvious that a man of your talents would be more helpful on the outside. I have made my mistakes and I will pay for them. But I would be happy if I could help you."

Peter held out the hand holding the *SS* knife and said earnestly, "Would you take my knife as a symbol of my trust?"

Otto hesitated, fully aware that in Hitler's glorious Third Reich no one was to be trusted.

Peter smiled and added, "Think what you could trade for it."

He handed the small knife to Otto who was nearly overcome by emotion. He had never expected to find such a comrade in the squalor of Dachau, a man of class and breeding like himself and a fellow *SS* member in the bargain. Giddy with excitement, he felt he could share anything with his new friend.

Otto began to speak of his life. He was hesitant at first but as he continued to speak and noted his friend's rapt attention, he warmed to his subject and the words tumbled from his lips. It was a great relief to finally unburden himself.

"I grew up in Michelstadt in southern Germany," he said. "In school I studied German history and languages. In the mid-1920s, I even studied law with an eye toward becoming an attorney.

"But I became sidetracked with what was to become the great interest of my life—Catharism."

"I have heard of the Cathars," commented his new friend. "Weren't they a strange Gnostic cult that flourished in the 12th century, primarily in southern France?"

Otto flushed with the first excitement he had felt in many months. He was intensely grateful to be able to share with a friend who was educated enough to at least comprehend his knowledge, if not fully share his enthusiasm. "Yes Peter; did you know that the Cathars were known as the pure ones?"

"They bathed often?" Peter asked, with an obvious attempt at levity. Otto didn't notice. He merely sat scowling, lost in thought.

"All right, why were they called the pure ones?" asked Peter. He was serious now and seemed genuinely interested in Otto's disclosures.

Otto Rahn smiled broadly. "Because they knew that their religion was closer to the truth of things, more pure, than the Roman Church of the time."

Raising an eyebrow, Peter questioned, "They knew, or they believed?"

Otto looked around to make certain they were not being overheard. Then he leaned toward Peter and said in a hushed voice, "They knew. They had proof that much of Church dogma was a later fabrication."

"How was that?" His countenance reflected genuine interest.

"Simple. When the Romans put down the Jewish Revolt of 70 A.D. they sacked Herod's palace in Jerusalem, which had been constructed over the ancient Temple of Solomon. Much of its wealth, including many of its most precious relics, artifacts and writings, were taken back to Rome as loot."

"So?"

"So, nearly 400 years later, Rome itself was sacked by the Goths, who acquired all of Solomon's Treasure for themselves and took it back to their native land."

"Which was where?"

Otto could see that Peter was now hanging on his every word. There was no pretense whatsoever in his interest. He was a captive audience.

"They buried the treasure in the Languedoc region of southern France, in the foothills of the Pyrenees Mountains that separate France from Spain. Originally called Occitania, the region was part of the old Septimanian kingdom peopled by a blending of Franks and Jews long before the nation of France was formed. They even developed their own language, the language of Occtitania or *Langue d'Oc*."

"So that is where the regional name Languedoc originated," Peter remarked with heightened interest.

"Correct. With the collapse of both the Roman and Charlemagne's Carolingian Empires, this area was ruled by a succession of kings of the Franks or *Francia*. Once consolidated, it became known as France."

"Yes, yes, I'm aware of all this history," interrupted Peter. "What about the treasure?"

Otto finished off the last of his portion of the beet and continued, "This area contains many craggy mountains and deep valleys riddled with thousands of caves and grottoes. It is the perfect hiding place for any treasure, especially one that might have thrown the new Catholic, or Universal Church, into chaos just as it was becoming firmly established.

"As a schoolboy, I became fascinated with the Cathars and with the legends surrounding them. I read about King Arthur and his Knights of the Round Table. I dreamt of the old Teutonic Knights and endlessly read Wolfram von Eschenbach's accounts of the hero Parzival."

"But those are just legends and myths," interjected Peter.

Leaning closer to his friend, his eyes glowing with excitement, Otto hissed, "Oh no, my friend, they are much more than legends. There is a reality hidden within the symbolism of these old stories. When Eschenbach told of Parzival's journey to the mysterious *Munsalvaesche*, the Mount of Salvation, seeking the Holy Grail, he was speaking of a real place. I know. I have been there!"

"The Holy Grail? The chalice of Jesus?" asked Peter with astonishment. "No! Are you joking with me?"

"Not at all, my friend, not at all. By 1931, I had come to the realization that the legends of a Holy Grail were based on reality, a reality involving the greatest treasure in the world. I even located the area where the treasure was hidden."

"Why would a treasure of silver and gold cause a problem for the early Church?" Peter was genuinely puzzled.

"Because," Otto added quickly with some irritation at his friend's lack of understanding, "this treasure was not simply gold and silver. It includes ancient scrolls, texts and even genealogies that could cause the Church irreparable harm."

"Genealogies?" Again, the conversation was taking Peter out of his depth.

"Yes, genealogies," whispered Otto with a small amount of exasperation. "Genealogies that reveal an unconventional knowledge of Jesus, his family and his progeny that the Church believes is best kept secret."

"Progeny? Are we speaking here of children? Are you saying that Jesus was married and produced offspring?"

Otto Rahn nodded, "That is the knowledge of the Cathars. There are those who believe that some of this family still lives in Europe today." He sat quietly staring at Peter, watching for any reaction.

There was a long pause. Then Peter asked evenly, "Are you some sort of heretic?"

Otto gasped and pulled back. He suddenly realized that he may have overestimated both his new friend's intellect and loyalty. He stared at Peter as he climbed to his feet and walked to a water bucket hanging from a nail on the wall. Otto's hands shook uncontrollably.

"Calm down," said Peter reassuringly as he dipped a ladle into the bucket. "I am not a particularly religious man. But your words would cause consternation among the faithful and condemnation among the many snitches around here."

Otto's narrow shoulders slumped. "I know you're right," he muttered. "This is why I am so happy to be able to speak to someone like yourself, a person of education and sophistication."

Peter took a sip of water from the metal ladle.

"I would not drink that if I were you," said Otto in a low but serious tone. Peter looked at him quizzically.

Making sure they were not being overheard, Otto confided, "Trust me, do not drink the water here any more than you must. They put fluoride in it to keep us passive and compliant."

"*Mein Gott!*" exclaimed Peter. "Fluoride is more poisonous than lead and only slightly less poisonous than arsenic." He seemed genuinely surprised to learn the lengths to which the Nazi concentration camp overseers would go to pacify their prisoners.

"I was told that as little as one part per million of sodium fluoride in the drinking water can chemically block the process of certain enzymes by the liver which protect us from any number of deadly toxins," said Otto. Walking to Peter, he took the water ladle from Peter's hand, studied it silently for a moment and tossed back into the hanging bucket.

"I'll risk death by dehydration rather than the agony of severe illness in this place." He added, and began pacing back and forth in front of the wooden bunk.

"There, there, *mein freund*, do not excite yourself," said Peter, placing his arm on Otto's shoulder in an amiable manner. "I am your friend and I want to hear more of your story. I mean, should you not make it out of this place, God forbid, someone must tell your story, *nicht wahr?*"

"Yes, that's true," agreed Otto. He sat down and stared down the long line of wooden bunks for some time. When he finally spoke, his voice seemed to come from the grave. "But let me tell you this. I am already a dead man."

"How can you say that?" Peter sat down beside Otto on the bunk.

Otto gave out a short and humorless laugh. "My death notice has already been published. I know this because some new arrivals told me. There was an article in the Berlin newspapers stating that I died more than a year ago, caught in a snow storm in the Tyrolean mountains."

With indignation, he added, "Those bastards! I am a much better mountaineer than that."

"But this is terrible, my friend. What are you going to do?" asked Peter, sympathy evident on his face.

Otto placed his head in his hands and muttered, "I don't know what to do. I'm only living from day to day here. Since everyone believes me dead, they can dispose of me at any time. I think the only reason I am still alive is that they are unsure whether or not I know the location of the treasure."

Otto suddenly turned, anger in his voice. "But I will never tell them where it is," he said vehemently. Taking Peter by the shoulder, he leaned close to his face and said, "Peter, I have seen National Socialism from the inside. It is not what we think. It is darkness and evil.

"I came to understand this while I worked here at this place. You would not believe the inhuman experiments that take place here. Young children immersed in freezing water, pregnant women … I don't want to think about it."

Otto turned and paced for a few moments before turning. "Peter, they must be stopped. But I don't know how. I tried to resign from the SS but my request was denied. I should have slipped away to some neutral country after the war started. But I couldn't find the strength to do it.

"All I wanted to do was to live quietly in the Languedoc and continue my study of Catharism. I have come to believe it is closer to the true religion of Jesus than anything promulgated from Rome."

"Tell me more about these Cathars," said Peter, lying back on the wooden bunk, which was covered only by a single gray woolen blanket. "All I know about them is what I was taught by the Church. And, I don't suppose the Church was very objective about them, do you?"

Otto finally smiled. "No, not very objective. You know about the Albigensian Crusade in which the Cathars were exterminated?" he asked quietly.

Peter nodded and replied, "Yes, in school we learned how an army funded by the Pope swept through southern France and exterminated everyone thought to be tainted with their beliefs. That was in the 13th century, wasn't it?"

"Between 1209 and 1244 to be exact," Otto said. He was pleased at his friend's knowledge of the subject.

"And I think I see something more to your story," continued Peter. "This extermination attempt was repeated about 100 years later against a later secret society which was quite famous at the time?"

Otto brightened, heartened that his friend might truly understand his narrative. "Yes," he exclaimed. "The Knights Templar!"

Peter nodded and mused, "The Knights Templar, the progenitors of all modern European esoteric thought. They were the ones who brought ancient knowledge of astronomy, architecture, medicine, navigation and many other things to medieval Europe."

"But where did the Knights get their knowledge?" asked Otto quietly.

Peter thought back over his knowledge of the greatest of the world's secret orders. "*Mein Gott!*" he suddenly exclaimed. "But, of course, the Poor Knights of the Temple were reported to have spent years excavating under…"

Peter looked at Otto, who was smiling and looking smug. As they both spoke, their words overlapped, "…the Temple of Solomon in Jerusalem!"

"And where was the center of the Knights Templar power?" asked Otto, a teasing look on his face. He watched Peter expectantly.

"Of course!" Peter almost shouted as he sat bolt upright on the bunk. "At the time of the Albigensian Crusade, they were centered in southern France, in the Languedoc region."

Peter grabbed Otto by his seedy coat and looked straight into his eyes.

"Then the fabled Treasure of Solomon must still be there, hidden in southern France. Am I right?"

Otto's eyes glittered with excitement and pride in his secret knowledge. He nodded enthusiastically.

"And you know where it is, don't you, *mein freund*?"

Otto said nothing. He merely looked up with a crooked smile that gave Peter the answer to his question.

"*Mein Gott*, Otto, have you told anyone about this?" asked Peter fervently, looking around to make certain they were not being overheard.

Otto got to his feet and began pacing in front of Peter. "Of course, I told someone. I am a loyal German. I told *Reichsführer* Himmler personally. But I'm not sure he believed me. I mean, look at my current situation."

"*Reichsführer* Himmler? You know Himmler? What did you do to be sent here to Dachau?"

Otto became pensive. His right hand flew to his mouth and he began chewing on a fingernail. "I'm really not sure," he muttered. "Let me explain.

"After traveling widely though France, Spain, Italy and Switzerland as a young student, I finally made my way to the Languedoc region in 1931. I was wearing a Boy Scout uniform to throw off the suspicion of the locals, but I was actually working for Himmler and other Nazi leaders."

Peter looked properly impressed.

"You see, I had met a man named Karl Maria Wiligut. At least that was the name he used when I first met him in the late 1920s. He is now a general in the *SS* and goes by the name of Weisthor. He was a long-time advisor on historical and metaphysical matters to Himmler. He is the person who introduced me to the *Reichsführer*."

"It's always nice to have friends in high places," muttered Peter without any apparent attempt at humor.

Otto ignored the remark and continued," You see, based on my studies, I had written a book about the Cathars entitled *Crusade Against the Grail*. I speculated on the whereabouts of Solomon's Treasure and it brought me to the attention of General Weisthor, who introduced me to Himmler. Before I knew it, I was employed as a member of a special *SS* division called the *Ahnenerbe*."

"I've never heard of it," murmured Peter, looking away.

"Few people have. By 1936, I was brought fully into the *SS* and promoted to sergeant and sent on an arduous trip to Iceland. A year later, I was commissioned as a second lieutenant and soon promoted to first lieutenant."

"It sounds like you were on your way up," said Peter. "But why send you to such a godforsaken place as Iceland?"

Whispering conspiratorially, Otto said with some excitement, "I was sent to locate the Kingdom of the Immortals, *Ultima Thule*."

"The source of our Germanic heritage," murmured Peter, thinking of his instruction in the infamous Thule Society.

Otto continued to pace the wooden plank floor of the barracks. Although an occasional prisoner had come and gone, no one seemed to be paying any attention to the two men quietly talking.

The pale January sun was waning. Realizing that the barrack would soon be filling, Otto hurried on with his explanation.

"You see, it is believed that in prehistoric times, beings from the stars came to the Earth and interbred with human women. They created seven races of humans, the purest being the Aryans. But these races over time lost awareness of their true origins and became mired in this physical world. That is, all but a select few, who handed down the sacred knowledge of their creators through a series of secret societies."

"Beings from the stars? Do you mean space men, like the American Buck Rogers? Surely an educated man like yourself does not take such ideas seriously?" Peter looked closely at Otto with questioning eyes.

"My friend, I have made a careful study of these matters for many years. I realize that the average man is both unaware and disinclined to think about such things. But that English playwright was correct when he wrote that there are more things under heaven and earth than are dreamt of in our philosophies," replied Otto calmly. Peter clearly saw the strength of his conviction.

"And this knowledge is available today?" asked Peter. He obviously was quite incredulous.

"Yes, but only within certain groups and only after much study and contemplation. It is far too much for the common masses to either understand or accept."

"And the Cathars and the Knights Templar were aware of this knowledge?"

"Yes, *natürlich*, they had the collection of ancient scrolls and texts from Jerusalem carefully hidden within caves in the Languedoc. These documents were filled with this ancient and hidden knowledge. Even the Vatican's 35-year crusade failed to discover their hiding place."

"But, you know where it is?" Peter was watching Otto carefully. Otto wondered if Peter was questioning his knowledge or his sanity.

"*Ja*, I think I know where it is," Otto finally replied without taking his eyes off of Peter. "I believe it to be in the caverns of Lombrives, near the Cathar mountaintop fortress of Montségur. There is one in particular which the local folk call the *Cathedral*. This magnificent cavern cathedral, a great hall, is more than 250 feet in height and is deep within a mountain. It can only be reached by descending a steep pathway deep into the bowels of the earth and passing through two large stalagmites. This is the mystic meeting place of the pure ones and their descendants. I wrote about this place but did not specify that I believe it to be the hiding place of Solomon's Treasure."

Peter's eyes were aglow. He had what he had come for. He had no more questions.

Overjoyed to have the opportunity to finally speak fully on his favorite subject, Otto's eyes took on a faraway look as he began to speak quietly but firmly.

"The Cathars believe that since the beginning of time, an eternal war has raged between the powers of Light and Dark. This struggle provides an ongoing balance to the universe. Lightness and Darkness. Knowledge and Ignorance. Positive and Negative. Without this balance, the universe would implode in on itself and be destroyed."

"That sounds worse than being in this place," muttered Peter with a slight smile. He glanced around restlessly, suddenly impatient to leave.

Agitated at this outburst of levity, Otto glanced at Peter with a scowl. But when he saw his friend's smile, he relaxed.

Returning the smile, Otto lamented, "I'm sure there are many things worse than being in this place but I can't think of any at the moment."

Peter's smile broadened and Otto went back to his discourse.

"The Cathars believe that all those who are not in the Light of reason, compassion and love are working for the Darkness. This includes political leaders and even high officials of the Catholic Church."

"I begin to see what got you thrown into this hellhole," said Peter under his breath.

Taking no notice of the remark, Otto continued. "*Amor* means love and *Amor* spelled backwards is Roma, or Rome. When the Roman Emperor Constantine folded Christianity into the Roman mythologies, he created a giant engine of conquest and control encompassing both church and state. This is what freedom-minded individuals have resisted ever since, beginning with the peaceful Cathars.

"Additionally, they knew that much of Church dogma was simply not true. They knew from the genealogies taken from Jerusalem that Jesus and Mary Magdalene were in fact husband and wife. Even the Church's closely edited version of the Bible refers to Jesus as a rabbi. Rabbis, according to both tradition and law, had to be married men.

"After its betrayal of the Merovingian kings, the Roman Church fathers felt it necessary to eliminate any mention of Jesus' family lest they become rivals to the power of the Church."

"But who would believe all that nonsense about children?" asked Peter, glancing around impatiently.

"Oh, it goes much deeper than just children," explained Otto, filled with enthusiasm for his subject. "The early Church began an internal crusade against women. Females have been prohibited from teaching or becoming priests. It went so far that priests were required to remain celibate, which has caused many problems right up to this day. And the problem centers on Mary, not the mother of Jesus, but the Magdalene, both his wife and successor as leader of his Church."

"Yes, well…" Peter tried to interrupt. "I have always been bored with the unproven claptrap and legends which always seem to attend any discussion of religion."

But Otto was undeterred. "According to the secret knowledge, Mary Magdalene along with her brother Lazarus, sister Martha, some servants and Jesus' children, Tamar, Jesus and Joseph, traveled by ship to the vicinity of Marseilles. They used the same route taken earlier by Joseph of Arimathea, whom some claim was actually Jesus' brother James rather than his uncle. A wealthy trader, Joseph had previously traveled to that area and perhaps even to southern England in search of tin. He reportedly was accompanied by the young Jesus."

"What happened to this family?" asked Peter. He seemed eager to bring Otto's dissertation to a close.

"Mary died at age 63 in what is now Saint Baume in southern France. Before her death, she and her children moved west into what is now the Languedoc region and there they intermarried with Frankish royalty engendering the Merovingian bloodline, which ruled the area until it was overthrown by minions of the Roman Church.

"For centuries, this legacy from Mary created the worst threat conceivable by Church fathers, yet they were hesitant to act until the time of the Albigensian Crusade. That's when they made their move to eradicate all knowledge and proof of this history.

"What Church fathers referred to as the Magdalene cult was most active in an area centered around a small Languedoc village by the name of Rennes-le-Château, located just south of Limoux in the foothills of the Pyrenees. And there may be an even darker secret."

"Really? What?" Despite his apparent impatience, Peter's interest was aroused.

"During the Albigensian Crusade, it was reported that certain Cathar leaders approached the commander of the Papal Army and asked if he would come and look at the body of their Lord."

Peter's mouth fell open and his eyes narrowed. "You mean the actual body of Jesus…" he began but stopped abruptly. "I have no time for irrelevant religious issues."

Taking Otto by the shoulders, he quickly asked, "You mentioned this town, Rennes-le-Château, is there anyone there with your knowledge?"

Otto smiled, still lost in the reverie of his thoughts. Speaking more to himself, he murmured, "Oh, yes. There is a woman there that I met each time I visited. She was very hard to convince to talk but once she understood my knowledge and my fervent belief in the ideals of Catharism, she opened up a bit."

He looked at Peter and gave him a knowing smile. "She was standoffish because I came to believe that many years before we met she had an affair with the village priest." Seeing Peter's look of renewed interest, Otto hastened to add, "Oh, he's been dead for many years."

"But the woman is still alive?"

"Yes, I believe so."

"What did you say her name was?"

"I didn't, but her name is Marie Denarnaud."

Peter's expression remained placid but it seemed to Otto that his thoughts were racing.

"Do you think this woman knows the full story?" he asked Otto, still lost in the philosophies of the Cathars.

Before Otto could reply, there was a clatter at the barrack door as a group of workers returned from their chores. More were following.

Looking around, Peter said, "I am sorry, Otto, but I must be leaving now. I can assure you that your secret is safe with me and, as I promised, I will do all I can to help you find release from this place."

With a faint and enigmatic smile, Peter moved toward the barrack door. He turned and said with a strange note of finality, "Good-bye, Otto."

Peter hurried down the *Langerstrasse*, only pausing to see if he was being followed, turned and moved quickly to the *Jourhaus* at the front gate. With his striped prisoner's cap in his hands, he entered.

"What do you want?" snarled the sergeant behind the desk.

"I respectfully request to see the duty officer, *Herr Feldwebel*," replied Peter.

Annoyed at this intrusion, the sergeant growled, "Just a moment." He stepped back into a rear office.

Returning, he gave Peter an odd look. It was not normal for prisoners to be admitted by the duty officer so readily. He motioned toward the office door, "You may go in now."

Entering the small office, Peter was relieved to recognize the duty officer, who was working feverishly at a mound of paperwork covering a large, worn wooden desk.

"I have what I need," he said simply.

"Excellent work," said the officer, without glancing up at Peter. "I can understand why *Reichsführer* Himmler chose you for this assignment, *Herr Sturmbannführer* Manteuffel."

Placing a sheaf of papers down on his desk, the officer looked at Peter with a broad smile. "You may use my private quarters to change back into your uniform, *Herr Sturmbannführer*. I am sure you are more than ready to get out of those disgusting prisoner's rags."

Peter nodded but said nothing. His mind was already formulating the next move in his plan to locate Solomon's Treasure.

"Have your people arrange travel for me to southern France," he suddenly ordered the officer. "And I need to travel in civilian clothes. I don't want any incidents with the Vichy government."

"*Jawohl, Herr Sturmbannführer*. And what about the prisoner Rahn?"

As Peter walked toward the officer's quarters, he waved a hand and said with disdain, "Dispose of him. And you need not make a record of it. The man died more than a year ago in a hiking accident."

He laughed loudly at the officer's puzzled expression.

CHAPTER 9

Northern France,
New Year, 1940-41

ON NEW YEAR'S EVE, JEAN Moulin arrived at the château by mid-morning
after being driven out from Chartres by one of the new recruits from
Giselle's Sisterhood. He arrived just minutes before Michel drove up in
the Nash carrying Marian, Irena and their precious Enigma machine.

Fully loaded, the old Nash touring car chugged off in a dense cloud
of smoke on a southwesterly course toward the coast.

After passing a road sign signaling their approach to Le Mans, Jean
spoke up from the back seat. "But we are heading south," he protested.
"Are we vacationing on the coast of Normandy? Calais is much farther
north."

Giselle turned in the front passenger seat and told them that she
knew German security was extremely tight in the area from Dunkerque
through Calais and on to Boulogne. Being the closest locations to England, security patrols and army checkpoints were everywhere.

"I decided to make the trip from St. Malo," explained Giselle. "It
will not be so heavily guarded. And on New Year's Eve, the sentries will
be even more lax in their patrols."

"And who was it that placed you in charge of this operation?" said
Jean testily from his position sandwiched on the rear seat. Giselle knew
he was still not accustomed to the idea of an organization of women

working against the Germans. While he was grateful enough for her help, she suspected that he considered her fledgling Sisterhood to be in competition with his own efforts to build an effective Resistance movement.

Receiving no immediate answer, Jean turned to Michel for support but Michel merely shrugged. Without taking his eyes from the road ahead, Michel said quietly, "It's a good plan." Realizing he was outvoted and dependent on their services, Jean sighed and settled back on the well-cushioned back seat between Marian and Irena.

Giselle turned and explained that she and Michel had managed to secure the services of one Gaston Soutre who before the war had operated several excursion boats from St. Malo.

"Each summer, he takes boatloads of tourists along the sandy beaches all the way to the rocky outcrops at Cherbourg at the tip of the Cotentin Peninsula. Now, with his larger boats confiscated by the Germans for their delayed invasion of England, Soutre has fallen on hard times.

"Michel worked in the Secret Service with one of this man's relatives. We met with him at St. Malo in late November. He was hesitant at first, knowing full well the dangers of a channel crossing in both winter and darkness, not to mention the German patrols.

"But the man's hatred of the Germans is strong. He has every good reason for detesting the Germans, but the primary one is a piece of shrapnel made from Krupp steel which remains lodged in his left thigh. He received it less than two weeks before the 1918 Armistice while serving in the French Army.

"After appealing to the man's patriotism plus overpaying him outrageously, we secured the services of his aging but capable trawler."

Giselle leaned over the front seat and continued her explanation. "Shortly before Christmas, Michel and I began to monitor the weather reports. Winter storms come up suddenly in the English Channel. I finally received a wire from a meteorology student at the Sorbonne who informed me that the weather on New Year's Eve should be perfect for a holiday on the coast. I knew this meant that weather for a channel crossing was optimal and our plan was ready to be put into operation."

It was dark by the time the travelers reached St. Malo and everyone was famished.

Michel located a small restaurant just outside the famed walled city of *Intra Muros*, which had been designated as their rendezvous point. They all enjoyed their dinner despite the tiring drive and nervous anticipation of what lay ahead.

Near closing time, a young boy of no more than 15 years entered and discreetly announced himself as François, their guide. Large, alert brown eyes peered out from under a tousle of dark wavy hair that stuck out from the woolen knit cap he wore. He was thin but moved with an agility born of hard work on the docks of St. Malo. He said they must be at *Fort National* precisely at 10 o'clock to rendezvous with his uncle Gaston.

He explained that his uncle had left the Port de Plaisance before dark under the pretext of moving his boat to dry dock for repairs. The German authorities had searched the vessel but found nothing suspicious.

Giselle's group would be picked up at *Fort National* and taken close along the western coast of the Cotentin Peninsula to avoid the channel islands of Guernsey and Jersey, which had been promptly garrisoned by the Germans after the fall of France. With a slightly north-eastern heading, they hoped to reach Portsmouth by morning.

Only Jean Moulin and Irena would accompany the Enigma decoding machine to England. Giselle and Michel would remain behind and return to Paris to continue their Resistance work. Marian would journey on to a secret French-Polish Intelligence center in southern France called *Cadix*. There he would continue work on the mathematical formulas so crucial to understanding the German code sequences.

Michel promised Jean that he would continue to try to reach someone in England to alert them of their attempt. Jean merely nodded quietly. He well knew that the normal Secret Service Intelligence channels were in disarray and that the British were very unlikely to take notice of any radio signals that were unofficial and not in code.

After warm *adieus* and much wishing of good luck, Giselle and Michel departed in the Nash to deliver Marian to *Cadix*.

Jean and Irena set off with young François on foot to the north corner of the ancient walled city. Looking out over the battlements, Jean saw the large stone fort, which had been built in 1689 to protect St. Malo from the English. He was thinking how ironic it was that now the English were allies and the old fort was a first step in putting him together with them, when he saw the lights of the city glittering off the water surrounding the island fort.

"But how are we supposed to get to the fort?" he asked François, pointing toward the island and the intervening water. Irena too now was leaning far over the stone wall and peering at the island.

François just laughed. "Look down," he said to Irena with a broad grin. The youngster had been watching Irena's girlish figure ever since they met. As she looked down into the darkness, he explained, "The tide is going out and before long, we can walk to the fort. But we must hurry as the tide comes in all too soon. Just ask some of my friends who have gotten soaked by staying too long." Jean laughed along with the lad, yet felt some concern for the boy. It was all like a game to him.

Irena could just barely make out the edge of the sea as it was a good distance from the battlement wall. "He's right," she said, "Look it is merely sand up near the wall."

"*Oui*, but we must wait until the course is dry. I don't want to risk being spotted by the *Boche*. And that is always a chance, even though we are fortunate your little trip is on a moonless night. We'll wait here for a little while longer," François explained.

Although there was no rain, a winter mist had fortuitously blanketed the city, cutting down on visibility and muffling sounds. It also soon chilled the small party and Jean became impatient.

"Can't we start yet? I'm freezing and think of poor Irena here," he motioned to the girl who was shivering despite her large woolen overcoat.

François had been checking a small wristwatch with such regularity that Jean had decided it must have been a recent present from his uncle Gaston. He checked it yet again and muttered, "Not much longer."

But nearly 30 minutes passed before the young man proclaimed the time had come to move. He led the shivering Irena and Jean, who was clutching the oilskin wrapped Enigma machine close to his chest, down an aged stone walkway to the sand. After listening carefully for any sign of movement nearby, François whispered, "Now, hurry!"

The youngster set out jogging at a punishing pace. Quickly, Jean was panting for breath but was more concerned with Irena who struggled along to bring up the rear. Once when he stopped to help her catch up, François hissed, "Hurry, we can't be caught out here in the open."

The run to the old fort seemed to take forever, especially since at any moment Jean expected to hear a sentry's challenge followed by gunshots. He did not want to think about the pain of a 7.92-millimeter slug slamming into his back.

But there were neither shouts nor shots and soon all three were huddled in the shadow of the fort, which loomed over them like a protective cover. Clutching the decoding machine, Jean slumped down to a sitting position gasping for breath while Irena leaned against the old stone wall with both hands, her chest heaving from the exertion.

The young François seemed hardly out of breath at all. Jean glowered disgustedly at the youth as he dabbed his forehead with a handkerchief and tried to slow his breathing.

As the ache in Jean's side began to subside, he noticed that François had squatted down next to Irena and was engaging the pretty Polish girl in conversation. He probably hasn't had much opportunity to meet girls from outside the city, Jean thought. He was filled with sudden sadness thinking about how the war had disrupted so many young lives.

As his thoughts turned to the hope that life would return to normal after the war ended and France was rid of the Germans, he was startled to hear a voice say quite distinctly, "Are you here to catch the Bournemouth Express?"

Jean jumped to his feet reaching desperately in his jacket pocket for his service pistol. François merely laughed softly.

"*Oncle* Gaston! You are right on time," said the boy peering into the darkness.

Suddenly the man was amongst them. Gaston Soutre was a huge bear of a man. He wore a dark heavy pea jacket with a woolen knit cap pulled down over a shaggy mane of long dark hair. A full bristling beard added to the impression of his being more animal than man. But his laugh was infectious and Jean watched approvingly as the big man hugged François.

"Aha, *mon petit*, I see you have carried out your mission quite well and you didn't lose track of the time," said Gaston loudly. François held his watch up and looked at it admiringly. Jean looked around nervously and hoped that the big man might be a bit quieter.

"Hurry, my friends, I have a small skiff nearby." Gaston seemed to have trouble muting his booming voice.

Jean was relieved when the group was finally settled in the skiff without incident. He helped Gaston push it out into deeper water and soon the two men were rowing at a slow but rhythmic pace. François kept lookout in the bow.

After several minutes, Jean could discern the black bulk of a larger wooden boat from the darkness of the water. Soon, they were all climbing aboard a 42-foot trawler that was originally built as a fishing boat that since the mid-1930s had been used to haul sightseers along the sandy beaches stretching both north and south from the city of St. Malo.

While Jean and Irena found a secure place for their special cargo inside the pilothouse, Gaston and François readied the aging craft for its voyage across the channel. François checked to see that everything was secure while the burly Gaston climbed down a hatch into the dark recesses of the boat and worked to start its single Peugeot diesel engine. Finally, after much coaxing mixed with an abundance of French curses worthy of the sailors they were, the veteran engine coughed to life.

Returning to the pilothouse, which Gaston referred to as the "dog house," the hulking seaman wiped his grimy face with an oily rag and set a course due north for the Cotentin Peninsula.

Without running lights, the creaking trawler moved through the foggy darkness at a slow pace of less than five knots. "We must conserve both the fuel and this old engine," explained Gaston. He picked up a stubby cigar from the plotting table and lit it. Irena grimaced as the cigar's acrid smoke filled the small cabin but said nothing.

"Once we clear the peninsula we will make a real run for it," laughed the big captain, as he tried unsuccessfully to blow a smoke ring.

Jean reached in a jacket pocket and produced a small brandy flask. Opening it, he offered it to Irena, who took a swig, grateful for the liquid's warmth. François looked at the flask longingly but Jean took a pull for himself and placed it back in his pocket.

As a blackout was in force, they could not see any lights along the shore, which itself was largely unseen except for occasional thinning of the fog when the lighter tone of the sand beaches or rocky cliffs became visible.

Some time passed with Gaston humming loudly from nervous tension. He continually peered through the windows on all sides. No one wanted to think about the prospect of a nighttime collision or interception by the Germans.

François and Irena were both soon nodding in an exhausted sleep while Jean sat awake, laying plans for his stay in England. He intended to meet with General De Gaulle and, putting aside whatever political differences they might have, pledge himself to assist the general to free all France. With the authority provided by De Gaulle, he hoped to consolidate the bickering Resistance movements into a formidable offensive weapon.

At the point of falling asleep himself, Jean was rudely shaken by Gaston, who leaned over him with a broad smile on his hirsute face. "Wake up, *Monsieur* Moulin," he said through the cigar butt still held in his clenched teeth. "We are now passing the *Cap de la Haie* and Cherbourg is to our right. We are now moving into *La Manche*. With any luck we proceed in a northerly direction for about 60 miles and we should reach Bournemouth by dawn."

The big man then woke François, whom he placed at the wheel, while he again climbed into the engine room. Soon, the chuff-chuff of the aging diesel engine had changed to a high-pitched roar and the speed of the trawler increased.

After a bit, François turned with a smile and said, "My uncle is a master of the machinery. Under his expert hands, we are making almost nine knots."

Awakened by the noise but uncomprehending, Irena looked to Jean. Was this a good thing? Jean returned the young boy's smile and nodded his head to Irena, acknowledging that this indeed was a good thing. But his smile was tight and unnatural. Jean was still very concerned over the possibility of collision. After all, the war was continuing and there was a multitude of craft in the channel. Everything from small torpedo boats to naval destroyers and cruisers could be expected in the channel at any time.

More than 30 minutes later, Jean was still worrying about being intercepted when François abruptly shut down the engine. The old trawler was suddenly silent except for swells splashing against the sides.

Bam! The hatch to the engine room flew open and Gaston climbed out onto the deck waving a greasy cloth. "What is the meaning of this? Why have we stopped?" he growled.

"*Oncle*! Please, be quiet. I thought I heard something," said François frantically. Stunned by his words, Gaston stepped to the doorway and stuck his head out listening intently. Jean and Irena were fully awake and straining their ears for any sound.

At first Jean heard nothing but as the minutes passed, he thought he could distinctly hear laughter, rough male laughter.

No one stirred. No one moved. All ears listened for the sound to repeat itself. Then came the deep throb of engines on the water. Jean looked around, desperately. If only there was a fog bank in which to hide. But there was none. If they were seen, they'd be arrested for certain, if not worse.

"They're passing aft," whispered François and everyone turned to look.

There in the darkness, a huge black hulk was looming ever closer in the fog. The shape grew and grew until the little group in the trawler braced for a collision that fortunately never came.

As the large boat passed within 30 yards of the trawler's stern, everyone held their breath. The big boat was also blacked out but they could see faint light leaking from under the curtains drawn inside the cabin. There was the faint sound of a radio playing. They could just make out the tune.

"We're going to hang out the washing on the Siegfried Line … Have you any dirty washing, mother dear? We're going to hang out the washing on the Siegfried Line, if that Siegfried Line's still there…"

"It's an English tune," whispered Irena with glee. She started to rise from her seat. "We must stop them. They can escort us to their base."

Jean quickly placed his arm across her, blocking further movement. Holding one finger to his lips, he said, "We don't know they're British. Anyone can pick up the English stations out here. There are still British citizens on the channel islands."

As if to confirm Jean's fear, a strong male voice suddenly called out in German, *"Emil, hast du eine zigarette?"* Another voice, full of authority, growled, *"Bist du schwachsinnig? Ruhe, dummkopf!"* The voices became hushed and unintelligible.

"They are definitely not British," whispered Irena, her eyes round and large with fright. Jean reached for the automatic in his coat pocket knowing at the same time that it was be useless against a fully manned German patrol boat.

But as the throb of the big twin Mercedes engines grew fainter, he relaxed. They were not spotted. Gaston turned and took the cigar stub from his mouth before grinning broadly and murmuring, *"Merci, mon Dieu."* The cigar fell to pieces in his hand. He had chewed it to shreds during the tense moments as the patrol boat passed.

Jean returned the big man's smile and was about to produce his flask for a small celebration when the throb of the patrol boat's engines suddenly changed pitch.

Rushing to the cabin door, Gaston peered into the darkness to

the Sisterhood of the Rose

their rear and said with great resignation, "They are coming about, my friends, I'm afraid it's all over for us."

"No!" said Jean vehemently. "We don't matter. But this package must reach England. Thousands, perhaps millions, of lives are in the balance." Pulling the automatic from his jacket, he said tensely, "*Monsieur*, we must make a run for it. Everything is lost if we quietly accept arrest."

"A run for it?" growled Gaston. "You must be mad! They have more than twice our power. Not to mention their guns. No, we must accept our fate. Think of these youngsters." He motioned toward François and Irena.

"They knew the dangers when we set out," replied Jean grimly, bringing his service automatic up to a raised position though not pointing directly at the wide-eyed captain. "I really do not want to threaten you with this pistol, but we must try to escape."

"He's right, *Oncle*," said François with an intensity Gaston had never heard before from the boy. The big man turned to Irena. "I too think it is our duty to try to escape," agreed the girl quietly, her face fearful and drawn.

Faced with a minor mutiny and never taking his eyes from Jean's pistol, Gaston shrugged and muttered, "Well, if we are going to do it, we must do it now. François, take the wheel. Stay on course until I tell you to take evasive action. You two stay low to the deck. I will see what this old work horse can really do."

With that he climbed down into the engine room, which quickly reverberated with sounds of the diesel cranking up. This time, there was no hesitation. As though sensing the critical nature of the moment, the aging Peugeot roared to life and the trawler began to pick up speed as it sliced through the dark channel waters.

Suddenly, the pilothouse was bathed in light. Everyone stood and looked at each other in shock until Jean finally peered out the door.

The large German patrol boat was gaining from the rear and one of the crewmembers had switched on a large spotlight on the foredeck. Jean could just make out the shape of a large weapon positioned near the light. It was a 20-millimeter cannon.

A loud amplified voice boomed out of the night. "*Achtung! Achtung! Hier ist der Deutsche Kriegsmarine.*" In English, the voice added, "Heave to, immediately, or we will open fire!"

Gaston poke his head out of the engine room hatch. "It would seem that we need more speed," he said jauntily. Apparently, once the decision was made and he began pushing the engine for all it was worth, Gaston had gained some newfound courage.

"Everybody down!" cried Jean. Turning to Gaston, he said with a determined smile, "Full speed ahead, Captain." The oily captain disappeared down the hatch, still grinning.

The trawler's engine strained and the boat cut neatly through the low swells of the relatively calm channel but Jean could see the spotlight growing larger and brighter behind them. Suddenly, there was a burst of fire from the boat's cannon and the trawler's cabin began to fly apart.

The stern of the boat bore the brunt of the attack, immediately turning into a shamble of holes, torn rigging and shattered planks. Rounds penetrated deep into the engine room. Shots that went high ripped holes in the pilothouse and shattered the windows, showering its occupants with slivers of glass.

Jean was horrified to see François' chest burst outward as the youth turned the wheel frantically in an effort to move out of the patrol boat's path. Without a sound, the boy dropped heavily to the deck. Jean clutched Irena and could only pray that the next salvo didn't destroy the trawler totally. Black smoke boiled into the cabin as the engine room hatch flew open and Gaston appeared, yelling, "It's no use! We're losing oil. The engine will seize up any moment."

He stopped, seeing the body of François lying in a spreading pool of blood. "*Mon Dieu!*" he cried, rushing to the boy. Cradling François' head in his arms, he moaned loudly, "What have I done? What will my sister say?"

Jean felt intense sympathy for the man but knew that François was not the first nor would be the last victim of this senseless war. Taking the package containing the Enigma machine, he snatched a life preserver and crawled toward the cabin door. The shooting had stopped, presumably as the German sailors were surveying the frightful damage.

The old trawler was already stern down as water poured into the damaged rear end. The engines had stopped and a mixture of oil smoke and steam was pouring from the stern.

"Where are you going?" called Irena, too terrified to move from her place on the deck.

Calling back over his shoulder, Jean yelled, "Stay here with the Gaston. The *Boche* will not harm you if you surrender peacefully. I must try and get this machine to England even if I have to swim. Others have swum the channel. I can too."

But as he slipped into the icy channel water, Jean knew in his heart of hearts that he would never make it. The water was numbingly cold, the distance was too great and he was not in the same physical condition he had been in his youth.

Bobbing in the cold water, clutching the Enigma machine with one hand and trying to wrestle on the life preserver with the other, Jean looked back.

The trawler was wallowing in the water, listing heavily to one side. The water line was halfway up the boat's deck. Irena was pulling herself out of the cabin door trying to hold onto the topside of the listing boat. There was no sign of Gaston.

The Germans, now close enough to see the sinking boat plainly, continued their ceasefire. They were slowing and making ready to bring the survivors on board as they approached.

Jean's heart sank. It had all been for nothing. He and the decoding machine were either going to end up in German hands or at the bottom of the channel. Having managed to pull on the life preserver, he reached in his jacket pocket and felt the cold steel of the automatic. Questions were racing through his head. Should he try to fight it out with the Germans, go down fighting? Or should he surrender and live to fight another time?

Or should he end his life right here and now and deprive his enemies the satisfaction of his capture and eventual torture?

Before any answer came, the night turned bright as a brilliant ball of fire erupted within the German patrol boat. There was a brief, but blinding, flash of yellow, which quickly turned to orange and then to deeper tones. The patrol boat literally exploded in one tremendous blast. Pieces of decking, railings, human bodies, equipment and weapons were flung high into the air.

The shock wave of the explosion pushed Jean underwater momentarily. When he resurfaced, it seemed the entire world was on fire. The blazing carcass of the patrol boat was settling into the sea in the midst of a ring of burning oil. Debris was raining down about him.

Jean swam frantically back toward the sinking trawler, ignoring the falling bits of the patrol boat. There was no sign of Gaston.

Irena was still clinging to the side that was jutting in the air but the boat's descent was gaining speed. It would soon slip under the waves and Jean knew that the suction would pull the heroic Polish girl with it.

"You must get away from the boat," he yelled as he reached for her. Overjoyed to find companionship at such a desperate time, Irena offered no protest as she slid into the water beside Jean. Both began paddling frantically away from the dying boat.

With little more than some hissing of steam from the hot engines, the trawler slid rapidly under water leaving behind only an expanding circle of debris. The still burning hulk of the German vessel also disappeared into the water. The burning surface oil lit up the scene in a ghastly display of undulating shadows.

"What happened?" murmured Irena, looking wide-eyed at the slowly diminishing flames while clinging tightly to Jean.

"I have no idea ... wait! Look!"

Far outside the dwindling ring of fire, they saw a huge dark bulk rising out of the water. Their shock and amazement could not have been greater if it had been some primeval sea monster.

They heard the clang of a metal hatch and the sounds of men running along a deck. Then a high-pitched voice was hailing them. "Ahoy, you chaps, hold fast. We'll have you out of there in a jiffy."

It may have been the cold water or the effects of his recent experience, but whatever the cause, Jean's mind was numbed. Unable to think clearly, he was more of an observer than a participant as two men appeared out of the night and pulled the pair toward what now was clearly a surfaced submarine. He could only think of poor François, a brave young man who never had a chance to truly live life. And he thought of Gaston, a brave captain who apparently chose to go down with his boat in the dark channel.

Friendly hands hauled Jean and Irena on deck as someone threw a blanket over their soaked bodies. "'*Allo*, this one's a girl!" exclaimed one of the men as he covered the shivering Irena.

A seaman off to one side was staring at the last flames still licking at the spilled oil. "*Blimey*! I always wondered what a torpedo would do to one of them little boats."

"Well, now you know, Teddy. No sense searching for survivors, eh?" answered a comrade.

The crewmen's conversation brought Jean back to consciousness. He knew that torpedoes were made to be used against large steel-hulled ships, not small wooden patrol boats. It was like shooting a small rabbit with a 50-caliber bullet. Total destruction.

Soon, he and Irena were sitting in the submarine's galley sipping hot tea and trying to respond to a barrage of questions from the curious crew. The talk stopped as the crew snapped to attention with the arrival of the sub's captain, a young slender, competent-looking man who smiled broadly and shook their hands.

The captain explained that the British Admiralty had received a furtive broadcast from France and, based on the possibility of recovering a German Enigma machine, had dispatched his submarine.

"Damned lucky we were in the area," said the captain, adding with a conspiratorial wink, "And I've always wanted to pot one of those *Jerry* patrol boats but I could never justify wasting a torpedo until now."

Reaching across the metal table, Jean unwrapped the oilcloth package he had kept gripped in his hands while being brought aboard.

"I think your superiors will feel that your efforts this day were well justified," he said, folding back the oil wrapping and opening the wooden Enigma case. "*Voila!*"

The captain looked at the device very carefully before replying. "I say," he finally said in his clipped British accent, "this must be the new four-wheeled decoding machine that we've all been after for so long. Nice work. This may be just the thing to shorten the war."

Despite their losses, Jean found himself feeling better than he had in weeks. He settled back, took a sip of the steaming tea and thought to himself, "Giselle and her Sisterhood are truly off to a great start in their fight against the Nazis."

CHAPTER 10

Chartres, France
Early Spring, 1941

IT WAS MARCH AND SOME buds were already appearing in the garden near *Château les Fleurs* when Giselle was ambushed from behind.

She had been creeping silently through the hedges of the garden concentrating on the best way to hold the British Sten gun when the figure had suddenly crashed through the foliage knocking her down. Before she could mount a counteroffensive, the weight of her attacker pinned her to the ground. She could feel the cold sharp blade of a knife at her throat.

"I'm afraid you're dead, my dear." Michel's voice whispered harshly in her ear. There was a hard edge to his words. Her lover had grown more callous since the Resistance began.

Pulling Giselle to her feet, he added soberly, "Remember what I have taught you. Always remain aware of your surroundings. A split second can mean the difference between life and death."

He smiled and put his arm around her shoulder as they made their way to the château. "I wouldn't want to lose you again."

Giselle smiled. She was pleasantly surprised that her feelings for Michel had not diminished over the months since her arrival in France. Back in the States, she usually lost interest in a man after the first date. Jim had been the only man that held her interest for long and she now was realizing that connection was due more to their mutual interest in archeology than any deep attachment.

Beginning shortly after New Year's Day, Michel and a few of his trusted agent friends had begun to teach Giselle the finer points of Resistance work—the use of various weapons, demolition and sabotage, the Japanese art of hand-to-hand Jujitsu fighting and how to kill quickly and efficiently. The pace of the training was grueling and learning to kill was an affront to her finer sensibilities. But Giselle knew that in war, such skills were necessary against a ruthless foe.

Looking down at her mud-covered trousers and the Sten gun in her hands, she thought how far the young ballet dancer had come in only a few short years.

She noticed that the flowers along the garden path were not yet budding. Spring was slow arriving at the château and she wondered if this was a harbinger for the new year. 1941 was certain to be a time of building and preparation, both for the Sisterhood and for herself.

Word of the successful transfer of the German Enigma machine to England reached France near the end of January through a wireless code worked out with Jean Moulin. Though saddened by the losses suffered, Giselle, Michel, Gabby and Charles celebrated their victory with a dinner in Paris.

Lifting their glasses high, the foursome toasted their success, not only in delivering the all-important decoding machine to the Allies but also the rapid growth of the Sisterhood. Many more university students had been recruited for a variety of operations against the Nazi occupation and Giselle had managed to enlist some of her old contacts in Paris. Already, vital information was filtering in from the growing network of agents, many of whom also were working for the fledgling French Resistance.

Women from all walks of life, including students, housewives, mistresses, servants and even prostitutes, were applying their age-old feminine charms to the war effort. Files on both German and Vichy officials, their idiosyncrasies and habits, were quickly filling filing cabinets in the château's hidden office.

Michel had been quite successful in establishing more reliable contact with his English counterparts and the information was being freely shared with Allied Intelligence in Britain.

February and early March had brought delays due to the chill winter weather, but it also provided time for Giselle to draw up her plans as well as practice the arts of war. She knew that her organization would have to expand beyond the boundaries of France to become truly effective against the Axis onslaught, which by early spring appeared unstoppable despite short-lived successes by the British.

The German Army had moved into Greece during the first week of April and revived the stalled Italian attack against that peninsular nation. At the same time, the newly formed *Afrika Korps* led by a successful *panzer* general named Erwin Rommel arrived in North Africa and quickly reversed the successful British invasion of Italian-held Libya. The British were pushed back eastward through El Agheila and Rommel eventually besieged the vital port of Tobruk.

With the military reverses of the Italians in both North Africa and Greece, Giselle decided she should lay plans against this weaker Axis partner. She also needed a source who might connect her to higher levels of the Axis leaders. And she knew just the place to start.

* * *

Northern Italy,
Spring, 1941

In early April, Giselle started to put her plans into action. She and Gabby motored toward Italy in the big Nash sedan with Michel at the wheel. It was an unusually mild day and beside her on the rear seat, Gabby was admiring the passing countryside as though they were simply out for a Sunday spin.

Charles had to remain in Paris to teach his classes at the Sorbonne, but had spent a considerable amount of time in coaching Giselle for an operation in Switzerland, the next destination after Italy.

She had agreed to aid British Intelligence in a scheme to hoodwink a top Nazi through his astrologers. Giselle was astounded to discover how deep the belief in the occult ran in the highest of Nazi Party circles. This knowledge only reinforced her belief that Peter and the skull were playing a large role in Hitler's quest for world domination.

The plan had been arranged through Michel and his British contacts. It sounded offbeat and chancy, but it would give her an opportunity to meet with ranking Nazi occultists who might give her a lead on Peter. Besides, the meeting was to take place in neutral Switzerland and she would not be using her true identity, so even if the scheme backfired, there seemed little harm in the effort.

Primarily Giselle was making this lengthy trip south in hopes that an old family friend might be persuaded to play a part in the new Sisterhood. She knew the high-level connections of this woman might help her immeasurably.

Talk had circulated for some time in the highest social circles that Mussolini had taken a mistress back in the early 1930s. Giselle knew that if anyone would have knowledge of the inner secrets of the Fascists, it would be this woman; her friend would know how to put them in touch.

South of Orléans, during a particularly long stretch of road through the rolling vineyard-covered countryside, Michel turned and asked, "*Ma chère*, how can you be so sure that this woman we are visiting will be sympathetic to our organization? Did you not say that she helped put that idiot Mussolini in power?"

Gabby, in an irrepressible holiday mood, jutted her chin in the air, raised her right arm in the Fascist salute and shouted, "*Viva Il Duce!*" As was becoming his habit, Michel tried to silence the young woman with an intimidating scowl, but to no avail.

Giselle merely smiled. She was perfectly happy to find some humor and gaiety in Gabby's youthful exuberance. She was still saddened by the deaths of the boat captain and his nephew and was beginning to be concerned about Charles' health. The winter had been hard on the older man.

Ignoring Gabby, who continued to mimic the Italian dictator by leaning out the car window and shouting "*Viva Il Duce!*" as they passed some startled villagers, Giselle leaned forward and spoke, emphasizing each word.

"This woman, as you call her, is Francesca Dellaporte Delano Tagliani and she is one of my aunt's dearest friends. They have been quite close since they both were children," she said. "If anyone can help us penetrate the Axis hierarchy, it would be her. And I feel certain she will help us. Although she is about the same age as my Aunt Gez, she always treated me more like a sister."

"Then she is from America?" asked Michel without taking his eyes from the road.

"Oh yes, she's as apple pie as I am," said Giselle with a small laugh.

"I've always called her my Aunt Fran, although there is no relation. She was born to an Italian émigré family in New York State, not far from my home. Fran grew up in our same social circles as Aunt Gez. I've always had the greatest admiration for her."

Placing both hands on the front seat, Giselle leaned even closer to Michel so he could hear her without shouting over the rumble of the straight 6-cylinder engine. "She always got whatever she went after. She married a wealthy stock broker, a member of the Delano family, in the early 1920s. But she was never content to stay home to cook and mend. She became one of the first women allowed on the floor of the Wall Street Stock Exchange and got her broker's license just before the Crash."

"Ah, that must have been terrible, to lose everything so soon after joining the game," said Michel with a groan.

"Oh, no," said Giselle brightly, "the Crash was what brought her great fortune and the love of her life. She paid attention to the latest gossip and the conversation of her well-connected friends and associates. She knew that the big wealthy financiers had encouraged speculation to balloon up the costs of stocks and bonds."

"How did that work?" asked Michel. He was genuinely interested as, being a creative artist and government functionary, he had never paid much attention to business.

Giselle frowned. "She once tried to explain it all to me but I'm not sure I understood it all. It was something about the inflation following World War I. The Federal Reserve first raised interest rates and when that caused a recession and the loss of many independent banks, they were raised even further. This, coupled with more money pumped into the system in 1927, prompted a boom period with thousands of small investors buying stocks and bonds.

"Aunt Fran once said she learned of a meeting in February, 1929, between the head of the Bank of England and officers of the Federal Reserve. Before the end of that month, the Federal Reserve began advising its member banks to get out of the stock market. She also noticed that Bernard Baruch and Joseph P. Kennedy, among others, got out early. So Aunt Fran followed suit and advised her clients to do the same."

"This Federal Reserve," interrupted Michel, "is that your central bank?"

"Yes," replied Giselle with a laugh, "only we are never supposed to call it that. The question of a central bank has been a contentious issue ever since the founding of the Republic."

She paused to look at a particularly beautiful vineyard as they passed, then returned to her explanation of the stock market crash. "By August, 1929, the Federal Reserve suddenly reversed its policy of expansion and the money supply began to contract. The balloon finally burst on October 29th, Black Tuesday. Those heavily in debt lost everything. Those that got out early were still there to pick up the pieces."

"Aunt Fran watched the big guys carefully and when they began quietly selling, Fran did too. When they started buying, she started buying up everything in sight for pennies on the dollar. She became fabulously rich."

Michel laughed. "It sounds like a Hollywood motion picture success story."

Giselle slumped, laying her head on the back of the driver's seat. As she gazed at Michel, her expression darkened. "Not really, *mon cher*, her husband was not so fortunate. She tried to warn him but he had too much male pride. He wouldn't listen. He stayed till the end and lost everything. He might have survived his personal loss, but he lost the money of his friends and clients. He couldn't stand it. He took his own life."

Hearing a gasp, Giselle turned to her right. Gabby was staring at her with a horrified expression. She had been listening to Giselle's story all the while.

"Quite right, my dear," said Giselle, her eyes reflecting the sadness evident in Gabby's face, "it was a terrible time. I think this is when Fran and Aunt Gez became even closer as friends and confidantes."

Hoping to break the gloomy silence in the car, Giselle cleared her throat and continued her story in a brighter tone. "After the Crash, she met a wealthy Italian banker named Rudolfo Tagliani and traveled home with him to assist the rise of Mussolini's Fascist Party. She actually thought it was the wave of the future and the beginning of a New World Order. Due to her Italian heritage, Fran could speak fluent Italian and, thanks to her connections in banking circles, she had learned plenty of insider information concerning world politics and finances. She and her Italian boyfriend became very influential, both with Mussolini and with some members of the royalty."

"Are we really going to meet a real prince?" asked Gabby with keen anticipation. Giselle laughed. "Don't get too excited, my little social climber. I merely said that Aunt Fran knows some members of King Victor Emmanuel's family. Her friend Rudolfo owns several vineyards and has a villa on the *Via Nomentana* in the outskirts of Rome near a close family friend, Prince Giovanni Torlonia. I think I told you that the prince once allowed Mussolini to use his family home on the *Via Nomentana* to entertain Emperor Haile Selassie of Ethiopia."

"Do you think I might get to meet the prince?" asked Gabby. Despite being a product of France's merchant class and an avowed socialist, she was nevertheless enthralled with the idea of actually meeting royalty.

"Probably not." said Giselle with compassion. "We are not going all the way to Rome, only to her vineyard home in Tuscany, *Villa Tagliani*."

Seeing the look of disappointment on Gabby's face, Giselle quickly added, "But you never know. My Aunt Fran has many powerful and well-connected friends. There's always a count or duke around, not to mention the young Italian men and you know what they say about them."

Gabby blushed but brightened.

"And how do you know she is not still a loyal Fascist?" Michel's eyes never left the road, but his pointed question clearly reflected the suspicion he felt. After many of his fellow agents had joined the Nazis, he had learned the consequences of trusting the wrong people.

"Well, I can't be certain, but from the tone of some letters that Aunt Gez showed me before I left to go back to the Yucatan, I distinctly got the impression that the bloom was off the lily."

Gabby looked at her quizzically. "I think that she has begun to question the correctness of the Fascist cause," Giselle explained with a gentle smile.

"But that doesn't mean she is ready to join ours," said Gabby, echoing some of Michel's suspicion.

"And what about her husband?" added Michel.

Giselle sighed at their lack of trust and sat back on the seat. She leaned back. "I guess we'll just have to wait and see," she said closing her eyes and accepting the rocking rhythm of the big sedan. She was asleep as it rolled through Avignon. Belching smoke from the wood-burning gas generator, the big sedan skirted Marseille to the north thus bypassing the taller of the Alps. It was well into the night when the travelers drove through Cannes and Nice and finally arrived in Genoa. They found a small but comfortable hotel there as it was decided not to barge in on Aunt Fran late at night. They would get an early start the next day.

"*Accoglienza! Accoglienza!*" The cry of welcome by the short woman standing in the cobblestone driveway of the large villa was taken up by some of the workers on the grounds. Even an upstairs maid was waving from a corner window.

The long blue Nash cruised through large wrought iron gates which arched upward to a stylish metal adornment of blue grapes clustered at the apex. Almost before Giselle could exit the car, the woman had grabbed her in her arms and was hugging with all her might.

Pushing Giselle away but holding her at arm's length, the woman beamed and exclaimed, "Oh, Giselle, I can't tell you how happy I am to see you. You're the best thing that has happened to me since this terrible war began. Let me look at you. Why you hardly look a day older than when I last saw you."

Despite herself, or perhaps because of Michel's presence, Giselle found herself actually blushing slightly. It had been more than seven years since she had been with Aunt Fran. She knew that she had changed considerably during that time but it was always nice to hear someone say the opposite.

Introductions were made and, as Aunt Fran welcomed Michel and Gabby, Giselle took a long appraising look at the woman she had loved and admired for so many years. In her late thirties, Fran was still a fine example of womanhood. Her figure was in full flower but without the paunchiness suffered by many older Italian women. Her dark hair still shone with brilliance in sunlight. As Giselle remembered, she used to wear it up, perhaps to appear more businesslike. But on this day it was long and flowing. Her light-colored print dress was moving in the slight breeze. Although the sun was bright and warm, summer had not yet arrived and she wore a gray woolen sweater over her dress.

"It is so pleasant today, let's sit on the veranda," suggested Fran, calling to the servants to bring a bottle of Tuscan Chianti. It proved to be chilled and delicious, not the raw wine served in cheaper restaurants in Rome.

Giselle savored the cool wine and looked about her at the sprawling *Villa Tagliani*. The main house was a two-story stucco building with a terracotta tile roof. Around it lay several outbuildings—a barn, stable, winery, tool shed and servants' quarters. A long driveway passed through row after row of vineyards and culminated in a well-kept plaza, complete with classic Roman statuary and fountains. The total ambiance of the villa and its grounds brought her an unaccustomed feeling of calm. After the weeks of stress and tension in Paris, the serenity of the Tuscan countryside had a relaxing yet invigorating effect on Giselle.

Early that morning, her group had driven southeast from Genoa to the small seaside town of Livorno. Aunt Fran's villa lay to the south and included a stretch of beachfront along the Ligurian Sea.

The villa was situated in a rich agricultural district that exported a disproportionate amount of Italy's wheat, wine, olives and olive oil. Giselle noted it was close enough to drive to Florence and the island of Corsica was easily reached by boat. She also was impressed with the long fertile valleys separating the Tuscan Apennines and the Apuan Alps.

She expressed this admiration to Aunt Fran, who became quite animated as she began a dissertation on the history of the region. Because of her loquaciousness, it became clear to Giselle that it must have been some time since Fran had felt fully comfortable conversing with anyone freely.

Aunt Fran described how the area was originally settled by the Franks but that a long series of wars between the city-states had left it in a shambles. The region was finally consolidated under the brutal tyranny of the Medici family.

"I was always told that I was named after Tuscany's Grand Duke Francesco I, a member of the third line of Medicis," explained Fran with a broad smile. She lifted her wine glass and offered, "Here's to the grand duke." Everyone lifted their glasses.

"And was it the grand duke who joined this area with Italy?" asked Gabby, apparently quite intrigued with this small history lesson.

"Oh, heavens no, my dear," replied Fran. "There was a plebiscite…" She paused at Gabby's look of puzzlement. "…a general vote, in 1861," she explained with a slight smile. "And the principality became attached to Italy the following year."

"And now you are part of the glorious Fascist state," said Giselle brightly, all the while closely watching Aunt Fran's reaction, which was quick in coming.

The older woman's eyes flashed and she started to speak, but instead glanced at Gabby and Michel. Quietly she muttered, "Giselle, darling, may I assume that I am among friends?"

Giselle looked her straight in the eyes. "These are my friends. I keep nothing from them. We are comrades in arms…" She paused, looking deep into Fran's eyes. Apparently satisfied with what she sensed there, Giselle added, "…against the brutality and tyranny of the Axis."

No one spoke. Michel and Gabby looked at each other in alarm.

Fran relaxed and broke into a large smile. "I knew I could trust you, *la mia cara*. I know both you and Gez well enough to know where your sympathies lie in the struggle taking place in the world today."

Looking about to make certain none of the servants were near, Fran suddenly spat on the ground, "That damned Mussolini has dragged us into this terrible war and I fear the only outcome will be defeat for my country."

"You mean the United States?" Gabby was confused.

"No, my dear, I mean my new country, Italy," replied Fran with a laugh. Becoming serious, she glanced about and said in a lowered voice, "But you must be careful what you say in front of the help. You never know for sure where their loyalties lie."

Everyone at the table sat still, not knowing quite what to say. Giselle broke the ice by walking to Aunt Fran and taking her hand.

Laughing with warmth and delight, she said, "Dearest Aunt Fran, I knew you'd feel this way. We are here to help."

"But what about *Signore* Tagliani?" asked Michel, not sure whether to refer to him as her husband or lover. He also could never entirely shake his suspicious nature. "Can he be trusted?"

Fran laughed without humor. "Ha! Rudolfo may hate Mussolini even worse than I do, if that is possible," she said with deep bitterness.

"But both you and your friend are still counted as big Mussolini supporters," said Michel. He would not let the issue go. Seeing the quizzical look on Giselle's face, he explained quietly, "I took the trouble to check them out with some friends in the bureau."

Giselle's questioning look turned to anger. How dare he check on her friends without informing her?

But before Giselle could say anything, Fran said, "*Attenzione*, my children, let's not start any arguments at this happiest of moments. Let me explain a few things."

She told how her lover Rudolfo Vallesanti Tagliani had been one of Mussolini's earliest supporters. He had even helped organize the famous March on Rome in late October, 1922, and had aided in the early funding of the Nazi Party, which in turn, supported the Italian Fascists. As a wealthy landowner, vintner and banker, Rudolfo had been among those who arranged a meeting between *Il Duce* and Kurt Ludecke, Hitler's personal representative.

"They met in September, 1922, at Mussolini's office in the Milan building housing his Fascist newspaper *Popolo d'Italia*," Fran said. "Since neither man spoke the other's language, they conducted their conversation in French."

Giselle smiled and nodded, pleased to think how French had been the language of diplomats for so many decades.

"Ludecke was quite impressed with Mussolini and agreed with him that the best way to achieve control of Italy was through the political process," explained Fran. "Rudolfo said Ludecke was absolutely amazed to learn that our glorious leader knew nothing of Hitler or the National Socialist movement. He had to spend considerable time explaining to Mussolini the political situation in Germany. But by the end of the conversation, Mussolini was quite sympathetic and interested in Nazi ideals.

"When Ludecke asked if he was prepared to use force to gain control of the government, our *Duce* told him straight out, 'We shall be the state because we will it so.'" She mimicked the blustery voice of Mussolini.

Fran looked at Giselle with sad eyes. "From that point on there was covert assistance to Hitler and fascism in general. We supplied military goods to nationalists in Germany and Hungary as well as in Corsica, Malta, Macedonia and Croatia. You may recall that Italy supplied hundreds of aircraft, equipment and some 50,000 soldiers to Franco's Fascist regime during the recent civil war in Spain."

Giselle pursed her lips and said with a thoughtful expression, "This means Hitler has been indebted to Mussolini right from the beginning."

"That's true," agreed Fran. "It was the beginning of the Berlin-Rome Axis and what is so ironic is the fact that Mussolini had not even heard of Hitler before this meeting." She shook her head in disgust. "And to think that today that German nobody has our *Duce* dancing to his tune."

Giselle noticed Gabby appeared somewhat bored with all the political discussion. With a broad smile, she turned to Fran, and changed the subject by asking, "But, now, I must hear all about the little *bambinos*."

The sad and serious countenance of Aunt Fran immediately blossomed into one of joy and love. "Ah, *si*, but of course." She turned in her chair and shouted, "Rosa, bring the boys, *per favore.*"

A heavyset woman stepped from a doorway of the home, waved and disappeared back inside. Moments later, she returned carrying a child in each arm. The two boys, not much more than a year old, were obviously twins. Their large dark eyes peered out from under a tousle of thick wavy black hair. Both were smiling and seemed quite at ease.

"What delightful children," cooed Gabby. Even the normally reserved Michel seemed taken by the two handsome youngsters.

Proudly, Fran introduced her sons. "This is Rudolfo," she said, as she touched one child on the head. Taking the other from Rosa's arms, she held him out as if exhibiting a magnum of prize-winning wine. "And this is Randolfo," said Fran, her face aglow with motherly pride.

Gabby took both boys and sat them on the well-tended lawn. She began playfully tickling them and making funny noises until both were squealing with delight. Even Michel joined in, swinging Rudolfo round and round while making airplane sounds.

Giselle watched the play with keen interest. It was the first time she had thought of Michel as a father figure. Instinctive thoughts of marriage and domesticity flickered through her mind. While her feelings for Jim and the desire to avenge his death were still quite strong, she felt the love for her former dance partner was growing into a solid commitment. She wondered what the future might hold for them.

Her reverie was cut short when she noticed Aunt Fran motioning her aside with a tilt of her head.

Unobtrusively, the older woman took Giselle by the arm and led her to a well-manicured garden that abutted the rows of grape vines already budding in the warmer spring weather.

When they were well out of earshot, Fran turned to Giselle and said with great feeling, "Your friends are very nice, just what I would expect from you. Giselle, my dear, I can't tell you what a breath of fresh air your visit means to me. Rudolfo and I love each other very much but these are dangerous times. He is well connected with the government but secretly works against Mussolini and his crew every chance he gets. He has his own apartment in Rome. He wants me to stay here so that I will be safe from the intrigues of politics. Occasionally we meet at Prince Torlonia's villa near Rome. It's all so clandestine."

"I think we visited there once years ago," said Giselle. "It's in Frascati, isn't it?"

'That's right, about thirteen miles southeast of the city. It's a beautiful and restful place."

Fran glanced about and smiled conspiratorially. "The prince still entertains Mussolini and his mistress there on occasion but he lost any enthusiasm for the Fascist cause when the war began."

"Aunt Fran," interrupted Giselle, "this actually brings me to the purpose of my visit. I am sure you know something of the woman that Mussolini has taken up with."

Fran laughed. "But of course. It is one of the worst kept secrets in Italy, at least among *Il Duce*'s entourage. Everyone talks about how this 28-year-old Air Force lieutenant's wife slips up a secret staircase in the *Palazzo Venezia* to have romantic trysts with our 58-year-old dictator. Most of his inner circle disapproves. They think he is making a mockery of his marriage to Rachele. But I think what they are really concerned about is what the Vatican might say if his affair was brought into the open."

"Tell me about this woman." said Giselle, hoping that the woman might be of use to the Sisterhood.

"Her name is Claretta Petacci, but everyone calls her Clara. There is much gossip about her and our leader and their possible connection to the death of Pope Pius XI."

"Really?" said Giselle as she moved closer to Aunt Fran. "Do tell me more."

With no awareness that she was behaving like a town gossip, Fran continued. "Well, you see, Clara's father is Dr. Francesco Petacci, doctor to the Pope. A little more than a year ago, when Pius died, many people think he was injected with poison by Petacci to prevent the Pope from speaking out against Mussolini's affair with his daughter. The official verdict was a massive heart attack."

"Do you think there is any truth to such rumors?" asked Giselle, who had always been fascinated by accounts of behind-the-scenes conspiracies and intrigue.

Fran merely shrugged her shoulders. "Who can say? It is well known that the elderly Pope fought long and hard against fascism, both here and in Germany, although he did reach an accommodation with Mussolini with the Lateran Treaty in 1929. But, of course, that treaty was a major concession to the Church. The Vatican city-state was created and the Italian government paid almost a billion *lire* in gold as compensation for Church property taken over during the 19th century *Risorgimento* that created modern Italy. The new Pope, who was a guest at the society wedding of Clara and Lieutenant Federici in 1934, is another story. There are many rumors about lucrative financial deals being conducted between the Vatican and the Rome-Berlin Axis."

Giselle made a mental note to keep a sharp eye on the Catholic Church and its dealings. She already had heard that the Church and Hitler had struck some kind of a live-and-let-live agreement. "At least we don't have to worry about a Vatican embassy in the United States. The public would never stand for such an intrusion on separation of church and state."

Fran merely smiled knowingly, "I don't know. I wouldn't be surprised to see the U.S. recognize the Vatican state at some point. There is too much power there, considering it has its own embassies, banks, currency and courts."

Giselle sat contemplating the idea that any U.S. president would openly recognize a religious institution as a sovereign state. Finally, she asked, "But what about this Clara? Do you think she truly loves Mussolini or is she simply drawn to his power?"

"I know the woman," replied Fran, who noted Giselle's look of surprise and interest. "She has visited here a few times."

Fran made an impish grin and whispered confidentially, "In fact, I may have a surprise for you later today."

Giselle raised an eyebrow in question.

"*Si*, knowing of your visit, I took the liberty of inviting her here today. I hope you don't mind." Aunt Fran smile was mischievous.

"I'm delighted," replied Giselle with sincerity. This was working out better than she had hoped. She knew it was contacts like this that would bring her closer to Peter and the skull.

Returning to the conversation, Fran said, "Clara is very brave and enthusiastic, but quite naïve about many things. She confides in Rudolfo and myself as well as many others, including Prince Torlonia."

"What about this prince?" Giselle thought of Gabby's desire to meet royalty. "Can he be trusted?"

"I think so," said Fran. Her face reflected serious consideration. "He works closely with Rudolfo and would never betray us. They get along very well together. Perhaps it's Rudolfo's great wealth or it could be due to his lineage. Would you believe this little New York girl is now associating with royalty?"

"Your highness," quipped Giselle and gave a short curtsy. Both women laughed.

"Tell me more about Rudolfo," implored Giselle.

She and Fran moved to a wrought iron bench and sat in the shadow of a tall poplar tree.

"Well, he was born in the south, the son of a very wealthy vineyard owner. You may recall we met in New York at that Christmas party at your Aunt Gez's apartment on Park Avenue."

Giselle frowned. "I remember hearing about the party but I wasn't there. That was 1932, wasn't it?"

"That's correct."

"Remember, that was the Christmas I was in bed with flu."

"Of course," said Fran, gently clapping her hands. "We were all so worried about you, but as I recall, you were over the worst of it at the time of the grand party."

Giselle nodded silently and frowned. She suddenly recalled the anger and hurt when she was not allowed to join the revelers. She had so wanted to dance for the adults but the fear of influenza was still strong following the great outbreak a decade earlier.

Sensing her thoughts, Fran quickly continued her account. "There was magic when we first saw each other across the room. I couldn't take my eyes off him. I was quite brazen but then I was a recently widowed woman in the prime of my life. He asked me to dance and when I felt myself in his arms it was as though the world faded away. There was just the two of us."

Giselle smiled dreamily as Fran continued her romantic account. "He was unmarried. He told me that between politics and business he had never had time for a family. But he apparently had second thoughts. We had such a wonderful time in New York that when it came time for his return to Italy, at his insistence, I went with him. Although he's Italian, he is very much an American at heart. We came here and had several idyllic years before the war began."

"You never married?"

Fran looked away with a faint smile on her face. "There seemed no point to it. I already had been married and he never pushed the matter. Then the twins were born and it was too late."

Fran pursed her lips and shook her head. "It would have been a scandal and bad for business," she said mocking Rudolfo. "So whenever anyone calls here, we just tell them the twins are Rudolfo's nephews. He says it's less complicated this way. I do not know what the future may bring but for now, I'm quite happy with my little family."

"Rudolfo sounds like quite a man," said Giselle with a grin. "I've always been sorry I didn't get the chance to meet him before you left the States."

Fran lowered her eyes and grinned widely, almost as wide as when she introduced her twins. "Yes, he is quite a man."

She turned and there was a sparkle in her deep brown eyes. "Picture one of my boys as a grown man," she said with a slight giggle. "He is tall but not too tall, just under six feet, slender and has long dark wavy hair."

Fran's shoulders wiggled ever so slightly as she said with girlish enthusiasm, "He is quite handsome and devoted to me. He's tender but strong, very much a man."

She lowered her voice. "Even though he more and more disapproves of Mussolini, *Il Duce* continues to have confidence in him. He trusts him implicitly and still shares secrets with him. He is quite a power in Rome."

Giselle leaned forward and took Aunt Fran's hands in hers. "This could be very important for us," she said with great solemnity, a plan already growing in her mind. Without going into great detail about the death of Jim and the stolen crystal skull, she explained what had prompted her to fight the Axis powers through a secret Sisterhood. As she talked, Aunt Fran's eye grew wider and wider.

Finally the woman could contain herself no longer. As Giselle was explaining about the creation of the French Resistance, Fran interrupted. "Oh, Giselle, this is marvelous. I've been searching for some way to do my part in ending this horrible war and the Fascist dictatorship. I might have known that you, of all people, would show the way. I must make amends for the support I gave Mussolini in past years. Please tell me what I can do."

Giselle sat in thought for long moments, then blurted out, "I have it. This place would be the perfect meeting place for the Sisterhood. It's secluded yet within reach of Europe's capitals."

"It is more perfect than you know," said Fran. Excitement was growing within her and her features were becoming animated. "Come, let me show you."

Leading Giselle by the hand, Fran walked through a small wooden gate leading into the vineyard. She snickered slightly at Giselle's puzzled expression as they walked down a furrow separating the long rows of grape vines. Giselle's bewilderment increased as the pair walked past the edge of the vineyard and moved toward a rocky incline in the adjacent foothills.

Glancing about to make certain they were unobserved, Fran pulled Giselle behind some tall and imposing boulders where she saw a human-size opening into the hillside.

"There are underground chambers here dating back to the time of the Romans. They have been long forgotten. We only discovered them when the winery was enlarged. They would make an ideal location for meetings or storage, don't you think?" Aunt Fran's excitement was infectious.

Delighted, Giselle merely nodded. Already, her mind was racing with ideas of how to put this secluded and protected location to use.

"This is wonderful, Aunt Fran. I have some ideas of how to make this place more effective and secure. But there is yet another way you could help," she turned and looked into her companion's eyes. In a somber tone, she added, "But it could be quite dangerous."

The older woman looked back, her eyes steady and hard. "I have made my decision to help."

"Very well, from what you have told me, I think that, through Rudolfo, you might be able to gain intelligence valuable for the Allies."

With a sly look, Fran whispered, "I may already have."

She smiled broadly at Giselle's quizzical expression. "Dear Rudolfo let me in on a little secret, one that no one is supposed to know."

"Well, what is it?" Giselle could hardly contain her curiosity. She was well aware of the high-level connections of both Aunt Fran and her wealthy man. She knew this secret would be more than gossip about marital infidelity or petty grafting.

Fran leaned close to her and said, "He learned from a very highly-placed source in Germany that many troops are quietly being withdrawn from France and sent to the East."

"Yes, we already know that," said Giselle. "But aren't they being sent to bolster the Axis efforts in the Balkans and Greece?"

"Oh, no, dear, Rudolfo said he has it on good authority that Hitler plans to attack Russia at the earliest opportunity."

Giselle gasped. "Why this monstrous! Why would he do such a thing? He made it very plain in his book *Mein Kampf* that Germany should never again fight a two-front war. He still hasn't conquered England and now he plans to attack Russia?"

Fran looked at her with narrowed eyes. "Apparently, Stalin is planning to launch an all-out invasion of Europe and Hitler must beat him to the punch or suffer defeat, considering Russia's overwhelming superiority in tanks and manpower."

Giselle stood still, shocked into silence.

"It's all very hush-hush," Fran continued. "Hitler's only hope lies in complete surprise and Stalin doesn't dare let the world know of his intentions. Even *Il Duce* doesn't know any of this. It is only known to a handful of our leaders. And no one wants to be the one to tell Mussolini since he is already in such a state at having to play second fiddle to that German corporal."

Giselle sat stunned. Finally, she sputtered, "But the Germans have a non-aggression pact with the Soviet government."

Fran shrugged. "I can only tell you what I know. Neither Hitler nor Stalin can be trusted. You know that."

"When is this to happen?"

"Soon, very soon. Perhaps before summer."

"Good God!" exclaimed Giselle. She had been struck by a sudden realization. "I have relatives in Russia. My father's brother and his wife are in Moscow and there are others. They must be warned. How do you suppose I can get to Moscow?"

Fran placed her hand on Giselle's shoulder. "Don't fret, my dear. I think that Rudolfo may be able to help you in that. He has friends in the diplomatic corps who travel back and forth to Moscow on a regular basis. We are still friendly with the Russians, you know."

Giselle's eyes took on a new sparkle at the thought of being able to travel to the Soviet Union.

Just then the faint beeping of an automobile horn interrupted the conversation. Aunt Fran looked toward the sound and tapped Giselle on the shoulder. "Your surprise is here," she said with a broad smile. "And in light of our discussion about your Sisterhood, it might truly delight you. But, please, not a word about Hitler's invasion."

Giselle nodded her agreement as the pair retraced their steps through the vineyard. While Fran hurried toward the villa, Giselle trudged slowly behind, deep in thought over the ramifications of the news about the coming invasion. The horror of war was spreading and her relatives must be warned. Thankfully, Fran had anticipated her thought of asking Rudolfo to help arrange her passage on a flight to Moscow.

As she approached the house, she noticed a sporty black car in the drive next to her big Nash sedan. A uniformed driver stood off to one side while Gabby and Michel, still holding the twins, walked around the vehicle admiringly. A smartly dressed and pleasant-looking woman stood by the right front fender.

Aunt Fran turned and came back to Giselle. Taking her by the arm, she whispered, "Hurry along, my dear. This is the woman we mentioned earlier. She told me she might drop by today."

As they approached the car, the woman was speaking, apparently bragging about the car. It was a sporty black two-door with red leather trim and somewhat gaudy wire hubcaps.

Although Giselle had been conversing with Aunt Fran in English, her Italian was quite passable. Michel was translating for Gabby. "This lady said it is a Fiat 2800 *Berlinetta* and that it handles beautifully," he said.

"How would she know?" Aunt Fran whispered in Giselle's ear with a laugh. "She can't drive."

The woman was dressed in a mid-calf length gabardine skirt with a rust-colored military-style double-breasted jacket. This was covered with a full-length brushed cotton duster topped by a wide-brim straw hat covered in silk flowers. A long white silk scarf completed this stylish touring costume.

She was not truly beautiful but exuded a powerful presence. Her short-cut dark, curly hair accentuated wide, dark eyebrows. Her nose was somewhat long but classically Roman and her lips were sensuous and highlighted by dark red lipstick. All this, coupled with a well-tanned complexion, gave the woman an exotic attraction that far exceeded her features alone.

She was obviously proud of her car. "*Uno 1940 modelo. Molto moderno,*" said the woman with a sweep of her hand along the chassis.

"Come, Giselle," said Aunt Fran in a loud voice, guiding her toward the group by the Fiat. "Let me introduce you to my friend Clara Petacci."

Overwhelmed by the news of the upcoming invasion of Russia and concerned for her relatives there, Giselle could only nod silently as she allowed herself to be introduced to Mussolini's mistress.

CHAPTER 11

Zürich, Switzerland
April, 1941

GISELLE STOOD OUTSIDE AUNT FRAN'S home and watched the tail lights of Clara Petacci's Fiat disappear into the Tuscan night. Her mind was in a whirl, not only from drinking more wine than usual, but from the implications of her conversation with Mussolini's mistress.

"It's a good thing she has a driver," murmured Michel, who stood with his arm around her waist. It was late and the servants had retired. Gabby had long since fallen asleep on a divan in the living room from the effects of the wine and the travel. Only Aunt Fran remained with them, now a full-fledged member of the Sisterhood. It was safe to display his affection for Giselle openly.

"*Oui, mon cher*," agreed Giselle slowly. "One more glass of that delicious Chianti and we would have had to carry her to her car." Beside them Aunt Fran nodded in agreement.

"I think it's time that we all went to bed," said Giselle with a sigh of fatigue. Inwardly, her mind was groping toward an audacious plan not yet fully formed.

"A splendid idea, my sweet," said Michel, hugging her closer to him with obvious intentions other than sleep.

Pulling away from him, Giselle rolled her eyes. "You must be kidding, my darling. After that drive this morning and all that's happened today, I am not feeling very amorous. Like Gabby, I need to sleep."

"Actually, I agree," said Michel, running his hand down her backside. "But we will speak more on this matter in the morning."

Aunt Fran looked at Giselle. The lights of the villa spilling out onto the driveway highlighted her knowing smile.

Giselle merely tittered and snuggled up once again up next to her lover. "Speak?" she asked coyly. "Well, more like make a point," replied Michel with a licentious smile as they returned to the house on unsteady feet. They all laughed. But, at Fran's suggestion, they all agreed to have one final nightcap.

It had been a very long day. Giselle had learned of the coming invasion of Russia by the Germans to stop a Russian invasion of Europe. It was all very confusing but she knew she must pass this information to her Allied contacts as quickly as possible.

It was further confusing to learn from Aunt Fran that for several years, German military men had secretly trained in the Soviet Union. Such exercises were prohibited by the Versailles Treaty but had taken place far from the watchful eyes of Allied authorities.

She had thought it quite ironic that the Soviet Union, which she now learned had helped give birth to the Germans' *Blitzkrieg* tactics, was about to feel the brunt of them.

But her excitement over the news of the coming invasion was overshadowed by something Clara Petacci had said during their lengthy conversations before and during dinner. The germ of an idea kept growing.

Despite the pleasantness of the day, the night had turned chilly. Giselle shivered next to Michel as they entered the villa.

Sitting next to a warm fire and sipping on snifters of Cognac, they discussed the day's visitor.

"Did you hear her discourse on world politics?" said Giselle to Aunt Fran, as though they were gossiping about a neighbor's latest affair. "She obviously has a lot to learn." Upon some reflection, she added with a faint smile, "As I do myself."

Fran patted her on the arm and said, "Don't fret, my dear, you seem to be doing splendidly."

"I don't trust her," said Michel matter-of-factly. Both women turned to look at him. His expression was sullen and distrustful.

"My dear Michel, you are always the suspicious one," said Giselle in a soothing tone.

"I don't think I trust her either," agreed Fran in a quiet voice. "She is bright and compassionate, but I think she is truly infatuated with Mussolini and that could be dangerous."

"*Oui*," chimed in Michel. "One romantic interlude with *Il Duce* and she might give away the game."

Giselle rose to her feet and faced her two closest friends. "Now it is your turn not to be fretful. After all, we didn't tell her everything about our organization, its activities or its members. She only knows that we hope to restore a peaceful balance to the world. And she seemed quite agreeable to that."

"Yes, but if that means the loss of power for her lover, then…" Michel's response was cut short by Giselle, who said blithely, "We'll burn that bridge when we come to it."

Aunt Fran giggled at Giselle's mangling of clichés.

"Aunt Fran?" Giselle turned to her. "Can you arrange for a flight to Moscow? It's essential that I warn my relatives."

Fran grew serious. "I don't know about that, *mia cara*. It would not be easy for Rudolfo to arrange a ride with the military and you have no exit visa for a commercial flight. You must also think of Rudolfo. I would not like him to take too many chances."

"I agree," replied Giselle soberly. "I won't put my personal concerns ahead of our overall effort. I'm sure I can find a way to warn my relatives."

"I don't like it," said Michel, who was looking at the floor as though he could see some dire catastrophe drawn there. "Every time we send a communication, we run the risk of discovery. Let the Russians take care of themselves. If what Fran told you is true, they are planning to take over all of Europe."

"Michel, how can you say that? These are my relatives. My uncle and his family live near Moscow." Giselle's anger was growing.

Putting both hands out in front of him, Michel turned conciliatory. "Relax, *ma chère*. It was thoughtless of me to express reservations about contacting your family." He knew better than to argue with Giselle on certain matters, and family was one of them. Besides, he had another argument.

"Giselle, my dear," added Fran, "I only said it would not be easy for Rudolfo to arrange passage for you on a military or diplomatic flight. I did not say it was impossible. I will contact him tomorrow and see what can be done."

"And if you will remember, we have business in Switzerland. We have someone to meet in Zürich before we return to Paris," reminded Michel.

Giselle's anger was deflected but still present. "Business? Someone? Michel, please don't play games. Fran is one of my closest friends. She is one of us now. We can be open with her."

Ignoring Michel's frown of disapproval, she turned to Fran with excitement. "Oh, Aunt Fran, it's just too juicy. We are to meet a British secret agent in Zürich. He has a plan to remove one of Hitler's closest associates."

"No," exclaimed Fran. "Whatever can it be?"

Michel climbed to his feet. He was a bit unsteady after all the drinking, but his voice was clear and strong. "That's enough, Giselle. It is not a matter of trusting Fran. It is a matter of protecting her. What she does not know, she cannot be forced to tell. Even Gabby doesn't know full details of the plan."

Giselle was shocked. This was the first time that Michel had spoken harshly to her and she couldn't decide whether to feel angry or mastered.

Fran made the decision for her. "He's right, my dear," she said softly.

Giselle sat silently for several moments. Her intellect gained the upper hand and she slapped both hands on her knees. "Yes, my darling, you are right. We must stay guarded at all times, for everyone's sake."

Everyone nodded in agreement, ending the debate.

"Oh, I just love the spy business already," effused Fran, who also had gone noticeably beyond her usual daily wine consumption. "It's so exciting to think I might be involved in espionage and such."

She suddenly stopped. "But what about a recognition sign. Aren't spies supposed to have a sign so that they can recognize each other? I read that somewhere in a book."

Giselle sat down beside her and smiled. "But, of course," she said. "The Sisterhood recognizes each other by a single long-stemmed red rose. The rose has been used by male secret societies throughout history, such as the Illuminati, the Rosicrucians and others. So why not us?"

"It is quite ironic to think that we will use their own symbol against them," chuckled Fran.

"And you already have a rose on your thigh," said Michel knowingly. Despite her worldly sophistication, Giselle felt a blush rising to her cheeks. But Aunt Fran merely smiled with understanding.

"Aunt Fran, as you might as well know, Michel and I..." she began haltingly.

Fran's smile broadened as she said, "Tut, tut, my dear, do not think me some old fogy. I have eyes and I have experience. You are a grown woman now and obviously capable of making your own decisions, especially when it comes to matters of the heart."

With a smile of gratitude for Fran's understanding, Giselle continued her explanation of the use of the rose. "Did you know that throughout the ages, the rose has always typified secrecy, as in the Latin *sub rosa*, meaning 'under the rose' or 'in confidence.' Also, the rose has been connected with the cross. The color fluctuates from red to white, such as the 'rose of Sharon' or the 'lily of the valley.'"

Giselle stopped abruptly. Her eyes wide and sparkling with inspiration, she exclaimed, "In fact, why not take the names of flowers as our code names?"

"Code names from flowers?" Michel shook his head. "How melodramatic."

"No, it's perfect," said Fran. "I love lilies. I will be the lily, a beautiful white lily of the valley." She raised her arms and spread them as though she was a flower opening its petals to the summer rain.

"Yes, your code name can be Lily White," agreed Giselle. The warm glow of the wine and the presence of Aunt Fran had revived some of her girlish enthusiasm.

"And what about you?" asked Michel with a broad smile. He found himself caught up in this wine-induced reverie in spite of his usual cynicism. "Will you be Rose Early?" He chuckled at his attempt at humor.

Giselle stood thoughtfully for a moment before replying. "No, despite my rose birthmark, I have always liked Violets. I will be Velva Violet," she proclaimed, spinning and striking a pose next to Fran.

"Sort of like Mata Hari, eh, *ma chére*? And what about me? Do I get a code name?" Michel was still grinning at the wistful conversation as well as Giselle's unexpected levity toward the dangerous business of espionage.

She looked at him with a serious expression. "But of course, my darling. You will simply be known as the Chauffeur."

Poor Michel stood stock-still for a long moment. His smile faded. An anger began rising within him and his face became flushed. But then he noticed that Fran was laughing and he saw the merry gleam in Giselle's eyes.

All three burst out laughing.

A faint voice came from the couch. "Hey, am I missing the party?" Gabby struggled to pull herself up from her sleep. Giselle perched herself on one of the couch's arms and said soothingly, "No, *ma petite*, there's no party. We are all going to bed. Go back to sleep."

Eyes closing, Gabby sagged back into her sleeping position as the others moved off to their rooms.

The next morning was spent laying plans for the mission in Zürich while Fran made a telephone call to Rudolfo to discretely ask his help in securing Giselle a flight to Moscow.

Giselle took more than an hour coaching Gabby for her role in the scheme. The young Parisian student was keen to play her part and paid close attention to Giselle's instructions, only rarely asking questions to clarify a point.

Aunt Fran arranged an early lunch consisting of an elaborate *insalata Fiorentina*, with fresh spinach, orzo pasta and grilled chicken in a roasted garlic lemon vinaigrette topped by shaved parmesan cheese. The sun-dried tomatoes, black olives, capers and pine nuts all came from the villa's extensive garden.

After packing their belongings and saying their good-byes to Fran, the threesome drove off shortly after noon in the big Nash.

By late afternoon, they reached Milan, stopping only for a brief meal of cheese and salami. Their pace slowed considerably as they entered the Alps to cross from Italy to Switzerland and the road became narrow and twisting.

It was nearing midnight when the Nash, blowing wood smoke and covered with grime and road dust pulled into *Bürkliplatz* near the center of Zürich, a quayside situated on the *Zürichsee* at the upper end of the stylish *Bahnhofstrasse*. It was the scene of hectic activity during the day, but this late at night it was dark except for the streetlights and there were few people on the street.

"Here we are," said Michel, gently nudging the sleeping Giselle beside him. She roused herself and looked about.

"It looks deserted," she muttered.

"That's because it's almost midnight, my sweet. Wake Gabby and grab the luggage. We'll get to our rooms and have a real sleep."

Although the threesome considered themselves to be traveling light, their baggage still consisted of three large suitcases, a satchel and a cosmetic bag, which they lugged across *Talstrasse* to a large, squat multi-storied building flying the flags of several nations.

The luggage was dropped to the ground when they found the front door of the *Hotel Baur au Lac* locked for the night.

After a few insistent rings, the concierge, struggling to button his uniform tunic, finally arrived to open the door.

"I apologize for our late arrival but we had difficulty in crossing the mountains," Michel explained to the sleepy-eyed staff member. "We do have reservations."

"There is no problem, sir," replied the man with little conviction. He dutifully led the pair to the registration desk and began the necessary registration paperwork. Both Michel and Gabby looked about at the sumptuous lobby of the old hotel. Elaborate chandeliers lighted the wood-paneled walls and stairway.

"*Magnifique,*" murmured Gabby in admiration of the ornate surroundings. Michel smiled and said to the concierge, "We have not been here before." The man nodded indifferently as he continued to fill out the register.

Michel, who was not accustomed to staying in luxury hotels, was still trying to get used to the idea that money was no longer a stumbling block in his life. Yet, his initial happiness to be rid of the financial worries that had plagued him both as an artist and an agent of the *Deuxième Bureau* had recently been shifting into a certain uneasiness about becoming dependent on a woman, even if it was a woman such as Giselle. The fact that he was relegated to chauffeur status did little to assuage this affront to his ego.

Michel was still musing about this strange turn in his life as he and the women were led upstairs to their rooms. Giselle and Gabby had registered for one room together while he had signed for a single room in keeping with their identity papers. But he knew Giselle would share his room as soon as practical.

As they parted, he said to Gabby, "Our meeting is scheduled for tomorrow afternoon in the bar. Come to our room when you wake up and we'll eat breakfast together and finalize our plans."

Gabby nodded in agreement and stood on her toes to give him a good-night kiss on the cheek. "Thank you for being such a fine driver," she said with all sincerity. Michel frowned as he walked down the hall-way to his room, again reminded of his role.

Once in their room, he and Giselle looked at each other and smiled weakly. The long and arduous drive over the Alps had so drained them that all they could do was fall into an exhausted sleep in each other's arms.

By 7 p.m. the following evening, Michel was perplexed. He, Giselle and Gabby had been waiting in the hotel bar since three that afternoon but no one had entered except for the usual businessmen stopping for a drink after work.

"I don't understand this," he said to Giselle, who was obviously be-coming impatient with the long wait. The young and impatient Gabby had been fidgeting for some time. "Our contact should have been here long before now," she whispered.

As evening drew on, the group decided to take shifts leaving for dinner as all were hungry and in need of a break from the monotonous wait. Gabby went first but when she returned, she found Michel and Giselle still sitting at the same cloth-covered table nursing a *Cinzano* and listening to Maurice Chevalier sing "*Il y a de la joie*" over a radio that was amplified through the lounge.

However, as Gabby sat down and was about to complain about the delay, a tall man approached their table. He had a long and somewhat bulbous nose, dark brown hair and the long smooth fingers of a person accustomed to working more with his brains than with his hands. He looked quite British, yet he spoke in immaculate French.

"Am I addressing *Monsignor* Devereaux?" the man asked quietly. "*Oui*," replied Michel cautiously.

The man leaned closer and said softly, "The chrysanthemums will soon be in bloom." It was the recognition sign that Michel had received from his agent friends in Paris.

Michel dutifully responded, "Yes, but they will be small this year."

With this proper countersign, the man smiled broadly and extend-ed his hand. "I'm Fleming, Ian Fleming."

The man pulled off his dark wool overcoat revealing a tan tweed jacket. His expertly knotted brown bow tie and a straight-stemmed pipe completed the impression of an Oxford professor. He sat down and Michel motioned the waiter over.

"And what will you have?" he asked the new arrival. Without looking at the hovering waiter, Fleming said, "Vodka martini, shaken, not stirred."

Fleming waited until after the waiter had left and, after glancing about to see if anyone was paying attention to them, said, "I'm dreadfully sorry for making you wait. I was detained on other matters and then I took the liberty of scouting this place for some time before making contact. Can't be too careful these days, you know."

Michel merely nodded in agreement. He was well aware that Zürich was brimming with spies from every nation.

"You must be Michel Devereaux of the French Secret Service?" continued Fleming.

"And you are with British Naval Intelligence," Michel responded matter-of-factly.

Fleming turned to Gabby. "But I have not had the pleasure of meeting the young ladies." He took Giselle's hand and brushed it with his lips as introductions were made. She smiled in acknowledgement.

The man did not notice Gabby's look of surprise as Giselle was introduced as Velva Violet. When it came Gabby's turn, the young student blushed slightly, unaccustomed to the courtly attentions of older men.

"How do you do, Mr. Fleming," she managed to say. "I am Fifi LeGonne."

She was pleased to see the surprised looks from Giselle and Michel. I, too, can have a cover name, she thought smugly.

Without responding, Fleming turned to Giselle. Now he was all business. "Are you to be our astrologer?"

Nodding, Giselle started to say something but was cut short. "Is it necessary to have the young girl present?" asked Fleming brusquely. "This is a delicate operation."

Gabby, her dander up, was about to protest what she considered his premature judgment, when Michel said, "We have already discussed this with our number one and it was agreed that Gabby ... er, Fifi will be assisting Velva at the meeting."

"And just who is your number one?" asked Fleming somewhat haughtily.

"I am," replied Giselle. She gave the British agent a cool and determined look.

Realizing that there appeared no room for argument, Fleming shrugged his shoulders as the waiter returned with drinks for all. Once left to themselves, Michel asked, "Is the meeting all set?"

"Yes," replied the British agent. "I have arranged it through one of our more infamous occultists. A fellow named Aleister Crowley. Have you heard of him?" Michel and Giselle shook their heads. "Well, it doesn't matter. He's an odd duck. He was well connected with the Germans during the last war and has many contacts here on the Continent. We think he's with us this time. He's useful, regardless of his true sympathies."

"And exactly who is it that we are supposed to meet tomorrow?" asked Michel. He remembered perfectly well but, suspicious as usual, he wanted to double check Fleming's knowledge.

Fleming smiled as if he entirely guessed Michel's ploy, but with no indication of having taken insult, he replied, "I should have thought you would have been briefed on that. And you and I are meeting no one. Only Miss Violet and…" he paused and looked at Gabby. "Miss Le-Gonne will attend the meeting. I am too well known in certain circles. I am merely the facilitator for this meeting, although I should like an account from you when it's over."

"But of course," agreed Michel.

Turning to Giselle and Gabby, he continued. "You two will be meeting with a pair of ranking Nazis, one Karl Haushofer and a Dr. Ernst Schulte-Strethaus."

"I have heard of Haushofer." Michel said. "He's a major Nazi theologian and the architect of the concept of *lebensraum*, living space for the new Germany."

"That's correct. He founded the Institute for Geopolitics at the University of Munich. He envisions a Third Reich that will gain its *Lebensraum* by expansion to the East."

"That chance may come sooner than anyone thinks," muttered Giselle, thinking of the coming invasion. Fleming gave her a quizzical look. Apparently he was unaware of the Nazis' next move.

"Why do you say that?" asked Fleming.

"Because I have just learned that Hitler is planning to attack Russia, possibly before the summer." Giselle saw the look of surprise on Fleming's face and was delighted to have shared information that this haughty British agent obviously did not know.

"We've suspected this for some time. Both Russia and Germany have been massing troops along their borders," Fleming mused to himself. "But I'm wondering why I haven't been told about it while you seem to know it for certain."

Giselle smiled. "It's a secret, my dear sir."

"Yes, well, I have been away from London for some time now," muttered Fleming, somewhat embarrassed to find an American woman passing him top-secret information.

"What about the other man?" Michel asked, bringing the conversation back to the point. "I don't believe I've heard of him."

Fleming leaned back in his chair and lit his pipe before confiding, "This is the one we want to work on, old chap. He is the astrological adviser to *Herr* Rudolf Hess, deputy *Führer* of the Third Reich."

Michel gulped and took a big swallow of his vermouth. "Well, your people certainly don't aim low," he said.

Giselle merely smiled and nodded in appreciation of the magnitude of the plan.

Gabby sat wide-eyed, already agog that she was involved in derring-do with a British agent. She had participated in several student demonstrations against the Nazis and was prepared to risk her life for a free France. But she had never imagined that she would be plotting against the man closest to Hitler himself.

Fleming seemed totally at ease. He tapped his pipe against a table leg and re-lit it. "It's simply part of the game, old man. If we are going to mount such a bizarre operation, we might as well go directly to the top, agreed?"

Michel could only nod slowly. "Of course," replied Giselle. "We simply did not know British Intelligence was aiming that high. Is our meeting still scheduled for tomorrow morning?"

"Right," said Fleming with a smile. "Are you all prepared?"

"As prepared as we'll ever be," said Michel with a concerned look at Gabby, who was still nodding as though she were some broken toy.

"Splendid," said Fleming, climbing to his feet and pulling a slip of paper from the pocket of his overcoat. Handing it to Michel, he said, "They will arrive at your hotel suite at 10 o'clock. Here are the pseudonyms they will be using. I suggest you address them as such, although they understand that you know their true identities. I went to some difficulty to arrange this meeting through occult circles here. I wouldn't want to lose our big fish through some silly mistake or lack of preparation."

He stared archly at Gabby. Giselle quickly interjected, "I have every confidence that the meeting will go exactly as planned. What you need be concerned about is whether or not the fish takes the bait."

"Yes, well, I suppose that depends on how well the hook is baited." Fleming responded pointedly as he pulled his overcoat about him. With one last doubtful look at Gabby, he touched two fingers to his forehead, said "Ta, ta, all. Good luck," and was gone.

"The English, ptah!" spat Gabby who finally found her voice. "First they flee from the Germans and then come to Switzerland to tell us what to do."

"He certainly didn't seem to take your report on the invasion of Russia very seriously," muttered Michel, adding with a smile, "Apparently, if such information doesn't come straight from Whitehall, it doesn't carry much weight. And I don't think he appreciated being told by a woman."

"That's his problem," replied Giselle indifferently. "He is from the old school, those that think women are only ornaments in a man's world."

"He's just an upper-class, how do the English say, twit. He probably has no idea how a real spy operates," said Gabby with a show of distaste.

"Now, now," said Giselle, trying to placate her young charge. "Possibly not, but he did arrange this meeting and now it is up to us to see that it succeeds.

"Besides, this may give me the opportunity to learn about Peter and the skull. The men we are meeting are the top occultists of the Third Reich. If anyone might know of their whereabouts, it would be them."

Gabby nodded, her indignation giving way to underlying nervousness. "I just wish I didn't have such stage fright, Giselle. I don't know if I..."

"You mean Velva Violet," interrupted Michel sharply. It was not a correction but an order.

Chagrined, Gabby said, "Yes, I meant Velva. We must all use our *nom de guerre* now I suppose. But, don't I get a codename of my own?" asked Gabby.

"Certainly, my dear," replied Giselle with good humor. "You will be the Laughing Lilac."

"Is that the best you can do?" asked Gabby. She appeared dubious over the name.

"I don't think you have any room to talk, Fifi." Giselle emphasized the name and laughed heartily. Gabby laughed even harder, almost spilling her drink. Even the moody Michel joined in.

Giselle was pleased to see that the young girl was regaining her self-confidence and good humor. Downing the last of her drink, she got to her feet and announced, "Accompany me to dinner, my dears, and then we'll turn in early. I want us all fully rested tomorrow morning."

However, as Giselle lay in bed after dinner, she found she could not sleep. There was her concern over the fate of her relatives in Russia. She kept trying to think of ways of contacting them after returning to Paris. It was terrible not to know how much time was left before the Germans launched themselves against the Soviet Union. And she knew she must communicate in such a manner that would not draw attention to her own foreknowledge. Perhaps Rudolfo could somehow arrange for her to visit Moscow, she thought.

She also was full of anxiety about the morning meeting. As an experienced dancer, she was accustomed to audiences while on the stage. She also knew she could handle herself around men in almost any setting. But this would be different. It was more personal, more immediate. And this role was to be played against ranking members of her avowed enemies. One slip and the entire game could become quite deadly. She secretly wished that Michel could be with her.

Thoughts of her dear Michel invariably led to thoughts of poor Jim. During the past months of planning and training, she had been saddened to find herself thinking of Jim less and less. Her initial heated determination to avenge his death had cooled into a calculating resolve.

Her biggest problem so far was in not knowing the whereabouts of Peter Freiherr von Manteuffel. None of her Sisterhood sources, not even those within the Resistance, could learn of him or his location. She knew intuitively that the skull had reached Hitler, but where was Peter? It was as though he was hidden away in some remote place.

She was still pondering the problem when she fell into a fitful sleep.

Promptly at 10 o'clock the next morning there was a loud knock on the door to Giselle's suite in the *Hotel Baur au Lac*.

She took one last look around before sending Gabby to open the heavy carved wood door. The young girl had bristled briefly at wearing a maid's uniform, but relented after Giselle pointed out the necessity of projecting just the right image for a renowned and wealthy astrologer.

The sitting room was tidy and Giselle was draped on a chaise longue dressed in a flowing white chiffon gown discretely covered with a diaphanous dressing gown. A well-practiced makeup job and a wig made her look ten years older. A silk scarf was tied around her head turban-style and she wore a pair of dark glasses. To aid in the illusion the curtains were drawn, leaving the room dimly lit. On a center table rested a single lighted candle.

Satisfied with the preparations, she motioned to Gabby who opened the door and ushered two men into the foyer. The larger of the men introduced himself as *Herr* Meinz from Frankfurt. Giselle knew this was Karl Haushofer, the so-called "man behind Hitler." His definitions of geopolitics had provided Hitler with scientific-sounding justifications for his dreams of national expansion.

Haushofer was a large, solid man in his seventies, immaculately dressed in an older fashion, complete with starched collar, black frock coat and Homburg hat. His long, aquiline nose drooped over a broad white mustache, which matched the silver hair circumventing rather large ears. His attitude was amiable and he appeared quite eager to commence the conversation.

The other man was younger and shorter, perhaps in his mid-fifties and dressed in a single-breasted blue serge suit with matching waistcoat and a black Fedora. He was introduced as *Herr* Hoffman and obviously was Ernst Schulte-Strathaus. His small, dark eyes darted about the suite and he appeared somewhat nervous.

"*Mademoiselle* Amadou will see you now," announced Gabby in a far-too-loud voice that made Giselle wince. As they entered the sitting room, Gabby almost shouted, "*Herr* Hoffman and *Herr* Mainz, may I present *Mademoiselle* Henriette Amadou?"

"*Enchanté, Mademoiselle*," said Haushofer with a courtly bow. "*Sehr angenehm*," said his companion without much enthusiasm. Both men stood waiting for the famous astrologer to initiate the conversation.

"I hope this meeting in Zürich has not caused you any difficulty, *meine Herren*," said Giselle softly as Gabby helped them with their coats and hats. "You may leave us, Fifi," she added with a perfunctory wave toward Gabby. The young girl's glare of displeasure at being dismissed was unseen by the two men but not Giselle.

Turning to her two visitors, Giselle explained, "We have heard that *Herr* Hitler does not take kindly to spiritualists and thought it better to meet outside Germany."

"Nonsense, my dear lady," replied Haushofer expansively. "That is all twaddle for the press. I can assure you that our *Führer* is an ardent student of the occult. My friend here is regarded as something of an expert on astrology. And he has the ear of many high-ranking party leaders, many of whom would be most impressed to meet the most renowned astrologer and spiritualist in the French colonies."

"It is strange that I have never heard of so illustrious an astrologer as yourself," interjected his companion. He looked around the suite with suspicious eyes.

Haushofer glowered at Schulte-Strathaus but continued smoothly, "I must admit, my dear lady, that I had not heard of you until recent weeks. Your name was passed along by some colleagues in France."

"That may be due to the fact that, until recently, I only practiced in the French colonies. The name *Mademoiselle* Henriette Amadou is not well known in my homeland," responded Giselle with a glibness she did not feel. "Additionally, there are certain aspects of my astrological chart that are only now becoming manifest."

She fervently prayed that the instruction in astrology she had received from Charles would see her through this subterfuge. "Please be seated, gentlemen." She indicated two armchairs situated in front of the chaise longue.

"May I offer you some refreshment?" she added. Both men declined.

Looking from one to the other, Giselle announced, "Well, gentlemen, it appears you would prefer to get to the point of this meeting. I am sure your time is most valuable. I know mine is. I have some astrological calculations and some private communications that I think you will find most interesting."

With that, she handed each man a set of papers filled with astrological charts and computations, which had been prepared by Charles then copied into her own handwriting. As they leafed through them, she slowly paced in front of the seated men. She was both pleased and slightly embarrassed to feel their eyes on her supple feminine form. She smiled inwardly, aware that any sexual thoughts would distract them from questioning her at length.

Speaking with authority, Giselle said, "As I am sure you are aware, a most unusual conjunction of six planets will occur near mid-May of this year. This will signal highly significant events of great magnitude on this plane."

Schulte-Strathaus looked at his wristwatch and said, "And what might these significant events be? We are well aware of the conjunction." He looked bored, a bit suspicious of the whole meeting and anxious to leave.

"I see this as an auspicious time for ending this terrible war between Germany and England. Such a peace might even lead to a partnership against the real enemy to the East," replied Giselle. She knew she must be careful not to give any indication that she knew of the invasion plans on both sides.

The two Germans looked at each other sharply. Giselle knew they were wondering if she was merely making a shrewd guess. She hoped they might believe that she was tapped into a higher consciousness. Otherwise, they would suspect she possessed unauthorized knowledge of the invasion of Russia.

Schulte-Strathaus looked befuddled. Giselle knew the man had dealt with many charlatans in the past and was not about to fall for some phony now. But she hoped she had given him an indication of some inner knowledge. She could see that his initial distrust was shaken. Haushofer, on the other hand, was effusive.

"Yes, that is exactly what is needed," he said enthusiastically. "The combined might of the *Reich* and Great Britain could crush the Bolsheviks once and for all. It is as I have said for some time, the only living space open to Germany is to the East, the open steppes of Russia.

"Just imagine combining the agricultural expanse of the Ukraine with the industrial strength of Germany's *Herzland*, especially in the Ruhr. More food, more production, more *Lebensraum* for Germany."

"Not to mention the Caucasian oil fields," added Schulte-Strathaus dryly. But his sudden interest in the conversation was noted by Giselle.

Haushofer frowned at his companion but continued his dissertation. "It is well accepted that political power can be equated to the amount of land held by a nation as well as its character. As I have often said, space is a factor of great power." His eyes were sparkling with enthusiasm for his vision of a Continent shared by the two great empires.

Giselle quickly added to his enthusiasm. "An end to communism could bring peace and stability to all the nations of Europe," she said with true conviction. Her whole upbringing had inured her against socialism in any form. She also knew well enough that communism had been a creation of Western financiers. These same men would be dismayed to see their carefully constructed balance of power upset by Hitler or Stalin.

Schulte-Strathaus, though obviously interested, did not seem to share the enthusiasm. Coolly he asked, "And just how could such a peace be arranged?"

Giselle inwardly breathed a sigh of relief. The older man had broached the subject on his own. He would now be much more receptive to their scheme, thinking it was his idea.

She proclaimed theatrically, "It would take a daring move by courageous and forward-thinking leaders on both sides. We already have found such a man in England."

"And who might that be?" asked Haushofer. His eyes were gleaming with excitement and interest.

"No less a personage than the Duke of Hamilton," responded Giselle with a note of triumph in her voice. "He has indicated a willingness to negotiate a peace with some ranking official of the *Reich*." She added confidentially, "There are Tory members of Parliament—and even some Royals—who would look quite favorably on securing peace with Germany, should there be a direct confrontation with Russia."

"What do you know of such a confrontation?" asked Schulte-Strathaus. His eyes were narrow and suspicious. He was obviously concerned that this woman might know something of the *Reich*'s secret invasion plans. He still appeared to be dubious about this female astrologer but was becoming intrigued with her message, especially as he knew that the Duke of Hamilton was an acquaintance of his boss, Rudolf Hess.

Giselle realized she had to be careful. She must not let her visitors think that she had inside knowledge of the coming invasion. "I only know what the stars portend," she said calmly. "I have seen that Mars, the planet of war, will soon be in aspect with Jupiter. This indicates a new expansion of the war and since your battle against England has not…" She glanced up to see Schulte-Strathaus glaring at her. Realizing that she must not speak of defeat, she quickly said, "…yet been concluded, I see this to mean war between the *Reich* and its natural enemy, Soviet Russia."

Before the Nazi astrologers could consider the shallowness of her interpretation, Giselle added with fervor, "This may present us with a unique opportunity to unite the Western nations against the Bolsheviks."

"I agree emphatically," said Haushofer loudly, punching his left palm with his right fist.

"And exactly whom do you claim to represent in this matter?"

Schulte-Strathaus was still suspicious but the implications were dawning on him and his interest was growing.

"Let us just say that, while I claim no official standing with the British government, I do speak for certain interested parties, parties that would not appreciate word of our discussion getting back to Churchill," replied Giselle. She looked slyly at each of her visitors.

"I fully understand, *Mademoiselle* Henriette," said Haushofer affably. "Any negotiated peace could only take place with a government that did not include that lying sea dog." Giselle knew he was referring to Churchill's position during the last war as First Lord of the Admiralty.

Still not fully convinced, Schulte-Strathaus asked, "Who then would represent our National Socialist regime? Our *Führer* would never humble himself to personally seek peace with the English."

"I have had a vision," responded Giselle, dramatically pinching the bridge of her nose. Her voice lowered, she spoke as though actually seeing the scene in her mind. "I see a man, a great German, walking calmly through the halls of an English castle. The stone floor echoes with his footsteps and his shadow passes along huge tapestries on the walls."

"Yes, yes, I too have seen such things," said Haushofer, speaking more to himself than the others.

Giselle continued to slowly pace about the room as she proclaimed, "It is the castle of a man well connected with the throne and one who will aid in bringing together two great Nordic nations. When the planets are in the proper conjunction, this will come to pass."

"But who represents the *Reich*?" Schulte-Strathaus was impatient, though he already suspected what the answer would be. Only one Nazi leader had the connections in England and the standing to bring peace between the two warring nations.

"I see a man in a flight suit, a man with bushy eyebrows, a man already well known in both countries. I see Cabinet Minister Rudolf Hess." Giselle collapsed onto the chaise longue. Her hand again covered her forehead as though exhausted by her psychic ordeal.

Haushofer was on his feet. "*Ja, ja,* I can see this plainly. It is the destiny of these two Aryan empires. This is most exciting."

Schulte-Strathaus sat still, slowly warming to the scheme. "Hess did meet the duke at the 1936 Olympics in Berlin," he muttered to himself. Peering out from under the hand on her forehead, Giselle saw the plan was forming in his mind.

She knew Schulte-Strathaus was thinking that a separate peace with England would allow Hitler to unleash his full force against the Soviet Union in the coming invasion. Its success would be assured.

There was also the consideration that Hess' stature in the Nazi hierarchy had slipped in recent years. Although he was still next in line to be Hitler's successor after *Luftwaffe* Chief Göring, his position as deputy *Führer* had moved Hess out of the sphere of military and foreign policy decision-making. If Hess could arrange peace with England, his standing with the party and with his *Führer* would be undisputed.

Giselle could see that Schulte-Strathaus was realizing that as Hess' fortunes grew, so would his own. His enthusiasm visibly increased as he considered the full scope of the plan.

Soon the three were discussing their plan for peace between Germany and England as if it were an accomplished fact.

Schulte-Strathaus seemed lost in thought as he analyzed each ramification of the scheme. Haushofer, on the other hand, became effusive and launched into anecdotes regarding his research into the supernatural.

"You would be amazed, *Mademoiselle* Henriette," he gushed, "at the communications we have received from supernatural sources. We have learned much in the way of technology, astrology and many other fields. We have seen strange and distant visions. We don't even know for certain if we are contacting our future or other planets or other realms of reality. It's most astonishing. Why we have even…"

Schulte-Strathaus quickly interrupted. "I'm sure *Mademoiselle* Henriette has better things to think about than some of your daydreams, *Herr* Professor," he said thought tightly clenched teeth. It was clear to all that he wanted Haushofer to close off this flow of information to the woman before him. Haushofer caught the hint and went silent.

Sensing her chance to change the subject and interrogate him about Peter, she asked with sincere interest, "Your research must have taken you to the four corners of the world?"

"Yes, of course, *meine liebe*, You may not have heard about it, but we have sent expeditions to many exotic locations, such as Iceland, Tibet and even Antarctica, in search of occult relics and objects," he answered boastfully, glancing at Schulte-Strathaus. The younger man appeared disinterested in his travel stories.

Seizing the opportunity, Giselle casually asked, "And have you found any objects of significance?"

Still thinking with pride of his country's successes in that field, Haushofer replied absently, "It is interesting that you ask. Just last year, we had a loyal German appear with a crystal skull of immense power. It is a most potent talisman. I have been studying it for several months now. It is quite similar to the one in Britain."

"You mean the Mitchell-Hedges skull," said Giselle matter-of-factly.

Haushofer seemed pleased that an astrologer would be knowledgeable on such a topic, especially a female.

"Yes, indeed. Except the one we have appears to harness immense power," Haushofer added with evident pride. He failed to notice a look of disapproval from Schulte-Strathaus, who once again appeared concerned that his companion was talking too much.

But Giselle noticed. Sitting upright on the chaise longue, she leaned closer hoping to distract Haushofer. Her senses were at their peak of perception. It took all her willpower to remain calm at this news.

Trying to act only mildly interested, she asked softly, "A crystal skull more powerful than that of Mitchell-Hedges? Where did it come from?"

"Some sort of lost Mayan temple in Central America, I believe. Himmler is most excited about it. He ranks it right up there with the Holy Lance, the Grail Cup and other powerful occult objects."

"Who discovered it?" asked Giselle, trying hard to act as though this was merely a routine follow-up question.

"Some archeologist fellow named Peter something, as I recall. I heard he is an officer in the *Ahnenerbe-SS* today."

"You bring the *Führer* a powerful talisman and you move up quickly. That's the way to get ahead these days," Schulte-Strathaus interrupted with a forced laugh. He plainly wished to close off the discussion.

Giselle and Haushofer joined his laughter. But Giselle felt no humor. She was dwelling on Haushofer's remarks. An archeologist named Peter? A crystal skull? Giselle knew this was no coincidence. She was both elated and subdued, elated by this first news of Peter and subdued by the fact that she was sitting across from two powerful Nazis. She knew she must keep her wits about her.

As she sat and tried to think of how to question the pair about the skull without arousing suspicion, Haushofer suddenly asked, "*Mademoiselle* Henriette, are you familiar with any of the legends and material that has been written about the ancient Cathars in southern France?" He lit a cigarette and cocked his head expectantly.

Giselle was taken aback. She sensed that the man was now trying to interrogate her.

Searching her memory, she replied honestly, "Well, I am certainly aware of the massacre of the Cathars, there but I confess that I really don't know much about them." The question made Giselle uneasy. She knew any in-depth discussion of occult matters might reveal her lack of familiarity with the subject.

"Have you ever heard of a small village by the name of Rennes-le-Château?"

"No, again you have the better of me, *mein Herr*." Giselle was becoming even more uneasy. The conversation was drifting and there was no prepared script. She glanced about apprehensively. There was perspiration on her neck and forehead despite the coolness of the room.

Walking to retrieve an ashtray, Haushofer waved an arm. "Well, no matter. We have been looking into some legends in that area but information is hard to come by. It's not like ancient secrets just fall into your lap."

He drew deeply on his cigarette. Exhaling a large amount of white smoke, Haushofer made a sound halfway between a grunt and a laugh.

Giselle fought to remain calm in light of Haushofer's startling revelations. Finally, she had a lead to Peter and the Skull of Fate. It was all she could do to control her impatience with the two Germans.

Luckily, Schulte-Strathaus reflected her impatience. He turned to Haushofer and said loudly, "Enough conversation, we must return to Germany and meet with Hess immediately." Haushofer nodded enthusiastically, obviously impressed with the plan devised with such a noteworthy and glamorous psychic.

As Gabby helped the two visitors with their coats and hats, Giselle had already lost all interest in helping the British to flummox the German occultists. Her thoughts were now on how to locate Peter through any contact within the *SS* that she could develop.

She was also planning her next operation, this time aimed at the heart of the Nazi beast, armed with information gained from its own southern ally.

Giselle was filled with a grim exuberance, sensing that her time for retribution was near at hand.

CHAPTER 12

Moscow
May, 1941

WHEN THE LARGE ITALIAN FIAT BR.20 bomber finally sat down on the grassy runway at Tushino Airport outside Moscow in early May, no one was more relieved to disembark than Giselle.

Rudolfo had been as helpful as possible, but it had taken a number of days before a seat on a courier flight could be arranged. Giselle contented herself with sightseeing around Rome and making plans for the Sisterhood with Aunt Fran at her estate, *Villa Tagliani*.

The flight had originated in Rome but made a stop in Athens, Greece, which had been occupied by the Germans on April 27th. She was glad to see some of the Italian officers deplane as it considerably lessened the overcrowding in the bomber-turned-transport.

Nearly every one of the dozen Italian attachés and liaison officers on board had made advances to her. They were a gregarious lot, mostly young men her own age, and they meant no real harm. Some of the older officers remembered seeing her name in lights or in the newspaper in the past when she had performed in Rome and Venice and were impressed to be flying with a celebrity even if many years had passed since she had appeared in public.

Giselle had learned at an early age how to gently rebuff the advances of men but this time she was preoccupied. The impending attack on Russia, concern over the safety of her relatives and the activities of the Sisterhood were dominating her thoughts. She was hard pressed to maintain her lighthearted composure during the lengthy flight and was relieved when it ended.

She also had spent a considerable portion of the long journey to Moscow wondering if the mission to Switzerland would pay off. She had carefully kept an eye on the news and even sent feelers through her newly established intelligence contacts in an effort to determine if Hess had taken the bait. Her efforts were fruitless. There was no word of any attempt by the Nazis to make peace with England.

Once on the ground, Giselle made an unsuccessful effort to reach her uncle by telephone. The lines were primitive, and more often than not, completely dysfunctional. Finally she accepted a ride into the capital city with one of the senior Italian officers who had the use of a staff car. It was small and cramped but she was thankful she did not have to spend hours waiting at Tushino. The officer, a member of the Italian embassy staff, was pleasant enough and she came to enjoy his small talk on the drive into the city.

The officer was kind enough to drop her off at the National Hotel. It was not her first choice, but rooms in the city were at a premium and the National did cater to foreigners. Wiring ahead for reservations, Giselle had hoped that she might encounter someone there that could be of benefit to the Sisterhood. She also hoped she might pick up war news that had not been filtered through the Communist propaganda ministry.

As she stood and watched a doorman unload her luggage, Giselle wondered if a decent room was being held for her.

To her great relief, her reservations were in order and it was not long before Giselle was luxuriating in a large claw-foot bathtub that undoubtedly dated to the time of the Romanovs. The room was chilly and the bath water was not as hot as she preferred, but after her lengthy journey she was in no mood to quibble.

It was well past nightfall before she was able to get a telephone connection to her uncle, Sergei Alexander Chernyakovski. Her uncle, who liked to be called Alexander in honor of his American brother, had changed his family name years earlier to avoid the lingering discrimination against Jews in the Soviet Union. The ploy had worked well, as Alexander now was a ranking officer in the MVD, the Soviet Ministry of Internal Affairs.

But Giselle suspected that her father's brother could never be a fully committed Soviet. She felt strongly that his commitment was simply a means of survival in Comrade Stalin's Communist state.

Bathed and dressed in a stylish gray heavy wool suit with a bright yellow silk scarf to ward off the chill of the hotel, Giselle had just found a settee in the lobby and taken a *Gauloise* from the silver cigarette case Michel had given her when she caught sight of her uncle.

Alexander was tall and angular, just like her father. But where her father was always fastidious in his dress and grooming, Alexander looked as if he had just come from a fight. His round face was flushed and his blue serge double-breasted suit with very wide lapels was rumpled. His pocket handkerchief hung a full three inches down the front of his suit coat. His long salt-and-pepper hair was flying in the air as he entered the lobby and his features were partially obscured by a dense cloud of smoke from a cigarette dangling from his thick lips.

"Uncle Alexander!" Giselle shouted with unaffected delight, oblivious to the startled looks about her. She rushed to him and they embraced. She hugged him with genuine warmth while he exhibited a certain hesitation. Giselle was somewhat puzzled at this lukewarm greeting from a relative for whom she had such fond memories.

"My dear, you look radiant," Alexander said in a friendly but formal tone as he quickly released her.

"Oh, Uncle, come and sit with me. Let's talk and catch up," said Giselle with a light laugh. She began leading him toward the settee. But she felt resistance on his part.

Looking up, she caught a certain look of anxiety flash across his face as he quickly and surreptitiously surveyed the hotel lobby. "I would prefer we talk in your room, if you don't mind, dear," he said in a low tone that was almost a whisper.

Giselle immediately understood his concern. Stalin's spies were everywhere. She gathered her purse and unlit cigarette and moved with him toward the hotel's one decrepit elevator. As the machine creaked its way upward, she said quietly, "I understand."

Once in her sparse but well-kept room, Alexander's demeanor changed completely. Before she could speak, he embraced her once again, this time in a bear hug that made her catch her breath.

"Giselle, my little sunflower," he roared. "It's wonderful to see you again."

Holding her at arm's length, he said in a booming voice, "Let me look at my little fairy princess."

Giselle smiled at the mention of her role in Swan Lake, the last performance she had given in Moscow. She knew the ballet was one of Uncle Alexander's favorite and that he had been especially captivated by her performance back in 1931 during her tour of Russia.

In response, she performed a pirouette that provoked a delighted laugh and brief applause.

Giselle took Alexander by the hand and they both sat on a small ottoman located under a huge painting of a rearing cavalryman in a uniform from Napoleon's era.

"Tell me all about yourself," she said warmly, "and Aunt Misha. How is she?"

"Misha is just fine," he replied but his countenance grew solemn and pinched. "Ah, my little sunflower, these are bad times for my be-loved Russia. I did not even feel comfortable talking with you in the lobby of one of our finest hotels. It seems that today, even the walls themselves have ears. The state has encouraged everyone to report on everyone else and it is making life miserable for all."

"So much for the Worker's Paradise," said Giselle with mock concern.

Alexander proceeded to tell Giselle of the increasing horror of the Stalin regime. She gasped as he recounted the misery and deaths caused by Stalin's purges and collectivization programs over the past decade.

"Oh, my dear, it has been terrible," he said, shaking his shaggy head. "I was there. I saw the figures. More than 12 million dead, whole vast territories emptied of their populations. I tell you, that man Stalin will be remembered for centuries for his role in this holocaust. And now rumor has it that he is preparing to invade Europe. His rule is proving to be a disaster for us all."

Giselle smiled inwardly. Her intuition had been correct once again. Despite his government post, Uncle Alexander was no loyal supporter of Stalin's regime. She also took note that her uncle in some way knew about Stalin's plan for the conquest of Europe.

"The man's an out-and-out criminal," declared Alexander, who be-gan to pace about the room. "You would not believe what he has done to the officer corps. Over the past four years, despite his grandiose plans, he has virtually destroyed our army's ability to fight a war. More than 30,000 army and navy officers have been executed. Executed, Giselle, never to fight again. This included all but 10 percent of our generals and all but 20 percent of our colonels. And now he wants to bring all of Europe under his control?

"One million Russians cannot even defeat the Finns with their mere 200,000 troops. Invading Finland—another colossal mistake. I really don't know where it will all end."

Sitting next to Giselle and slumping over, he put his head in his hands.

Giselle placed her hand on his back and said gently, "Then you will not be happy with the news that I have brought."

Alexander looked up with questioning eyes bloodshot with worry.

Giselle took his head in her hands and said soberly, "Russia must prepare at once. Stalin's plans are known to Hitler. That swine at this very moment is preparing to launch a massive attack on Russia."

She paused to let the impact of her news sink in. But Uncle Alexander showed no surprise. "A preemptive strike," he muttered as much to himself as to Giselle.

"You already knew?" asked Giselle.

Alexander's voice was soft, his face filled with weariness. "No, darling, I didn't know. But many of us have suspected as much. We have tried to tell the 'Man of Steel,' but Stalin will not listen. He lives in his own little dream world, cut off from reality."

"But I have this on good authority…" began Giselle but was cut off.

"I'm sure you do, dear, but no matter. Our glorious leader only believes what he wants."

"But there must be some way to make him understand the threat?" she mused.

After a long moment of silence, Uncle Alexander suddenly jumped to his feet. "There might be a way. I just thought of something."

Grabbing Giselle by the arms and grinning, he asked, "How would you like to visit the ballet with me tomorrow night?"

His grin was infectious and Giselle found herself smiling, "I had wanted to visit the ballet while I was here. Tomorrow would be perfect. But what is your plan?"

"I think I shall keep that to myself for the time being," replied Alexander. He was staring beyond Giselle, apparently lost in thought. Looking her in the eye, he added, "I don't want you to get your hopes up in case I cannot arrange this."

Giselle merely nodded. "I understand."

Walking to a sideboard standing against one wall, she said primly, "Now then, the hotel management left me a vase of freshly-cut flowers in water and a complimentary bottle of vodka. Which would you prefer to drink?"

They both laughed. Uncle and niece sipped on the vodka and talked about family matters and remembrances into the early morning hours before Alexander bid farewell with the promise to return for her that evening.

Giselle felt better than she had in weeks as she sat in excellent seats within the opulent Bolshoi Theater and watched a presentation by its famous ballet company. She basked in the near perfect acoustics of the neo-Grecian theater on Petrovskaya Street, which had been rebuilt several times since 1781.

This night in Moscow was a genuine treat. She and Uncle Alexander had consumed a wonderful meal beforehand, beginning with delicious Black Sea caviar and ending with brandy-soaked apricots from Georgia.

Midway through the performance, Uncle Alexander had excused himself. Upon his return, he whispered cryptically, "It has been arranged."

As she sat watching the superb dancing of the Russian prima ballerina Olga Vasiliyevna Lepeshinskaya, Giselle pondered on whom she might be meeting at the close of the performance. As the production ended to a standing ovation, her curiosity was at fever pitch.

Uncle Alexander led her backstage, pushing along with a throng of friends and well-wishers, until they reached the dressing room of *Mademoiselle* Lepeshinskaya. Giselle now guessed that Alexander's mysterious contact would be the famous *danseuse*. Although Olga had been with the Bolshoi when Giselle had visited in 1931, they'd had conflicting engagements and had never met. However, after introductions and compliments on her performance, Giselle was surprised to see one of her managers escort the dancer out, leaving her and Alexander alone.

"I explained our need for privacy and *Mademoiselle* Lepeshinskaya was quite understanding," he explained with a smile and a wink. "Besides, she was quite honored to meet the famous Giselle Tchaikovsky and is on her way to a private reception," he added.

Moments later, he opened the door and motioned for someone to enter. Giselle was all expectation. Was this to be a leading Soviet military officer? Or perhaps a cabinet minister?

Giselle was shocked to see a young girl enter the room and look hesitantly about. Outside the door, Uncle Alexander was speaking to a burly uniformed Russian, apparently some sort of security guard. Quickly regaining her composure, she stepped forward and said with a smile, "Well, hello, young lady. How do you do?" She extended her hand.

The girl smiled back shyly and shook her hand. "Are you *Mademoiselle* Tchaikovsky, the famous *danseuse*?" she asked in a small voice.

Giselle laughed and replied, "I don't know about the famous, but I am indeed a dancer. Or, at least, I was until a few years ago."

"I have heard of you," said the girl matter-of-factly.

She was a cute thing, about 15 years old, with an impish gleam in her eyes. Her round cherubic face was framed by dark auburn hair, parted down the middle and pulled back in pigtails.

Giselle got a second surprise when Uncle Alexander stepped forward and made the introductions. "Giselle, I have the pleasure of introducing you to Svetlana Alliluyeva, the young daughter of our leader Joseph Stalin."

Although somewhat stunned at meeting the daughter of the Soviet dictator, Giselle was quick to say, "It is a distinct honor to meet you, Svetlana. Are you interested in the ballet?"

The girl brightened visibly and replied, "Oh, yes, *Mademoiselle*, I have always liked all aspects of the theater. I come as often as I can."

Her voice carried a certain soft Georgian accent. Undoubtedly, she picked this up from her father who was born in Gori, a small village in southern Russia, Giselle reasoned.

"That's wonderful," said Giselle. "Do you manage to attend very often?"

"Oh, yes," replied Svetlana brightly. "We live in the Kremlin and it's quite close."

"Do you know your sign?" asked Giselle, hoping to turn the conversation to the direction she desired.

"My sign?" Svetlana was puzzled.

"Oh, I mean your astrological sign," said Giselle, laughing. Her Russian, while passable, still was not as fluent as she would have wished.

Svetlana laughed too. "Oh, of course. Yes, I was born on February 28th. I am a fish."

"You mean Pisces."

"Yes, that's it."

"Do you know what that means?"

Svetlana looked blank. "Not really." Uncle Alexander, standing by the door, also looked perplexed by Giselle's line of questioning.

"It means, my sweet, that you are a very sensitive person who always sees the goodness in others," Giselle said gently. Svetlana smiled and nodded her head. Giselle knew she was on the right track and she inwardly thanked heaven for the knowledge of astrology she had picked up from her aunts and Charles.

"And you would like to help make this world a better place, wouldn't you?" she continued.

Svetlana nodded slowly. Her eyes were questioning. She wasn't sure where this conversation was going.

"You realize that there is a war going on in Europe?"

"Yes, I've heard my father talk about it and I read the newspapers."

"And you know that war is a terrible thing. People are killed and cities destroyed."

"Yes."

"You would do most anything to prevent a war from coming to Russia, wouldn't you?"

Svetlana was now on her guard but she mumbled an answer, "I suppose so."

Giselle knelt in front of the young girl and took her hands, saying, "Svetlana, we have only just met but you know that, as a ballet dancer, I have traveled the world. I have played in London, Paris, Rome, Berlin and even here in Moscow."

Svetlana's eyes were wide and somewhat glazed as she pictured all these wonderful places she had always wanted to visit.

"Did you know that in all these cities there are women, very special women, who are working for peace in the world?"

"No," mumbled the girl, still trying to picture herself in one of the great European capitals.

Standing and placing an arm around Svetlana's shoulders, Giselle whispered, "How would you like to become one of those special women who desire peace above all else?"

Svetlana, caught up in a wave of emotion born of altruism and teenage dreams, eagerly nodded and said, "Oh, could I?"

"Yes, Svetlana, you can. You can even have your own secret designation, the sign of a flower."

"Oh, yes, but which flower?"

"The sun flower, a true symbol of the Russian steppes, don't you think?"

Svetlana now was excited and enthused. "Oh, yes, it's perfect. But what do I have to do?"

"It's very simple. You simply have to speak to your father. You can do that, can't you?"

"Oh, yes," The girl was still in a state of dreamy excitement. "I talk to him all the time. He loves me very much but he can be cruel sometimes. He's always blowing pipe smoke in my brother's face. He calls me his 'little sparrow' and says I make him laugh."

"Well, now that you are part of this special Sisterhood, you must take a warning to your father," said Giselle in a serious tone.

"What kind of warning?"

"The most serious kind," answered Giselle, taking Svetlana by the shoulders and looking directly into her eyes. "You must tell your father that the rumors of German troops moving eastward are true and that Hitler plans to attack Russia in the very near future, perhaps before summer."

Svetlana stood still, contemplating the seriousness of what had been said. Her bottom lip began to quiver and she said haltingly, "But I'm only 15 and barely that. He will never listen to me."

Giselle shook her gently. "Svetlana, you must make him listen. You must convince him that he should listen to his ministers and officers. They know what they are talking about. I know this thanks to my sources in Italy. I cannot tell you who they are but they have very high-level connections within the government If Russia is not prepared when the Germans attack, it will be a disaster for your country."

Her eyes moist, near tears, the young girl responded, "I'll try."

Giselle, sensing that she had pushed the girl as hard as she dared, gave her a hug and said, "I know you will do your best. Just keep in mind all that is at stake and never speak of the special Sisterhood that now counts you as a member. Now go."

Svetlana made a faint smile and turned to leave. Uncle Alexander opened the door for her while Giselle called out, "Good-bye, Sunflower."

Svetlana's smile grew and she waved as she left.

Giselle and Alexander stood watching the young girl leave, accompanied by two security men. "I hope we've done the right thing," muttered Giselle. She turned to her uncle. "And I hope your efforts won't get you in trouble."

Uncle Alexander smiled and placed his arm around her shoulder. "Don't worry, my sweet, it won't be the first time Stalin has heard this warning. I just hope that he is not too caught up in his own plans for aggression and that he will listen to his own daughter."

Several days passed and there was no encouraging word from the Kremlin. Uncle Alexander could find no sign that anything had changed in Stalin's perceptions. Giselle accepted his conclusion that the plan to use Svetlana was not working out.

While waiting on word from the Kremlin, Giselle had made another valuable contact. She had overheard a well-dressed woman speaking with an American accent in the hotel bar.

Although the woman appeared older than Giselle, she had no compunction in introducing herself and hoping that their common nationality would ease any irritation over the intrusion. After all, compatriots in a distant country tend to group together.

Giselle was surprised and delighted to find that the woman was the noted *Life* magazine photographer, Margaret Bourke-White and that her husband was none other than the novelist, Erskine Caldwell. Giselle was familiar with his work, having read *Tobacco Road* and *God's Little Ace* while on a ballet tour in the early 1930s.

Bourke-White and her famous husband had arrived in Moscow only days before and had taken up residence in the National. Despite her own fame, Giselle felt just a bit in awe in the presence of such a notable couple.

Although Margaret, or Peg as she preferred to be called, was more than 10 years her senior, she and Giselle hit it off right from the start. They were both women who had gained fame and fortune in a man's world. They were both worldly wise and very much their own person. They even had mutual friends. Peg mentioned that she had taken a short vacation with Papa Hemingway in 1935.

"I'll bet that was an experience," said Giselle with a knowing look that Peg immediately understood.

"Oh, yes, I certainly got plenty of exercise trying to stay out of his reach." They both chuckled, each recalling their own experiences with the amorous author.

Despite their age difference, they struck up a close, almost girlish friendship, acting like two sisters off on a holiday lark. More than once, the pair had closed the bar at the National Hotel, drinking and giggling into the morning hours. The Russian waiters soon quit betting on which American woman would pass out first. They were always wrong. Both held their liquor like a veteran *Cossack*.

It was in these private discussions that Giselle had confided to Peg her plans and actions in combating Hitler and his Nazis. At first, she was circumspect, unsure of her friend's allegiances. But she quickly found a comrade in arms in the well-dressed and dedicated photographer.

Finally, Peg had confided her darkest secret to Giselle, who then realized she had found a trustworthy ally.

It was late one night, not long after Peg's husband had departed for bed leaving the two women alone at a far table of the hotel lounge. "Good night, Skinny," Peg had called after him. It tickled Giselle to hear Erskine Caldwell, already acknowledged as one of the world's greatest authors and playwrights, called Skinny, especially since the handsomely freckled and muscular Caldwell was anything but skinny.

After his departure, their conversation grew serious, with Giselle telling of her adventures in Mexico and how she was building the Sisterhood to aid in the final victory over Fascist tyranny.

After several Vodka Collins, Giselle gave her new friend a detailed account of her experience in the Yucatan, the death of Jim, and Peter's expropriation of the crystal Skull of Fate. Peg was engrossed by the story, commenting, "That would make a great Hollywood movie plot."

Giselle merely laughed. "They'd probably turn it down. They'd say it was too unbelievable.

"But then I don't have time for Hollywood anyway. I have much more important business at hand." She confided her plan to discredit the Third Reich's deputy *Führer* with a ruse involving occultism and astrology.

Peg's eyes grew bright with merriment. "Oh, that's just too delicious," she cooed. "Have you heard anything from this yet?"

Giselle shook her head. She then proceeded to tell her new ally about her code name, Velva Violet. Peg was fascinated by such intrigue. "Perhaps I should be called Morning Glory," she laughed. "Just ask Skinny. He's the one who has to face me in the morning."

Giselle smiled but continued her explanation as to why she felt obligated to fight Nazism. "My father is a Russian Jew," she said, wondering how Peg would take this information. Discrimination against Jews was still very much alive in many parts of the United States.

Peg grew quite somber and revealed the secret in her past. She said her father's original name was not White, but Weiss. His parents were Polish Orthodox Jews. She had said this in a matter-of-fact manner, apparently neither proud nor ashamed of her heritage. But Giselle, from her own experience, knew that this was a confession meant to be kept strictly between the two of them. The older woman did talk freely about her antagonism toward repressive political systems.

"Why, my dear, did you know that both Skinny and I helped raise money for the American Relief ship which took needed supplies to the anti-Fascist forces in Spain just before the war?" Peg had confided over a fresh vodka and tonic. "We were always getting involved in some socialist activity or the other," she laughed. "Of course, that was earlier in the Depression when leftist politics were socially acceptable.

"Recently I severed all my connections with any political activity when I decided as a photo-journalist I must be perceived as objective and above such things." She made it sound more like an apology than an explanation.

It was then that Giselle knew without question that Margaret Bourke-White, though too publicly visible to be a fully operational member of the Sisterhood, could still be counted on as a resource in the fight against fascism.

"I have another secret that might interest you," said Giselle in a confidential tone.

Peg cocked one eyebrow. "Oh?" was her only reply.

With the slight smugness often found in one who knows secrets, Giselle said in a conspiratorial voice, "I have it on good authority that Hitler at this very moment is preparing to attack Russia. It would have already happened if that idiot Mussolini hadn't gotten bogged down in the Balkans and Greece and needed his help."

"But Germany and Russia have signed a non-aggression pact," gasped Peg, quickly grasping the implications of Giselle's revelation.

Giselle smiled but there was no humor in it. "You must also know that Stalin at this moment is planning to launch an all-out assault through Poland, Germany and Romania. Hitler knows this and, being outnumbered in both men and weapons, must strike first if he is to have any chance at all of preventing the conquest of all Europe. Besides, since when has any pact or treaty meant anything to Hitler?"

"You're right, of course," agreed Peg with a snort. Then she lightly banged her drink on the table. "Damn! You know, Giselle, that's exactly what my editor told me. Old Hicks said he had a hunch Hitler would attack in the East and he wanted me right here to record it. I thought he was off his rocker at the time. Holy Cow! I've got things to do."

Tossing down the last of her vodka, Peg gathered up her things and bid a hasty farewell.

Giselle sat for some time, slowly finishing her drink and contemplating the possibilities of being a comrade in arms with the famous photographer, Margaret Bourke-White.

Late the next morning, Giselle entered the hotel lounge to find Peg holding up a newspaper and waving her over to her table. Her face was flushed, her excitement evident.

Hoping that perhaps her meeting with Svetlana Stalin had paid off, Giselle rushed to the table and sat down next to her new friend.

"Has Stalin announced national mobilization?" she asked with excitement.

Momentarily sobered, Peg said, "No, I'm afraid not." Then she regained her excitement and handed a copy of London's *Daily Herald* to Giselle. "Percy Cudlipp is the editor and a friend of mine. He sent me this copy. Take a gander at this!"

Giselle read for several minutes, tossed the newspaper onto a nearby table and squealed with delight. Peg hoisted her drink and said loudly, "Here's to you, kid."

The paper's front page, dated May 11, 1941, was filled with an account of Rudolf Hess' aborted mission to England.

It reported that the day before, Deputy *Führer* Hess had taken off from Germany in a specially modified *Messerschmitt 110* twin-engine fighter plane he piloted alone to Scotland. Out of fuel, Hess bailed out near Glasgow and loudly proclaimed to a startled farmer that he was on a "special mission" to see the Duke of Hamilton. Armed only with a pitchfork, the farmer promptly had taken Hess into custody.

Hitler, embarrassed and fearful that his third-in-command might give away his impending attack on Russia, immediately pronounced

Hess insane. Furthermore, an item in the back of the paper reported that, in an operation known as *Aktion Hess*, the German dictator had all astrologers within reach arrested and sent to concentration camps. Haushofer and his son Albrecht were being held by the Gestapo. The British seemed disinclined to pay any serious attention to Hess and had him locked away in prison after treating his broken ankle.

Peg could not restrain her laughter. With an evil grin on her face, Giselle proclaimed, "One *Kraut* down, 60 million to go!" Peg roared louder.

The two women spent the rest of the afternoon downing vodkas and celebrating. As evening arrived and the room began filling, Giselle grew quiet.

Sitting back in her chair, Peg smiled knowingly. She recognized that Giselle's reflection was the result of her concern for the next move by the Sisterhood.

"Cat got your tongue?" Peg said after a long period of silence.

"I'm sorry, Mrs. Caldwell, but I can't stop thinking about Michel, Gabby and the others. I must return to Paris," said Giselle absently. She looked up with a weak smile. "Or should I say Miss Bourke-White."

"Giselle, don't play formal with me. I've asked that you call me Peg. All my close friends do. And after all we've shared, I consider you among them now. I mean, what's in a name anyway? You do know that I have retained my maiden name, Bourke-White, as my professional name?"

"Of course, everyone does," laughed Giselle, wondering to herself what educated person in either Europe or America did not know the name of the world's foremost female photographer.

"I am curious about one thing though," she added.

"And what is that, my dear?"

"Where did the name Bourke-White come from? It's an unusual name, isn't it?" asked Giselle, her voice dropping off as though she had made some terrible transgression.

Peg braced her right arm on her hip and leaned closer, nearly face to face with Giselle. "It's really quite simple. I took my mother's maiden name of Bourke, a good Irish name straight from Dublin where her grandfather was a builder. And I also took my father's name of White. Add a hyphen and you get Bourke-White."

Leaning even closer, Peg smiled knowingly, arched one eyebrow and said in a low voice, "After all, you of all people should know about the use of professional names, right Velva?"

Giselle bristled. Glaring at her companion, she whispered savagely, "I've told you, you must never mention that name. Things have moved too rapidly. You could put both of us in jeopardy."

Peg flashed her famous wide, toothy grin and said, "Calm yourself, honey. I'm perfectly capable of keeping secrets and, besides, no one can hear us over the din in this place. I can barely hear you myself." She leaned even closer to accentuate her statement.

Giselle's anger broke under Peg's unblinking gaze and smile. Settling back on her seat, she ordered yet another Vodka Collins. With its arrival, she took a sip and wiped her mouth daintily with a handkerchief and sat looking about at the people.

She sat looking about at the people. Giselle well knew that she was extremely fortunate to have such a person as Margaret Bourke-White on her side.

One of those possibilities had come to fruition only a few days later, when Peg sent word for Giselle to meet her in the hotel lobby.

Sitting in a quiet corner of the huge lobby late that evening, Peg shocked Giselle by suggesting that the pair make a quick and quiet trip to Germany.

"Whatever for?" gasped Giselle. "I would just as soon walk into a cage full of hungry lions."

With a knowing smile, Peg had only said, "There is someone I think you should meet."

"And who might that be?"

Holding an index finger up to her mouth, Peg replied, "I don't want to say until I can confirm that my plan is possible."

Giselle was miffed at this sudden secrecy from someone whom she had grown quite fond of in just a few short days. Evenings, actually, as her days had mostly been taken up making arrangements for the Sisterhood's activities in Stalin's "Worker's Paradise." It was evenings spent in the National Hotel and a few surrounding restaurants that had sealed their friendship.

"But I think it can be arranged," added Peg with a large smile. "Let's adjourn to the bar and I'll fill you in as best I can."

After drinks, Peg unobtrusively checked to see if they were being watched. Satisfied they were not under observation, she leaned closer and said, "Giselle, my dear, it's all arranged with a pilot I know. You and I will be making a brief trip to the *Vaterland*."

Giselle was shocked. "My God, Peg, do you really expect me to walk through *Herr* Hitler's playground? A certain name that begins with V is probably on a Gestapo watch list right now."

With a reassuring smile, Peg said, "Don't worry so much, honey. No guts, no glory, as they say. Besides, we'll be flying into Munich, making a short train ride to Berchtesgaden and then home again. No one will be the wiser. Skinny and I are planning some quiet time at a resort on the Black Sea. I'll just tell him I'm off to shoot some Soviet tractor factory in Smolensk or some other ungodly place and will meet him there. We'll be back before anyone knows we're gone."

Giselle sat quietly, nursing her drink. "I don't know, Peg," she said hesitantly. "I'm running too many risks as it is and I feel I still have work to complete here in Russia."

"It may mean nothing compared to what you might do in Germany," replied Peg, looking straight at Giselle with her large, unblinking blue eyes.

Intrigued in spite of herself, Giselle asked, "And just what is in Germany that would make such a hazardous trip worthwhile?"

Peg sat back in her chair and slowly sipped her vodka. "Oh, just a certain young lady I think you should meet," she said coyly.

"A young woman? Are you joking? I have dozens of young women both working with and for me at the moment. Why would I want to meet this person?"

"Oh, no real reason," Peg teased. "She's just a little older than you, about 29 I'd say and she is fascinated with artists of all kinds, especially film stars."

"But, I'm not a film star…" protested Giselle. But Peg interrupted.

"No, but you have a reputation as a dancer. She's also infatuated with strong women who lead adventurous lives."

Perplexed by this description of what could have been any one of millions of dreamy housewives, Giselle asked pointedly, "Who is this woman?"

Peg paused for effect, glanced about and whispered, "Eva Braun."

Giselle's face was blank as she wracked her brain for a few moments. Finally she asked, "So, who the hell is Eva Braun? I've never heard of her."

Peg was savoring the moment. She leaned forward to place her drink on the table and said, "Not many people have. She's Hitler's mistress."

Giselle was shocked into silence. Suddenly aware that someone might notice her paralysis, she gulped her drink and looked intently at Peg for any signs of a joke.

Her voice still lowered, Peg said confidentially, "It's one of the best kept secrets of the *Reich*. I myself only heard of this through one of my top-level sources and he only passed it along as idle gossip.

"But it turns out that I vaguely knew the woman years ago. She used to be an assistant to Heinrich Hoffman."

Giselle blinked hard. "Hitler's personal photographer?"

"That's the one," agreed Peg. "I met her in the early '30s while I was photographing the I.G. Farben plant near Berlin. She was quite attentive to me, apparently impressed with a well-known American photographer who was also a woman. I recall that she was quite taken with celebrities of all stripes. I got the sense that she might be open to more modern ways of thinking. I have a feeling she might be receptive to you and your Sisterhood. Just think what she might be able to do for you."

Giselle, her mind flooded with the possibilities of such an ally, could only mumble, "When do we leave?"

CHAPTER 13

Bavaria, Germany
June, 1941

GISELLE CHUCKLED QUIETLY TO HERSELF as she sat with Peg in a compartment of the *Suddeutschland* Express. She was glad the two women were alone. Her good humor would most certainly have been unappreciated by other passengers traveling through wartime Germany.

She had been again thinking of the successful operation against Rudolf Hess. She also thought how lucky she had been to meet Margaret Bourke-White. After all, who else but the well-connected *Life* magazine photographer could have managed to get them both on a transport flight from Moscow to Munich along with American news dispatches and newsreel film?

Accustomed to ferrying newsmen along with his cargo, the transport pilot, plied both with bottles of vodka and American dollars, had agreed to allow both women on his flight to Munich. As Germany was making every effort keep America in its professed neutral status, there had been no problem entering the country since both carried U.S. passports along with Peg's press credentials.

Following the customs formalities and a light breakfast, the pair had boarded the *Suddeutschland* Express for the short ride to Berchtesgaden.

As the train rumbled southward, her good humor faded into philosophic contemplation. She well knew that the loss of one deputy

Führer, while a masterstroke of psychological warfare, would most probably not substantially hinder Hitler's Third Reich.

But her reason for this trip into Germany just might.

Staring out at the passing Bavarian countryside, Giselle knew it was more than simple luck that had put her in contact with Margaret Bourke-White. She was still amazed that she also had met with Clara Petacci. There was a fateful plan unfolding, although she could not yet see the end results.

She leaned back against the cushioned train seat and thought back to that idyllic afternoon at Aunt Fran's *Villa Tagliani* and her conversation with Mussolini's mistress.

Following a lively conversation and afternoon tea, Giselle and Clara Petacci had left the others to wander off to a far corner of the estate. She had offered Clara an American cigarette, which was gratefully accepted. Taking seats on a wooden bench, they conversed quietly and intimately.

Giselle had been trying to think of a way to broach the subject on her mind, but could not. At a pause in the conversation, she simply blurted it out, "Clara, have you heard anything about a crystal skull and a man named Peter who is connected to it?"

She watched Clara's face carefully for any sign of subterfuge but saw none as the woman answered, "I'm sorry, my dear, but I have no idea what you are talking about. What's this about a skull?"

Giselle realized the woman was telling the truth and ignorant of deeper issues. With an air of nonchalance, she dismissed the subject saying, "Oh, it's really nothing, just some accessory for my home that I am trying to track down."

She then steered the conversation back to home decoration. Soon they moved on to current events and Giselle was impressed to find the woman was more knowledgeable about world affairs than she had thought. Clara even exhibited a certain sympathy for those whose lives were being disrupted by the war.

Sensing an opportunity, Giselle said softly, "Especially the poor Jews."

Clara gave her a sharp look. "You know we are supposed to think of the Jews as our enemy?"

"Yes," Giselle replied evenly, "but what have they ever done to us? They only want to live, just like the rest of us. It's not right for Hitler to demonize an entire people simply to drum up support for his war."

Clara had contemplated this idea for a moment, then spoke, "Do you know that Hitler is constantly encouraging *Il Duce* to hand over the Italian Jews for transport to concentration camps in Poland?"

"Really?" Giselle acted surprised at this revelation. But she had heard such talk for some time from Resistance members in southeast France along the Italian border where many Jewish refugees crossed seeking asylum. She also had learned that some Italian generals in the Italian occupation zone in southern France were preventing Vichy officials from deporting Jews. Similar hesitation on the part of Italian authorities was taking place in Greece. It was clear that many Italians were not supportive of Nazi measures against the Jews. Giselle hoped Clara might be one of them.

"I have heard *Il Duce* say that the Jews should simply be sent to Italian Somaliland in Africa," Clara continued. "But he is under such pressure from the Germans."

"No civilized nation should make war on innocent women and children," said Giselle, watching Clara's reaction carefully.

The dark-haired woman appeared sincere when she responded, "Yes, I just wish there was something I could do to help those poor unfortunates. But *Il Duce* is walking a thin line. He must placate the Germans if he is to have their continued support."

"Words and actions do not always have to be the same." Giselle gave Clara a shrewd grin. Her meaning was not lost on the older woman. Clara smiled and replied softly, "I will speak to him on this."

It was the best Giselle could have hoped for from the lover of the Italian dictator. If she might save the life of even one person, this effort to sway Mussolini through his mistress would be well worth it.

"I just want to do what I can to end this frightful war and save lives," muttered Giselle. "I know there must be people close to Hitler and Mussolini who feel the same." She watched Clara to see her reaction.

An imperfection on the tracks caused a particularly heavy jolt to the *Suddeutschland* Express and brought Giselle back from her reveries. She shook her head and looked down at the ornate platinum cigarette case cradled in her hand. The metal case with its beautifully engraved fleur-de-lis gleamed as a ray of Bavarian sunshine glanced through the train compartment window and reflected off its burnished surface.

She slowly and thoughtfully turned the case in her hand to reveal the elaborately engraved design with the initials "VV" for Velva Violet subtly weaved into the intricate design.

Peg turned from looking out of the window and saw her studying the ornately engraved case. "It is rather beautiful," she commented.

"It was a present from Michel," explained Giselle. Several members of the fast-growing Sisterhood had lavished gifts on her as tokens of their esteem. Most were engraved, with the initials "VV" carefully hidden within intricate designs. Anyone casually looking at the engravings would likely not notice the initials hidden in the patterns. Next to Michel's cigarette case, her favorite gift was a sterling silver necklace containing a beautiful moonstone.

"And the initials 'VV' obviously stand for…" began Peg but she was cut short by a sharp look from Giselle. Sheepishly, she muttered, "Oh, yes, we're not supposed to say that name in public." Glancing around the compartment, she added dryly, "I don't see any public here."

Giselle ignored her but smiled to show there were no hard feelings over her *faux pas*. Inwardly, she reveled in her *nom de guerre*, Velva Violet. While it provided a new identity bringing new opportunity, more importantly it gave her the chance to make a difference in the world. Who could imagine a world-class ballerina literally fighting against the Axis? Who would imagine a woman working in 1941 other than in the kitchen?

The codename still caused a thrill of excitement to course through her body even though she was already beginning to dread the constant tension, bordering on fear, brought on by her new vocation as espionage agent.

"We must never mention that name," she said quietly as much to herself as to her companion. "One slip of the tongue, one wrong move and the game will be up."

She did not want a slip of the tongue to cost her the Sisterhood. What had begun as a simple desire for vengeance and penance for the loss of the Skull of Fate had slowly evolved into a pyramidal organization encompassing old friends and social contacts. Almost single-handedly, she had created a whole new level of espionage in Europe from a broad and divergent group of women.

Much to the amazement of more than a few of the "old boys" in London's Whitehall as well as back in Washington at the War Department, the Sisterhood had already produced impressive results. She felt pride welling up within her for the successful delivery of the Enigma decoding machine to England and for the defection of Rudolf Hess.

There had been other missions too since Jean Moulin had departed with the Enigma machine. The sudden death of a certain foreign minister in Belgrade, a slowdown in the development of Axis rocket science, the loss of vital heavy water in Norway destined for Nazi atomic research and more. All were part of a covert war rarely mentioned in the news headlines.

She noticed Peg looking at her with a puzzled expression and shook her head. This was no time for complacency. I must be in top shape for this little job, she thought. Little job indeed. This one contact might prove to be the most important Velva Violet might ever make. Danger was now her constant companion since her plan involved a journey into the heart of Nazi Germany. She was glad that she had the company of the well-known photographer.

"Please understand," Giselle said to Peg as she stroked the cool metal of the cigarette case. "The American dancer Giselle Tchaikovsky was a well-known performer with connections to the highest social circles. Even though she hasn't been on the scene in some years, her name and reputation still linger. She continues to be above suspicion." she explained.

"But Velva Violet is another story. Unfortunately, that name is becoming known to the *Gestapo*. Although they have not yet learned of Velva Violet's identity, they have begun to suspect a force is working against them that they cannot identify. Their male arrogance will keep them from suspecting an organization of women for some time. But one whisper of that name and the balloon will do much more than go up. Mum's the word, as they say."

Peg nodded thoughtfully as Giselle settled back on the padded seat and gazed out the window at the passing Bavarian countryside.

Now looking out the large window of the speeding train, Giselle found the immediate scenery merely a blur, but it was the horizon that really caught her attention. The Bavarian Alps rose majestically to form a jagged, bluish-gray backdrop to the small villages that dotted the well-maintained countryside. Every movement of her eyes offered a new panorama of postcard portraits of towering mountains, picturesque alpine villages and dense green forests, all perfectly arranged as though pre-planned by some omnipotent landscape artist. She saw the broad blue expanse of the *Chiemsee* and knew that the train would arrive in Berchtesgaden soon.

Berchtesgaden. She remembered the small vacation town from a visit while on a ballet tour in the early 1930s. Until now, she had fond remembrances of the town, located just 74 kilometers southeast of Munich and initially made famous by the nearby salt mines. She recalled the pleasant well-kept park in the shadow of the twin spires of the 12th century *Stiftskirche* cathedral.

Now the little resort town had another reputation—it had become Hitler's mountain retreat.

Giselle had learned that additional rings of fortifications were being added to the growing compound on the Obersalzberg, built over the site of the old *Haus Wachenfeld*.

With the added construction of Hitler's *Berghof*, the town's pre-war population of a mere 4,000 people had swollen to nearly 20,000, some 15,000 of these being heavily-armed troops stationed there to protect their *Führer*'s retreat.

A bile of fear rose within her. Her mouth was suddenly very dry. Why on earth was she venturing into Berchtesgaden, the beast's lair?

She noticed that Peg had grown quiet and somber. Giselle wondered if she too was having second thoughts about traveling into the heart of the Nazi empire.

Unbidden, doubts began to flirt around the edges of her consciousness, hazy mental pictures of arrest and imprisonment. But she shook them off. Hazardous though it may be, this one visit might accomplish more than the entire previous nine months spent constructing her underground organization.

While conquering her hesitations, Giselle noticed the train was slowing. Gradually the foreground of her vision coalesced into a slow-motion panorama of gingerbread cottages and red-roofed chalets.

As the train pulled to a stop in the station set in the midst of the Bavarian beauty, she saw a large red banner flapping just outside the compartment window. Highlighted against a brilliant white circle in its center was a giant *swastika*, which momentarily pressed against the glass.

Giselle gave an involuntary shudder at the sight. Screwing up her courage, she looked at Peg who gave her a salute and said weakly, "We who are about to die salute you."

"That's not funny," said Giselle as she gathered up her belongings. Within minutes, both women alighted onto the station platform.

Looking about, they suddenly found themselves flanked by two tall and muscular young men dressed in the stylish but sinister black uniforms of the SS.

"*Fräulein* Bourke-White? *Mademoiselle* Tchaikovsky?" One of the men placed his hand on Giselle's elbow. She noticed the sleeve band that designated the trooper a member of the *Leibstandarte-SS Adolf Hitler*, Hitler's personal bodyguard regiment. "Please come with us."

A jumble of thoughts raced through Giselle's mind. Warning bells were going off. Had they been found out? Were they to be arrested? Was this the end of the line for Velva Violet?

Although Giselle maintained an outward calm, her stomach was churning at the sight of the black-clad Stormtroopers. One of the troopers suddenly bent over and began gathering up their luggage while the other said pleasantly, "*Fräulein* Bourke-White, *Mademoiselle* Tchaikovsky, I am under orders to escort you to the *Berghof*. There is a car waiting out front."

Still unsure if she was under arrest, Giselle decided to play out the scene with confidence. She placed a hand affectionately on the trooper's arm, partially covering the blood red *swastika* armband.

"You boys do a magnificent job," she gushed. "And you are so punctual. Such healthy looking boys." She gazed admiringly at the SS man, who tried to maintain his military bearing even as his cheeks flushed slightly with embarrassment.

As she and the trooper passed Peg, she saw the photographer roll her eyes. "We all have to play the game," Giselle thought with a faint smile. "We can't all be intimidating photographers with press credentials."

Her poise fully recovered, Giselle marched for the station entrance with the young trooper hurrying to keep pace. Peg trailed behind with a nonchalant stride. The second trooper struggled along last with the pair's luggage.

In his haste to be courtly, the SS man accompanying Giselle fumbled clumsily with the door of a big wine-colored Mercedes 230 Saloon parked outside the station. After securing the luggage, the two men took their places in the front seats and, with a low roar of the six-cylinder engine, the big Mercedes quickly left Berchtesgaden behind.

The 3.5-kilometer drive to the *Berghof* passed quickly. "You must be quite honored to have been selected to protect the *Führer*," said Giselle, leaning forward toward the driver. "You must enjoy duty in this beautiful place very much." She waved a hand vaguely out the car window at the huge, dark fir trees they passed.

The square-jawed trooper in the passenger seat said nothing but the round-faced blond driver for the first time smiled and replied, "Oh, yes, madam, it is very beautiful here, especially for a boy from the industrial Ruhr."

"Perhaps you could show us the sights," cooed Giselle, much to the driver's delight.

"Of course, madam," he answered. With a wide grin, he sat up a bit and straightened his black peaked cap.

Once through the first security checkpoint, he relaxed somewhat and began to act the part of tour guide. As they accelerated past the *SS* guard post, he pointed to some buildings on their left. "Here is our post office and the driver's quarters. And the long building behind there is the *Autogarage* where they service the cars and trucks," he explained. "And to our right is the barracks that houses the guards. And on the left again are the movie theater and a kindergarten."

As the big dark red Mercedes pulled past the barracks, the driver nodded toward a large multi-story wooden home with two balconies that completely encircled the building. "That's *Reichsleiter* Bormann's house," he said in a reverent tone.

Giselle knew that since the flight of Deputy *Führer* Rudolf Hess to England, Martin Bormann, Hitler's chief of staff, had become the most powerful man in the *Reich*. Few people, outside the upper levels of the intelligence community, realized what a power Bormann had become in recent months. No one saw the *Führer* without going through him.

Just ahead on their left, there loomed the famous *Hotel Zum Türken*, now headquarters for the security services, *Reichssicherheitsdienst* and the *Gestapo*. A long column of troops dressed in field gray uniforms with rifles resting on their left shoulders marched along the pavement while several young women dressed in traditional Bavarian dirndls waved approvingly from the stone patio in front of the hotel.

Thanks to some intelligence research, Giselle knew that the main entrance to a vast underground bunker system was located on the east side of the *Hotel Zum Türken*. She silently hoped that she would never have to go there as dark cramped places gave her claustrophobia. She had heard outlandish tales of dark ceremonies and blood rituals being conducted in cavernous rooms deep within the bunker system.

"And, of course, the famous *Berghof* villa of our beloved *Führer*," said the driver proudly, breaking Giselle's reveries. Both she and Peg turned and gazed with interest at the sprawling mountain complex. Its large white facade was broken by windows with colorfully painted shutters and a wide wooden balcony on the second floor shading an enormous picture window on the first.

The Mercedes appeared to be leaving the *Berghof* complex and Giselle felt her apprehension return. Where were they taking her? She sneaked a glance at Peg but the American only gave a small shrug of her shoulders. She didn't know either.

Ahead the road passed through a phalanx of tall trees. Glancing between the trees to her right, Giselle saw the unmistakable manicured greens and flags of a golf course. A little further on, the large four-door touring car swung off onto a small gravel road, leading to a small gingerbread cottage sitting in the center of a circular drive.

As the car rolled to a stop, a slender woman with light brown braided hair came out of the cottage door and approached them. She was dressed in a traditional dirndl, complete with short white apron. She was about five-feet, three-inches tall with well-proportioned, shapely legs. She was in her late twenties and still quite attractive, thanks in large part to a pleasant smile. As the woman neared, Giselle realized her attractiveness stemmed more from her trim, fit figure and healthy tan than from any innate beauty.

The woman's smile was open and cordial as she beat the SS man to the rear door. Having recovered his military bearing, the driver stared straight ahead while his companion stood at attention behind the woman as she opened the car door.

"Miss Bourke-White, I'm delighted that you could make this visit," she said taking Peg's hand. "It is so nice to see you again after so many years. I was delighted to get your telegram requesting a visit."

"The delight is all mine," said Peg amiably. Looking about at the scenic mountains and forests, she added, "Berchtesgaden is certainly a change from that photography studio in Munich."

The woman seemed to blush slightly. "Yes, my situation has changed quite a bit since we last met."

Peg, unsure of the protocol for meeting a powerful dictator's mistress and fearing she might have offended their hostess, said quickly, "Let me introduce you to my friend." She pulled Giselle forward a bit. "Eva Braun, this is *Mademoiselle* Tchaikovsky, well known in France as an exceptional young ballerina and patron of the arts."

Taking Giselle's hand, Eva made a slight curtsy and said, "I am honored to meet you, *Mademoiselle* Tchaikovsky."

"Please call me Giselle," responded Giselle as she watched the effect this offer of friendship had on her hostess. Despite the near-daily parade of the pompous and mighty through the *Berghof*, Eva obviously was excited to be in the company of a famous American photographer and a woman of means.

Suppressing a slight giggle, Eva said, "I have so looked forward to your visit. I don't get to meet many people these days." She looked quickly at the two *SS* men.

Sensing that Eva may have entered a sensitive area of conversation by implying she was being kept incommunicado, Giselle quickly said, "Peg here…" she looked at her companion. "You don't mind if Eva calls you Peg do you dear?"

"Why not?" responded Peg, with a wave of her hand. "It's just us women here."

"Peg has told me so much about you," said Giselle.

Eva giggled again and whispered, "I hope she didn't tell you everything. We women must have some secrets."

Giselle put on her best smile and responded, "She told me just enough to convince me that I must stop in and meet with you, as I am making a tour through Bavaria anyway. I understand that you are also a patron of the arts?"

"I am and I must say I'm delighted to meet such a notable dancer. And I have always had great respect for talented artists of all kinds," replied Eva, exuding enthusiasm.

"Oh, she's not just another performer," said Peg with a wide sweep of her hand. "She was toasted as a prima ballerina on the Continent for many years."

"Yes, I do recall that name." Eva turned to Giselle and said, "It is a great pleasure to meet someone so connected to the fine arts world. And your German is excellent."

"Thank you. I assure you the pleasure is all mine," replied Giselle in her most humble tone. She knew that a true admirer of creative artists could never resist being shown respect and attention by their icons.

"Oh, I just know that we are going to have a wonderful time together," said Eva, placing her hand on Giselle's arm. "But come, we'll retire to a place with more privacy." She motioned for Giselle and Peg to reenter the Mercedes and climbed in after them.

As the *SS* man climbed back into the passenger side of the car, Eva's friendly tone changed to the impersonal arrogance of one who is accustomed to obedience from subordinates. "Driver, you will take us to the *Kehlsteinhaus*."

"*Jawohl, Fräulein* Braun," snapped the driver. The big red Saloon pulled away, its tires crunching on the gravel drive.

Indicating the small cottage, Eva explained, "This is the *Bechstein Haus*, a guest house for special visitors. It's small but cozy. Most of the *Führer*'s guests stay at the *Platterhof*, which is better equipped to host guests accustomed to luxury. Only special friends stay there."

"We would like to be special friends to you," said Peg bluntly.

Somewhat embarrassed, Eva said quickly, "I didn't mean you weren't … I just thought we might have more privacy at the *Kehlsteinhaus*…*" She became even more embarrassed. "I mean, of course I would like for you both to be special friends, it's just that…"

Giselle smiled at her discomfort. "I quite understand, Eva," she said in a soothing tone. "You would prefer not to be seen with Americans at a time when relations between our two countries are, shall we say, strained."

Eva smiled sheepishly as though caught in some distasteful act and admitted, "Well, you realize that I have to be very careful about what I do and whom I see. I must avoid any circumstances that might reflect poorly on the *Führer*, even when he is not in residence like now."

"I quite understand," said Giselle sympathetically. "Peg explained all. You must be very lonely here on occasion."

Eva looked out of the car window past her guests and sighed. "It is difficult sometimes. Whenever important visitors come, especially Party officials, I am not to be seen. Sometimes I could just…"

She caught herself, realizing that these friendly women also were citizens of a nation that might soon be at war with Germany.

Stiffly, almost as though reciting a learned speech, she added, "Of course, it is my duty to serve my *Führer* and my Fatherland in whatever manner is necessary. We are all soldiers now that we are locked in a struggle to bring the New Order to Europe."

Giselle and Peg remained silent.

Eva leaned back on the broad leather car seat and sighed. "But let's not discuss politics. I have been so excited since receiving your telegram. I am absolutely famished for news of the theater and the arts."

Looking at Giselle, she added, "I recall your name from some years ago. You danced in the Berlin Opera House in the early '30s, didn't you?"

"Yes, as a young girl," smiled Giselle. "It's kind of you to remember."

"How could I forget," said Eva with a sparkle in her eyes. "That was about the same time that my boss first introduced me to the *Führer*. Those were exciting days."

From her briefing by Peg before leaving for Bavaria, Giselle knew that Eva had been an assistant to Heinrich Hoffman, Hitler's personal photographer. Hoffman was a man quite close to the German *Führer*. In the mid-1930s it had been Hoffman who had convinced Hitler to undergo treatment by his own physician, Dr. Theodor Morell. And Hoffman's daughter, Henrietta, had a short-lived marriage to Baldur von Schirach, the Hitler Youth leader.

It was also Hoffman, along with the ubiquitous Bormann, who had insisted that Hitler receive royalties on each German postage stamp carrying his likeness. The immense wealth accumulated in this manner had provided Hitler with the funds to purchase his retreat at Berchtesgaden.

Giselle kept this information to herself. She did not want Eva to know the depth of her interest or research on her. Giselle also was careful to avoid showing any enmity toward the Third Reich. She merely smiled and nodded during the ensuing inconsequential conversation as they rode, awaiting an opportunity to question Eva as to her own personal beliefs.

The afternoon sun was bright and Giselle wished she could remove her overcoat but there was no room to maneuver wedged in between Eva and Peg on the leather rear seat of the Mercedes. She sat quietly as the car retraced its earlier drive through the *Berghof* area. But instead of turning onto the road to Berchtesgaden, the big convertible eased to the right onto a narrow mountainous road marked "*Kehlsteinstrasse.*"

Conversation waned as the large Daimler-Benz 2.3-liter engine strained to pull the car up the twisting, mountainous road. Several times, they passed through tunnels cut into the mountainside.

Peg seemed lost in the moment, staring with unabashed interest at the mountain scenery. Giselle could just imagine how she was seeing photographic opportunities in her mind.

Giselle too became totally absorbed with the panoramic view of the Alps and was somewhat surprised when they came to a stop in a circular parking lot. The two *SS* men remained with the Mercedes. Giselle, Peg and Eva walked between two concrete retaining walls that grew in height as they approached a large arched entranceway cut into the side of the *Kelhstein* peak.

Walking in the bright Bavarian noonday sun, Giselle felt lightheaded. The long journey, the apprehension of arrest and the meeting with Hitler's mistress were a dizzying combination. Then she remembered the altitude. Their drive had begun at 3,300 feet, then moved in a zigzag manner up the mountain to more than 6,000 feet. No wonder she was lightheaded, she thought. Smiling, she relaxed and allowed herself to enjoy the scenery, which was quickly lost to sight as Eva led her into the darkly shadowed entrance to a rock tunnel.

The heels of their shoes reverberated loudly on the stone floor of the passageway. Giselle noticed that Eva had matched her steps to hers. Peg joined in and soon the trio were marching in unison, as though members of some military unit.

Marching along in the echoing tunnel, it seemed unnatural to speak. Giselle ogled the arched stone block walls and contemplated the woman beside her.

Though seemingly a superficial blonde more interested in film stars than history or politics, Giselle realized there seemed to be much more to this woman. She wondered if she should share some of her adventures in Central America and Mexico. She decided against it, as the less Eva knew about her, the safer it would be. Giselle was well aware of the brutal interrogation methods of the Nazis. And she knew she could never be entirely certain as to Eva's true loyalties.

Looking ahead, she saw a small doorway flanked by electric candles. Inside was a glint of golden light that immediately engaged her attention.

With Eva standing to one side smiling and extending her arm in invitation, Giselle and Peg entered a large elevator the size of a small room. A circular lighting fixture inset in the ceiling cast off light that bounced off the highly polished brass walls creating a golden glow within the elevator. Green leather cushioned benches lined three sides of the space and each woman took a separate bench, relieved at the chance for a rest.

Somewhere deep within the bowels of the mountain an engine throbbed to life and the elevator began to rise swiftly.

Looking around her, Peg shook her head. "This is incredible," she muttered.

Eva smiled proudly, "Yes, my *Führer* spared no expense in the construction of what he likes to call his Eagle's Nest. The tunnel we just passed through is more than 120 meters in length. The road here is only four miles from the *Obersalzberg* but it passes through five tunnels. It really is quite an engineering achievement."

"I wish I hadn't left my camera in the car," groaned Peg, admiring the golden opulence surrounding her.

Moments later, the lift reached the apex of the shaft and bumped to a halt. Exiting, the three women entered a large room with long square wooden beams supporting the ceiling. Glancing about, Giselle decided the room looked big enough to house a good sized restaurant.

An enormous bright-red Persian rug covered much of the floor and situated near its center was a large round dining table covered with a white cloth. A bouquet of wild mountain flowers in the center was the only decoration. Steam rose from an elaborate tea service. Near the table was a large stone fireplace over which hung an intricate medieval tapestry.

Giselle noticed the odd assortment of stuffed chairs placed around the table. Several were covered in solid red while others were in different colors and patterns. It looked like an expanded version of any bourgeoisie living room.

She particularly noticed the number. There were 12 chairs, a sacred number with numerous historical and metaphysical implications. She wondered if it was sheer accident that 12 chairs surrounded the table in Hitler's most personal place.

The walls were made of slate gray stone blocks and appeared to be of the same material used to construct the elevator tunnel. Walking to one of the large windows set in a slight alcove, Giselle gave a small gasp at the vista outside.

The *Kehlsteinhaus* was situated on an outcropping, a narrow finger of rock jutting from the side of the mountain. Behind the building a pathway wound toward the summit in the near distance. The other three sides faced out to a breathtaking view of the Alps, some covered with snow and others with bright-green meadows and woods.

"On a clear day, one can see all the way to the *Dachstein*," Eva said excitedly, pointing as if she were a tour guide. "Munich is over there and Vienna is in that direction."

"No wonder Hitler thinks he's master of the world," muttered Peg with awe. Eva turned and looked at her quizzically, uncertain of her words. Deflecting her curiosity, Giselle took her by the arm and gushed, "Oh, this is simply amazing. I feel I'm on top of the world."

Giselle and Peg stood staring out the large window at the mountainous panorama while Eva moved to the center table.

"Won't you be seated? I had some tea ordered. I'll pour," said Eva as she busied herself over an engraved silver tea set.

"I'll stand for a moment, if you don't mind," replied Peg, taking a slow walk around the large single room. "I need to stretch my legs after that ride."

"Please make yourself comfortable," said Eva, pouring tea.

Giselle joined Eva at the table and asked, "And where is your *Führer*? I thought that during the summer months, we would find him here among the beauty of the mountains."

With no hesitation, Eva replied, "Oh, he is in East Prussia, closeted with the generals. They've been at it for weeks now. It must have something to do with the Mediterranean theater. We seem to be pushing the British back in North Africa but I understand that plans are afoot to evacuate Crete, which is sad after all the heavy fighting there."

Eva suddenly stopped and glanced at her guests as though she had just spilled some state secret. "Oh, but we decided not to discuss politics," she said apologetically.

Seizing the opportunity, Giselle spoke up. "It's quite all right. I would like to count you as a friend and, in fact, this is the real reason I came to see you."

"Oh?" asked Eva, arching her eyebrows in wary puzzlement.

"I thought you might be interested to know why your *Führer* has been spending so much time at his Prussian headquarters."

"It's not another woman, is it?" Eva asked, suddenly concerned.

Peg turned from the window and laughed gently. "No, no, nothing like that." Eva's face softened in relief.

Growing quite serious, Giselle moved to a stuffed chair next to Eva. She leaned forward and said bluntly, "Hitler is planning to attack Russia."

Eva looked shocked. Her eyes narrowed. "No one is supposed to know. How did you learn that?" she asked warily.

"There is a non-aggression pact with Stalin…" began Giselle.

"But don't you understand," interrupted Eva, becoming emotional, "Stalin has massed his armies on his western border. He intends to invade all Europe. The German Army is outnumbered in tanks, planes and men. We must strike first. It is our only chance."

After waiting a moment for Eva to regain her composure, Giselle said gently, "I understand. But don't you see what this means?"

After a few moments of silence, Eva looked up nodding. "The war will spread. It may engulf the entire world," she said somberly. "This is terrible. This is monstrous. How can such a thing happen?"

Sensing a momentary loss of faith in the infallibility of her nation's policies, Giselle said, "Do you realize that all this is following a plan dictated by the forces that are at work around Hitler?"

Eva sat back in her chair and looked at Giselle in silence.

"Are you trying to get information out of me?" she asked in a suspicious tone.

"Quite the contrary," replied Giselle soothingly. "I am here to give you information."

After another long silence, Giselle added softly, "And I am here to enlist your help."

"My help? Help in what? You are an American. I would never betray the Fatherland!" said Eva indignantly.

"Of course not. No one is asking you to betray your country," said Giselle quickly. "All I am asking is for you to help save lives, not only in Germany but throughout the whole world."

"Save lives? I don't understand," said Eva. Her features pinched into a puzzled expression.

Getting to her feet, Giselle paced lithely back and forth in front of the large stone fireplace while Peg backed a short distance from Eva. She did not want to seem intimidating.

After a moment, Giselle moved to Eva and said gently, "Do you understand that there have been forces at play throughout history trying to fragment humanity, separating men from women, the righteous from the unrighteous."

Eva scowled. "Are you talking about the occult?" she asked, her eyes narrowing.

Giselle smiled. "Some people call it the occult. But I'm sure you realize that the word 'occult' only means information that is hidden or beyond the range of common knowledge."

Eva looked at her shrewdly. "You are speaking of ancient knowledge that has been handed down over the centuries by secret societies." Her response was really more of a statement than a question.

"Exactly!" exclaimed Giselle, obviously surprised that Eva would exhibit any understanding of such subjects.

Giselle and Eva stared at each other for some time.

Giselle broke the silence by softly saying, "You really do understand about these things, don't you?"

Very quietly, Eva replied, "I have had access to certain understandings and even documents. Addie has spoken on occasion about these subjects," she added, unconsciously using her familiar name for Hitler. "I used to pay no attention when I was younger because I didn't understand, in fact, really didn't want to believe in such things. But that was before I studied the documents."

"What documents?" asked Peg. Giselle became intensely interested.

"The *Ahnenerbe-SS* have been excavating in southern France. They have discovered and impounded some very rare and significant documents," Eva explained, adding with a conspiratorial smile, "The *Führer* was more concerned with the political aspects of their work and dismissed these papers as irrelevant. I took some for myself, for they spoke of ancient secrets and reportedly were brought to France by Mary Magdalene herself."

Peg stared at her wide-eyed. "You mean the Mary Magdalene of the Bible?" she exclaimed.

Eva's smile grew. "The very same."

"I have heard stories…" Giselle muttered to herself.

Eva placed her teacup on the small table and sat looking at her companions with a thoughtful expression.

Giselle broke the ice. "You do know something about the ancient Sisterhood, don't you." It was not a question.

Eva looked at her for a moment and then seemed to make up her mind to confide in her new American friends.

"Do you like our little teahouse?" she asked quietly. It was the first time she had even intimated a close connection to Hitler.

"Like it? I love it. What an amazing place." Peg gestured to the view outside the oversized windows.

Eva leaned forward. "It's even more amazing than you think," she said cryptically.

Peg, expecting to learn some new fact about its construction, replied, "Oh, and how is that?"

Eva sighed and slumped a bit into her stuffed chair. Looking from Giselle to Peg, she seemed like a petulant teenager when she asked, "I guess you know that I have a certain special relationship with our *Führer*?"

Giselle didn't know whether to laugh or not. But she decided to err on the side of caution. She simply nodded seriously. Peg simply stared.

"Oh, everybody knows and nobody knows," exclaimed Eva, "It's enough to drive me mad."

Regaining her composure, she leaned across the table and confided, "My *Führer* has studied the occult for many years. He was first indoctrinated into the Secret Doctrine while an art student in Vienna before the Great War. He became knowledgeable as a grand master architect and used this wisdom from secret societies when he designed the Eagle's Nest. He used the same dimensions, positions and alignments found on the Giza Plateau to construct the *Berghof* as a center of power."

Giselle's eyes widened. She was stunned. She knew about Hitler's desire for ancient artifacts, his quest for esoteric knowledge and, or course, the crystal Skull of Fate that Peter had brought him from Central America. But she had never considered the extent of his knowledge or ambition.

"Really?" was all she managed to say in response. Peg was speechless. She was not prepared for such talk.

Becoming excited with the rare chance to demonstrate her knowledge, Eva walked to a sideboard and produced a piece of paper. Returning to the large table, she began sketching with a free-flowing fountain pen.

"Look, The Eagle's Nest is aligned with the Great Pyramid, including its hidden passageways. There are similar passageways in this mountain. The *Kehlsteinhaus* is the capstone of the tower over the King's Chamber in the Great Pyramid. The elevator shaft represents the tower itself.

"Hitler told you all of this?" Giselle was incredulous.

Eva laughed lightly, "Oh, no. Not in its entirety. But he often has used me as a sounding board, never thinking that I actually might listen to his musings. And he certainly never thought that I would be so stimulated by the energy he has created here in this place. I have been piecing things together on my own and gaining my own power."

She sat back and folded her arms proudly. Eva appeared elated to finally share her confidence with others who actually might understand the strange and wondrous learning process she had experienced.

Returning to her sketch, Eva drew further lines and said, "There are secret passageways beneath us, and one represents the Queen's Chamber in the pyramid. No one will ever discover it. That is where I have hidden the documents I obtained from the work in France."

"And who discovered these documents?" asked Giselle. Her interest was intensifying.

"A fellow named Otto Rahn had written extensively about the legends and stories of southern France. He spent some time there researching. I believe he brought back some of the knowledge which was handed over to Heinrich Himmler. Some of it was passed along to me by my friends in the *Ahnenerbe-SS*," explained Eva.

Ahnenerbe-SS! There was that name again, the same one mentioned by Haushofer in Zürich. She had been unable to learn much about the organization, but she knew it was her one link to Peter and the skull.

As casually as she could, Giselle asked, "Have you met a man named Peter Freiherr von Manteuffel? He's with the *Ahnenerbe-SS*."

Eva's forehead furrowed in concentration. Slowly, she replied, "No, I don't recall anyone by that name."

"Never mind," said Giselle, realizing she had hit a dead end. "Where exactly in France did this Otto Rahn fellow find this knowledge?" asked Giselle. She was intrigued but trying hard not to sound too inquisitive.

"I'm not sure," Eva said pondering the question. "All I know is that he journeyed to a small village called Rennes-le-Château and returned with documents attributed to an ancient and secret society. Addie paid them little attention once he realized they had no strategic value in his conduct of the war. He lost interest in them and that's when I managed to obtain them for myself."

"Didn't the SS want them back?" Peg asked, trying to rejoin the conversation even though she obviously had no idea what was being discussed. Giselle was desperately trying to think of some way to elicit more information from their hostess.

"They do what I command," replied Eva haughtily.

Giselle smiled and said, "I'll bet they do. But tell me more of this *SS* bunch. It sounds as if they are most efficient."

"Yes, they are. The *Ahnenerbe-SS* has contributed much to the war effort, more than anyone is likely to know. They are very secretive you know. A man named Hermann Wirth helped organize the unit. He has proven most helpful to me. I have learned much from him. Do you know he has documents referring to ancient Atlantis?"

Trying to act uninformed in such matters, Giselle laughed and looked incredulous. "I thought Atlantis was just a myth," she said blithely. Peg's being uninformed was no act. She stared at both Eva and Giselle with incredulous eyes.

"The name may be wrong, but from what I've learned, there may be much truth to the stories of an ancient and great prehistoric civilization. We are still learning about this," said Eva in a serious tone. "We have made expeditions to Antarctica, Iceland and even Tibet in search of such knowledge. Dr. Ernst Schafer of the Sven Hedin Institute headed the expedition to the Himalayas. We have learned much from our investigations."

Giselle thought this information might explain her inability to locate Peter, despite her growing web of agents and contacts. He may have been sent to some secret retreat in a far corner of the world.

Eva was still talking. "The documents Otto Rahn produced from his research in France contain the divine principles of creation written in the language of light, very similar to old runes. Did you know that runes stemmed from ancient Sumerian tablets only discovered in the last century? These elder documents speak of many arcane things, such as the divine seed, the secrets of crystals and stones, energy fields known as ley lines, other star systems associated with such energy and even contact with other worlds. Such knowledge is well kept within a highly secret program within the *Ahnenerbe-SS* code named *Majik*."

Giselle realized that this woman was much more educated in esoteric knowledge than she would have ever imagined. Peg finally remembered to close her gaping mouth.

Still bubbling with enthusiasm for her subject, Eva continued. "I must tell you that Addie…" This time she caught herself in her familiarity. "I mean my *Führer*, is not so knowledgeable as he thinks he is. I have found several references to things he has left out of his occult practices.

Either he doesn't recognize the importance of such things or he was never informed. I suspect the latter. I think that one of his early mentors intentionally withheld vital information."

"Who was that?" asked Giselle casually while every fiber of her being focused on Eva's words.

"Well, I am not supposed to know these things but playing the role of a dumb woman sometimes has its advantages." Eva smiled, then continued earnestly. "You may have heard of Rudolf Steiner, the Theosophist who formed the Anthroposophical Society in 1912?"

The name meant nothing to Giselle yet she nodded in silent acknowledgement. Peg brightened. "I've heard of this guy. He developed the concept that humans can access universal truths with the need *of* the five material senses or something like that."

"Yes, he assisted in some of our *Führer*'s early esoteric education. Apparently, *Herr* Steiner did not fully trust him and withheld some important aspects of his teachings." She gave a short laugh. "He is dead now, of course, but I think that he now would realize his mistake. Clearly, our *Führer* was destined to know such things, *nicht wahr?*"

Giselle again nodded. She was shocked to learn that such intelligent and highly placed persons took such matters seriously. Yet, her own experiences indicated the truth behind philosophies she once considered preposterous.

Realizing the need for caution, Giselle nevertheless could not help but chance the question that was foremost on her mind. "Have you heard anything regarding a crystal skull?" She asked as casually as possible. Peg's eyes widened. Due to their conversations in Moscow, she knew what Giselle was attempting to learn.

Eva looked at Giselle with quizzical eyes that were beginning to harden with suspicion. "Yes, I know about the skull. Why do you ask? How do you know about this?"

Giselle decided her best tactic would be the truth. "I was involved in its discovery," she said.

She decided to take another, greater chance.

Taking Eva's hands in her, Giselle looked deep into her eyes, the mirror of the soul. "Since you know so much of the hidden knowledge, you must know that once the world was run by a matriarchal system bound in love to the earth and to humanity."

Without dropping her gaze, Eva slowly nodded.

"Eva, then you must know that it is up to us to stop the carnage that is engulfing the world," said Giselle softly. "We must help make the world safe for everyone, Germans and others alike."

Caught between the thinking and feeling sides of her nature, Eva protested, "But, we must have *lebensraum*, living space, and we must protect the purity of our Aryan race from the sub-humans…"

"That's just political talk," said Giselle angrily. "We must look above that and take into consideration what's good for everyone, not just the Germans, the French, the British or anyone else. Eva, with the attack on Russia and the rising tensions in the Far East, the entire world may soon be engulfed in war. We must do something to stop this."

"What can we do? We're not in charge," she objected. After a moment of silence, Eva shook her head slightly and muttered, "After all, I'm just one person."

"That is so," agreed Giselle in a calmer tone. "But that doesn't mean you can't make a significant impact on the events and people around us."

Eva sat quietly, considering her statement. Peg had seated herself nearby and also was deep in thought. She had expected some womanly chitchat and an attempt to swap information. She had never envisioned delving into such esoteric topics with the mistress of Adolf Hitler.

"Look, we all have our own special talents and abilities. I understand that you like to make your own perfumes," said Giselle, trying to engage Eva's self interest.

"Oh, yes," she responded with some enthusiasm. "I have long worked on developing scents. I enjoy the study of flowers, herbs, and certain essences. I'm afraid poor Addie is oblivious to scents. But he has tried some of my preparations just to be kind."

Giggling like a schoolgirl caught in some infraction, Eva whispered, "I have been particularly interested in a white powder made from pure gold through a heating process mentioned in those papers I obtained from the SS. I mentioned this to Addie but he said he checked with some chemists who assured him there was nothing to it, that it was just modern-day alchemy. But I actually had some of this powder produced and slipped it to him once during dinner. The effect was quite noticeable to me although I'm sure he did not realize its true source. He became quite animated and spoke on any number of topics for several hours."

"There, you see," exclaimed Giselle, "you are already practicing female alchemy. You can change a man's attitude and perceptions by the use of elixirs and scents." Inwardly, she wondered what could possibly produce powder from metal.

Eva laughed. "Giselle, you can change a man's attitude even more quickly with other tools," she said imitating the slapping of a whip into her left hand.

Giselle laughed. Peg joined in the laughter, thinking to herself this was an important insight into a sado-masochistic relationship between this woman and the German *Führer*. She couldn't wait to share this with her peers at *Life*.

Quick to take advantage of this moment of female camaraderie, Giselle offered, "That's all fine and good, but sometimes you might prepare a potion that will make your man more contemplative, more understanding. You have the power to shift his thoughts toward peace."

"And if that doesn't work?" asked Eva absently, still contemplating Giselle's exhortation.

Giselle looked straight into Eva's eyes and said seriously, "Then you should consider taking more serious steps. Chemicals can be used for purposes other than making perfumes and aphrodisiacs."

Eva looked shocked and Giselle realized that she might have overstepped herself. Quickly, she asked, "Have you met Clara Petacci?"

The question caught Eva off guard and Giselle saw her thoughts shift. "I haven't seen her since we met in 1937 during her visit to Germany. I liked her well enough"

She dropped her eyes. "She is a kindred spirit. We found we were both in much the same situation. We were carefully kept out of sight. But we managed to meet in Berlin. She's a very interesting woman."

"You should know that Clara is one of those working for world peace," said Giselle quietly. Eva looked up.

"Really?" she said with a trace of astonishment.

"I'll be damned," exclaimed Peg. Giselle had not mentioned the involvement of Mussolini's mistress. She shook her head. This conversation was going from the bizarre to the sublime.

Eva sat quietly, contemplating.

Giselle decided to allow Eva time to think on her proposal. She reached into the floral arrangement on the table and withdrew two small flowers. She examined closely the two small white woolly flowers, each with several points emanating from a central head. When Giselle finally spoke, she said, "This is Edelweiss, I believe. "

"Yes, they are," replied Eva, rousing herself from her contemplation. She added with pride, "Their tiny blossoms are considered quite a rarity as they only bloom at the highest altitudes of the Alps."

Giselle handed Eva one of the Edelweiss and said softly, "Remember this, Eva. With worldwide war looming, we may never be able to meet again.

"If we ever need to communicate, your recognition sign will be a single Edelweiss. Mine is a single long-stemmed rose. This way we'll know it came from the other. All of the women I speak of have taken names of flowers. Their overall symbol is a single red rose."

Eva smiled, intrigued with the idea of the use of secret signs like some secret agent. "Does Clara Petacci have a flower code?" she asked.

"She's the Black Iris," Giselle said in a quiet but serious tone. Eva's smile slowly faded as she grasped the implications of such secrecy.

"Giselle, can you stay with me for a few days? There is so much for us to talk about." Eva asked. Her request was almost a plea. Behind her back, Peg was shaking her head. In her mind, it was time to leave.

"Eva, you know I would love to stay with you," replied Giselle with a sincere sorrow. "But I must get back to Paris as soon as possible. I have responsibilities and commitments I cannot break. I'm sure you understand." She could not tell Eva that she was impatient to return to Paris to question Charles about this *Ahnenerbe-SS*. It was, after all, her first major lead in finding Peter and taking the powerful skull from Eva's lover.

Eva smiled and said, "Certainly, dear, I truly understand. Are you certain you won't have any problem with the border checkpoints?"

Peg laughed softly. "I shouldn't think so. An American passport and American cash can still move mountains. We're not in this war yet."

Giselle thought it wise not to tell Eva their travel plans. She did not want to reveal that Peg had already made arrangements to fly back to Moscow on another transport flight. She knew that the photographer was anxious to join her husband as soon as possible. And she too was more than ready to leave the German *Reich*. Just before boarding the *Suddeutschland* Express, Giselle had purchased a train ticket for Paris.

Eva nodded silently and soon the women left the *Kehlsteinhaus*.

The return trip down the elevator and the long walk through the tunnel was uneventful as the pair swapped innocuous pleasantries. Eva was for the most part deep in thought. Giselle felt encouraged by the meeting and already was entertaining optimistic thoughts of promoting worldwide peace.

The big red Mercedes was still in the parking lot and soon the trio was motoring back down the winding road to the *Berghof*.

After some banter in front of Hitler's large two-story villa, the women made their farewells. As Giselle and Peg climbed into the car, Eva suddenly exclaimed, "Giselle, wait one moment. I have something for you." With that she turned and ran up the steps to the house.

Giselle and Peg looked at each other with questioning eyes. Looking toward the steps of the *Berghof*, Giselle hoped her new acquaintance would find the spirit and strength to aid the Sisterhood in its struggle for justice and peace. She knew that only the purest of hearts would be able to access the highest spiritual knowledge and wisdom necessary to stop this conspiracy of hate. She also knew she must quickly find out about the *Ahnenerbe-SS* and its link to Peter.

As the moments dragged on, doubts and fears welled up in her mind. Peg too was looking worried. What if Eva was not the thoughtful person she seemed? What if she had only played Giselle along until she was safe back in the *Berghof*? What if she even now was calling the guards to arrest the meddling Americans? She found herself sweating despite the cool mountain air.

Suddenly Eva returned alone. As the driver was putting the Mercedes into gear, she reached through open side of the touring car and handed Giselle a single red rose bud.

Peg's eyes grew large and a broad smile came to her face. Giselle also smiled, relaxed on the back seat and mouthed a "thank you" over the roar of the engine. Quickly Hitler's home and woman were lost to sight.

CHAPTER 14

Tuscany, Italy
January, 1942

GISELLE HAD THOUGHT IT LUCKY that no one but a few local peasants would pass the *Villa Tagliani* on that chilly January evening in 1942. Anyone else might have commented on the number of cars parked about the sprawling estate.

The locals would simply assume that the wealthy owners were having another of their famed parties. The few that did pass probably would not take notice that the villa sat dark and quiet under a full moon.

Beyond the villa and deep underground in one of the recently discovered Roman chambers, Giselle pushed a fork into her salad and surveyed the scene before her.

The large cavern-like chamber was warm and a bit smoky from the series of flaming braziers that ran along the sides of the rectangular room that had been carved out of the rocky hillside. Two long tables ran nearly the length of the chamber and flanked a large round table. Both men and women were seated at random down the long tables. But sitting at the round table were only Giselle and the 12 inner members of the Sisterhood of the Rose. They were all females. And what a variety there was. One thin blonde could have passed for a Parisian magazine model while a young woman with short-cropped dark hair would have looked quite at home digging beets outside a Russian *dacha*. One older woman, a dowager queen, was laughing while sharing some jest with Aunt Fran.

The gathering was still wearing the robes worn earlier during a sacred goddess ceremony. For the Sisterhood, the robes reflected the colors of their flower codenames. Now, with hoods pulled back, they all were embarking on the ritual feast that followed such ceremonies. It was the first occasion for many of the attendees to meet the others. Giselle was gratified at the ease with which these women of varied backgrounds and circumstances were able to blend with each other in solidarity of purpose.

Gabby was at the round table sitting next to her favorite aunt, one that had made a significant addition to the Sisterhood. Married to a Swiss businessman, she held Swiss citizenship. This, along with her profession as an art broker, allowed her to move in a wide variety of circles and countries. The Sisterhood put this privilege to good use.

However, Gabby was not facing her aunt, but instead turned toward one of the long tables, flirting with Jean Paul, who carried dual membership in the Sisterhood and the growing French Resistance. At that same table sat Michel, his dark features pinched in concentration as Charles, with scholarly patience, attempted to explain some point of argument.

There had been a brief brouhaha with Gabby's aunt when it was learned that she had planned to bring along a German, an officer no less. The woman had argued that the man was well connected to the Nazi hierarchy yet swore that he was open to the principles of peace and justice. Giselle's Aunt Fran had been livid at the prospect of placing both the Sisterhood and her beloved villa at risk. Giselle had finally managed to soothe things over by having Gabby's aunt promise to leave the man behind and not reveal anything of consequence to him. It had been like this from the beginning, each member of the Sisterhood bringing her own pet peeves and desires to the table.

But at the moment, Giselle was not consciously taking note of Gabby or the other guests nor did she hear the soft murmur of dinner conversation as the group savored the fine meal prepared by Aunt Fran and her staff. She was deep in thought, pondering the news of the past few months. None of it was very good.

Her elation the past June following the meeting with Eva Braun and the success of their mission to Switzerland had been dampened by the news that it was now beyond dispute that Peter had delivered the Skull of Fate to Hitler. But where was he? How could she ever retrieve the skull if she could not locate Peter? It grated on her to know that her worst enemy was also her only hope of finding the artifact.

Eva Braun had been no help in locating Peter and, despite the temptation to remain with her in Berchtesgaden to glean more information on activities within the *Reich*, Giselle had decided it would be both safer and more productive to return home. After voicing respect for each other's work, Giselle had bid farewell to Peg after they arrived in Munich.

It had taken two days for her to travel by train from Munich to Paris. The rail trip had been slow. Many times her train was stopped or shunted onto a siding to make way for military traffic moving eastward. The Pullman porter had explained it was due to the German and Italian operations in Greece and Yugoslavia, but Giselle knew it had to do with the upcoming invasion of Russia. Despite the delays, the journey was bearable. Once again, the power of her American passport and currency had afforded her the luxury of a private compartment.

When she had finally arrived in Paris on June 23rd, Michel had met her at the *Gare de l'Est* station with a handful of newspapers proclaiming the news that German troops were moving almost unhindered into the Soviet Union in an operation called *Barbarossa*. It had occurred exactly as she had been warned months previously.

At dawn on June 22, 1941, Hitler's Directive Number 21 had ordered more than 3 million German soldiers utilizing 3,580 tanks, 600,000 vehicles and supported by 7,184 artillery pieces to pour across Russia's western border, launching a *Blitzkrieg* that would lock the two great nations in the greatest military struggle in the history of the world.

Tears of sadness and frustration had trickled down her cheeks as she read about the ease with which the initial German attack rolled forward. Entire Russian armies were encircled by the rampaging *panzers*. Mechanized units were counting their daily advances in the hundreds of kilometers.

The Nazi-controlled radio commentators in Paris were enthusiastically announcing the news of German victories and citizens were awestruck with the success of the unexpected attack.

Even though Giselle suspected that the number of captured or destroyed units was inflated by the German propagandists, she also knew that even they could not deviate too far from the truth. If even half of what was being reported was true, *Barbarossa* was a mind-boggling success.

Giselle realized she was one of the very few who knew the success of *Barbarossa* stemmed from the fact that the Russians were not prepared for defense but had been set in offensive positions in preparation for the all-out assault on Europe. Nevertheless, she was despondent over the turn of events.

"I should have prevented this," Giselle had muttered to herself as she read the early reports of the invasion. Inwardly she knew the Skull of Fate had once again given the advantage to Hitler. She also was concerned for the safety of her Uncle Alexander and her other relatives as well as her new friend Peg.

Adding to her concern was the event that had occurred less than a month before the Sisterhood gathering in Tuscany. On December 7, 1941, Giselle's world had turned upside down as America entered the war.

Giselle and Michel were well aware that circumstances were pointing to an eventual war with Japan. Even so, the attack on Pearl Harbor had come as a complete surprise to her.

Even as they read about Hitler's astounding success in Russia in the summer of 1941, they had taken note of the news reports concerning events in the Orient. They had the added benefit of their own private sources of information. Both were well aware that President Roosevelt had denied Japan necessary oil supplies, secretly funded Major General Claire Chennault's "Flying Tigers" in China, ordered attacks against German U-boats in the Atlantic and sent Britain war materials. By repeatedly violating the Neutrality Act, he had all but declared open war against the Axis on his own initiative.

Nevertheless, the news of the devastating attack on the Pacific Fleet in Hawaii both shocked and saddened Giselle. Just as she had so feared, the entire world now was involved in a deadly conflagration.

As 1941 had come to a close, the news only grew worse. Beginning just two days after the United States and Britain declared war on Japan, troops of the Empire of the Rising Sun seized the U.S. base on Guam, the southernmost island in the Mariana chain, attacked the mid-Pacific island of Wake and invaded the Philippines. By December 11th, Japanese troops advanced into Burma and by the 18th, they were circling Hong Kong, which surrendered on Christmas Day.

The news on her quest for Peter was equally bad. Despite numerous inquiries and the questioning of every one of the Sisterhood's growing number of contacts, there was still no trace of the man. There was only the word that he had been enrolled as an officer in the *Ahnen-*

erbe-SS. It was as if the man had dropped off the face of the Earth.

The lack of information concerning Peter and the skull cast a pall over her success in ridding the *Reich* of Rudolf Hess as well as her other Sisterhood activities.

The organization was rapidly growing in both numbers and strength. Already there had been operations in conjunction with the British as well as some sporadic attacks on the occupation forces. It was a far cry from the simple demonstrations Giselle had helped organize early on for Gabby and her fellow students.

Shortly after New Year's Day, 1942, Giselle had decided to call a conference at Aunt Fran's villa in Italy for all ranking members of the Sisterhood to lay plans for the coming year. One particular concern was a recent meeting of high-level Nazi officials on the *Wannsee.* Information had leaked back to the Sisterhood that plans had been laid for a "Final Solution" to the Jewish question. Giselle had shuddered to think what this diabolical plan might entail. The man chosen to administer this horrific program was *SS Obergruppenführer* Reinhard Heydrich, already notorious for his brutal methods as deputy *Reich* protector for Bohemia and Moravia. Plans were already in motion for an assassination attempt against Heydrich.

Toward the end of January, members of the Sisterhood had begun arriving at *Villa Tagliani,* their vehicles passing quietly under the blue grapes motif of the huge gates. Many had driven there from various locations in Europe. Others had traveled by boat, entering the chamber through a narrow back tunnel that had been constructed to connect with a boat dock within a grotto on the Ligurian Sea.

All had brought their letter of invitation signed only "VV" along with a long-stem rose as their bona fides. All letters had been sealed with wax in the form of a red rose. No one entered without displaying the rose. It was Giselle's scheme for preventing infiltration by enemy agents.

Michel, Charles and Gabby had accompanied her on the long drive down from Paris. The visit was looked on as a combination of work and play. All four were glad for a respite from the pressures of Paris and their double lives. They had enjoyed two days of peace and quiet at the *Villa Tagliani* as they waited for all the guests to arrive.

Now Giselle found herself anxiously picking at her salad plate. Her stomach was in knots. She knew she must address this gathering and somehow bind the attendees into the common cause. She looked up from her dinner and inspected each face before her. Her heart swelled with pride, knowing that these women were risking everything for the cause of peace and justice.

Now, as dinner drew to a close, she knew it was time. Giselle reluctantly rose from her chair and tapped her wine glass for attention. A hush fell over the chamber and all eyes looked toward her. Giselle's voice gained volume echoing off the rocky walls of the grotto.

"Greetings, it is good to be together … again," she began, smiling at the looks of puzzlement on some of the faces. She had not met many of the attendees and she knew they might not catch the inference to their connection in past lives.

"As you all know, we of the Sisterhood go by codenames for security purposes. Let me introduce myself. I am Velva Violet."

A wave of whispering swept through the chamber. All Sisterhood communications carried the name Velva Violet. Many attendees were excited to finally put a face to that name.

Again waving for silence, Giselle smiled and continued, "I want to thank each and every one of you for making the time-consuming—and in some cases, dangerous—trip to be with us here tonight under this lovely Tuscan moon. Some of you know each other and I would ask that you not reveal any real identities. Others of you we have not yet met but I assure you that your patriotism and concern for humanity are known to us.

"Friends," she continued, noting with amusement that many of the women appeared to understand her remark about meeting again. "I know we all share in the sorrow for what has happened to America. But I think we can agree that this one despicable act by Japan may have done more to aid our cause than anything up to this point."

There was general head nodding. Those in attendance well understood the need for American intervention if the Nazi grip on Europe was ever to be loosened.

"And there is one bright spot in this picture of which some of you may not be aware," she continued. "We have just received word om our contacts within the occupation forces that the Germans have ulled back from Moscow. They are now dug in on the west bank of the Ioskva-Volga Canal."

A buzz of excitement passed through the room. One of the new-leaders called out, "But I thought the *Boche* announced they had aptured one of the city's main power stations and that the Moscow

Highway was within reach. They said that white flags of surrender were flying in the city's streets and that the government had evacuated."

Giselle remembered the woman because of her name. It was Madeleine Braun, a Parisian some 10 years older than Giselle who had devoted her life to easing the plight of workers and political refugees. She was now acting as a liaison agent in southern France between the Sisterhood and the Resistance.

Giselle smiled. "Do I understand then that you now take seriously *Herr* Goebbels' propaganda?" The woman blushed with embarrassment but quickly joined Giselle and others in the general laughter.

"I was only teasing, my dear," Giselle smiled. Turning more serious, she continued, "Apparently, the mighty German *Wehrmacht*, in its haste to attack Russia, neglected to take along winter clothing. Now, even the slightest wound is resulting in death due to shock as temperatures have dropped to more than 50 degrees below zero Fahrenheit." Gasps were heard from around the room. "Even their antifreeze is freezing. Automatic weapons will not fire and fires must be lit under tanks to warm them enough to start."

"It sounds like the Soviets have found a formidable ally," a man shouted from the rear. More laughter came but it carried an undercurrent of cruel satisfaction more than humor.

"It demonstrates that the Germans are not the supermen they would have us believe," continued Giselle, waving for quiet. "I have received word that Army Group Center has called off its expected attack against the Russian capital and that fresh Mongolian troops, well equipped for winter fighting, have launched a counteroffensive. It seems the danger to Moscow is over for the time being." There was general applause, especially from some in the audience that Giselle knew were members of the Communist Party.

She knew the time was quickly coming when she and other leaders in the newly formed Resistance movement would have to deal with the question of how to handle these former political opponents. But now i' was time to energize her followers.

"You are not here by accident. An ancient plan is unfolding to night. We may not realize or accept this on a conscious and intellectu level, but soon the purpose will become clear.

"It pleases my heart to see the legacy of the eternal Sisterhood con together once again. Throughout the ages on this world there have bee those women who have assembled themselves inside the sacred numbers to preserve the Goddess energy until such time as she is resurrected.

"I and some of your fellow members are working with secrets that have only been passed down through secret brotherhoods and secret sisterhoods. For centuries, many of these brotherhoods have distorted these sacred principles for their own goal of controlling the world. Women were left out and, in fact, made into second-class citizens."

Mouths were gaping open around the large chamber. Few of those assembled had ever heard such talk, especially spoken by a woman openly.

"My friends, it is the duty of those gathered here under this full moon to pledge our unconditional allegiance to world peace and harmony. We must end the madness of war and financial manipulation. We must restore the natural balance between the divine feminine and the divine masculine. And it falls to women to lead the way."

"Hear, hear! Yes!" The cries echoed about the chamber.

"We are gathered to battle against the very antithesis of the Goddess, a warmongering, spiritually-distorted, patriarchal-dominated world that serves very few people on this planet—men or women—least of all the divine feminine."

Moving more confidently into her speech, Giselle's voice rose as she proclaimed, "We are now at a crossroads in world events. Either we see that this is the last of planet-wide warfare or we doom future generations to an endless cycle of hatred and violence.

"The path before us is uncharted. The going will be difficult. But it's just such an uncharted path that provides unparalleled opportunities to end, or at least diminish, the pain and suffering we see about us."

Placing both hands on the large round table, Giselle lowered her voice and looked from face to face. Deep inside, she found herself surprised at both the content and intensity of the words that began to flow for her lips. It was as though some separate spirit had taken control of her speech.

"You see, my friends, it is the imbalance of energy in our world that has brought us to the present sad state of affairs. And energy is the basic building block that binds the universe together.

"This loss of balance is not by accident. It is a strategy that was developed long before our present history was first written down, before the time of Noah's Flood. This strategy is designed to maintain control over humanity by perpetuating a constant state of disharmony and the vibration of fear. Agitated and disharmonious people soon become frightened people and frightened people are quick to embrace hatred and violence.

"The female energy, the mothering aspect of humanity, is necessary to maintain the balance of energy on this world. But much of this has been conditioned out of the male psyche. Men have been taught that to be a real man is to deny both their own intuition and higher consciousness. They have been trained to live in their lower consciousness and ladies, I think we all know where that low spot is.

"Women still hold strong to their 'woman's intuition.' This is why so many of our psychics and oracles are female. Throughout history, there have been ongoing efforts to prevent this energy from being used for peaceful purposes. Organized religion and the political systems have relegated women to a subservient role. In the name of honoring women, they have prevented us from attaining positions of power in the male-dominated social structures.

"This is nothing new, my friends. We here tonight are operating from the energy of love, the same energy that lay behind the great matriarchal societies of the past. We are the descendants of these ancient leaders and we are gathered together at this time of trial and tribulation to carry on their work."

Giselle took a long-stemmed rose from the table in front of her and held it high in the air. "The symbol of the rose stretches back before the beginning of history. The rose is composed of five petals surrounded by eight petals. This is why you see before you the thirteen members of the Sisterhood's inner circle, myself and twelve members of equal standing. We have seen this throughout history in Jesus and his twelve disciples and the thirteen members of a witch's coven. King Arthur made a round table to avoid elevating any of his twelve knights over another. Thirteen is the number of transformation. The powers that be, political and religious, have no interest in the people having access to transformation, so they mislead us by keeping our attention on twelve.

"In geometric terms, we see a pentagram within an eight-pointed star, the ancient Star of Isis. The Egyptian goddess Isis, long revered as the goddess of total femininity, has been worshipped for centuries under the various names given to her individual aspects, such as Hathor, Meri and Sochit.

"The Sumerians called her Ninhursag; the Greeks named her Athena and to the Romans, she was Minerva. But these names all referred to the same feminine principle.

"The male secret societies know this, which is why we see the Star

depicted on the red sash of the old Knights Templar. Today we
e rose playing a large role in the societies of the Freemasons and
osicrucians.

"This force has been used for both good and evil throughout the
For, after all, energy has both positive and negative aspects.

"Well, my friends, today we have this power and I would like for
f you to pledge yourselves to use this recovered power for the bet-
nent of this world."

With a great sense of pride, Giselle looked out at the faces before
: She waited for applause to die down before she continued.

"Swift and effective work by our Sisterhood is now needed more
n ever," she said loudly over the hubbub of the group. "I want each
you to return to your homes and jobs with a solid commitment to do
1atever you can, whatever is asked of you, so that we may achieve the
final victory as quickly as possible. I think we all realize that we have
roles in the grand drama that is being played out on this world.

"We have all been conditioned and educated for this very moment
and many of us realize that spiritual assistance has guided us to this point.
The male dominated societies have had their way for millennia and, frankly, they've made a mess of it. Now it's our turn, so let's get on with it."

Almost shouting over growing applause, Giselle proclaimed, "Our
mission is a sacred one as well as a dangerous one. But in the end, regardless
of the risks, it is a mission worth living for … and dying for if we must."

After the hearty applause subsided, Giselle motioned for Gabby to
rise and announced, "Our own Laughing Lilac will now give each of you
assignments for the coming weeks as well as the name of your immediate
Sisterhood contact. You may discuss any problems or details with them.

"Since I may not see many of you for some time, let me say *bonne
année* to each and every one of you." A chorus of "Happy New Year!" was
returned. As Gabby rose and began shouting out individual instructions,
Giselle held the rose high in the air and shouted, "Long live the rose!"

Moments later, as Giselle pushed through a throng of well-wishers
gathering by the large round table, she motioned for Michel and Charles
to join her. Once seated in a small adjoining chamber, she poured each a
glass of wine, then dropped wearily into a chair and fixed her two close
friends with a serious gaze.

"The attack on Pearl Harbor has been a boon to the Sisterhood,"
she began, "but it has created a gigantic personal problem for me."

"Would you be talking about the fact that now war has been declared between your country and Germany, you are an enemy alien?" asked Michel casually. A flicker of humor danced around his eyes.

"*Oui*, of course," responded Giselle with irritation. She was irked by his light tone. "Michel, this is a serious problem. The authorities may be waiting at the château to arrest me when we return."

"But, *ma chère*, don't you recall we have already planned for this eventuality? I have all the paperwork prepared. Giselle Tchaikovsky is no longer here. She left quite suddenly for America. Only her aunt, the reclusive Giselle St. Clair, an upstanding citizen of France, remains at the family château."

With that, Michel stood and produced a packet of official documents from his coat pocket. He handed them over to Giselle with a formal bow. She took them and saw a passport, birth certificate, travel permits and various other credentials.

"A little makeup, some old clothing and..." Michel's words were cut off as Giselle, with a small squeal of delight, grabbed him around the neck and gave him a long, lingering kiss. "Oh, my darling, this is such a load off my mind..." she murmured, finally pulling her lips from his.

"Yes, well, perhaps I should remove myself," muttered Charles with some embarrassment. The professor started to stand up but Giselle put out a hand and said, "That will not be necessary, Charles. We can continue this later." She gave Michel a knowing look. "Right now, I have another problem."

Smiling, the older man resumed his seat. "And what might that be, my dear?"

Giselle walked slowly to the chamber's door and stood quietly for some time watching the Sisterhood members in the large assembly hall disperse into smaller groups.

Finally, she turned and said, "I'm sure I don't have to tell either of you how important it is that I find Peter and retrieve the Skull of Fate."

When neither man spoke, she continued, "Michel, as you well know, we have tried everything within our power, contacted every source we have and still have no lead to Peter's whereabouts. There must be something that we've overlooked."

"What about those German astrologers in Zürich?" asked Charles. "They knew about the skull, there must be some clue in what they said."

"I have already told you," replied Giselle with an irritation she regretted as soon as she said it. "I'm sorry, Charles. It's just that I feel while I have the necessary clues, I just can't seem to put them together properly. They did not even know the name of the man who brought the skull to Hitler. They merely said a man had shown up with a crystal skull. I did not want to press them. I was scared to death as it was."

Michel peered at her intently. "They didn't mention any other names or locations?"

Giselle thought for a moment, straining to regain memories of the hotel conversation. Finally, she said, "Well, they mentioned expeditions to Tibet and Antarctica, but surely they have no connection to Peter and the skull."

"You don't know that for certain," admonished Charles. Giselle nodded and began to consider the idea that Peter was in one of those far off locations. It would certainly account for his seemingly total disappearance.

Michel was now pressing the point. "Giselle, think. Was there anything else they said that might give us a lead?"

Brows furrowed, Giselle replied through pinched lips, "I do recall that Haushofer mentioned something about a village in southern France. He mentioned studying legends in that area…"

Giselle paused and stood still. Was this the lead she was looking for? Something about this line of inquiry was tickling her memory.

"That may be it, Michel!" she exclaimed. "What was the name of that village he mentioned?"

"I don't recall," mumbled Michel, looking hurt that he was not being more helpful.

"Don't worry, darling, I can't think of it either." Giselle's mind was racing. "But we did speak about it following the Zürich meeting. Would you recognize it if you saw it?"

"I think so."

"Drink your wine. I'll be right back."

Moments later Giselle returned with a Michelin map entitled "Pyrenees, Languedoc, Roussillon." Spreading it on a table, she peered at it carefully. "Professor, here is Beziers. Wasn't that one of the cities involved in the destruction of the Cathars?"

Peering over her shoulder, Charles quickly answered. "Yes, it was one of the first cities to be attacked in what became known as the Albigensian Crusade. From there the Papal Army marched westward, deeper into the Languedoc region."

"Now, Michel. What was the name of the village?" Michel peered closely at the map but nothing registered. He was shaking his head. Giselle realized her pressure on Michel was actually pressure on herself. The name was dancing about just on the fringe of her conscious memory. It was maddening.

Thinking hard, Michel responded, "I'm sorry *ma chère*, I just can't remember."

Staring up, Giselle said absently, "I think it began with Rennes something."

Pulling his finger down the index of the map before him, Michel stopped. "Here's a Rennes-les-Bains. Is that it?"

Giselle slowly shook her head. "I don't think so."

Moving ahead in the map's index, he asked, "Then how about Rennes-le-Château?"

"Yes, that's it!" shouted Giselle leaping from her seat. "I'm certain." Charles clapped his hands in delight.

Giselle bent over the map and then straightened up to face both men with a dazed look in her eyes. The name had struck a receptive cord somewhere deep within her memory. Suddenly, she blinked as the name manifested itself in her mind.

"Oh, my God!" she shouted. Both men turned to stare. Her hands were over her mouth and her eyes were wide.

In a whisper, she muttered, "That's the village Eva Braun mentioned. Some man with the SS brought back documents from that place. Apparently, they were quite old and contained information that Eva found fascinating. This will be where we'll find Peter. I just know it."

"I might have known," said Charles quietly. "I have studied about that village. I have been told things by some colleagues and seen references to it in old documents and manuscripts dating back to the last century. There is some sort of mystery connected to the place."

"A mystery?" echoed Michel.

Folding up the map, Giselle threw it on the table. "Mystery or no, we must make a trip to this Rennes-le-Château. This is the break I've been waiting for."

Giselle pulled up one of the wooden chairs and sat down facing the professor. "Charles, dear, now is as good a time as any to explain this mystery."

Charles, his silvery hair dipping over his steel-framed glasses, sat thoughtfully for a few moments. "It is a strange story and one that I'm afraid I cannot make much sense of," he began. "I became very interested in this story some years ago when colleagues in Toulouse first mentioned it. But when it seemed to have no solution, I lost interest."

He settled back in his chair and placed both hands to his chin. His eyes roamed upward as if in deep concentration. "It seems that in June of 1885, a young Catholic priest named Francois Bérenger Saunière arrived in the small Languedoc village of Rennes-le-Château. He had been appointed to the small Church of St. Mary Magdalene there. It is a very old church, having been mentioned in writings of the Knights of Jerusalem in 1185. It is said to have been built over the ruins of a Visigoth structure dating back to the 6th century.

"This Saunière had his work cut out for him as the church had fallen into disrepair and was nearly roofless," said Charles with a secretive smile. "And it appears that this Rennes-le-Château is at the center of one of the most active of the Magdalene sects."

Michel looked puzzled. "Magdalene sects?"

"These sects believe that Mary Magdalene lived and died in southern France following Jesus' crucifixion," explained Giselle. She had heard such stories since she first visited France as a young girl, but she had never placed much stock in them before now. But all the talk about the feminine side of spirituality being blotted out by the male-dominated Roman Church had caused her to reconsider her skepticism.

"That's correct," agreed Charles. "In fact, there are many so-called *Black Madonnas* throughout France that reportedly allude to this idea. Since the Roman Church shifted the focus of veneration to Mary, the mother of Jesus, and exterminated the region's Cathars, the Magdalene tradition was forced underground. The Black Madonnas were painted in that manner as a secret code to let the aware know they represented the Magdalene. It is even widely believed that many of the great cathedrals of Europe, especially those built by the Knights Templar, who inherited much of the Cathari traditions, originally were dedicated to Mary Magdalene, not Jesus' mother."

"And how does this connect to Rennes-le-Château?" asked Giselle. She was becoming impatient to learn how this small French village might have anything to do with Peter or the Skull of Fate.

"Please let me finish," answered Charles evenly. "You see, the area has been a hotbed of alternative beliefs since the time of the Merovingian kings. The Merovingians evolved from the intermarriage between the early Franks and a Jewish community that grew with refugees fleeing the Jewish Revolt against Rome in 70 A.D. The Merovingians were said to carry within them the *Sangreal*, or Royal Davidic Bloodline, which gave them the divine right to kingship. Even the Roman Church pledged eternal fealty to the Merovingian bloodline until it arranged to have the royal line overthrown and the Carolingian royalty substituted. This was a stunning act of treachery the Church has long tried to suppress and forget."

Trying to be as kind as possible, Giselle asked gently. "Yes, but what has all this to do with the priest in Rennes-le-Château?"

"Yes, of course, I'm getting to that," muttered Charles. "I have, you see, some associates in Toulouse who were aware of this story and I am only repeating some of what I learned in our conversations. I have a book with me that may provide some details. May I fetch it?"

"By all means," replied Giselle graciously with a patient smile. Inside, she fought hard to bring her impatience under control.

Shortly, Charles returned to the small anteroom and pulled several old bound volumes from a weather-beaten leather satchel. After a few moments, which seemed like hours to Giselle, he exclaimed, "Oh, yes, here it is."

Scanning through the book, Charles paraphrased the story. "In 1891, Father Saunière managed to secure a small loan to repair the Magdalene church. In the course of this restoration, one of the supporting columns of the altar was moved and inside he discovered some old documents."

"What kind of documents?" asked Giselle, her interest reviving.

"There were genealogical charts which some have claimed detailed the descending bloodline of Jesus through the Merovingians."

"I'm beginning to see the connection," muttered Giselle. "Please go on."

"There were also documents written in Latin, but coded in such a manner that no one has managed to make sense of them. They were written by a former parish priest," he paused to refer to his book. "One Abbot Antoine Bigou."

Looking up, he continued, "One night, Father Saunière defaced the tombstone of a local family named Blanchefort that apparently was connected to this mystery. But the priest failed to realize that others had already made a rubbing of the inscription, so its message has since become known.

"Here is the translation: 'To Dagobert II, king, and to Sion belongs this treasure and he is there dead.' Dagobert was the last of the Merovingian royal line. He was murdered in 679 A.D. by one of his own officials who had close ties with the Roman Church. But the remainder makes little sense."

"But it does refer to a treasure," said Michel. He too was becoming excited as the story came together.

"That's right. Please continue, Charles," added Giselle, who was staring at the wall of the chamber without really seeing it. She suspected that the documents Charles was describing and the ones mentioned by Eva Braun were one and the same.

"Father Saunière took his discovery to Church authorities in Carcassonne," continued Charles, glancing at his book, "where he was directed to the St. Sulpice Seminary in Paris. St. Sulpice, I might add, is considered the foremost center for occult studies by the Church in France. It was here that the life of this young and inexperienced village priest suddenly took a new turn. He found himself surrounded by wealthy and powerful Parisians, many of whom were known to dabble in the occult arts. It was even rumored that he had an affair with the famed opera star Emma Calvé, high priestess of the Paris underground."

"I remember her," said Giselle, somewhat astonished to find someone she knew involved in Charles' tale. "I met her once in Paris many years ago. Although she was getting along in years, she was still quite beautiful. She was most complimentary about my dancing."

"I note here that she visited Saunière many times in Rennes-le-Château after his time in Paris," Charles said, after checking his book. "After his stay in Paris, Saunière's financial problems seemed to have vanished. In fact, over the next few years, he spent millions of francs not only restoring the Magdalene church but building a lavish country home he called *Villa Bethania* and a round tower overlooking the valley in honor of Mary Magdalene. He also upgraded the town's road and water supply and amassed a great library."

"Where did the money come from?" asked Michel.

"Ah, there is the mystery," replied Charles. "Why should some dusty old parchments bring sudden wealth? One source of his money may have been Archduke Johanne von Habsburg, a cousin to Austrian Emperor Franz Joseph. It was found that a considerable amount of

JIM MARRS

money was transferred from the archduke's account to that of Saunière shortly after the two met in Rennes-le-Château.

"Of course, it is also suspected that the Vatican paid large sums for Saunière's silence. They did not want stories spread of past transgressions by the Church. It was also reported that Father Saunière made further discoveries, strange and unusual discoveries involving some antique gold coins or jewels and even reportedly a crypt containing human skeletons. There was definitely something quite extraordinary that he discovered about Rennes-le-Château."

Once again Giselle found herself wondering if the priest had indeed discovered the documents mentioned by Eva Braun.

Charles continued his account in his most vibrant classroom demeanor. "I found it interesting to note that Saunière had inscribed over the door to his renovated church the Latin words 'Terribilis Est Locus Iste.'"

"This is a terrible place," murmured Giselle, recalling her first-year Latin class.

"Why would he have that placed on his church?" asked Michel.

"When I first heard this inscription, I thought of Genesis 28:17 in the Bible. This was Jacob's exclamation upon discovering the Gate of Heaven," replied Charles.

"Hmm, the Gate of Heaven," mused Giselle, who then asked, "Where is this Father Saunière today?"

"Oh, he died in 1917, about the time you were born, I believe."

Giselle merely nodded, still deep in thought. Her excitement was growing. It could not be mere coincidence that Eva Braun had mentioned this same obscure Languedoc village as Haushofer. She knew she was on the right track.

"There were even mysterious aspects to his death," continued Charles. "Let me see. I have it here." He shuffled through the pages of his book. "Ah, yes. It seems that Father Saunière died of a sudden stroke on January 17, 1917."

"So?" asked Michel.

"That just happened to have been the same date he had obliterated the Blanchefort tombstone, the same day as the official feast day at St. Sulpice where he had taken his discovered documents and just five days after his housekeeper had inexplicably ordered a coffin. Furthermore, when a nearby priest was called to administer last rites, he refused after hearing Saunière's dying confession, which was never made public."

"That must have been some confession," snorted Michel.

"I assure you it was," came a voice from the doorway. "In fact, the young priest who took Saunière's confession reportedly committed suicide shortly afterwards."

"Jean Paul? Is that you?" asked Giselle, squinting into the shadows. Everyone in the room was on their feet.

Stepping into the light, Jean Paul said quietly, "I'm sorry, I didn't mean to startle everyone. But I happened to hear what was being discussed and I thought I might add to the conversation."

"You know of such things?" said Charles, eyeing the young man sharply. "I think you've been holding out on me."

"Yes," agreed Giselle, her eyes also suspicious. "How have you come by such knowledge?"

Jean Paul took a calculated look around the room, closed the door behind him and faced the group. "What I am about to reveal to you must remain in this room. It must be kept secret at all costs, even at the cost of your very life. Is this agreed?"

The young man peered first at Charles, then Michel and finally Giselle. Only after they each indicated their assent, did he begin to speak.

"Have any of you here heard of the Emerald Brotherhood?"

When the only replies were blank expressions he smiled slightly and said, "I will take that as a no."

Beginning to pace somewhat, Jean Paul said, "I will begin with what you call the ancient times, although they are not so ancient in the grand scheme of things. There once was a wise king who we have come to know as Solomon.

"King Solomon was in contact with a certain group that sought to control the entire world through a network of patriarchal monarchies. On the surface, he appeared to go along with their plans and was greatly rewarded financially. However, being the wise leader that he was, he could plainly see that such a plan would upset the balance of God's nature and ultimately destroy humanity. So he sought a way to protect the future generations.

"He permitted the formation of a mystical sect which set up shop on the outskirts of his domain in Palestine. This group was quite eclectic as it included the teachings of the Isis tradition from Egypt, the Cabalistic knowledge of Solomon's own Hebrew heritage as well as the Tantric and mystical principles of the Eastern philosophies.

"This secret society was created to prevent the masculine power-control group from completely suppressing, if not obliterating, the sacred feminine."

"Solomon had great admiration for the feminine aspect of the world," muttered Charles in agreement. Everyone else was standing slack-jawed at Jean Paul's revelation.

"Solomon gave this sect a charter to protect this sacred information—the knowledge of the divine masculine and the divine feminine co-creating in balance. The yin and yang of the interconnected energies of Earth. The most important aspect of this charter was to protect the precious feminine energy as it had the power one day to save all humanity once it is brought back into balance with the masculine.

"This sect chartered by Solomon eventually evolved into the Essene community and many of their records much later became known as the Mary Records in honor of the three Marys—Mother Mary, Mary Magdala and Mary Bethany. Selected members of the Essenes were sent off for training in Egypt and the East. They returned to the community at Qumran to integrate their learning into the whole. This was done by both men and women."

"Okay, but how do you fit into all this?" Giselle asked.

"I'm coming to that," replied Jean Paul holding up one hand as a sign for patience. "To protect both the Essenes and their knowledge, Solomon created a sort of royal secret guard known only to a select few. They are called the Emerald Brotherhood. Their commission is to be both protector and partner to the Sacred Sisterhood, the keepers of the Goddess wisdom. This Brotherhood consists of 12 Guardians and one Overseer."

"You keep speaking in the present tense," said Michel still eyeing Jean Paul with suspicion. "Are you saying that this Brotherhood still exists?"

"I am telling you that I am a member of the Brotherhood," replied Jean Paul. He stood and fixed the group with a steady and solemn gaze. "As the son of a Jewish rabbi who was specially trained in the mystical aspects of the Cabbala, I am now one of the 12 Guardians. I have sworn an oath to protect the secrets that have been hidden in southern France."

"What are the secrets?" asked Giselle in a quiet voice. She was still awed by the information pouring from this man she had worked beside for so many months.

"I am not at liberty to divulge that at this time." His voice carried a note of sincerity and apology. "I am revealing myself to you now because you have already figured out much on your own and I don't want to see you wasting more time in research."

Jean Paul looked a bit sheepish when he added, "And I need your help."

"I am the only Guardian left in Europe. The others have all been sent to safer places. Should something happen to me, another will be called to take my place. You will never know who that is unless he chooses to reveal himself to you. I will also tell you this—there are others pledged to protect the secrets of the Knights Templar, the Cathari families and Father Saunière but they do not know of the existence of my Brotherhood. They believe themselves to be the last line of defense."

"How can we help?" Giselle asked with concerned sincerity.

"You must make plans to travel to Rennes-le-Château soon. I am told a man connected to the Nazi SS has made several trips to the area. I am afraid that his knowledge of the area's secrets may have been passed to SS Chief Himmler or even higher."

"We will make plans immediately," responded Giselle as Charles and Michel nodded their assent. "But, Jean Paul, let me ask you, do I understand that a Sisterhood has existed secretly throughout all time carrying the divine feminine aspects?"

"That's correct."

"Then where is this Sisterhood today?"

"The existence of the Sisterhood is enigmatic at best," replied Jean Paul with a slight sign. It was always difficult to explain to persons who had been conditioned throughout their lives to conventional belief systems.

"It doesn't always exist as a formal organization. The Sisterhood comes together when it is needed. Members' souls pass through many different times and places."

Giselle was insistent. "But you still haven't answered my question."

Jean Paul sighed again. "In recent years, the Sisterhood has not existed in a formal way. We are trained to recognize Sisters when they show up on this material plane. I was looking for the signs when I joined with you. My Overseer predicted that the next Sisterhood would be represented by a rose, a flower whose essence holds the highest energy vibration of any of the Earth's flora."

Giselle was stunned. She had had no concept of such things when she formed the Sisterhood of the Rose.

Jean Paul smiled. "Is my meaning clear?"

Giselle could only nod in the affirmative, but she still felt some confusion. She had not been conditioned to such esoteric concepts.

"Then perhaps you really are the Magdala," he said with an enigmatic smile.

Uncertain if Jean Paul was serious or joking, Giselle finally found her voice. "Do you think that we will find Peter and the Skull of Fate at Rennes-le-Château?"

"I think that if the man you seek is dedicated to finding the most valuable objects in the world then he will most certainly end up there."

Giselle nodded. "Yes, it definitely sounds as though that small village is at the center of our search." Turning to the professor, she asked, "Charles, you mentioned a housekeeper. Is she still alive?"

"As far as I know, she is," replied Charles, peering down at his book. "Here it is. Her name is Marie Denarnaud. She was quite young when she began working for the newly arrived Father Saunière. Just 18 years, I believe. There were rumors that she may have been much more than just his housekeeper. After the priest's death, Marie continued to live in the *Villa Bethania*. I do remember one of my colleagues mentioning this woman just a few years ago."

"She would be in her mid-70s today," Giselle said quietly after some calculation.

Jumping to her feet, she turned to her two friends. Her mind was made up. "We must pay a visit to Rennes-le-Château and *Mademoiselle* Denarnaud," said Giselle emphatically.

"It won't be easy," groused Michel. "The village is in Vichy and it is a mountainous and desolated area."

"It's very far and isolated," cautioned Charles.

Noticing the hesitation on her friends' face, Giselle said pleadingly, "After all we've learned, do we have any choice?" Both men shook their heads resignedly while Jean Paul nodded approvingly.

To Giselle, it seemed that a giant puzzle was beginning to come into focus, although the overall picture was not yet clear.

Just then, Gabby burst through the door. Her eyes were wide with fear and excitement. "You'd better wrap up your little *kaffeeklatsch*. The police are here!"

CHAPTER 15

Southern France
March, 1942

A SURGE OF ADRENALINE HAD coursed through Giselle's entire being with word that the police were outside *Villa Tagliani*.

Leaping from her chair, she had raced into the large meeting chamber and began barking orders.

"All those who arrived here by water, return to the boat dock immediately and disperse," she yelled over the tumult created by Gabby's warning. "Those who have automobiles outside the villa, come with me and do not make any more noise than necessary."

As she led the group back to the cavern's entrance and through the dark vineyard, she considered their situation.

Situated in such a remote area of Tuscany, she had thought Aunt Fran's home a safe haven for the Sisterhood. She and Aunt Fran had failed to take nosy neighbors into consideration. Someone must have notified the local police that there were a suspicious number of automobiles parked around the darkened estate. She could envision members of the local constabulary, grumpy at being dragged out late at night, dutifully driving out to the villa to investigate.

Giselle had suggested to Aunt Fran during their meeting the previous summer that she should order tunnels built between the Ligurian Sea and the villa. Fortunately for the Sisterhood, no one in the area knew of these tunnels since both workmen and materials had been brought in all the way from Genoa, another of Giselle's suggestions.

Arriving at the rear of the villa, Giselle learned that lookouts had spotted a police car slowly motoring up the long drive to the villa. One had rushed to the grotto to alert the Sisterhood while the other hid herself.

Peering around one corner of the villa's main house, Giselle could see that there were two policemen in a small sedan. They had just arrived and were climbing out of the car to approach the front door.

She, along with Gabby and Aunt Fran, quickly herded everyone into the villa through a side entrance. A few were told to hide themselves about the grounds.

A loud knocking had begun at the front of the house as they entered. Motioning for absolute silence, Giselle had cautiously led them down a hallway to the villa's large dining room and placed them all in chairs while whispering her plan. After placing one lighted candle in the center of the dining table, Giselle had taken a seat while Aunt Fran hurried to the sound of knocking on the front door.

She had listened intently as the conversation between Aunt Fran and the policemen grew louder as they approached the dining hall.

"I can assure you that there is nothing untoward taking place in my home." Giselle had heard Aunt Fran's voice rising in indignation. "I am more than willing to let you see for yourselves."

"*Scusi, Signora.* Please understand that we have received a report and I am required to investigate," one officer had explained in an apologetic tone. Giselle had a clear picture of this man, undoubtedly one of those simpering bureaucrats who attempted to curry favor with persons of social standing that he encountered in his work.

"I only understand that you are disturbing a very delicate experiment," Fran had replied with obvious irritation.

"Experiment? What kind of…" the officer's question had ended in mid-sentence as he burst through the dining room doors and stopped, transfixed by the scene in front of him.

There in the darkness broken only by a single candle burning on the large dining room table were eighteen women sitting silently around the room. Their heads were bowed and their eyes closed. No one moved nor acknowledged the policemen's presence. It was most unsettling to the official who was generally accustomed to respect when he entered a room. The puzzled officer looked from face to face, trying to judge the situation.

Just a group of women, he thought, and well connected to judge by their clothing and automobiles. In a lowered voice, he whispered, "What is happening here? Is this some sort of séance?"

"Some people call it that," Fran had replied with indignation. "We prefer to say that we are attempting spiritual communication with the dearly departed."

"You mean dead people?" muttered the officer, his eyes narrowing. His partner crossed himself and glanced about uneasily.

Smoothly and quickly, Fran took the policemen by the arm and escorted both back out the door and down the hallway. "Yes, well, I did say it was an experiment," she said, adding pointedly, "And you have spoiled it with your rude interruption. I shall tell *Signor* Tagliani that you disrupted our meeting and frightened our friends."

She paused for effect and added, "He will return soon from Rome where he is meeting with Mussolini."

The officer's eyes widened at the name-dropping, but it had the desired effect. "No, No, *Signora* Tagliani, surely that will not be necessary."

Almost pleading, he had added, "You must understand. It's the Germans. They pressure our superiors to investigate every little thing. My report will make it clear that our visit was purely routine and that there is nothing here to report. I am very sorry to have disturbed you."

Shifting to her sweetest tone, Fran had smiled and taken the policeman's hand in hers. "*Grazie*, I understand. These times are stressful on us all. Please give my regards to your chief."

Smiling broadly, the short man bowed slightly and climbed into the police car. He watched the woman wave them good-bye in the rear view mirror as he pulled off down the long driveway.

Glancing at his companion, his smile dropped quickly and he muttered, "Stupid women. Even with a war on, they waste their time trying to contact the spirit world."

Long after the incident at Aunt Fran's villa, Giselle, Gabby and Charles were still talking about it.

"I can still see the looks on their faces," said Gabby with a giggle. She had lost interest in the rolling wine country of central France and was regaling her fellow passengers with her recollection of that night.

Resting her head on the back of her seat with her eyes closed, Giselle smiled. She too still recalled with glee the expressions of the two Italian policemen when they entered the main dining room of *Villa Tagliani* to find the room nearly full of women sitting in the dark.

Glancing out a rear window of the big Nash, Giselle opened her eyes and watched the vineyards pass by. She was amused at Gabby's laughter. The young girl obviously had forgotten her stark terror the night the police arrived at the *Villa Tagliani*.

She continued smiling at the recollection, thinking how easily some people could be manipulated. Watching the passing countryside, Giselle's eyelids began to droop. She soon was dozing until a blast of the car's horn startled her awake.

She glanced up in time to see an irate farmer make an obscene sign as the big Nash swerved around his hay cart, missing it by inches. Giselle's annoyance with Charles' driving returned. She had become impatient soon after leaving Chartres but had tried to suppress the feeling by sleeping. Now he had almost collided with a hay wagon.

Her irritation was exacerbated by her anger with Michel. Ever since the name Rennes-le-Château had surfaced in their meeting at Aunt Fran's, Giselle had been eager to leave for southern France.

She had wanted to drive straight there from Italy but Michel had been adamant. It was the first real argument they had ever had.

Shortly before the Sisterhood meeting in Tuscany, Jean Moulin had arrived back in France by parachute and began consolidating the Resistance under the authority of the absent Charles De Gaulle.

At a joyful reunion with Giselle and Michel in *La Coupole*, Jean explained that he hoped not only to create a force to combat the German occupation but also a military organization that would unify the disparate and often feuding factions of the Resistance.

Using information and contacts supplied by Giselle and her Sisterhood, he began building a secret internal French Army called the *Forces Françaises De L'Intérieur* or simply the FFI. The work was time consuming as well as hazardous, and Jean had begged off attending the Sisterhood meeting in Italy.

She knew that Jean Moulin had his own work with the ever-growing Resistance, but she needed Michel, both as driver and her right arm. Michel had wanted to stay behind to help his old boss but finally capitulated to Giselle's entreaty.

But following the episode with the Italian *polizia*, he had put his foot down.

"I must return to Paris now, *ma chère*," he argued. "I owe Jean Moulin so much and he needs my help."

When she saw that the usually obliging Michel was not to be moved from his position, Giselle had grudgingly accepted defeat. After all, if she was going to spend the rest of her life with this man, she would have to learn to compromise. In addition, it had been almost two years since the murders in the Mayan pyramid. Surely a few more days would not matter.

Once back in Chartres, Giselle had spent every day imploring Michel to take her to southern France but each time he had some excuse for postponing the trip. Finally Giselle had taken matters into her own hands. If Michel was too busy to drive, then she would simply go on her own.

She enlisted Jean Paul to drive her and Charles had agreed to accompany them as he had a reciprocal teaching arrangement with the University of Toulouse and had a working knowledge of the area. The ever-faithful and enthusiastic Gabby also agreed to go. She had all but stopped attending classes due to her growing commitment to the Sisterhood.

After further conversations with Jean Paul, Giselle realized that his quiet and unassuming demeanor masked a real sharpness of wit. The man missed very little and had an uncanny ability to pass through life virtually unnoticed by those about him. It was a very valuable attribute and Giselle believe it would serve the Sisterhood well.

One of Jean Paul's assignments had been to investigate the SS officer that Gabby's aunt had attempted to bring with her to Tuscany. Utilizing the resources of the Emerald Brotherhood, Jean Paul had the man tailed to Argentina where he met personally with Eva Duarte, a stage actress who was mistress to a Colonel Juan Peron. Peron had recently returned to Argentina from Italy where he had served as military attaché and had developed a fondness for both the Nazis and fascism. Giselle had made a note to keep this woman in mind for future use.

Another distraction was the assassination of SS *Obergruppenführer* Reinhard Heydrich. Using information supplied by the Sisterhood, British Intelligence had dropped three young men of the Czech Resistance by parachute in the vicinity of Prague. On May 29th, they ambushed Heydrich as he motored into the city. One of the Resistance fighters had tossed a hand grenade under the officer's car where it exploded causing fatal wounds. Heydrich suffered for a week before dying.

But elation at the successful operation was dampened by the brutal retaliation of the Nazis. More than 1,000 Czechs were condemned to death by German courts martial and the entire town of Lidice was obliterated, its citizens either scattered or executed.

The Sisterhood was kept busy arranging for the escape of both Czech partisans and civilians targeted as hostages by the Nazis.

It was late February before Giselle had set out on the long journey to the Languedoc region. Michel, with the aid of his mechanic friend Claude, had tuned up the Nash. With extra wood strapped to the roof, Claude thought there should be no problem with fuel. "It's not very pretty but it should work," he pronounced. "Just be sure to hit some bumps now and then to settle the firebox."

Giselle worked to make her appearance more compatible with that of an older woman.

Placing an antique pair of glasses on her nose, she bundled herself into a dowdy outfit she had purchased in Paris and put on a pair of box-like black shoes that previously she would never have given a second glance. As an afterthought, she found one of Aunt Gez's old hats, one with a medium wide brim and some black netting pulled down to obscure her face.

Giselle slouched and studied herself in the mirror. "Not too bad," she said with approval. "My own mother wouldn't recognize me."

"I should hope not," retorted Michel. "You look like a frump." Giselle threw the hat at him.

Giselle and her three companions had departed in the morning and by afternoon were well south of Paris, nearing Bourges, where they planned to spend the night.

Jean Paul drove with Charles beside him while Giselle and Gabby rode in the rear seat.

Once away from the February chill in Paris, the sun felt warm and they were able to ride comfortably with two windows partially down. The rolling countryside appeared green and lush, with only a few leafless trees to show that it was still wintertime.

They stopped for an early supper and found a small hotel for the night. The next morning they proceeded without difficulty through the border checkpoint into Vichy France.

Charles had offered to take a turn at driving but along the way to Toulouse, Giselle had grown increasingly impatient with his slow and inattentive driving, especially after his near miss with the hay wagon.

Like many men who had come of age before the time of the automobile, Charles drove with hesitation and caution.

Giselle kept her irritation in check by listening with genuine interest as Jean Paul launched into a dissertation concerning the background of the rose, a symbol that could be traced back to the goddess Isis. The symbol was then copied by Greeks and then usurped by the Romans. A symbol of life, love and rebirth, the rose also was known to represent confidentiality and secret knowledge.

"As you said in your speech, Giselle, the rose typically has five inner petals. Five is the number of the divine feminine principle," Jean Paul explained. "To suppress this power, the patriarchal brotherhoods took this sacred pentagram and inverted it, just as the Nazis took the ancient spiritual-based *swastika* and rotated it. Around the outside of a rose are eight petals. Again, eight is the number of Isis, signifying creation and power. Together they add up to 13, the number of transformation."

"Isn't it amazing how such numbers continually show up in various ways?" said Charles turning to look at Giselle. "And consider that the prominent colors of the rose, red and white, represented duality to the alchemists. These colors have been used to represent the sacred feminine energy in the Church for centuries. Overtly, the colors red and white are associated with the Virgin Mary. They were prominent on the surcoats and Maltese crosses of the Knights Templar. Covertly they were often used in stained-glass windows that faced west, the legendary direction of matriarchal power. You find this in the cathedral at Chartres. There must be more to this than sheer coincidence. Surely this is a sign of the divine blueprint at work."

Giselle sat silently contemplating their words.

The next day, following a pleasant night's rest in a small hotel on the Rue de Metz in Toulouse, Giselle announced that she would like to drive the rest of the way. Charles argued that it wasn't proper for a wealthy French dowager to be driving herself, and Giselle readily agreed to let Jean Paul resume the driving chores.

With Jean Paul again at the wheel, they made better time, arriving in the ancient fortress city of Carcassonne well before noon. The city had borne the brunt of wars and plagues since the 1st century when it was attacked by Roman legions and later by Visigoths, Moors and the Albigensian Crusaders. As they passed through, Giselle could not help but feel pity for the city's present population, now suffering under the privations brought on by yet another war.

Yet, Giselle found herself enjoying the ride as the Nash turned toward the Pyrenees Mountains already visible to the south. Thanks to wartime shortages, traffic was virtually non-existent. By mid-afternoon, they reached Limoux where they stopped for tea and fresh croissants in the small, picturesque village.

Giselle was thankful that Jean Paul knew the way to Rennes-le-Château as it was not even listed on some maps and her otherwise complete Michelin map provided no real details.

Late in the day, the foursome reached the river front community of Couiza. A cloud cover had moved in and it had begun to rain. No one seemed inclined to tell the travelers anything about their neighboring village. But finally one old man tapped his pipe against a lamppost and pointed to a narrow road leading southward. Further down this road, Gabby spotted a small sign that indicated Rennes-le-Château was four and a half kilometers away.

As they proceeded slowly in the rain, the travelers were awed by the wild and desolate countryside. Craggy peaks rose on all sides, while deep chasms and ravines formed large gashes in the limestone earth. The fractured and jagged soil was often dominated by crumbling ancient ruins on many of the high points. The undulating ridges of the area increased in number as they became the foothills of the Pyrenees. There was a scent of dampness and wild mint in the air, intensified by the drizzling rain, which kept odors close to the ground.

"There doesn't seem to be many people here," Giselle commented after failing to notice a house or barn for some time.

"Whoever survived the Albigensian Crusade likely died of the Bubonic Plague," responded Charles dryly from the passenger seat. "The entire area was largely unpopulated until the last century."

Billowing wood smoke, the big Nash Landau slowly made its way along a narrow roadway that twisted and turned following the contour of a large hill. Giselle was thinking they would spiral right into the sky when a gate appeared and suddenly they found themselves in a tiny village perched on the crest of the hill. The buildings were small and old and hunched together as if seeking mutual protection from the misting rain.

They parked near a large water cistern. Despite the rain, Gabby jumped from the car and ran to a low stone wall overlooking the valley.

"Oh, you must come and see this," she called, laughing with pleasure. The rain and wind plastered her long dark hair to her face.

Equally glad to have finally reached their destination after the long and arduous drive, Giselle stepped from the car and walked to join her friend.

In spite of the rain and gloom, the vista was magnificent. No longer could one only see the peak or ridge in front of them as they passed through the innumerable valleys. Here was a panorama worthy of a king. A good portion of the Languedoc lay spread before her, a long stretch of the Corbières mountain chain with the Pyrenees dimly seen towering in the background.

Giselle suddenly became aware that the rain was no long splattering her face. Looking around she found Charles had joined her with an umbrella.

"Always prepared," she said with a smile.

"Look to your right, my dear," he replied. "I do believe that is the *Tour Magdala*, the Tower of Magdalene, I mentioned."

Looking along the stone wall, Giselle saw it ended at a small castle-like edifice with a single tower protruding out over the valley on one side.

"Why it looks like it was made for dwarves," snickered Gabby, joining them under the umbrella.

"Actually, I think it was only meant to be a library for the priest Saunière," explained Charles. "But it must have cost a small fortune. Look at the workmanship and the ornate design of the battlements. See how the single turret juts out over the valley below. That takes skill and manpower. And it's not done cheaply."

"So the mystery continues," said Giselle with a smile. "Let's see to our accommodations."

After making inquiries in the town, the travelers were directed to a large ivy-covered, two-story farm at the base of the hill called Les Labadous. The couple who lived there were gracious and most happy to share their home, especially after Giselle made them a generous offer of compensation.

By morning, the rain had stopped and the sun had returned bringing a cloying fresh smell to the countryside and filling the valleys and ravines with a light ground fog.

After a meager breakfast of coffee, homemade bread and grape jam, the foursome split up. Enthralled by stories their hosts had told the night before of a nearby cave where in legend Mary Magdalene had met with others to worship, Gabby declared she would trek to the cavern.

Jean Paul excused himself by saying he had Brotherhood business to conduct in the area but assured Giselle that he would discretely keep an eye on her and her friends.

Charles welcomed the opportunity to study the strange adornments and sculptures in the Church of St. Mary Magdalene.

Giselle had already decided to meet with Marie Denarnaud even though her hosts had warned her that the elderly woman was for all practical purposes a recluse, seen only rarely on the street and then only on brief shopping trips for necessities.

Undaunted, Giselle drove Charles and herself back to the town, taking care to park out of sight of the woman's home. She had decided there was no point in making the woman think that wealthy sightseers were coming to intrude.

As Charles went up the short walkway to the church's entrance, Giselle turned to her right and walked the short distance to the *Villa Bethania*. She stood for a moment looking at the ornate two-story building, with twin chimneys on each end of its high, slanting gray slate roof, and two gabled windows flanking an alcove containing a statue of Mary Magdalene. Giselle quickly realized that this was no simple priest's rectory. The building reflected grace, style, an intricate knowledge of architecture and, most of all, costly materials and craftsmanship.

Having no idea what she would say to the woman but knowing that she must make the attempt, Giselle glanced about at the red rooftops of the village that lay behind her, sucked in a mouthful of the clean air and gently knocked on the thick wooden door.

There was a rustle of movement inside and a thin voice called, "Who is it?"

Here goes nothing, thought Giselle, replying, "*Mademoiselle* Denarnaud? I am Giselle Tchaikovsky and I need to speak with you."

"Go away," came the reply. "There is nothing to speak about."

Desperately casting about for a topic to prolong the conversation, Giselle called, "You may recall my name. Some time ago I was well known for my career in the Paris theater."

"Theater?" There was a long pause then the voice came again. "Did *Madame* Calvé send you?"

Thinking quickly, Giselle crossed her fingers and replied, "Yes, she sent me." She realized the woman was speaking of the opera singer Emma Calvé and since she had met the diva once, she hoped she could continue the charade.

There was the sound of a lock bolt being thrown back and the large door creaked open a bit revealing the face of an elderly woman. Suspicion mixed with hope shone from her bright, intelligent eyes set back in a weathered face.

"Do you bring news?" the woman finally asked.

"Why, yes, I have news," lied Giselle, adding, "And I was hoping you might have some as well. May I come in?"

Glancing about nervously, the woman seemed to hesitate before making up her mind. "Yes, please, come in," she said finally, opening the door wider.

Giselle stepped into the foyer of the house and stood surveying its interior. The place was small and compact, yet full of *objets d'art*, elaborate tapestries hung from the wall and statuary stood in every corner. And, rocks, all kinds of rocks, from dull sandstone to glittering quartz, were displayed everywhere.

The furnishings were old and simple but obviously of good quality. With the outside shutters closed, the interior was dim and carried a smell of dust and antiquity.

After the two women were seated, the older woman waved her arm indicating the room. "You will have to excuse the rock collection. It belonged to Father Saunière. He gathered them from all around this area. He was quite an outdoorsman, you know. I haven't had the heart to get rid of them."

"It's most interesting," replied Giselle noncommittally.

Marie Denarnaud leaned forward and peered at Giselle closely, "And how is my favorite cigarette girl?"

Giselle inwardly thanked her lucky stars that she had a background in the theater for she was well aware that Emma Calvé was most famous for her role as Carmen, the cigarette factory girl, in Georges Bizet's opera of the same name.

"She's still smoking," replied Giselle with a laugh.

The woman looked surprised. "Your French is excellent, but that colloquialism comes from somewhere else. You are American, no?"

"Yes, I am and I..." Giselle began.

"You must leave immediately! I want no more trouble. Please, go!" The older woman was on her feet and pointing to the door.

"Please, listen to me," pleaded Giselle, seeing her only clue to Peter and the skull about to be closed off. "I am here to help you. I don't mean to bring you any trouble."

"But, you will, don't you understand. He said they would arrest me and put me in a camp if I spoke to anyone. I am an old woman. I thought all the intrigue was over many years ago. Then he came and now you. Just leave me alone!" The woman was pacing back and forth in agitation.

Giselle's mind was racing. Who did she mean? Who threatened her?

Taking a chance, Giselle looked the woman in the eyes and asked coolly, "Are you speaking of Peter?"

Marie Denarnaud could not have looked more shocked if Giselle had slapped her in the face. She stared at Giselle, her eyes narrowing in suspicion.

"You know this man?"

Without changing her look or her tone, Giselle replied, "He killed the man I loved."

Even as she spoke the words, Giselle felt a pang of conscience. She had loved Jim and she was as determined as ever to avenge his death. But, as the days with Michel had grown longer, she found her thoughts of Jim did not carry the deep emotional resonance they once had. She knew that soon she would have to deal with this duality in her feelings. But now was not the time.

Seeing a look of pity and sorrow on the older woman's face, Giselle quickly pressed the advantage. "Whatever this man has told you, *Mademoiselle* Denarnaud, whatever threats he has made, let me assure you that I have many powerful friends and we stand ready to help you."

The woman sank wearily onto a divan. "Powerful friends, hah!" she snorted. "I have heard all that once before. That is what François, … I mean Father Saunière, said and look what it got him."

"But, *Mademoiselle*, I can protect you," protested Giselle.

"You? Protect me? That man showed me credentials. He is an *SS* man. How can you protect me?" The elderly woman shook her head wearily.

Silent for a moment, Giselle spoke softly and slowly, "I am going to take a great chance on you. I want to indicate the trust and faith I have in you. I am with an organization that is fighting against men like Peter. We have resources and we are operating on behalf of higher powers."

Giselle saw a spark of interest flash in the woman's eyes. "What higher powers?"

Realizing that she now had the woman's full attention, Giselle said quickly, "The powers that I suspect you know something about, *Mademoiselle*, the powers that you and Father Saunière learned about through your discoveries here."

Giselle knew this was a stab in the dark. Yet, with what she knew from her talk with Eva Braun and what she had learned from Charles, she knew it must be close to the truth.

Looking up at her guest with suspicious eyes, Marie said quietly, "You don't come from *Madame* Calvé do you?"

Giselle sat beside and took her thin hands in hers. "No, my dear, I don't. But what I said was not entirely a lie. I met her years ago when I was performing in Paris. But I was just a child then."

Marie sighed and smiled wanly. "Yes, we all were at one time."

"Let me be honest with you," continued Giselle. "I know all about the stories of mystery and buried treasure. I want you to know that I care nothing for all that. I must find this Peter and stop him. He has provided Hitler with a talisman of great power that I found. I feel a personal responsibility for what is happening in the world today. I must make it right for the good of humanity."

Marie snorted. "The good of humanity? The vast number of humanity don't have the vaguest idea of what is happening, or about to happen, to them, much less what is in their best interest."

"But you do?"

The woman looked up at Giselle and said with a secretive smile, "Oh, *oui*, I know things, some things that it would be better that I didn't know."

Taking the woman's hands, Giselle said gently, "I sense that you understand that something must be done to counteract the chaos being caused by the secret brotherhoods. Their perversions of the ancient knowledge and their exclusion of the female aspect in this world's energy must be stopped. The old balance must be restored to ensure peace and harmony." Every word gave proof of Giselle's sincerity and determination.

Marie Denarnaud sat staring at this stranger in her home. Giselle could see that her sincerity and energy had impressed the older woman.

Sensing her hesitation, Giselle once more pressed her advantage. "Let's take this one step at a time," she said gently, not wanting to reawaken the woman's suspicious nature. "Please tell me about Peter.

Everything, you can remember. Anything you tell me can only benefit France, *Mademoiselle*."

"You may call me Marie," said the woman. She then sat deep in thought for long silent moments.

When she finally spoke, it was in a sad and weary voice. "I must admit there is something about you that inspires my confidence. It would be a great relief to finally talk to someone of education and sophistication like yourself. You are so unlike my neighbors here in Rennes-le-Château. They farm or manage their shops, go to church every Sunday. Their world is narrow and tightly structured.

"You are young and open to new ideas. You have traveled and seen the world for what it is. I could share things with you that would be unbelievable to my neighbors here. But, I don't know if I can take the chance. The need for secrecy is greater than you can imagine. Such secrets could prove fatal to you."

Giselle took the woman's hands and said gently, "*Mademoiselle* Denarnaud, we all must die sometime. It is not death that matters, but how we live our lives."

"You don't understand," replied the woman. "I don't care about my own life. I am an old woman. My time is drawing to a close. I speak of the lives of others, including yours. I speak of ancient secrets that are a danger to whoever knows about them."

Giselle was casting about for anything she could say to draw the woman out. "Marie, you are a religious woman, you live next door to the church. Don't you realize the benefits of confession, catharsis of the soul?"

Knowing she could at any moment send this visitor away and never see her again, Marie nevertheless poured out feelings that had built up within her for years, "The Church? What do you know about the Church? I go through the motions because I have to live in this village but I care little for the Church. The Church has brought me nothing but pain and loss. I have found my spirituality elsewhere."

"Yes, I understand," said Giselle, still holding her hands. "We all must find our own way to God. I also understand the pressure you must feel."

Marie pulled her hands away and stared at Giselle for long silent moments.

Giselle sensed that somewhere deep inside the woman a door opened bringing light and relief, a chance to unburden years of pent up emotions, a chance to pass along hidden information to a new generation. A decision was made.

"Listen my dear, this man, Peter, is connected to the SS and I know what they seek. Now you claim to be working against them and you know *Madame* Calvé. I know sooner or later, I must make a choice. So, I suppose I'll choose to trust you. I certainly don't trust that man Peter."

"You won't regret this," replied Giselle with sincerity. "I think you know that what you do from now on may have a great impact on the lives of many, perhaps millions, of people. Please help me stop the violence and cruelty that is sweeping the world."

Marie sighed. "Very well," she said finally, "I will tell you about this Peter but that is all." The woman obviously still held out some suspicion of Giselle and her motives. "Right now, let me make us some tea."

After the tea was poured, Marie began to speak, "This Peter fellow came here almost a year ago. It must have been in the late spring as I was already harvesting vegetables from my garden.

"He showed me SS credentials but he was not in uniform. Instead he was dressed for the outdoors. I believe he said he hiked here from Limoux. We have not seen any German soldiers this far south. In fact, if it weren't for the headlines and the few refugees who have come to stay with relatives in this area, we wouldn't know the war was going on.

"This man Peter said he wanted to ask me some questions. At first he was polite enough. He said he worked for something called the German *Ahnenerbe* Society and was interested in the history of this area. After some time, he became quite insistent in his questioning. He mentioned a young man named Otto Rahn whom I recall visiting here several times in past years. That's when I knew what this Peter fellow was really after."

"And what was that?" asked Giselle.

"Why the treasure, of course!" said Marie with some indignation. She thought everyone knew the legends of hidden treasure. But Giselle, her mind still fixed on Peter, continued to look at her with a blank expression.

"Treasure?" asked Giselle.

"The Treasure of Solomon." Marie spoke as though pointing out an obvious fact to a child.

Giselle sat stunned. Bits and pieces of knowledge swirled through her head. Jews fleeing Roman Palestine. Romans looting the temple. Goths looting Rome. The Cathars holding to their secrets. The Knights Templar returning from Jerusalem with treasure from Solomon's Temple. Stories concerning the resting place of the Ark of the Covenant, the Grail Cup and other legendary objects. It all fell into place.

"The treasure is intact and is here?" She finally asked. There was awe in her voice.

"Yes, and curse it for all the trouble it has brought. The Church tried to get their hands on it but failed, as have the various secret brotherhoods. *Herr* Peter failed too. I sent him off on a series of wild goose chases and feigned ignorance of the exact location. He appeared to believe me. He did not learn anything from the villagers, of course, as they know nothing at all of this. Most of them are just hard-working churchgoers."

"So he found nothing?" asked Giselle, impressed by the strong will of the small woman seated before her.

Smiling with pride, Marie replied, "Nothing. I could tell he was uncertain as to the extent of my knowledge and he hesitated in harming his one lead to the treasure. I believe he was actually on the verge of physically abusing me when thankfully he received a telegram calling him back to Germany. I believe his superiors were exasperated with the time he wasted here."

The woman's eyes grew dark and angry. "Before he left, he actually threatened me … me, an old woman! He told me he would return and that if I breathed a word about the treasure, he would have me arrested and locked away. I have feared his return ever since. Do you really think he could do that?"

Giselle sighed. "My dear Marie, the world today is distorted. The *Boche* control the Vichy government and certainly all of the occupied north. I'm sure he meant what he said."

"*Mon Dieu!* This is terrible. Whatever has become of my beloved country? It was bad enough that I had to watch what I say because of the Vatican and powerful officials with ties to certain secret societies. But now I must toe the mark for some Germans. Bah! I certainly am glad that I did not tell that man anything that he didn't already know. I can keep my mouth shut when I put my mind to it."

Giselle laughed. "I like your spirit, dear lady. I want us to be good friends, especially as I know we are on the same side.

"One further question, did this man mention a human skull made out of crystal?"

Now it was Marie's turn to look puzzled. "A crystal skull? How odd. Why would he have mentioned something like that?"

Giselle sighed. Here was another dead end. She was beginning to wonder if she would ever locate Peter and the skull. But at least now she knew what game Peter was playing. He was after Solomon's Treasure. She wondered why Peter had not returned to the village with a battalion of troops with shovels to search for it.

With a shrug of her shoulders, Giselle looked steadily at Marie. "Since you have opened up to me, I am going to tell you an unbelievable story. But it is a true story."

Marie's tea grew cold as she sat spellbound listening to Giselle describe her adventures in Mexico, the death of Jim and Katrina and the theft of the Skull of Fate. Her eyes grew wide as she learned of Giselle's efforts to form not only a Resistance to the German occupation but a Sisterhood to advance love and light in this world.

Marie sat contemplating Giselle for long moments. Finally, with a note of thankfulness in her voice, she said, "So you are not seeking the treasure." This was a statement, not a question.

"I told you I am not," responded Giselle with a warm smile. "Perhaps it's because I have always had all the money I need, but I truly believe that there are more important things in life than money."

"That is what … ah, Father Saunière said too. He spent lavishly to renovate the church and the town but it only brought him trouble."

"Would you feel comfortable in telling me about Father Saunière?" asked Giselle softly.

"Yes, my dear, I think I would. It's been so long since I have had a woman to talk to that I trusted. The townspeople here are kind enough but they are quite provincial in their thinking. Come, the sun is out today and the rain has cleared the air. Let us walk in the garden and I will share with you my story."

Exiting from a rear door of the *Villa Bethania*, the pair strolled through a well-kept garden area, up some stone steps and into the small cemetery adjacent to the Church of the Magdalene. Perched atop the hillside, the cemetery had an unobstructed view of the hills and valleys north toward Couiza and Limoux. Marie began to unburden herself.

"I was born in this area and grew up in Couiza. I never expected to see much of the world. I knew my place was right here. I was only 18 years old when Father Saunière was posted here in 1885. He was young and virile and quite handsome. I was ecstatic when I was hired to be his housekeeper. We became quite close. Over time, he taught me many things."

Despite her age, the woman actually blushed. Smiling, Giselle said gently, "I understand."

"During renovation on the church, he discovered some old documents written by a previous priest. They contained genealogies pertaining to Jesus, Mary Magdalene and the Merovingian rulers. But more importantly, there were coded instructions for locating a fabulous treasure. We kept the treasure map to ourselves but he took the genealogies to St. Sulpice in Paris and was astounded when Church officials paid him large sums of money, some through the Habsburg family, to keep quiet about his find. You can well imagine how proof of Jesus' ongoing lineage might damage Church dogma."

Marie stared out at the mountainous vista before them. Her mind drifted back almost 60 years. Unconsciously, she lapsed, using the priest's first name.

"But François was less intrigued by the genealogies than by the prospect of the treasure. Not the gold or jewels, though there is plenty enough, but by the description of ancient texts, knowledge from our past. This is why he kept some of the documents secret from everyone but myself. He did everything he could to throw off later investigators. He was determined that only those whose hearts were in the right place might have access to the knowledge.

"But the parchments were not easy to decipher. For instance, one translated, 'Shepherdess no temptation that Poussin Teniers hold the key peace 681 by the cross and this horse of God I complete this demon of the guardian at noon blue apples.'"

"Blue apples? It sounds like gibberish," said Giselle. "But Nicolas Poussin and David Teniers are the names of two well-known painters, aren't they?"

"That is correct," replied Marie. "And both of them were connected to our mystery as well as others, such as the musicians Richard Wagner, Claude Debussy and the author Jules Verne, who combined science with his fiction. They and many others were involved in studying and keeping the secrets.

"These secrets, along with the treasure's location, had been handed down through the Blanchefort family for centuries. Bertrand de Blanchefort was the fourth Grand Master of the Knights Templar and one of the Order's most capable leaders. He turned the Order into a highly effective organization. He was also from a Cathari family and held their most cherished secrets."

"So the Templars brought the treasure here to the Languedoc from Jerusalem," said Giselle.

"Yes, and it was added to that portion of Solomon's Treasure which was hidden here by the Visigoths under the rule of Alaric. He sacked Rome in 410 A.D. and made off with much of the treasure the Romans had originally taken from Jerusalem following the Jewish Revolt. Knowledge of the location of this treasure was handed down through the Cathari."

Giselle snapped her fingers. "Yes, I'm beginning to see it all," she said. "Many of the leaders of the Templars were Cathars. They were aware of the treasure's existence all along. It was scattered among the caverns here in the Languedoc."

"Exactly," agreed Marie. "These treasures were eventually combined and coded maps were kept. One such map to the Templar treasure went from Bertrand de Blanchefort until it passed into the hands of Dame d'Hautpoul de Blanchefort, whose family château is just there." She pointed toward the ruined turret of the château just visible to the southeast down the narrow road that passed in front of the *Villa Bethania*.

"The Dame gave them to the local priest, *Abbé* Antoine Bigou, for safekeeping during the French Revolution. He later fled to Spain, but not before copying the coded instructions on several parchments and concealing them in the altar pillar. This is, of course, where François..." Marie caught her familiarity. "Rather, Father Saunière discovered them when I was a young girl."

"Hello!" Voices came from behind them. Startled from their deep conversation, the two women turned to see Charles approaching accompanied by a chunky dark-haired man dressed in black.

Charles was plainly excited as he approached the women. "Oh, Giselle, you must take a look inside the church. It's more amazing than I ever thought. It's simply overflowing with strange and wonderful things that are obviously meant to convey secret messages. Why, there's a statute of a demon just inside the front door, horns and all. And the place is resplendent with statues and paintings of the Magdalene, one shown with a human skull. I'm almost certain this is meant to refer to the Johnnite Heresy."

Marie's eyes were sparkling and she wore a secretive smile. She was pleased that someone appreciated the esoteric symbolism of the church.

"The what?" asked Giselle.

"The Johnnite Heresy," repeated Charles. Taking on his best professorial tone, he explained, "It sprang from the intense rivalry between the followers of Jesus and those of John the Baptist prior to the crucifixion. The followers of John believed that he was the true messiah. The early Roman Church largely eradicated this idea, although it has been demonstrated that the concept continued through modern times within certain elements of Freemasonry as well as some Middle-Eastern sects.

"The symbol of the skull became quite popular after the death of John the Baptist," Charles continued. "To his followers, the skull signified the cycle of death and rebirth, an opportunity for another chance, as offered by John through baptism. It is most interesting how the symbol of the skull crops up throughout history. The Knights Templar used a skull with crossed bones on their ships, an affectation apparently appropriated by latter-day pirates. And, of course, the Nazi *SS* is not called the Order of the Death's Head for nothing.

"In fact, even today on June 24th, the birthday of John the Baptist, thousands of pilgrims gather at Amiens north of Paris, the supposed site of the final resting place of his skull. Although by now it may be in the hands of our enemies."

Charles suddenly noticed that during this soliloquy, Marie had embraced his short companion. Embarrassed, he quickly turned to Giselle.

"Oh, my dear, I am so sorry. In my excitement, I completely forgot my manners. Please allow me to introduce you to an associate of mine, Bernard Fauseau, professor of history at the University of Toulouse, a practicing Cathar and, I might add, a delightful fellow."

"*Enchantée*, Professor Fauseau," said Giselle, offering her hand.

Taking her hand in one of his, while the other pulled aside a lock of his bushy black hair that had blown across his pleasant round face, the man smiled broadly, "No, by the account of you given to me by my friend Charles, it is I who should be enchanted, *Mademoiselle*. And please, call me Bernard. I do not much care for titles or stations in life. The Lord God has made us all from the same clay."

Giselle looked sharply at Charles. In these times, one could not be too careful about sharing one's activities.

Charles, noticing her unease, quickly said, "*Pardon, ma chère,* I assure you that we may speak freely in front of Bernard. We have been both friends and associates for many years. He is the one who has provided me with much of the information about this place." He stopped and seemed to notice Marie for the first time. Now it was Charles' turn to be concerned about saying too much before a stranger. Then he noticed that everyone but him was smiling.

"I'm quite sorry for bursting in on you this way, my dear," Charles stammered. "I realize that I was not to disturb you while you were making your visit, but I was so excited after seeing the church and when I saw you here in the cemetery…"

Giselle placed her hand on his shoulder. "That's quite all right, Charles. Calm down. I believe that we are all friends here. Permit me to introduce you to this grand lady, *Mademoiselle* Marie Denarnaud. This is Professor Charles Richer of the Sorbonne."

"Delighted to make your acquaintance, dear lady," said Charles with a slight bow.

Marie nodded in acknowledgment and said testily, "The delight is all mine, young man, but you must know that except for meeting this insightful and determined young woman, not to mention the fact that you are friends with Bernard, I would have nothing to do with you."

Taking Bernard by the arm, she added, "Bernard and I go way back. There are no secrets between us. We share common beliefs."

Giselle looked surprised. "Do you mean that you too are a practicing Cathar?"

"Well, I cannot very well go around advertising the fact in my position here, now can I?" she replied, squeezing Bernard's arm and giving him a quick wink. "After all, the Cathari and the Roman Church have been sworn enemies for centuries now."

"After the unnatural death of Father Saunière, I found I could no longer blindly accept the tenants of the Catholicism," she explained. "Yet, I was stuck here and pledged to protect the secrets. The villagers are kind and well meaning, but they are woefully ignorant. They are suspicious of anyone who does not adhere to their provincial lifestyle."

She shrugged her shoulders. "So, I attend services at the chapel each Sunday so as not to arouse the suspicions of the villagers. But my faith lies with Bernard and the handful of those who still practice the religion of the Cathari."

In the awkward silence that followed, she added, "Shall we retire to my home? I will prepare lunch for all of us."

With words of gratitude, the newfound friends adjourned to *Villa Bethania*.

During the next two days, everyone spent long hours discussing the history and mystery of Rennes-le-Château. Gabby, fresh from her hike to the cave of Mary Magdalene, told of her adventurous descent into the hillside cavern. "There are tunnels in the rear that extend for a great distance," she related, "but I didn't have the time or equipment to explore them."

"You were on the right track," said Marie enigmatically.

"Then I shall continue my explorations," said Gabby with a self-assured smile.

During this time, they became closer than friends; they became comrades in arms, sharing in secrets kept well away from the general public and most especially from the Germans. Marie, with Bernard's help, fleshed out the details of her story of treasure and intrigue in Rennes-le-Château during the time of Father Saunière. Gabby continued her exploration of the cavern systems around the village and Charles spent much of his time in the small but endlessly fascinating chapel.

At Marie's request, Giselle even moved into *Villa Bethania*, taking a small but comfortable room in the back. She and Marie sat up into the early morning hours discussing philosophy, history and the need for bringing balance back to the world.

Each day, Charles, Gabby and Bernard would join them for lengthy discussions. Marie and Bernard explained the philosophy of the Cathars as Giselle, Charles and Gabby sat enraptured.

They learned that the remnants of this early-day Gnostic sect believed in a dual universe, one divided into good versus evil. Evil was represented by the material world with all its illness, death, wars and seductive pleasures that turned humanity away from the Divine. Good was defined as nothing less than the Kingdom of God as understood by the earliest Christians. They believed humankind had to ascend from the material world through a joining of both spirit and soul, a co-mingling they termed "consolament."

The Cathar community, still suspicious of the outside world even in the enlightened mid-20th century, was somewhat reclusive. It was divided into believers, the *croyants*, and a small number of priests or *parfaits*. No distinction was made between male or female *parfaits*, who usually wore garments of traditional black. They did not believe in the construction of elaborate and costly churches and often met outdoors. They, like their ancestors, were vegetarians, supported equality of the sexes and fought against distinctions of class and position.

Giselle and Gabby in particular were greatly impressed and even swayed by the dedication to such ideals.

For their part, both Bernard and Marie were also impressed by their new friends, for they saw the Nazis as the epitome of the materialistic evil they abhorred so much. They were greatly impressed to learn of the Sisterhood and its efforts to rid all Europe of this scourge.

Yet, though all the discussions, Giselle noted that neither Marie nor Bernard ever mentioned the exact location of the treasure. Each time she tried to bring the subject up, her question was deflected in one way or another.

On the third day of their visit, with Gabby still exploring the cave systems, Giselle announced following a pleasant lunch that they intended to make their good-byes. "There is so much work to do. We must be leaving tomorrow," she explained to Marie as the two women sat with Charles and Bernard in the villa's drawing room. "But we have thoroughly enjoyed our visit. This has turned out to be most instructive. I have known for some time about the power struggles within the upper circles of society, but I had no idea of the deep and ancient secrets that bind these circles and the secret societies together."

"Alas, you have only begun to scratch the surface, my dear," replied Marie with a knowing smile. She looked to Bernard, who gave her a slight nod of approval. "Bernard and I have discussed this and we have decided that you and your Sisterhood might just be the best chance we may have for preventing our secrets from falling into the hands of that Peter character and his kind.

"You have been most patient, though I know that you are curious about the treasure's whereabouts. Come with us and we will show you a secret that has been kept for many, many years."

Intrigued, Giselle trailed behind as the group got to their feet and followed the spry little woman out a rear door. She was not prepared for the shocking impact of Marie's secret.

The entourage made its way to the Church of the Magdalene and once inside, Marie and Bernard each searched around to make certain they were alone. It was mid-day and still early spring. The small church was empty. Bernard closed the bolt, locking the small wooden door.

Walking to the altar, Marie turned and said, "Bernard, if you please."

The portly man in his black double-breasted suit, stepped to the altar and pressed a protruding stone under the ornate altar, which began slowly moving to one side with a low grinding sound revealing a narrow, circular staircase leading into blackness below.

Everyone stood in shocked silence for some time. "This is unbelievable," muttered Charles.

Marie's high-pitched voice broke their reverie. "Bernard, would you please lead the way, in case I should fall?"

The short man grinned and replied, "Do not worry, I will catch you. How long has it been since you last went down these stairs?"

Marie smiled wanly. "It has been a number of years. At my age, I do not make this trip lightly. But I think it is most important that our friends see for themselves that which must be preserved at all costs."

The elderly woman slowly and carefully followed Bernard down into the inky darkness. The others followed quietly, still somewhat dazed to find themselves climbing downward under the church.

Just as the daylight from the church was closed off by the altar returning to its original position, Bernard produced a small flashlight from his pocket. From that point, they all followed the small circular spot of light that bobbed up and down as he took each step slowly and methodically, in deference to Marie's age.

Little by little they moved down the steps for what seemed an eternity to Giselle until they stepped onto a smooth stone floor. There was an audible click and the room lit up with light. Marie had found an old-style light switch on the wall near the stairway.

Giselle could see two rows of wrapped wires leading down the rock limestone tunnel quarried deep inside the hill beneath the village of Rennes-le-Château.

Marie stopped to catch her breath and muttered, "François had this lighting system installed shortly before his death. It was quite modern then." She laughed softly. "He was overcharged, as usual. He never could handle money very well, that's why he left the bookkeeping to me."

"Further down this tunnel is a fork," said Bernard. "Near there is a small opening which leads to one of the old ruins at the base of the hill. You may enter the tunnel system from there."

"I'll keep that in mind," murmured Giselle, as much to herself as her interlocutor.

Pointing to the lighted tunnel stretching away into the distance, Marie wheezed, "The way to the treasure from the fork is to the right but it will take you some amount of time."

"Yes," agreed Giselle, "Montségur is more than 21 kilometers to the west."

Marie's eyes were sparkling with humor as she said, "But this tunnel leads to the northeast."

"Northeast?" Giselle was puzzled. "Everything I have learned about this matter indicates the treasure should be somewhere near the Cathar stronghold of Montségur."

"That's what everyone thinks," said Marie with a laugh, "including that swine Peter. Misdirection has been our greatest advantage in keeping the treasure safe. Actually, the treasure lies beneath *Pech Cardou*, a mountain to the northeast, where it was moved at the time of the Albigensian Crusade."

"Why are you revealing this to us now?" asked Charles, still amazed at the reality of what he was experiencing. In all his years of travel and research, he never suspected this legendary treasure might truly exist.

"Marie and I have decided that the Sisterhood with its close connections to the Resistance may be our best chance of keeping the treasure from the Germans," explained Bernard. Marie nodded her assent. "We feel certain *Herr* Peter will return and next time he won't come alone."

"Quite simply, we need your help," she added.

"We will help you all we can," said Giselle with all sincerity.

Giselle was already formulating plans to deal with such an event. "How far is it from here to the treasure?" she asked absently.

"Just more than 10 kilometers," answered Bernard.

"Father Saunière tunneled more than six miles?" asked Giselle, skeptical of such an achievement.

"Oh no, *ma chère*." Marie scoffed. "Not that much work. He merely had this tunnel and stairs built." She indicated the lighted tunnel before them. "After a short distance, this tunnel connects to the original system of caves and passageways which spread out in every direction. If you know the route, it will take you to the treasure."

"Amazing," Charles repeated himself, looking about in wonder. No one could have suspected that this vast interconnected cavern system lay under the small and sleepy village of Rennes-le-Château.

"The treasure lies in a great cavern called the Cathedral. I have seen it myself several times," said Bernard.

"And this is the lost Treasure of Solomon?" asked Charles, his eyes alight with excitement.

"Yes," replied Bernard, "the final resting place of the treasure cache of the Visigoths, the Cathari and the Templars. It is worth more than a king's ransom. It is the greatest treasure in the history of the world."

"Can you describe it?" asked Giselle, her archeological mind reeling with the prospects of actually locating such a find.

"I have seen many, many ancient gold coins and precious jewels of all sizes and shapes. I recall there is a wonderfully crafted silver chalice mounted on a three-prong base made of emerald or perhaps jasper."

"The Grail Cup?" gasped Giselle. She glanced at Charles, who stood with his mouth agape.

"Perhaps," replied Bernard in a reverent tone. "There are also many items which we believe came from Solomon's Temple, such as furniture, a golden urn, a harp, swords, plates and vessels, menorahs and other candelabras made of solid gold. There are also stone tablets bearing inscriptions which no one has been able to decipher."

"The Tablets of Testimony!" Now it was Charles' turn to gasp.

He looked to Giselle. "You do know about the Tablets which by the Biblical account were handed down to Moses at the same time as the Ten Commandants?"

She merely nodded, her mind reeling at the thought of actually locating such legendary treasures.

Turning back to their guide, Charles asked, "Are you certain these are the Tablets of Testimony?"

Bernard shrugged his shoulders. "No one knows for certain. They have not been translated. And, there are many religious objects, some undoubtedly early Christian since I recall seeing crosses of silver and gold, some inlaid with jewels and pearls."

"They must have been added during the time of the Templars," mused Charles.

Giselle stood still in amazement, trying to grasp the full impact of such a discovery. "The modern world would be agog at a find like this. It would make Howard Carter's discovery of King Tutankhamen's tomb pale by comparison."

Suddenly, her face turned dark with fury. "We can't allow such a treasure to fall into the hands of those Nazi swine. History would never forgive us."

"My people agree," said Bernard. "But we don't know what to do. We are a peaceful and passive people. We have managed to keep the secret so far by silence but we don't know what to do if the Germans return to search in force."

"And you'd better believe they will," said Charles with a fervor Giselle had never before seen in the man, "especially if they find a clue to the treasure's location."

They all stood in silence in the rock tunnel when Giselle edged past the professor to exclaim, "What's this?" Kneeling down, she picked up an object from the tunnel floor.

Even in the dim light of the tunnel, the coin she held up shone with a dull yellow finish. She held it closer to a light bulb and studied it. "The Emperor Nero, I believe," she concluded. "This one coin is worth several months pay to you, Charles."

Charles smiled and examined the coin. "But where did it come from?" he asked to no one in particular. He noticed that everyone was looking at Marie.

The older woman was somewhat embarrassed. "I brought some of the treasure up here many years ago and placed it in a nearby alcove," she admitted quietly, indicating an area just behind her.

"We needed money for the church and town and I couldn't very well keep trekking back and forth through this maze of tunnels and caverns," she explained defensively, looking from face to face.

"They do stretch for many miles, you know," added Bernard in Marie's defense. "I don't think anyone has actually determined the extent of this underground system. They claim you can walk all the way to the ancient Temple of Isis at Petra."

"Petra? The Rose-Red City?" exclaimed Giselle in disbelief. "But that's in British Transjordan."

"Yes, I know, near where the Jordan River once flowed into the Gulf of Aqaba," agreed Bernard calmly.

"My God! That's in the Middle East. You must be joking?"

"I'm just telling you what the ancient legends say, my dear," Bernard replied gently.

Giselle shook her head. "I'm sorry, but I am still having trouble with the whole idea of this fabulous treasure."

Marie leaned against the rocky wall of the tunnel and said, "May I rest a moment before we return?"

"But of course, you poor dear" replied Giselle. Placing a hand on the woman's shoulder, Giselle gazed deeply into her eyes saying, "While you rest, may I take some of these gold coins? I assure you they will be used to protect the treasure."

Marie again produced her tight and enigmatic smile and said, "Very well, *ma chère*. But, you must understand that this is not the true treasure."

Her offhanded remark caught everyone by surprise. They all turned to stare at the elderly woman. "Are you sure this is wise?" Bernard whispered softly to her.

"Yes, Bernard, I have given it much thought. I am not getting any younger and neither are you and your select *parfaits*. I think it is time we pass the secret on to a younger generation, especially one that will revere and protect it."

Bernard shrugged. "We have worked well together for many years, Marie. I will accede to your wishes if that is what you think right."

Turning to Giselle, she said solemnly, "Then let me rest a few moments more and we will return to the *Villa Bethania* where I will share with you the greatest secret in the world."

On the slow return trip to the spiral stairway and the climb upward, Giselle's impatience was nearly uncontrollable. Her mind was reeling. She found her thoughts of revenge and the recovery of the crystal skull muted, replaced by visions of the greatest discovery of all time.

Might she be the one to bring Solomon's Treasure, perhaps the greatest archeological find in history, to the world? She could hardly contain herself during the slow and laborious trip back up the stairs to the church.

One question nagged at her thoughts. What could possibly be a greater secret than the location of Solomon's Treasure?

Gabby and Jean Paul were waiting for the group when they arrived. As they all gathered in the living room, Marie produced a map of the region similar to the one that had guided Giselle and her friends to the Languedoc.

Stretching it out on the dining table, Giselle noticed Marie's map was different. Someone had drawn on it, making a circle with a protractor and sharp, distinct lines with blue ink and a straight edge.

"Bernard," Marie said, turning to her longtime friend and confidant, "would you explain our little secret? I'm afraid all that exercise has exhausted me." With an understanding smile, Bernard moved to the table.

Marie reclined on the divan watching as Giselle, Charles and Gabby peered over the map while Bernard began his explanation. The older woman pursed her lips as she expectantly waited for their reactions to the amazing story she knew so well.

Pointing at the geometric designs on the map as he spoke, Bernard began to lecture as though he was in his classroom in Toulouse.

"You see here a map of this area. To complete this circle here," he pointed to a large circle drawn on the map, "you need only connect these locations: Rennes-le-Château on the extreme west, then upward to Coustaussa, on through Cassaignes, over to Serres and on down to Bugarach, around to Saint-Just-et-le-Bézu. Within this circle is a pentagram centered on Rennes-les-Bains, but with its top angle extended northward to an arching rock at the summit of *la Berco Grando* mountain. This same significant outcropping can be seen in the background behind the effigy of Mary Magdalene carved on the altar in the church here and is a reference point. All of these places have been considered sacred sites as far back as anyone can remember.

"The geometric measurements of this design signify that the connection of these sacred sites is not coincidental. While there are certain slight distortions factored in by the original designers, nevertheless the mathematics of this gigantic design are impeccable and meant to convey a message."

"A message?" asked Gabby. "What sort of message?" Giselle frowned at the interruption. Charles was closely studying the designs on the map with a look of amazement on his face.

Bernard shrugged his broad shoulders. "We are not certain. But it has to do with human origins and perhaps even the future. You see, mathematics is the language of the spirit. There is no room for equivocation or deceit. Two plus two always and only equals four. This is a way to communicate through great gulfs of time and space, to reach intelligent beings regardless of their language or culture."

"But what does all this mean?" asked Gabby. Seeing Giselle's look of disapproval, the young girl contritely stepped back and waited for Bernard's reply.

"It means that you are standing at the edge of a great and ancient temple, much like Stonehenge, which was laid out many centuries ago to encompass 40 square miles of this countryside. This temple is dedicated to the Earth Mother, also called Astarte, Ishtar and Isis."

"Do you mean this is a place of prayer?" asked Gabby, still trying to grasp concepts far removed from her university education.

Marie uttered a sharp laugh laced with bitterness. "Oh no, my dear, this is a place of learning." She looked at her guests with sad eyes. "This place has indeed taught me much, although I have had to keep it secret for the most part. I have only shared what I have learned through Father Saunière with Bernard and a few select *parfaits* of the surviving Cathars. They are enlightened enough to know the danger of such knowledge falling into profane hands."

"But this is incredible," said Giselle. Her archeological instincts were fully aroused. "Surely in this enlightened age, the knowledge of this ancient formation must be shared with the world. I mean the Church might frown on such revelations, but they don't burn people at the stake any longer."

Marie looked at her with a great sadness in her eyes. "No, they don't. But surely you are aware of the secret and powerful forces that would gladly kill to gain any advantage over the population, not to mention what the lust for gold and wealth does to men. And there is an advantage to be had that makes the treasure of gold and silver trivial by comparison."

Charles, who had been standing silently amazed at what he was hearing and seeing, shook himself and said, "I can't imagine what that could possibly be."

Marie smiled and looked to Bernard. "Perhaps you should explain this too, my old friend. I suspect they already think I am just a crazy old fool."

The group began to protest, but were silenced by her raised hand.

Bernard, looking as though he had been asked to present a dissertation on fairies and goblins, nevertheless cleared his throat and in a serious tone stated, "Based on the work begun by Father Saunière and brought forward by my people, we have reason to believe that this gigantic ancient temple acts as a device for focusing natural Earth energies. By our calculations, if the proper harmonic frequencies can be produced within the temple's central chamber, an energy vortex, a portal can be opened to another realm."

"My God, Bernard," exclaimed Charles. "What do you mean to another world? Another planet? Another time? Perhaps some other dimension?"

"We don't know. It's never been done, that we know of," Bernard replied softly.

"Why not?" Giselle, always the scientist, was genuinely flabbergasted that if such a device existed, it had not been tested.

"As you already know, our world is out of balance. The feminine aspects of life's energy have been suppressed for many centuries. This device we call a Star Portal requires the proper balance between the masculine and feminine energy frequencies before it will open.

"This is why the Templars failed to make it work, as did certain Egyptian and Roman rulers in similar sites. Latter-day groups like the Rosicrucians, the Freemasons, the Illuminati and even the highly secretive, and possibly illusionary, Priory of Sion have all failed to activate this portal. And now the Nazis are sniffing around. If they were ever to discover the true secret of this place, they would stop at nothing to acquire such power."

"I agree," said Giselle, a hard and determined look growing in her eyes. She walked into the villa's kitchen area while Charles and Gabby continued to ask question after question about the large open-air Temple of Isis and its attendant Star Portal.

Recalling her own experience with the Skull of Fate and knowing of the many archeological anomalies around the world, she did not need convincing that Marie and Bernard might be telling the truth. She was well aware of many unpublicized anomalies in science that hinted at worlds beyond our own three-dimensional plane.

If any part of this account of a Star Portal were true, Giselle knew she must do everything in her power to prevent Peter and his *swastika*-clad friends from obtaining access to it. Already they were spreading across the globe like an infectious disease. She didn't even want to consider that they might be able to enter other worlds, whether material or ethereal.

Then she remembered Bernard's words. The Nazis, including Peter, would indeed stop at nothing to acquire the secrets of the portal. Perhaps she could use their greed against them, maybe even to regain the skull. A plan that had begun to form in her mind in the tunnel started to come into focus.

It was several minutes before she returned to the others, but when she did, it was with a newfound sense of purpose and determination.

"I have a plan," Giselle announced to the group, her eyes sparkling with intensity. "Marie, it will require you instantly alerting me should Peter return to Rennes-le-Château. A telegram will suffice."

"Certainly, but I cannot write openly. Shouldn't I use some sort of code?"

Thinking for a moment, Giselle smiled, "The code will simply be 'Blue Apples'—this will mean that Peter has returned. I'm sure you can remember that. Will you do this?"

"If this will thwart the *Boche*, I will see that it is done."

"Good." She turned to Bernard. "Can you gather some manpower, people who can be trusted to keep their mouths shut?"

"Yes, of course," he replied with a slight shrug of his shoulders. "My people have become quite proficient at keeping their mouths shut since the Papal Army of extermination swept through this area." His nonchalance was infectious.

Giselle smiled knowingly. "But, of course. And can you obtain some explosives?"

"I think so," replied Bernard. He did not seem concerned at all that her request could be exceedingly dangerous for him. "Some of my *croyants* are farmers. I think they keep dynamite for blasting tree stumps and damming gullies and such. But what do you have in mind?"

"What I have in mind, my dear friend, is to prevent the cursed *Boche* from taking the treasure. But it will require some strenuous labor on the part of you and your group."

Leaning on the table and searching the faces of her friends, Giselle explained, "Bernard, you and your people will close off all the tunnels leading to the treasure. Dig a new entrance that will be known only to us. Use dynamite if you must."

Bernard and Marie nodded approvingly.

Turning to Marie, she continued, "Marie, you will not know the new route so you cannot reveal it regardless of what happens. Hope-fully, this will protect the treasure.

"When Peter returns you must stall him and whoever is with him until we arrive and can take charge. I would stay here with you until then, but there is too much work to be done in the north and we have no idea when he may come back.

"Knowing the depths of greed within the man, I think I can con-vince him to bring the skull here. I shall simply reveal the Star Portal to him and inform him that the skull is critical to its operation. If he could not resist worldly power, how can he say no to universal power?"

"But won't you be taking a big chance in revealing to him the portal?" asked Marie. "What if he wants it for himself?" Bernard nodded in agreement.

Her eyes grew hard and cold. "This knowledge will do him no good because after we recover the skull, I will personally deal with Peter Freiherr von Manteuffel."

CHAPTER 16

Neuschwabenland, Antarctica
Fall, 1942

SS *STURMBANNFÜHRER* **PETER FREIHERR VON** Manteuffel sat dejectedly on his sparse steel bunk and looked about his small room.

In addition to the steel-framed bed, really little more than a cot, there was a small writing table with a flexible-necked lamp, a chair, a bookcase filled with his reference material and a metal wardrobe containing his uniforms and personal effects.

"I might as well be back in Dachau," Peter muttered to himself.

"Talking to yourself again?" The question came from a man standing in his doorway. Peter had not noticed him. Without looking up, Peter replied, "It's the only way I can get intelligent conversation in this place."

Pulling a cigarette from a red cardboard box labeled "Safari Orient," Peter lit one and made a face, "These damned canteen cigarettes taste like hay from the stables," he grumbled.

"That's because they're part of a shipment that arrived here more than two years ago," responded the man with a laugh. "Just be glad that you can still obtain cigarettes. Sometimes I think they have forgotten all about us back home. There's been no radio traffic for days."

The man was SS *Obersturmführer* Hans Langer, chief radio operator for the expedition. He was not tall but well built. His youthful good humor was usually quite infectious but on this day in the fall of 1942,

Peter was again experiencing a fit of depression. They seemed to be coming with more frequency.

"Yes, well, you told me yourself that there was to be a near black-out of communications lest the Allies discover our presence here."

Hans nodded thoughtfully. "This is true." Eyeing Peter's cigarettes, he held out his hand.

Peter stood up, handed Hans a cigarette and stepped through the door past his friend. Surveying the cramped hallway filled with crates stacked ceiling high on one side, he said, "I'm telling you, Hans, if I don't get out of this place soon, I swear I might crack up."

Hans laughed. "What do you mean *might?*" He had long since realized that Peter's rank of major was largely honorary, a reward for some special expertise or service to the *Reich*.

Peter smiled at this attempt at humor but his heart wasn't in it. He paced a few steps and turned to Hans. "I have been here for more than a year now and I am wasting my time. I should be home pursuing important work instead of buried here writing progress reports and studying the flora and fauna. But no, I'm stuck in this hole at the bottom of the world going slowly crazy from lack of anything meaningful to do."

"But you have conducted your studies here." objected Hans. "I have seen your light on late into the night on many occasions."

Peter nodded. "It is true that I have come to a greater understanding of many things, but it is all academic. I now have a good idea of how to accomplish my true mission and I am eager to get started. I've been here more than a year now. I must get back."

"Come, walk with me to *Agartha*. It always helps to get out of your room and exercise," said Hans, moving off down the corridor. With a sigh, Peter followed.

As they suited up in their cold weather gear of long padded jackets and fur-lined hoods, Peter moved to the small window on the outside door and stood looking into the bleak whiteness.

It was hard to believe that, after all his travels, he would end up at the one place he least expected—Antarctica, the world's seventh continent.

He had not even been aware that Germany had taken an interest in this continent, much less the amazing discovery that had been made. News of this discovery and subsequent exploitation had been virtually non-existent in the press outside Germany. Peter had been astounded when Himmler had told him to familiarize himself with its history.

His assignment had come in early May, 1941, just six weeks before the invasion of Russia and shortly after he had returned empty handed from the Languedoc region of France. Peter had heard rumors about the invasion but had no confirmation. And he knew better than to ask Himmler about anything so sensitive.

He still recalled the summons to the *Reichsführer*'s office. When Himmler told him he was to be assigned to Antarctica, he could not resist the impulse to protest.

"But, *Herr Reichsführer*, what about Solomon's Treasure? Surely, I am needed here. I've already made one trip to Rennes-le-Château and I think I have enough information now to begin closer field work." Peter was careful not to mention that he had had no luck drawing information from the woman who had been housekeeper to the village priest. "I am certain that with just a little more time I could have made a breakthrough."

Himmler rose from behind his large and ornate wood-carved desk and walked slowly across the spacious office festooned with flags, banners, runic carvings and paintings, which only a year previously had been hanging in museums. "Peter, *mein junge*, you must learn patience. All things come to those who combine patience with careful planning."

Peter snapped to attention, embarrassed and not just a little fearful that he had spoken out of turn. "Of course, *Herr Reichsführer*. I am sorry for questioning your orders."

Himmler paused and smiled benignly at the young officer before him. He had not forgotten the marvelous relic that Peter had placed in his hands. And he knew the young man would be needed in the future.

In a gentle voice, he said, "My dear boy, I should not have to explain myself to you, but please understand. Hunting for the treasure is a delicate matter. It lies in unoccupied France and there are niceties to be observed. Can you imagine what the Vichy government would think if I let you tear off through southern France with a convoy of troops and military equipment?

"There is a very big operation coming up soon and the *Führer* has made it quite clear that he wants no problems with the French. There are those of us who are not as satisfied as the *Führer* that Britain can cause us no more harm, so we certainly don't want to take the chance of creating new enemies."

Peter looked as if he wanted to say something, but Himmler continued, "Oh, I know, you'll say but why can't we simply ask for permission to conduct excavations in France?

"The *Führer* feels that would be a mistake. They quite naturally would ask what we were looking for and what would we say? Why, we're coming to take Solomon's Treasure from its hiding place in the Languedoc. They wouldn't like that, would they? Can you imagine the repercussions, both in France and abroad? The Jews in Britain and America would make much to do about this and raise the alarm. The United States might enter the war. No, dear boy, it is not yet time for that. We shall be patient and wait our chance. The treasure will still be there.

"And in the meantime, based on your background and training in both archeology and geology, I would like a report from you on our operation in the Antarctic. Only my most trusted officers even know of its existence. I will let you know when it is time to return and I will expect a comprehensive report."

"*Jawohl, Herr Reichsführer!*" shouted Peter, coming to attention. He pivoted on his left heel and stalked from Himmler's office as if on the parade ground.

Stomping down the marble-floor hallway, Peter glanced back and saw Himmler standing in the doorway watching him and polishing his pince-nez glasses.

He felt pride that the SS chief would count him among his most trusted lieutenants but at the same time he was suspicious. The bastard wants to be rid of me for some reason, he thought. Perhaps he fears that Hitler might decide to learn more of the treasures I recovered in the Yucatan. So far, he only has the Skull of Fate. Himmler must be determined to keep the remainder of my find.

Peter smiled to himself, thinking of the Mayan gold he had hidden away in Mexico for use after the war. Himmler will never get his hands on my retirement. He was somewhat surprised to realize how cynical he had become concerning the SS, the Party and the war. It was not at all like he had thought it would be.

Here he was, wasting his time and being sent to the bottom of the world and all for nothing more than a major's pay. His thoughts darkened as he marched from the massive government building housing Himmler's office.

On June 22, 1941, as millions of Axis troops crashed into the Soviet Union on a front stretching from the Baltic to the Black Sea, Peter had been traveling under the Atlantic in a supply submarine, designated U-530.

During the seemingly endless days of crossing the Atlantic submerged, Peter had discovered he carried with him a touch of claustrophobia. This was not helped by the stench of sweat, urine and diesel oil which permeated the submarine. He soon realized why they were nicknamed "pig boats."

No one had been more relieved than Peter when the U-boat reached the far South Atlantic and was able to run on the surface for hours at a time. Peter was finally allowed on deck. But the long entombed journey had provided Peter with time to study the background of Antarctica and the attraction it held for the Nazi leadership.

Their interest involved a section of the continent known as Queen Maud Land, situated east of the Weddell Sea well within the Antarctic Circle. Thought to be merely a land of ice and snow, Peter had read the 1823 reports of the English seal hunter James Weddell, who wrote, "The ice in this region had completely disappeared, the temperature is mild, birds were observed flying around the ship and groups of whales frolicked in the wake of the craft."

Amazed by this discovery, bad weather nevertheless forced Weddell to return home. Despite several subsequent expeditions, including those of the famous Commander Richard Byrd in the early 1930s, no one had found this sanctuary of warm water and thriving plant life until late in 1938.

It was then that *Kapitan* Alfred Ritscher, an arrogant but competent man, had renamed the area *Neuschwabenland* in honor of his flagship the *Schwabenland*, a floating laboratory that belonged to the *Lufthansa* airline. It carried two amphibian aircraft weighing 10 tons each as well as a complement of scientists and technicians.

Ritscher's expedition had been under the direct orders of *Reichsmarschall* Hermann Göring, Rudolf Hess and other influential members of the secretive Thule Society.

Officially on a mission to study the feasibility of whaling in those waters, Ritscher proceeded to drop small *swastika* flags along separate flight paths to the South Pole, eventually staking out more than 600,000 square kilometers for the *Reich*.

Within this immense area, Peter learned that the explorers discovered huge ice caverns filled with warm water and living plants. It was found that the soil of Antarctica was remarkably rich and could grow nearly any plant, once ice free. It was the perfect secluded hideaway, approximately 5,600 miles from Africa, 4,760 miles from Australia and 1,870 miles from the southernmost tip of South America.

Ritscher and the *Schwabenland* returned to Hamburg on April 12, 1939, amid much fanfare. Peter, however, was in Central America and never learned of the expedition until he was given the files by Himmler. With war fears rising that year and Hitler's attack on Poland in September, the German expedition was quickly forgotten by all but the Nazi High Command.

Peter learned that by mid-1940, submarine bases located in *Neuschwabenland* became the sites of a great buildup of supplies and materials in addition to servicing U-boats operating in the South Atlantic. Some time later, orders were issued that these U-boats should concentrate farther north and not engage in any hostilities in the South Atlantic. They hoped to draw attention away from the Antarctic bases, which were filled with planes, tractors, sleds, all the equipment and machinery necessary to create a new *Berchtesgaden* for the *Führer.*

Peter had been amazed to think that all this had gone unnoticed by the eyes of the world. But as he continued his studies, he realized that the great distances involved almost guaranteed secrecy. The continent of Antarctica was larger than the whole of Europe. Plus, he learned that the supply of this new world was accomplished entirely by the German submarine fleet.

As he and Hans walked from the living quarters to a huge hanger-like storage building that housed the opening to *Agartha*, Peter for the first time took real notice of the remarkable amount of supplies that had been shipped to this desolated place.

Tons of stored oil and gasoline, naphtha, clothing, canned foods, medicines, vitamins of every kind, water distillation equipment, generators, weapons, and communication equipment filled every available space under the roof. The sheer bulk of it was overwhelming. There was enough material stockpiled here to support thousands of people for many years.

When he and Hans reached the armed guards at the tunnel's entrance, there were no formalities or security checks. No one could get to this place without being brought by submarine and no one got out except the same way. The outside temperature at its highest hovered right at zero degrees Fahrenheit. Peter didn't want to even think about the lowest temperatures.

A burly SS trooper opened the heavy metal door with a clang and Hans and Peter stepped into a long corridor tunneled out of the rock and snow. It was brightly lit by incandescent lights powered by generators that were both out of sight and sound. The rocky corridor was silent but for the soft tread of their fur-covered boots.

A lighted area up ahead grew in intensity until they found themselves at the mouth of an immense cavern. To his left, Peter saw that the sub pens contained only two U-boats, one in dry dock and the other being provisioned for a return to sea. The narrow channel that would carry the sub to open sea was blocked by a huge steel door set back from the actual opening which carried the ships into the Atlantic.

To his right was a scene of bustling activity. Workers were constructing large living quarters, storage and power generation facilities and meeting halls. Already, some of the more ambitious workers had begun gardens in an area designated to become giant farms.

The whole scene was brilliantly lit by a thin translucent ice sheet that covered the rocks forming the cavern's ceiling. From the air above, it looked like one continuous reflective pane of ice. But from below, it acted as a giant skylight, bringing both light and heat from the sun to the area far below.

"It is truly an amazing sight, isn't it, Hans?" said Peter with awe. "I can't imagine that the rest of the world doesn't know about the warm water and vegetation here."

Hans shrugged. "It's too isolated. Everyone has been conditioned to think this place is nothing but ice and snow. Maybe sometime, years from now, they will discover that there's more to this continent than they have been told."

Peter stood taking in this scene of bustling construction. Suddenly a shiver passed through his body and it wasn't from the chilly Antarctic air inside the underground cavern.

Peter had long been speculating on the immense amount of supplies and materials cached at this secret and largely underground base. He also pondered the construction, which was continuing there at a rapid pace.

His first thought had been that this place was meant to be a secret base from which to launch an attack on the Americas. But that didn't make sense. Peter was well aware of the influence of his nation in South America, particularly Brazil, Argentina, Bolivia and Paraguay. For cash in hand, the friendly leaders of those nations would gladly have allowed Hitler to build a secret base.

No, this place was different. There was another reason for this hidden base.

It suddenly struck him. This was meant to be a refuge in case of defeat in the war, a refuge that no nation on the Earth could know about nor reach with ease.

Peter found himself sweating despite the chill of the cavern. It was the first time the idea of defeat had entered his thoughts. His thoughts took a darker turn. If the leadership was bearing the expense of constructing this sanctuary, it obviously meant they were seriously considering the prospects of losing the war. Perhaps, they included even the *Führer* himself. He must know about this project. It was too grandiose for him not to know.

Peter felt sick to his stomach. The thick wall of his National Socialist training was cracking. Doubts began to swirl in his head. All of the risks he had taken, the theft of the crystal skull, the death of Katrina, Giselle and Jim. If the *Führer*'s great experiment failed, would it all have been for nothing?

"I'm sorry, Hans," Peter said weakly. He leaned up against the rock wall of the cavern. "I'm not feeling well. I must go back. Besides, I still have much work to do."

"Very well, *kamerad*, but I'm warning you, I have marked the level of my bottle of *Schnapps*." Hans grinned and walked off toward the construction site.

Peter took one long look at the base that had been under construction since before his arrival more than a year ago. But today he saw it in an entirely new light. This was no hidden base from which to mount an invasion against the gangsters of the West. It was a last redoubt for National Socialism in defeat.

As the days turned into months, Peter began to wonder if he would ever leave this cold and confining place.

With each arrival of a supply submarine, Peter had joined the rush to get news from home just as he had done since his arrival in *Neuschwabenland* in August, 1941. He had kept up with the war news from arriving sailors and the newspapers that came with the mail. During the past years, he realized that the hostilities had turned into a see-saw battle of death and destruction.

Two weeks after Operation *Barbarossa* was launched against Russia, Soviet and British leaders had signed a mutual assistance pact in Moscow. Near the middle of August, the American president, Roosevelt, had met with Churchill on a ship off the coast of Newfoundland.

By late November, 1941, the German drive on Moscow had stalled and the Russians had struck back at bulges in the German front line at the small towns of Tula and Klin. The biggest news came on December 7th, when Hans had rushed into his room with shocking information.

"Peter, I was monitoring the South American radio stations and you won't believe what has happened," he said with great excitement.

"And what would that be," responded Peter calmly. The boring daily routine coupled with the isolation and drabness of Antarctica had brought him to a near zombie-like state.

"Japan has attacked the American fleet at Pearl Harbor," Hans was practically shouting. Others were crowding Peter's door to hear. "Early reports claim that the American Pacific Fleet has been crippled."

Peter jumped from his chair. This meant America would now be in the war.

Everyone followed Hans to the radio room where they stood around, speculating and gossiping for hours waiting to hear what the German response would be. But Peter knew what this attack meant. He had overheard Himmler mention that on April 4, 1941, Hitler himself had pledged to Japanese Foreign Minister Yosuke Matsuoka that should Japan become involved in a war with America, Germany would promptly take part. Hitler had only said this in an effort to move Japanese leaders into joining the war against Britain, particularly in attacking Singapore and thus tying up British troops in the Far East. He never thought his pledge would nudge Japan into attacking America, which he had gone to considerable lengths to keep neutral.

Having lived in both North and Central America, Peter had fully understood the gravity of the Japanese attack and was prepared for Germany's response.

Although as early as December 8th, the German *Kriegsmarine* received orders to attack American ships wherever they were found, a formal declaration of war did not come until December 11th.

That day, Peter had joined the hundreds of workers and technicians in *Agartha* listening to Radio Berlin. Listening intently through the static of the short-wave radio, they heard the *Führer* address the deputies of the *Reichstag.*

Hitler explained his attack on the Soviet Union by stating, "I may say this today: If the wave of more than 20,000 tanks, hundreds of divisions, tens of thousands of artillery pieces, along with more than 10,000 airplanes, had not been kept from being set into motion against the *Reich*, Europe would have been lost..."

The Nazi *Führer* went on to say that the cause of the war now encircling the globe could be laid at the feet of one man—Franklin Delano Roosevelt.

In terms he usually reserved for his hated enemy Churchill, Hitler railed against Roosevelt, his voice high-pitched and thin over the base's loudspeaker, "This man, who is the main culprit of this war, is guilty of a series of the worst crimes against international law. He has authorized the illegal seizure of ships and other property of German and Italian nationals..." Static interrupted the *Führer*'s words. "Roosevelt's ever increasing attacks finally went so far that he ordered the American Navy to attack everywhere ships under the German and Italian flags and to sink them—this in gross violation of international law.

"First he incites war, then falsifies the causes, then odiously wraps himself in a cloak of Christian hypocrisy and slowly but surely leads mankind to war, not without calling God to witness the honesty of his attack, but in the approved manner of an old Freemason..."

The *Führer* carried on for a length of time in this vein, accusing Roosevelt of stirring up war both to support his class peers in England, his Jewish backers and to distract public attention from his wrongheaded and failed New Deal policies.

"For years this man harbored one desire—that a conflict should break out somewhere in the world," Hitler thundered, finally stating, "I have therefore arranged for the passports to be handed to the American *chargé d'affaires* today, and the following..."

His words were drowned out by cheering, both from the packed *Reichstag* as well as from the workers at the *Agartha*, who clearly understood that a declaration of war had been made.

Peter had smiled and joined in the *Sieg Heil* salutes, but he could not bring himself to join in the celebration at the base. He had seen too much of America and he knew that victory would now be long in coming, if it came at all.

Trudging back to his little room, he could see how the world was lining up against his *Vaterland*. He had sat on his bed for a long time contemplating what only a few months before had seemed like such a bright future.

The specter of eventual defeat began to plague his waking hours, especially since his faith in the *Führer* and his New Order had been shaken by the knowledge of this underground retreat at the bottom of the world.

He only half-heartedly joined in the 1942 New Year's celebration at the base and throughout the spring and summer of that year, he went back to writing his reports without enthusiasm.

He spent many hours cataloging and identifying the minerals that the workers found during their excavations. In addition to large quantities of coal and iron, he had identified many other useful ores and minerals.

When he was not working in geology, he dabbled in whatever artifacts attracted his archeological interest. And he continued to pore over the old texts and esoteric papers he had brought with him along with the copious notes and publications of Otto Rahn.

Peter had learned much during his long months in Antarctica and as he thought over the knowledge he now had regarding the Treasure of Solomon, his devious mind began to form a plan.

During the next several months, Peter had reviewed his knowledge of the treasure and its origin. He used his friend Hans as a sounding board. Every hour Hans was off duty, Peter had regaled him with his findings and conclusions.

Hans was affable enough about this odd education process because he had nothing better to do during the long Antarctic days and nights. Then there was the fact that Peter's musings just went in one ear and out the other, relieving Hans of any painful thinking.

"Everyone has heard of the Holy Grail, right Hans?" announced Peter one day in the late fall of 1942. Hans dutifully smiled but shook his head.

Hans' negative response went unnoticed by Peter, who had already immersed himself in the subject long before the radio operator had joined him in his cramped living space.

"The definition of the Holy Grail has changed greatly over the centuries," Peter explained, as much to clarify his own thoughts as to illuminate Hans. "Today, most people think it means a silver chalice that once held the blood of Christ, either as a reality during the crucifixion or symbolically representing the wine of the Last Supper.

"But in ancient legends, the Grail was interpreted as many things— a meteorite from the skies, a jewel that fell from Lucifer's crown when he was cast out of heaven, a particularly precious stone from antiquity, even tablets inscribed with lost knowledge.

"Eirenaeus Philalethes, a 17th century alchemist, once wrote that the Grail, sometimes referred to as the Philosopher's Stone, was actually nothing but gold digested to..." Peter stopped to read from one of the books open before him, "'the highest degree of purity and subtle fixation ... a very fine powder.'

"Whatever it was, Hans, it appears as if it was a real, tangible object. And some researchers, particularly a young German named Otto Rahn, traced the legend back to the Biblical patriarch Abraham, who was said to have commissioned the original cup, later known as the Grail Cup. It is a talisman of great power."

Peter's eyes were shining. He was thinking of the strange and mysterious crystal skull, wondering if it carried the same power as the Grail. He was completely engrossed in his own rhetoric and did not even notice that the agreeable Hans was idly toying with his prized Olympia portable typewriter which he used to type his reports.

"Abraham was a direct descendent of Shem, one of the sons of Noah, but he was not an Israelite. They didn't exist at that time. No, Abraham was from Ur of Chaldea."

"Where's that?" asked Hans with no real curiosity.

"That, my *kamerad*, is the ancient term for Sumer, located between the Tigris and Euphrates rivers in Mesopotamia. This is the area where the city of Baghdad stands today. And this is where the world's very first recorded civilization arose."

"Really?" muttered Hans as he continued playing with the Olympia's keys.

"Really. We are only just now beginning to learn about the Sumerians. Excavation of their cities and stone tablets was only begun in the last century. Abraham was a believer in the one universal God, El, as well as the holder of ancient secrets including the fabled 'Tablet of Destinies' said to contain all human knowledge handed down since the time of the Great Flood."

Peter, captivated by the story he was recounting, did not even hear the clacking of the typewriter keys. Pacing about the room, he continued his oration:

"One of Abraham's relatives was a superior metallurgist working for the rulers of Babylon. He is the one who took a silver-like metal found in the mountains of Persia and fashioned it into a cup with places for three large precious stones. This cup, or bowl, sat on a three-footed base made from emerald. According to legend, this became known as the Emerald Cup and it was placed in the Temple of Ur, even while Abraham's god ordered him to move westward while promising to create a great nation from his descendants. Many years later, while living in Palestine, Abraham regained the cup from the legendary King of Jeru-Salem, Melchizedek, who used it to serve him wine.

"Prior to his death, Abraham gave the cup to his son Isaac, who in turn passed it to his son, Jacob, whose name change to Israel eventually came to refer to his entire people. I believe that name is nothing less than a combination of the ancient gods, Isis, Ra and El."

Finally, the clicking of his typewriter keys intruded on Peter's consciousness. "Will you please stop that!" he snapped, turning sharply on Hans. Hans gave him a hang-dog expression and placed his folded hands in his lap.

"As I was saying," said Peter with obvious irritation. "The cup then went through Levi and his descendants until eventually it came into the possession of Moses, who was of the House of Levi. Moses presented the cup to his brother Aaron, the original high priest of Israel. It is most likely then that the talisman was placed in the original Tabernacle along with the Ark of the Covenant."

"You certainly seem to know a lot about the Jews," said Hans, taking a sudden and suspicious interest in Peter's dissertation.

Peter, remembering the conditioning to report fellow SS men who might show sympathy or interest in anything Jewish, laughed and hastily replied, "Ah, Hans, to be truly effective, you must know your enemy."

Hans suspicious look transformed into one of understanding. "*Ja, richtig.*"

Peter hurriedly added, "And I must know every bit of information, no matter how trivial, if I am to secure a great treasure for *Reichsführer* Himmler."

"Treasure, you say?" Hans turned to look at Peter. He was now truly interested.

Peter had long considered whether he should share any information with Hans. Knowing the methods of Himmler and other Nazi leaders, he had finally come to the firm conclusion that neither Hans nor any of the other workers at this hidden base were likely ever see the outside world again. He had begun to wonder if he himself would ever leave. On several occasions he had caught himself thinking of the American gangster expression of keeping someone on ice. Was he being kept on ice, literally?

Yet he clung to the idea that his expertise was still needed, a faith that proved to be prophetic.

"Listen, Hans, and I will tell you a story, a story of the greatest treasure in the world." He paused allowing the import of his statement to sink in.

"When the Israelites left Egyptian bondage, Moses encouraged them to take from their former captors whatever was needed, to include gold, silver and precious jewels. This was the beginning of the fabled Treasure of Solomon. For more than 500 years, this treasure grew with each conquest and it was kept in the Tabernacle of the Israelites. With the death of King David, his son Solomon finally built the first permanent temple on Mount Moriah in what is now Jerusalem, a stationary repository for the treasure.

"The builders of the temple added a maze of tunnels, chambers, tombs and passageways beneath Moriah as they excavated for the foundations. It was the perfect hiding place for their treasure during times of hazard.

"Solomon, through his chief builder, Hiram, King of Tyre, covered the temple with gold, silver and precious gems. The Holy of Holies or inner sanctum, alone was 30-by-30 feet and covered with the finest gold from Parvaim to the east. This gold alone would be worth nearly two billion *Reichsmarks* today."

Hans, who had been reclining on Peter's bunk listening with ever-widening eyes, sat upright and gulped. "Did you say billion?"

"That's right, *kamerad*, two billion *Reichsmarks*." Peter went silent, thinking of such immense wealth. He had been thinking about it for months and had decided there would be something in it for him. The incredible amount he had just mentioned did not even include the incalculable worth of such relics as the Ark, the Cup, the Tablet of Destinies and other texts. It was wealth beyond imagination. He dared not speak further, fearful he might say something to indicate he intended to gain the treasure for himself.

Hans looked at Peter intently. "And you know where this treasure is?"

Realizing that he had said entirely too much, Peter hastened to reply, "Oh, no. Unfortunately, this great treasure was lost over the centuries, stolen and looted by everyone from the Romans to the Crusaders." He did not mention that he now was convinced the entire treasure was hidden in the vicinity of the Cathar stronghold of Montségur.

"But if it was hidden within that maze of passages and tombs, perhaps some of it is still there?" Hans' eyes still sparkled with a faint hope of instant wealth.

"Perhaps," replied Peter. "But the *verdammte Tommies* hold Jerusalem, remember?" Hans' face fell and his face returned to its usual expressionless mask.

Peter clapped his fellow *SS* man on the shoulder and said with some heartiness, "Don't look so glum, my friend. Perhaps after the war, you and I will make a pilgrimage to Jerusalem." He gave Hans a wink and the man visibly brightened. "Come along, *kamerad*, I will buy you a beer at the canteen."

As the pair tromped along the chilly corridor, Peter smiled inwardly. Within a day or two Hans would have forgotten all about the treasure. But Peter knew he would never forget. Since even his own superiors were planning for defeat, he had begun to picture himself as a man of independent means, lounging on some tropical beach surrounded by beautiful and willing women far from a Europe in ruins. He felt that the time for its recovery could not be far off.

That time came in mid-November of 1942. It began with the arrival of a supply submarine and a joyous message. The commander of the U-boat summoned Peter and informed him that he had brought papers ordering Peter back to Germany. Even more important, from Peter's standpoint, was the news that the Americans had invaded

French North Africa where they took control with a minimum of opposition by the French authorities. In anger, Hitler had ordered the occupation of all France.

Peter was elated. With the Nazis having the full run of France and with the United States already in the war, all the roadblocks had been removed. All the months of cold and boredom, all the claustrophobia, were forgotten. Peter would finally be able to put his plans into action. He knew that upon his return to Germany, he would be free to go after Solomon's Treasure.

Only now, he had more personal plans for the disposition of that wealth.

CHAPTER 17

Southern France
Summer, 1943

MANY MONTHS PASSED BEFORE GISELLE finally received a telegram from Marie Denarnaud containing the words, "Blue Apples." Accompanying the message was a single long-stemmed rose.

The months since her visit to Rennes-le-Château had been busy and exciting. There were periods when Giselle had nearly forgotten Marie's revelations and her pledge to sound the alert should Peter return. But she could never completely put out of her mind the fabulous treasure nor the incredible Star Portal revealed to her during her visit there.

Her studies with Charles, who continued to bring her many old and hard-to-find books from the libraries of the Sorbonne, had greatly increased her knowledge of pre-Biblical cultures and civilizations. Her growing awareness that very ancient peoples had traditions of a great antediluvian civilization, complete with wondrous technology and flying gods, only served to confirm her belief that the Isis Temple encompassing Rennes-le-Château was not just some latter-day fraud or misinterpretation.

Since her visit there, Giselle and her still-growing Sisterhood had participated in numerous hazardous adventures, some without the proverbial happy ending. Many people died or had been tortured and imprisoned. But Giselle and the principal Sisters were still actively involved in the struggle against the Axis war machine.

The year 1942 had proved a pivotal time for that particular machine. As the year drew on, the Axis remained strong but it was becoming evident that the forces of Germany, Italy and Japan were not invincible.

On April 18th, Brigadier General Jimmy Doolittle's B-25 bombers brought the war to Japan's doorstep and in early May, the Imperial Japanese Navy was turned back at the Battle of the Coral Sea off New Guinea, saving Port Moresby and Australia from invasion. One month later, the Battle of Midway turned the tide of war in the Pacific.

The tide also was turning in Europe. Before the war, German *Luftwaffe* Chief Hermann Göring had smugly boasted that if any allied bombs were to drop on the *Vaterland*, "my name is Meyer." By mid-1942, displaced residents of bombed-out German cities were calling him that Jewish name night after night.

Late in the year, the much-vaunted *Afrika Korps* was being pushed back into Libya by British Field Marshal Bernard Montgomery. In Russia, the handwriting was appearing on the wall as the summer German offensive against the Volga River industrial city of Stalingrad stalled in the late fall. In November, the Soviets attacked and penetrated both sides of the extended Axis lines leading to Stalingrad, much of which was manned by half-hearted Italian and Romanian troops. They soon encircled the city.

But the major event of 1942 for Giselle and her associates were the Allied landings in North Africa known as Operation *Torch*. They were joyful in the knowledge that French colonies were being taken from Vichy and that the Grand Alliance, as the allies of America, Britain and Russia now were being called, was taking the fight to the Axis.

Their excitement was curtailed, however, when Hitler accused the French of not resisting the landings sufficiently and ordered his forces to occupy the remainder of France. Giselle and Michel were convinced that the *Torch* invasion was merely an excuse for Hitler to consolidate his *Fortress Europe* in preparation for an Allied assault, which appeared more and more inevitable.

With all this activity, Giselle was somewhat surprised that she did not hear from Marie even after the New Year began. Apparently, Peter had not returned since his initial visit.

She also was at a loss to explain the total lack of information on Peter. Even some usually good sources with connections to the German

High Command could find no sign of the man. Gabby had suggested that perhaps he was dead but Giselle could not bring herself to believe it. Something deep inside told her he was still alive and preparing to carry out some plan to gain Solomon's Treasure. That feeling along with her thoughts of revenge kept the issue very much alive in her heart.

As 1943 began, successful operations by the German U-boat fleet in the Atlantic and at Kasserine Pass in Libya were overshadowed when the last German positions at Stalingrad fell to the Russians on February 2nd. The losses at Stalingrad were irreplaceable and even sparked an abortive attempt to overthrow the Hitler regime.

Heart-breaking news came in late February. Giselle had just returned to the château from yet another Sisterhood mission when she found Gabby sobbing on the staircase.

"What's happened?" she had asked trying to console her protégé.

"It's terrible and it's all my fault," was all that the young woman could say.

Dabbing at her puffy eyes with her handkerchief, Giselle said soothingly, "Just tell me all about it. It will help to talk about it."

Sitting up a bit straighter, Gabby began to speak. What began hesitantly quickly became a torrent of words.

"As you know I have been encouraging resistance to the Nazis through my contacts with other universities. One of the most active groups, believe it or not, has been at the University of Munich, the birthplace of Nazism. Isn't that ironic?"

Her sobbing renewed and it was some time before she could continue. "Two student recruits were this brother and sister, Hans and Sophie Scholl. Hans was a medical student and Sophie studied biology. They were both quite keen on opposing Hitler and, with our help they formed their own Resistance group. Because their work involved so many German students whose loyalty could not be counted on, they changed the name of their group to the *Weisse Rose*, the White Rose. They did not want to endanger our secrecy. The White Rose symbolized a Christian spirit which venerated love and justice and opposed what they called the Nazi's 'wall of fear and terror.'"

"Yes, I have heard of them," said Giselle softly. "Go on."

"Last week, the Scholls joined other students in a demonstration in Munich. The Scholls dropped leaflets from a balcony of the university's inner court and were recognized by the building superintendent. The leaflets read in part, 'Germany's name will remain disgraced forever unless German youth rises up immediately, takes revenge and atones, smashes its torturers, and builds a new spiritual Europe.' It was the first such protest in the Third Reich and Hitler was furious. The Scholls were reported to the *Gestapo*, arrested and hauled before the *Volksgericht*, the people's court. They said that Sophie appeared in court with a broken leg resulting from her interrogation by *Gestapo* agents."

"That's dreadful," said Giselle, shaking her head. "But surely, we can arrange for some competent legal counsel for them."

Gabby looked at her through tear-stained eyes. "It's too late," she cried. "They were both hanged yesterday."

"Oh, Gabby, I'm so sorry." Giselle held her shuddering body close to hers. "But you must not blame yourself for this."

"But I encouraged them," she sobbed. "I helped them organize the White Rose."

"Yes, but you did not execute them, my dear." Giselle pushed her away and looked into her face. "The only ones responsible for their deaths are the evil men responsible for all the death and destruction in the world today. We must face the fact that there will be losses in our fight to regain truth, justice and love. And we must pledge ourselves to fight even harder against such brutality."

"But it hurts so much," Gabby said in a little girl voice.

"I know, dear, I know."

Further deflating the Resistance in Germany carefully nurtured by the Sisterhood was a failed bomb plot against Hitler in mid-March.

Gabby's aunt had concealed a pressure-activated bomb within a small figurine by the famed sculptor Auguste Rodin, which had been purchased for Hitler. A Major General Henning von Tresckow managed to slip the statue aboard the *Führer*'s personal aircraft during a flight from Smolensk on the Eastern Front to his headquarters at Rastenberg, East Prussia. But, being sealed inside the artwork, the pressure activator failed and the bomb did not explode.

Despite these setbacks, the Sisterhood grew stronger as the year progressed and information gained through its activities was passed along to Allied Intelligence officers by Giselle, who maintained close connections to all participants.

Michel and his restored British contacts provided one conduit. This was augmented by Giselle's personal friendships in English and American high society. As Velva Violet, Giselle had developed deep and solid ties to Allied security officers. She sporadically received information about her relatives in Russia and she received regular information concerning the Italian war effort through Aunt Fran.

Nurses and some sympathetic doctors also proved a valuable source of information. Nurses, for the most part, were well disposed toward the humanitarian goals of the Sisterhood and produced prodigious amounts of information from wounded soldiers sent back from the front lines for convalescence. Such men were always ready to share their tales of battlefield glory or misery with an attentive nurse.

Daily, various Sisterhood agents came and went from *La Coupole* acting as messengers and couriers. Occasionally one was captured but so far, no one had traced Velva Violet's activities back to Giselle.

Despite her activity, Giselle's mind was never far from thoughts of Rennes-le-Château and its unbelievable secrets. She was becoming quite impatient over the matter when Marie's telegram carrying the words "Blue Apples" arrived on Thursday morning, July 15, 1943. She immediately prepared to take action.

Michel was fully engaged with the French Resistance in addition to his Sisterhood activities but he nevertheless made arrangements to drive Giselle south. He was excited and slightly incredulous after hearing the remarkable story brought back from her first visit. Charles and Gabby also volunteered to go, since it was summer and there was no pressing business at the Sorbonne. They too were eager to learn more about the amazing Star Portal.

Giselle was eager to confront Peter. She knew she had the advantage as she assumed he again would be alone, at least until he had located the treasure. That was an eventuality she hoped to prevent.

The group was in high spirits as Michel wheeled the big Nash toward Orleans. They were all glad to leave the summer heat in Paris behind. Michel stopped occasionally to shake the firebox within the generator that produced the wood gas fuel.

"This road is too good," he grumbled. "That firebox needs a few good jolts now and again."

In Toulouse, they encountered a German checkpoint, but passed without incident. Charles had his university credentials and it was explained that Gabby was a student traveling with her teacher along with her guardian and driver. The phony documents provided to Giselle and Michel by the Resistance passed inspection while Charles and Gabby used their own. Unbeknownst to all but Giselle, Jean Paul was following them at a discrete distance. It was a small measure of additional security.

It was in this historical city that Charles made contact with Bernard Fauseau, his university associate and leader of the local Cathars.

Over dinner at a small bistro, it was decided to drive only as far as Couiza. "There are Germans all over the area, most near Montségur. But a considerable number of Germans are digging in the Rennes-le-Château area," Bernard warned. "Some of the roads are blocked and they are checking identity papers very carefully. As I have a summer class, I'm afraid you will have to make your own way to *Mademoiselle* Marie. But I am leaving you the telephone number at the university should you need to contact me."

"May I speak to you outside," Bernard whispered to Giselle as the waiter took their orders. Somewhat surprised at his mysterious manner, she quietly excused herself and followed him to a small deserted patio.

"Why all the intrigue, Bernard," she asked as she lit a cigarette.

Slipping a piece of paper into her hand, Bernard glanced around and explained, "Here is a detailed map of the new route to the cavern containing the treasure and the Star Portal."

"The Cathedral?"

"*Oui*, I want to you to have this, but only you," he said. Glancing back at the table where their friends sat, he added, "Now, except for a select few of my people, you and I are the only ones to know its location. It must stay this way. This secret is too important. If Charles or your friends should be taken by the Germans..."

Giselle interrupted him by placing her hand to his mouth. "I quite understand, *mon ami*," she whispered. "I will commit this to memory and destroy it."

With a warm smile, she added, "You have been most helpful, as always. We shall leave for Rennes-le-Château in the morning. It will be best if we don't call attention to ourselves. When we arrive, I think we'll just slip in the back door."

Seeing Bernard's puzzled look, she explained, "We shall enter through the opening in the ruins at the base of the hill and climb the circular stairwell to the church."

Bernard smiled back and replied, "Ah, but of course. Shall we join the others?"

Moments later, when a delicious dinner of roast duck arrived, Bernard said, "Let us bow our heads and ask the Lord to bless and protect all of us."

Unconcerned about what the other customers in the bistro might think, the group honored Bernard's convictions by bowing their heads in prayer. Giselle and Michel exchanged a glance of appreciation as Bernard began his prayer. They both knew they would need all the help they could get as they drew nearer the elusive Peter.

Bernard's warning of German movement in the area proved prophetic. The small group encountered a German patrol as they made their way on foot to Rennes-le-Château the next afternoon.

Dressed in hiking gear and carrying knapsacks, Giselle, Michel, Gabby and Charles had made good time during the trek from Couiza, stopping only for short breaks and a light lunch of fresh bread, Pyrenees mountain cheese and red wine.

Gabby was the first to notice the patrol. "I think I see someone moving on top of the hill ahead," she whispered. Everyone scattered. It was easy to find hiding places among the rock-strewn hillside and they lay undetected as the four-man patrol passed well to their right. They could smell their acrid cigarette smoke and hear their guttural laughter. The clinking of their canteens and mess kits echoed over the hillside as they trod along a narrow cow path.

"Regular troops," whispered Michel to Giselle. He was clutching his 8-mm *Model d'Ordonnance* revolver in his right hand. "This may be a larger expedition than we counted on." He motioned for everyone to remain still long after the soldiers had gone in case they had thought to mount a rear guard. But no one else materialized and the group moved on.

They considered hiking to *Les Labadous* and resting for the night, but the owners had been so warm and kind on their last visit, no one wanted to place them at risk. So it was decided to trek straight on to the *Villa Bethania*.

The dim light from a half moon worked in their favor, as the small band laboriously climbed the rocky hillside atop which sat Rennes-le-Château.

In the gathering dusk, they entered the low ruins and found the opening to the tunnel system. After climbing the stairway into the chapel, they used a key given to them by Marie Denarnaud and made their way to her rear door. The only sounds to be heard were a dog barking in the distance and some chickens preparing to roost.

Giselle rapped quietly on the weathered wood door and soon heard a faint voice call, "Who is it that disturbs an old woman's quietude?"

"Blue apples," whispered Giselle loudly and the door was flung open. A small figure darted from the door and Giselle found herself being hugged tightly by Marie. The elderly woman's strength was surprising.

"Ah, *mes amis*, I was hoping it was you. The last several days have been a nightmare. I never knew what to expect," Marie said with obvious relief to see her northern friends.

"We are all glad to see you again too, Marie. Are you all right? Shouldn't we all get inside quickly?" Giselle looked around alertly. Michel had his hand in his jacket pocket, the one where he concealed his service revolver.

Marie only laughed. "Oh, do not concern yourself. The *Boche* left several days ago and I don't expect them back for awhile."

"They are gone?" Michel was surprised. All day, his nerves and instincts had been on full alert. Giselle and Gabby looked quizzically at each other.

"No, no, young man, they have not gone for good. They are now centering their search around Montségur," Marie explained. "In fact, I understand they are bivouacked near the ruins."

"They have found nothing?" asked Giselle.

"*Non*, just some old religious relics, nothing to mention..." The woman stopped talking suddenly and stood staring at Michel with suspicion.

"*Pardonnez moi*, dear Marie, This is Michel. Remember? I told you about him during our last visit. He drives me..." said Giselle.

"Yes, my dear, I recall you said Michel drove you to distraction," interrupted Marie. She broke into a broad smile and hugged Michel, winking at Giselle behind his back. Gabby giggled while Charles tried to suppress a laugh, recalling how Giselle had mentioned Michel's sensitivity at having to play her chauffeur.

Michel pulled himself away from the elderly woman and looked at Giselle with a perplexed expression.

Laughing, Giselle said, "You little tease. I said he drove me as a cover for his Resistance activities."

They were all laughing as Marie ushered them inside.

Once they were all gathered in the sitting room with cups of hot mint tea, Marie told of the events of the past week.

"That man Peter was accompanied by a civilian academic. They arrived here on the 28th. This time he wore his true colors, a black SS uniform with silver piping and *swastika* armband.

"He was cordial enough and explained that he was with a team of scientists searching for historical relics in the area. They consisted of historians, geologists and archeologists, all in the employ of the *Ahnenerbe-SS*. I knew full well their true goal but did not question his superficial explanation.

"After some pleasantries, the others left to find accommodations for the night. He remained behind and soon was pressing me for my knowledge of nearby caves and grottoes.

"I knew he needed my knowledge, so I feigned illness and asked him to come back the next week. I was hoping for time to contact you," she told the gathering in her sitting room. "He was most insistent but finally yielded and left. I did not dare leave the house for the entire week as I was certain I was being watched. It was difficult to find someone to help me but I was able to have a friend send the telegram from Couiza the day before Bastille Day. I apologize for being so tardy."

"Do not fret yourself, dear Marie," said Giselle in a soothing tone. "You have done well. We are here now." She stood to her feet and said, "So, where to begin? Where is Peter now?"

"I really don't know. He hasn't come back here since last Friday. I suspect he has joined the diggers at Montségur. That seems to be where the work is being concentrated although they have search parties scattered across the countryside. I fear they may be getting closer than we would like."

"Do you think they have found the treasure?" asked Giselle. She was becoming anxious. The German expedition was larger than expected and they might have learned of the cavern system. Peter was not in Rennes-le-Château. Nothing seemed to be working the way she had planned.

"I don't think so," replied Marie. "Bernard and his men did their work well. I could not trust the wires or the mail with the details. But they did exactly as you advised. Using explosives and with much digging, they blocked the main tunnel to the Cathedral under tons of earth leaving only a smaller passageway. I do not know the precise directions myself."

She laughed and added, "They opened several new passages that lead nowhere. With any luck, the *Boche* will wander around in those caverns for months without finding anything."

"But we can't be certain of that," argued Michel. "I think we should keep an eye on them in case they somehow discover the treasure. Can you imagine the harm should such wealth fall into the hands of the Nazis? Not to mention the loss to history."

"I agree, let's go find them," added Gabby. Her eyes reflected a fierce eagerness for action. Even Charles was nodding his assent.

Michel looked at Giselle and said quietly, "I must agree, *ma chère*. I don't like the idea of just sitting here when the *Boche* are so close to the treasure. Perhaps we should keep a close eye on them in case we need to call for reinforcements from the Resistance. I have already alerted a unit in Toulouse to be standing by."

Giselle arched an eyebrow at him. With a loving smile, he added, "You didn't expect me to allow you to take on Peter and the Third Reich by yourself, did you?"

Giselle sighed, wondering what he would think if he knew she had had Jean Paul follow them without telling him. She also knew he was right. They would need help. And she knew it would be difficult to keep her impetuous but well-meaning friends out of action. "Very well," she said. "Let's get a good night's sleep and you can get a fresh start in the morning. I will stay here with Marie in case Peter returns. I need the time to think. The treasure may be safe for a time but I must figure out a way to retrieve the crystal skull."

The next morning, after drinking the very strong coffee that Marie had been hoarding for some time and despite Giselle's qualms, Michel, Charles and Gabby set out on foot to observe the German expedition.

Giselle watched them go with trepidation. She did not like the idea of their moving across the Languedoc with the German patrols so active. Another part of her mind was concerned as to what she would do should Peter show up at the *Villa Bethania*.

Although the July sun was hot, the trio made good time, clambering over the rugged hills west of Rennes-le-Château until reaching some stone ruins shortly after noon. Michel checked their map and determined that they had covered a distance of more than 15 kilometers.

"Are these ruins Roman?" asked Gabby collapsing onto her back. She was panting and somewhat winded despite her young age and excellent condition.

Michel merely shrugged. "Some say they are Roman but others say they were left from the time of the Visigoths," explained Charles, breathing heavily from the long hike. "Still others claim some of these ruins pre-date modern history."

"The map makes no distinction," muttered Michel, who also was trying to catch his second wind and pouring over a Michelin map of the area.

As they rested and ate a lunch thoughtfully provided by Marie, Gabby decided Michel might have begun to have second thoughts about their mission. Charles was showing his age, sweating profusely, his chest heaving with exertion. Even Gabby had grown quiet with weariness. She noticed Michel looking at them with concern.

"A few more minutes and we must press on," he said without enthusiasm. Gabby and Charles both groaned at the thought of continuing. "Marie marked some ruins here," he added, pointing to the map. No one seemed to care enough to look. "It is *Castel d'Amont.* Somewhere just south of these ruins there is supposed to be a lookout point where we might get a view of Montségur."

"Can't we just remain here for awhile?" asked Gabby, who had found a shady spot beneath a bushy broom shrub.

"*Certainement, ma petite chou!*" replied Michel rising to his feet and pulling on his knapsack. "Stay here if you like, but for me, I don't want to spend the night on the open ground."

Gabby looked about at the open fields and considered the idea of sleeping on the ground and in the open. There was not much deliberation. She soon was on her feet and slipping the straps of her backpack over her shoulders.

The sun was quite low as the trio approached the ruined castle, which lay on a craggy hillside just southeast of the small hamlet of Belesta.

Michel unpacked his binoculars and scanned the area but saw nothing unusual. He could just barely make out the irregular outline of the ruined battlements at Montségur. The sun lay behind the ruins, causing a glare that prevented him from obtaining a good view.

"Let me have a look," said Gabby. "Perhaps younger eyes may see something you missed." She grinned at the disgusted look on Michel's face. Charles just shook his head at her cheek and sank wearily to the ground.

Gabby scanned the western horizon for some time before blurting, "Look! I think I see a truck moving near Montségur. I think we should get closer…"

"I think you should all stand up and place your hands on your heads." The gruff voice came from behind them. As one, the trio turned in shock to see two uniformed men standing with rifles leveled at them.

"What are you three doing here?" one of the men demanded. Gabby was momentarily relieved to see the pair wore police uniforms. Her relief was short-lived, however, when she saw their German canteens and gas mask canisters. She knew they must be part of a French militia force, undoubtedly working in concert with the Germans.

Charles calmly stepped toward the men. "I am Professor Charles Richer. I teach at the University of Toulouse. My companions and I are merely on an archeological outing," he explained.

"*Arrêtez!*" cried one, racking the bolt of his World War I vintage *Lebel* rifle. Charles stopped. "This area is off limits by order of the authorities," the man continued.

"What authorities?" asked Michel with a sneer. "You wear the uniform of the French police but you answer to those German dogs."

"You insolent whelp!" the man snarled, swiftly bringing his rifle around for a butt stroke to Michel's head. Gabby screamed, distracting his companion's attention.

Michel, expecting the move after his provocation, ducked under the swinging rifle and drove his right fist hard into the man's midsection. With a loud grunt the man sank to his knees, his eyes and mouth wide open as he tried desperately to draw in air. His rifle dropped to the ground beside him.

Gabby reached into her pack for the small *Walther PP* pistol she had been carrying for the past year. She was proud that Giselle had presented it to her as a sign of her trust and confidence. But she was not quick enough for the second policeman.

He quickly swung toward her and pointed his rifle squarely at her head. Gabby was both terrified and infuriated. Indecision was written on her face as she tried to decide if she had a chance of gaining the pistol.

"Don't, Gabby!" cried Michel. He looked from his two companions to the militiaman who was still on the ground gasping for air and back to the man holding the rifle on Gabby and Charles. Making his own decision in an instant, Michel leaped over some large boulders and ran helter-skelter down the steep hillside disappearing into a copse of trees.

The standing militiaman hesitated, undecided whether to chase after Michel or keep his captives secure. Realizing he could only fire at Michel by turning from his captives, the man decided to err on the side of caution. With an angry glance back at the vanishing Michel, he stood still, motioning both Gabby and Charles to their feet with the muzzle of his rifle as his gasping companion struggled to his feet cursing loudly.

After being relieved of their personal effects, Gabby and Charles were marched toward Montségur, all the while enduring curses and an occasional punch from the acrimonious militiamen.

Upon reaching a narrow dirt roadway, one of their captors fired his rifle into the air and before long an Opel *Blitz* military truck ground its way up the dirt track to their position. Gabby could not help but note the irony. Giselle had specifically mentioned the Opel trucks manufactured by the General Motors plant in Brandenburg as a clear example of certain powerful American companies that had continued their business operations in support of the Axis even after the United States entered the war.

The prisoners were loaded in the back accompanied by one of the men who had captured them and a soldier in the uniform of the *Waffen-SS*, the military arm of the Black Order. The trooper obviously was well trained. He held a very deadly looking MP-40 machine pistol on the captives the entire trip and his eyes never left them.

Charles seemed resigned to his fate. The long hike had taken much of his physical stamina. Gabby, on the other hand, kept glancing around, her mind racing to devise some plan of escape.

But nothing presented itself and soon they reached a small village at the base of a tall and craggy peak. At the top could be seen the lengthy stone parapets of Montségur. One of the few brick houses in the village flew a *swastika* and Gabby correctly guessed this was where they were to be taken.

As she and Charles were brought through the front door of what apparently had once been someone's fine home, Gabby saw it was filled with activity. Several typists, both male and female, and a radio operator sitting at a large console, provided a background clamor of clatter and conversation. She noticed a slender, blue-eyed SS officer striding toward her with an unpleasant look on his face. There was something about the man that drew her attention and chilled her. She was visibly relieved when the man passed her by and exited the front door.

Gabby and Charles sat for a long time on a window seat in a ground-floor room. It was bare except for a steely-eyed *Waffen-SS* man sitting in the room's only chair, his machine gun laying across his lap with the barrel pointed in their general direction. His attention never wavered.

Finally, the door was flung open and a senior non-commissioned officer stepped inside and ordered everyone to follow him.

A large room in the rear of the building had been converted into an office. There was a massive ornate wood desk sitting in front of a large bay window with an excellent overview to the west of the mountain known as *Fourcat*. The desk was flanked by Nazi flags in freestanding bases.

Sitting in an over-stuffed leather high-backed swivel chair was a large, almost obese, man in the field gray uniform of the German *Wehrmacht*.

Gabby somewhat dispassionately saw that the man was a colonel, judging from his silver braided shoulder boards. She also saw that the man carried a chest full of various medals, none for combat. She decided the man obviously was a rear-echelon paper shuffler. True to character, he was pouring through a sheaf of documents as though no one had entered the room.

To one side, sitting in an opulent French provincial chair was a much smaller man, dressed nattily in the gray uniform of the SS. He appeared to be eyeing the captives with a combination of interest and amusement. Gabby took this to be a good sign. Perhaps they had nothing on which to hold them except being in an unauthorized area. Her hope faded as she saw both the *Feldwebel* who had escorted them in and the *Waffen-SS* guard both take up positions along each wall.

After long moments of silence, the SS officer put a hand to his mouth and cleared his throat. As if it were a signal, the big man sitting at the desk put the papers down, finally looked at Gabby and Charles and said, "Well, well, what have we here?"

He got to his feet and struck a pose near one corner of the huge desk. "I am *Oberst* Konrad Fleischmann, the military governor of this department. And you are...?"

Charles stood up and seemed to come to attention. Gabby decided old habits die hard, but rose to her feet also. If they were not being charged with anything serious, it might be best to be cooperative and try to talk their way out.

"Col. Fleischmann, I am Professor Charles Richer of the Sorbonne and this is one of my students, Gabriella Duprey. Sir, if I may ask…"

"No, you may not!" snapped the colonel squinting at Charles through small piggish eyes. "You will speak when asked to. Now, what were you doing in an unauthorized area?"

With a conciliatory look, Charles began, "Well, you see, *Herr Oberst*, we came to this place to search for historical artifacts. I am preparing an academic paper for the university at Toulouse and I…"

"But you said you were from the Sorbonne," the colonel interrupted.

"I am from the Sorbonne. I have a guest professorship arrangement in Toulouse and I was merely…"

"Enough lies, you swine!" shouted the colonel, moving to a position directly in front of Charles. He looked as though he was about to strike him. "What do you know of treasure buried in this area?"

Gabby was stunned by such a direct question. She saw that Charles was trying desperately to remain impassive, but his lips were twitching. Gabby's brain was awhirl. How could this pig of a German officer in far southern France possibly know anything about the treasure?

She tried to remain unmoved by the colonel's question but her eyes were wide and round. Beads of perspiration were forming along her forehead.

As calmly as he could manage, Charles cleared his throat and stated, "I am sorry, *Herr Oberst*, but I don't know what you are talking about."

The colonel looked at Gabby, who had reined in her emotions and managed a blank expression.

Chagrined by not obtaining the response he had hoped for with his surprise question, the colonel turned and strutted in front of the desk before stopping by the gray-clad *SS* man in the chair.

"Allow me to introduce *SS Obersturmführer* Klaus Barbie, chief of the Fourth Section of the *Geheime Staatspolizei*," said the colonel perfunctorily. Gabby gasped. This man was no ordinary policeman. He represented the *Gestapo*, the secret state police. In fact, his name and brutality were already well known to the Sisterhood.

"He is visiting from Lyon and wanted to meet you. You should feel quite honored," said the colonel with a slight wave indicating the man in the chair.

The small dark man had eyes alive with intelligence but little else. He got to his feet and surveyed Gabby and Charles coldly. Gabby felt a chill. Barbie seemed to show a special interest in her.

Barbie leaned forward until his nose was inches from Charles, who continued to show no response.

Turning on his heel, the SS officer took two steps, turned and barked, "Where is Jean Moulin?"

"Who, sir?" asked Charles in a quiet voice. Gabby merely blinked hard.

"I thought as much," muttered the man. He stood quietly for a moment before he decided to ask a straightforward question.

"A car registered to a French widow, one *Madame* Giselle St. Clair, a prominent name if I'm not mistaken, passed through a checkpoint in this area recently." He pointed a finger in Charles' face. "Do you know this woman?"

"I have met her on occasion," replied Charles calmly.

Barbie's expression grew shrewd. "At *La Coupole* restaurant perhaps?"

"Perhaps," acknowledged Charles. "I eat there frequently. It is close to the university."

With a show of disgust, he turned to Fleischmann and said, "Colonel, take this man away." The *Oberst* waved his hand and the two soldiers grabbed Charles by each arm and led him through the doorway.

When the colonel turned to take Gabby, Barbie blocked the move with his hand. "Leave the girl with me," he said, his eyes glittering with a savage intensity.

Gabby's frightened eyes looked deep into those of Barbie. She shivered involuntarily. She saw they were the eyes of a man who welcomed a chance to combine business with his own twisted pleasure.

The big colonel gulped. "Very well, Klaus. I will excuse myself," he said and turned to leave with obvious relief.

CHAPTER 18

Rennes-le-Château
Summer, 1943

PETER FREIHERR VON MANTEUFFEL WAS in a foul mood as he stalked from *Oberst* Fleischmann's field headquarters at the base of Montségur, brushing past two civilians apparently being brought in for questioning.

He glanced at the tall, silver-haired man and the young girl being pushed along by a *Waffen-SS* trooper but decided they held no importance for him.

What was important was to find the treasure. Peter cursed inwardly as he climbed into the rear seat of the small *Kubelwagen* that had been assigned to him as director of the expedition. He and a large team of specialists had been in the Languedoc for almost a month now with nothing to show for their efforts but a few relics and artifacts, all of little worth.

Where could it be? He puzzled over the problem as his driver steered them along the narrow and winding mountain road. The four-cylinder, air-cooled Volkswagen engine whined loudly at the exertion.

His gloom was all the deeper due to the high expectations he had brought to this expedition. His elation at being summoned back to Germany from Antarctica was heightened when he learned that he was to lead a team of scientists to search for the greatest treasure trove in history. Armed with the information he had obtained from Otto Rahn in

Dachau plus his research while marooned at the South Pole, Peter had felt absolute confidence that he would uncover the treasure in short order once the expedition reached the Languedoc.

Instead, here he was almost a month later, utterly confounded in his attempt to retrieve the treasure. His failure was especially hurtful now that he had decided to try to take the fortune for himself if possible.

Things had gone well at first. The rather substantial number of scientists and academics gathered by the *Ahnenerbe-SS* had established a base camp close to Montségur and had made multiple searches, spreading out in a circular pattern as he had directed. They had searched caves and grottoes in the area, even finding some small tunnel systems.

Although some ancient Roman, Gothic and even Templar artifacts had been discovered in ruin sites and caverns, there was no indication of the great treasure.

If he couldn't produce it soon, his usefulness could be at an end and Peter did not want to think about that eventuality. A trip back to Antarctica or to the Eastern Front might be the best of alternatives.

Peter had visited the Denarnaud woman when he first arrived and made yet another effort to pry knowledge from her. While she was pleasant and cooperative enough as before, he had gained little to point him to the exact hiding place.

He could not be certain, but Peter nursed a deep suspicion that the elderly woman was not telling all that she knew. But he had been careful, as she was his only lead to the treasure.

Glancing at the last rays of the setting sun, Peter debated with himself. Should he return to his quarters or should he make one last effort to coax the treasure's location from Marie Denarnaud?

"Driver, take me to Rennes-le-Château," he ordered. His mind was made up. His patience was at an end. He would visit the Denarnaud woman and this time, he would learn all she knew. "No more coaxing," he thought. "It's time for coercion if necessary."

While Peter still harbored a genuine distaste for physical violence, he nevertheless had always adhered to the Nazi philosophy that "the end justifies the means." And if he didn't produce the promised treasure soon, Himmler would be sorely disappointed. This could mean his life would be at an end, figuratively and perhaps literally.

The sun was low by the time the Kubelwagen pulled to a stop in front of *Villa Bethania.* "Wait here for me," he instructed the driver, a large blond man with the round, weathered face of a farmer. The man, obviously untroubled by any serious thought, pulled a blue box of *Gitanes* cigarettes from his tunic pocket and settled back in his bucket seat.

Peter straightened his black uniform as he walked to the front door and rapped sharply.

The heavy carved wood door opened a crack through which Peter could see the small, bright eyes of Marie Denarnaud. "Oh, it is you," said the woman with just enough politeness to keep the greeting from being called surly.

"I am most sorry to intrude at this hour, *Madame* Denarnaud," replied Peter, bowing slightly from the waist, "but it is necessary that we speak. May I come in?"

The door opened wider and Marie extended her arm in invitation. Peter stepped into the home, grateful to be out of the July heat.

"Won't you sit down?" offered Marie as she took a seat in a large high-backed chair with padded arms.

"No, I will stand." he replied stiffly. Peter noticed that the woman glanced anxiously toward the kitchen.

"Have I disturbed your supper?" He asked with no real concern.

"Oh, no," responded Marie quickly with a look of guilt as through she had been caught at something.

Peter looked around the room. Now that he had gained entrance and was alone with the old woman, Peter felt secure in pressing his demand. "I am afraid the time for politeness has passed, dear lady. We have come up empty-handed again. You must give me precise directions to the cavern known as the Cathedral. And I want them now."

"But I already told you that I don't know the precise location," pleaded Marie.

"And I am telling you that I don't believe you," snapped Peter harshly. "You will give me the exact location and you will do it now."

Marie looked at him with a slightly amused expression masking her fear. "And if I don't?"

"Then, my dear, you will have bought yourself a one-way ticket to a concentration camp," Peter replied quietly but in a hard and unrelenting tone.

Marie sat quietly, contemplating this threat. Once more, she glanced toward the home's kitchen as if in expectation.

Peter glanced through the kitchen door but saw no one. His frustration and anger pushed beyond his normal limits, he walked to a position in front of the elderly woman. Peering closely into her lined face, he said with deadly earnest, "You will tell me, old woman, or I will be forced to take the harshest of methods." He extended a clenched fist toward her face.

"I think not." The full-throated feminine voice came from behind him, in the direction of the kitchen door. Whirling, Peter saw a slender blonde woman standing in the doorway, her face masked by shadow.

Straightening, Peter turned and said in his most commanding voice, "*Madame*, I have no idea who you are but I am an officer of the SS. If you have any concern for your personal safety and well-being, then I suggest that you leave this place immediately and do not speak of anything that has transpired here." To accentuate his remark, Peter placed both hands on his waist, imitating the authoritarian stance of his SS superiors.

"And I suggest that you take a seat on that couch and make no sudden movement or it will be your last," replied the woman as she stepped into the room. It was only then that Peter saw the Luger pistol she held pointed at his chest. His eyes widened in alarm. Since joining the Death's Head Order, Peter had experienced only fear and awe from the population. Although he well knew that a war was taking place throughout the world, he was unprepared for someone to use violence against him.

Shocked, he stumbled backwards almost tripping over an embroidered footstool. Peter regained his balance and stared at his captor's face as it moved into the dim light of the one electric lamp.

Shock piled upon shock as recognition dawned in Peter's eyes. "Giselle! *Mein Gott*! *Eines Gespenst*! You're a ghost. This cannot be." The color drained from his face and his knees sagged. He threw an arm up as though to ward off some terrible apparition. He appeared about to pass out.

Giselle looked at him with cruel delight. Quietly, she said, "Sit down, Peter, before you fall down."

Numbly, Peter stumbled to the divan and sank down on it. He sat staring at the woman before him. After long moments of silence, he shook his head as if to wake himself from a bad dream and muttered, "Giselle, is it really you?"

Giselle was enjoying the moment immensely. "What's the matter, Peter? Have you been laboring under the mistaken belief that I died in that Mayan pyramid? Did you think you could be rid of me so easily? You see, I even still have the pistol you gave me back in the jungle."

Peter stared dully at the weapon. "Giselle, I..." Peter left the sentence unfinished. He had started to offer some explanation or exhibit bravado, but he knew it was useless. There was no explanation for what had happened except that which both he and Giselle understood. He had wanted the skull and had taken the steps he felt necessary to obtain it, including the death of his wife and friends.

Marie sat stunned and frightened throughout the confrontation between Giselle and Peter. Now, through trembling lips, she asked in a dry and hoarse voice, "Is this the man who killed your friend and left you for dead?"

"The very one," replied Giselle coldly, advancing toward Peter. He shrank back on the couch. Sweat was beading on his forehead. It was not due to the warm summer evening. Fixing Peter with her gaze, Giselle said evenly, "Peter, there is only one thing that can save you."

Her statement hung in the air like a still, chill fog. Peter's eyes, which had been full of fear, grew shrewd. "And what would that be?"

"I want the skull." Giselle's voice was even and calm but there was no mistaking the iron will and determination behind her demand.

Peter sat still for a long moment then suddenly burst into laughter. "You want the skull? You must be insane. I don't even have the skull. You would not believe who now possesses the skull."

"Oh, I believe it," replied Giselle, "because I know that little Austrian paperhanger has it and I also know it is responsible for the chaos in the world today. I want it back and you're the only person who can get it for me."

Peter's laughter only increased. "Giselle, you little fool. You have never had a tight grip on reality in all the time I've known you. But you are really adrift now.

"How do you expect me to get the skull from Adolf Hitler, the current master of Europe and soon the entire world? I couldn't get the skull from him, even if I wanted to."

Peter's mocking laughter rose in pitch, bringing the anger that had been within Giselle for three long years to boiling point. "Shut up!" she screamed, stepping toward him and pointing the pistol at his head.

The move was a mistake on her part as Peter, though caught in a swirl of emotions, had quickly recovered from the initial numbing shock of seeing Giselle alive in front of him and had been seeking just such an opportunity.

In a sudden blur of motion from his seated position on the divan he lashed out with a high-topped riding boot and deftly kicked Giselle's gun hand. The Luger flew across the room, landing with a loud clatter on the hard wood floor near one corner. Marie screamed at the sudden violence in her sitting room and cowered in her chair.

Giselle cursed herself inwardly for being so foolish as to get that close to a man she knew was fully capable of taking her life without compunction. She steeled herself to strike him hard as he rose from the divan.

But again the crafty Peter was ahead of her. Instead of rising straight up from the couch, the lanky SS officer ducked under her set fists and launched himself like a pile driver into her midsection. Peter clung tight, his arms locked around her waist, pushing her across a coffee table. As though struck by a battering ram, Giselle was driven backwards over the low table and into a tall floor lamp, which fell with a clash.

Both combatants crashed heavily onto the polished wood floor, Peter's right shoulder driving the air from her lungs with a wheezy cough.

Outside, Peter's driver looked up from the issue of *Signal* he was reading and cocked his head. When he heard nothing further, he shrugged and resumed his perusal of the picture magazine.

Giselle tried desperately to regain her breath and make a move on her attacker. But Peter was not winded like her and he was stronger. Before she could resist, he was straddling her with his booted legs, his hands on her throat.

She could feel the strength of his fingers as they pressed down on her windpipe. She thrashed wildly in an effort to throw him off but he was too heavy and too strong. The fingers tightened their grip and Giselle could feel the edges of her vision beginning to blur as blood and oxygen were cut off from her brain.

In desperation, she looked toward Marie, but the elderly woman was curled up in her chair, her eyes wide with horror and her face paralyzed by fear. The world began spinning and growing dim.

Giselle grasped Peter's arms but there was no strength left in her hands. The darkness in her head was growing deeper and deeper. Giselle simultaneously feared and greeted a growing calmness within her. She knew that unconsciousness followed by death would soon be upon her.

As she was about to give herself up to the warm and engulfing darkness, she dimly felt the pressure on her neck release. Quickly, oxygen was reaching her starved brain cells and her vision returned, though initially blurry and indistinct.

She vaguely saw a mass of movement before her accompanied by a babble of indistinct sounds. Propping herself up on one arm, she tried to make sense of the scene in front of her.

Marie, immobilized by fear, was still cowering in her chair. On the floor in front of her, Giselle saw the moving shape was two men locked in mortal combat.

One was Michel and the other Peter. They were struggling over Michel's service revolver. Michel had entered the house to find Peter on Giselle and in his rush to pull Peter off her had left himself open to attack.

Both men now were struggling for the weapon. Michel had the revolver in his right hand, while Peter had a strong grip on his wrist. The hand with the pistol flailed wildly in the air and neither man seemed able to secure a useful grip on the weapon.

Giselle, realizing it would be dangerous to join the struggle on floor, crawled to her feet and, despite her grogginess, picked up the floor lamp. Stepping to the combatants, she brought the tall iron lamp over her head and struck downward, landing a heavy blow across Peter's upper back.

With a loud grunt, Peter collapsed and went limp. Michel quickly rolled from under him and jumped to his feet, the revolver triumphantly clutched in his hand.

Giselle stood gasping and rubbing her throat. As Michel pulled the groaning Peter up into a sitting position in front of the divan, he spoke rapidly in his excitement and exertion.

"Gabby and Charles have been captured," he stammered. "I managed to escape and made my way back as fast as I could." Yanking the semi-conscious Peter into a more upright position, he added, "It seems I arrived just in time."

"But how did you get here without being seen?" Giselle was still groggy.

"I came in…" he glanced from the reviving Peter back to her, "… the back way."

Giselle realized he had crept to the villa from the church after using the secret staircase under the altar.

Peter shook his head to clear it and glared at Giselle, who was looking at him without seeing him. She was still slightly numb with shock and pain. She was also angry with herself for allowing her companions to strike out across the countryside without her.

She realized that there was nothing she could do for them at the moment. Perhaps later she could arrange a rescue attempt aided by local Resistance members. For the moment, she must concentrate on Peter. The return of the skull in the interest of world peace superseded any personal considerations

Peter was now fully conscious. "You realize that I have a man just outside," he said through teeth clenched in hatred. "All I have to do is call out and it's over for you. Even if you stop him, the alarm will go out and you will never have rest until you are caught."

"You realize that all I have to do is say the word and my friend here will put a bullet right between your eyes. Then we'll take care of your man," responded Giselle as matter-of-factly as she could muster. "But, if I kill you, you'll never get to hear my proposition."

Peter looked genuinely puzzled. Glancing from Giselle to Michel, he said with some hesitancy, "What can you possibly propose that would mean anything to me?"

"Well, I could tell you where the treasure is located."

Peter sat bolt upright. His body tensed. His eyes narrowed. "You know about the treasure?"

"Yes, and I even know where the gold and jewels are hidden," said Giselle with a cryptic smile.

Now Peter was confused. "Are you talking about the Treasure of King Solomon?" he asked sharply.

"No, I'm talking about a treasure worth far more than that."

Peter looked at her, his eyes full of suspicion but also curiosity. He knew Giselle well enough to know that she did not talk of treasure lightly. He respected her background and competency enough to pay close attention to her words.

"What are you talking about?" he asked. He was more confused. He was still full of apprehension and suspicion, still not fully accepting that his old nemesis was alive and in control of him at the moment. The fact that Giselle would make him any kind of offer intrigued him.

Giselle knelt beside her captive and looked him in the eye while Michel stood to one side, out of reach, holding his aimed pistol at arm's length. Peter had no choice but to listen intently.

"There is a great secret in this place and it is more important than any amount of gold and silver," she said quietly.

"Pshaw!" Peter rolled his eyes. What possibly could be more important than the greatest cache of gold in the history of the world?

"Listen to me, Peter," she continued, shaking his shoulder. "There is an ancient temple in this place. You have walked across it many times now without realizing it. You cannot see it for what it is."

"And what is it?" Peter asked sarcastically.

"It is a Star Portal, a gateway to other worlds, other realms, other dimensions. Peter, why should you settle for the riches of this world when you could have the riches of all the worlds?"

Peter stared at her as though the intelligent and educated women he had known so well had gone stark, raving mad.

"I'm serious, Peter, this is the most amazing thing you could ever conceive of and it's right here beneath your feet."

"You have seen this portal?" Peter's curiosity was beginning to overcome his incredulity.

"Yes, I have." Giselle hoped the lie was not evident on her face. "And furthermore, I know how to activate it, but it requires the Skull of Fate."

Peter looked at her for a long period, trying to gauge her intent and seriousness. He finally muttered, "I have heard talk among some of the ranking *Ahnenerbe-SS* concerning matters which sounded out of this world. Expeditions to far-flung places have returned with strange and esoteric objects, similar to the skull.

"I even heard that we have recovered strange circular aircraft capable of attaining unbelievable speeds and distances. I was told they did not originate on this world. But I always thought this was just idle gossip or propaganda designed to throw our enemies into confusion."

He looked at Giselle. She could see his mind racing. She hoped her account of the Star Portal might make sense in light of his knowledge of esoteric matters.

Looking at her, Peter spoke through clenched teeth, "Why didn't you just kill me when you had the chance? I know I would kill you, if I had the chance."

"We need the crystal skull to open the portal and you are the only one who has a chance of getting it." She looked unblinkingly into his questioning eyes, eyes that now were filling with suspicion.

"So, this is your ploy. You are trying to regain the skull. Well, it will never work. The skull has proven most useful to the *Reich*."

In a voice husky with emotion, she added with an intense sincerity, "This is big, Peter. This is much bigger than the treasure, bigger than our personal enmity, even bigger than your *Reich*."

Knowing full well the extent of Peter's ego and greed, Giselle decided to play on his weaknesses.

"Think of it, Peter. You alone would have the means to traverse space, time and other realms. You could travel among the stars, look into the future and expand your consciousness farther than any living man. You could acquire the knowledge of the universe. You could become like a god. It could be all yours, Peter."

Peter was staring into space, his dreams of personal wealth and power rekindled by her words. Giselle had seen that same unfocused yet passionate gaze in the Yucatan pyramid.

Yet Peter remained confused. Was this some sort of trap or could she be telling him the truth.

Giselle continued to fuel his mental fire. "I'm not lying to you Peter. Why should I? What purpose would it serve? We are both scientists. We would scrap everything we hold dear to gain the knowledge the portal offers."

"But I can't open it alone, Peter," she implored. "There must be a unifying blend of the male and female energies activating the proper harmonic frequencies. And most importantly, we must have the skull to focus the energy in a precise manner that will open the Star Portal.

"I have studied this at great length, Peter. It's the only way."

Peter stared hard at Giselle, searching in her eyes for any sign of subterfuge or deceit. His mind was already sifting the possibilities. He had already decided to take Solomon's Treasure, or at least as much as he could purloin, for himself. Why not acquire what surely must be the greatest single prize on the planet?

But his suspicions had not been allayed. "Why should I trust you?" he asked in a sullen but earnest tone.

"Because of this," she replied, walking into the kitchen. Peter looked at Michel who still held the gun leveled at his head and relaxed.

Moments later, she returned with a small leather pouch. "Give me your hand."

Hesitantly, Peter held out his right hand. Giselle opened the pouch and poured out a number of glittering coins. Peter's eyes widened at the sight of the golden discs in his hands.

Holding one up for a better view, he muttered, "*Mein Gott*! Genuine Roman gold coins and in excellent condition. These must be worth…"

"…more than 10,000 *Reichsmarks*." Giselle finished his sentence. "That's more than 2,000 American Dollars and there's plenty more where they came from."

Looking up at Giselle, he said with a crooked smile, "So, you do know the location of Solomon's Treasure. Perhaps we should discuss this further."

With a small look of triumph, Giselle stood up and rubbed her neck. "Excellent."

Turning to Michel, she said, "Let's just make certain that we have no further trouble with our friend here."

Turning to Marie, who was still frozen in her chair, she said, "Marie, what do you have that we might use to tie him up. Any rope?"

Shaking her head as if awakening from some bad dream, Marie muttered, "I don't know of any." Glancing about, she pointed toward the heavy green velour curtains hanging over the front windows. "What about the drape cords?"

"Good idea," said Giselle, who began pulling down a length of the braided gold cord. Walking past Michel, who still held Peter at gun point, she knelt and began to truss up Peter's hands.

Just at the moment she realized that she had blocked the aim of Michel's revolver, Peter scooted backward and placed his boot in her midsection. Before she could avoid the move, he had kicked her backwards, knocking her into Michel, who was desperately trying to move out of her path and take aim at Peter at the same time.

Their bodies collided and entangled. Peter moved swiftly right behind Giselle. He knocked her to one side with a brutal clout from his left hand while grabbing Michel's pistol hand with his right. Already off balance from the collision, Giselle fell heavily to the floor.

The two men stood over her prone form, grappling for the weapon. Both men knew the other would grant no quarter and the struggle for the gun was quiet but desperate.

Before Giselle could get to her feet, Peter had brought his right knee up to strike savagely into Michel's groin. With a gasp of pain, Michel loosened his grip on the revolver just enough that Peter was able to procure the weapon for himself.

Fully realizing the deadly hazard he was in, Michel clenched his left fist and drove it hard into the side of Peter's face. With a grunt, the slender blond staggered backward but did not lose his grip on the gun.

"*Schweine!*" he hissed as he brought the heavy service revolver in a sweeping arc to connect with the side of Michel's head. There was a soft thud and unyielding steel connected with very yielding human tissue. Michel sank noiselessly to the floor.

Marie gave out a small sound, a whimpering sort of cry, and scuttled into a corner of the room where she curled up into a ball, staring with horror at the scene before her.

Giselle glanced at Michel's inert form on the floor and knew instantly that he would be no help to her. Desperately, she tried to scramble to her feet while making for the kitchen door. But it was no use. Time and distance were against her.

Peter righted himself and quickly stepped to her and grabbed a swatch of her blonde hair in his right hand. Yanking her off balance, he sent her careening across the room. She slammed against the far wall and fell to the floor. The impact knocked a painting off its hooks and it fell, striking her on the head. The heavy gilt frame gouged into her flesh.

Her vision blurred as unconsciousness approached and she felt something warm and wet on the side of her face. She placed one hand to her head and saw there was bright-red blood on it.

Looking up, she saw Peter towering over her, gloating with triumph. "Well, *meine liebe*," he said. "It appears we have come to the end of this adventure. I have won and the great Giselle Tchaikovsky has lost. I will get the location of the treasure from you one way or another."

"Although I am not normally a man of violence, after today I might prefer it in this case," he added with a malevolent smile on his face. The words were spoken in a low, ominous tone, which only made them the more chilling.

After making certain that Michel was unconscious, Peter moved closer to Giselle. The pain and the danger were bringing her back to full consciousness quickly. She glared up at Peter, who returned her look with a smirk.

"Before I learn what I want to know and finish the job I started in the Yucatan, I want you to answer one question," he said.

Kneeling beside the dazed woman, he placed Michel's revolver to her head and asked in a conversational tone, "All that talk about a Star Portal was *scheisse*, 'bullshit' as you say in America, intended to make me give up the skull, wasn't it?"

Giselle merely glowered at him, a thin trickle of the blood that stained her hair spreading down her cheek.

Peter was becoming impatient. "Tell me the truth, you cow! There was no truth to the talk about the portal, was there?" He cocked the hammer on the military revolver with an audible click.

Giselle was silent, as she judged her chances to escape what appeared to be certain death. If she confessed the Star Portal story was false, he would shoot her. If she gave him the location of the treasure, he would shoot her. If she made a sudden move, he would shoot her.

Looking directly into his angry blue eyes, she spoke softly and sincerely, "Peter, it is true. With your help and the skull, we can gain unimaginable power, more power than has ever been dreamed of by any mortal human."

"You lie!" Peter shouted, climbing to his feet and pointing the cocked revolver at her face. "It's all too fantastic. There is no such thing as a Star Portal. Tell me the truth."

With the knowledge that they might well be her last words, Giselle responded quietly, "It's all true, Peter. I swear. Compared to the Star Portal, the treasure is nothing."

Giselle knew she had little time left and spoke rapidly. "Listen to me, Peter. No one has had an opportunity like this. You may keep the treasure. Just help me open the portal."

Confused, Peter hesitated. She would allow him to keep Solomon's Treasure? Could her incredible story possibly be true? Could he be passing up the chance to gain unthinkable power for himself?

His rational mind, his Teutonic upbringing and his science-based education finally combined to override his sense of wonder.

"You lying bitch! Enough of your fantasies! I can't believe a person of your capabilities would fall for such rubbish. You can't be trusted. I left you for dead in the jungle, yet here you are. This time I will finish the job, right after you give me directions to the treasure."

Giselle closed her eyes, awaiting the torture she knew was coming.

She would not give up the secret of the treasure voluntarily but she did not know how much abuse she could take before breaking. Oddly enough, she did not think of her own peril. Her thoughts turned to Gabby and Charles and the harsh treatment they must be receiving at the hands of the Nazis. She steeled herself for the inevitable.

Instead, she heard the words, "I think not."

Opening her eyes, she saw Peter turn to face Marie, who was standing behind him aiming Giselle's Luger at his head. She realized with unbounded relief that Marie had found her pistol as well as the courage to pick it up and use it.

Giselle started to climb to her feet but Peter swung the revolver back toward her and she hesitated.

Peter rose slowly to his feet, his blue eyes never leaving the large automatic wavering in Marie's trembling fingers. He smiled but there was no warmth or humor in it.

Stepping toward her while reaching out his hand, Peter said soothingly, "Dearest lady, you don't want to use that. Why it might make a mess that would take days to clean."

Giselle glanced over at Michel, who was groaning and beginning to regain consciousness then back to Marie who was slowly backing away from Peter.

Sensing that Marie lacked the resolve to pull the trigger, Giselle cried, "Marie, throw me the gun." But the command was too late.

As Giselle spoke the words, Marie glanced in her direction. It was the moment Peter had been waiting for. He pounced with all the strength and fury of a predator. He grasped Marie around her waist and easily wrested the pistol from the elderly woman's hand, knocking it to the floor.

He took her shoulders in both hands and shook her, his fury rising to a fever pitch. "Enough nonsense!" he snarled over his shoulder. "Giselle, you will give me the exact location of the treasure right now or I will kill everyone in this room, beginning with this old crone."

The distraction had been just enough for Giselle to slide forward and gain possession of her Luger. She was now climbing to her feet, the automatic aimed steadily at Peter.

In the same instance, Peter saw her action and twisted his body toward Giselle. Flinging Marie effortlessly onto the divan, he pointed Michel's service revolver at Giselle's head.

The two stared at each other over the gun sights. Neither moved and neither spoke. It was a standoff.

Giselle knew she had to break the stalemate somehow. But a wrong move could lead to a blood bath and there was too much at stake for that.

"Peter, you must listen to me," she said with as much calm as she could muster. "Every fiber of my being wants you dead. I could have killed you earlier when my friend arrived, especially after learning the fate of my friends. But I didn't. Think about that. Also think about the treasure. If you kill us, there will be no one left to guide you to it."

Peter stood still, his aim unswerving. Yet, his eyes evidenced some hesitation and contemplation.

"And think of the Star Portal," Giselle implored. "It's real. It exists. I know this to be true, unbelievable as it may sound."

She saw a glimmer of interest in his eyes and pressed the advantage.

"Together, we can open it. Peter, the rewards will be unimaginable. You can keep all the treasure. You know I care little for material wealth. But I do care for the limitless knowledge that could be ours once the Star Portal is activated."

Peter glanced quickly at Marie, who lay sobbing on the couch. "Is this true, woman? Does such a Star Portal truly exist?"

Weakly, as though every last reserve of strength had been exhausted, Marie slowly raised her head and answered, "*Oui, Monsieur*, it is all true." It was obvious that the woman was too shaken and exhausted to be lying.

Peter looked back to Giselle, whom he had fully expected to fire on him when he looked away. She stood, still aiming the Luger but gave no indication she meant to use it. He looked over at Michel who was slowly rising to a sitting position. Peter knew he must make a decision soon before the odds shifted against him.

"Then this portal is the true secret of Rennes-le-Château?" he said to Marie, who merely nodded as she dabbed at her teary eyes with the hem of her cotton dress.

Greed, self-protection, scientific curiosity and the knowledge that this might be the chance to make himself indispensable to the highest authorities if not master of the world all vied in Peter's imagination. The current expedition was a failure. Unless he brought something back to Himmler, he could well end up spending the rest of the war back in Dachau, only this time he would not just walk away.

"Very well, what do you propose?" Peter had made his decision. He lowered the revolver and watched warily for Giselle's reaction. Realizing that greed and self-preservation had overcome Peter's innate skepticism, she smiled slightly and lowered the Luger.

Moments later, when Michel gained full consciousness, he was amazed to see Giselle engaged in conversation with Peter, who was sitting calmly in the chair previously occupied by Marie. Marie was sitting on the divan with Giselle, tending to her head wound with a clean cloth.

Michel regained his feet and tensed, looking about rapidly for some weapon or advantage over the situation.

"It's all right, *mon cher*," said Giselle reassuringly seeing him rise to his feet. "Peter and I now have an agreement. Let us finish this and I will care for your head in a moment, my brave hero."

Her words reminded Michel of the blinding pain that filled his head. Taking a chair, he sat quietly holding his head. He was still confused, but there did not seem to be any immediate danger and it appeared that somehow Giselle was advancing her scheme to regain the skull.

He saw Peter lean forward and ask with interest, "Again, what is the significance of March 16th?"

"There are many aspects to the Star Portal opening that must be taken into consideration," explained Giselle, trying to remember the information she had gleaned during long conversations with Marie and Bernard. "There are far too many things to explain to you right now. But one aspect involves a certain planetary alignment that will only occur next March 16th.

"It marks the 700-year anniversary of the fall of the Montségur fortress and the end of the Albigensian Crusade. It was a date full of power and portents, according to the Cathars."

"This is unbelievable," muttered Peter. "First you want me to sell this fantastic story to Himmler and Hitler? Then, assuming they accept it, I must tell them to wait for almost a year before taking action?" He shook his head.

"Look, it will take some time for you to obtain the skull, won't it?" she offered.

"That's true enough. Even with great luck and assuming they will believe such a fantastic story, there will still be meetings, conferences, memoranda. Such things take time."

Giselle shrugged. "Draw things out as much as possible. Tell them you have to research the whole subject thoroughly before activating the portal. Tell them anything."

Suddenly smiling, she offered, "Perhaps if you make your requests through *SS Obergruppenführer* Kammler, the way might be opened for you."

Peter sat bolt upright and stared at Giselle. "You know of Hans Kammler?"

"I know many things, including the location of the treasure." Giselle sat smugly, gratified that her shot in the dark had paid off. Hans Kammler was the name of the *SS* officer that Gabby's aunt had tried to bring to Tuscany prompting an investigation by Giselle. He was an inconspicuous but steadily growing power within the *SS*. It was rumored that he had connections with almost all of the *Reich*'s most top-secret technology. It had seemed a safe bet that Kammler would be included in any discussions concerning the Star Portal.

"How do you know of Kammler?" Again Peter asked the question.

Giselle replied steadily, "He is even now waiting on a report from me." It was a complete lie. Giselle barely knew anything about the man but she relished the look on Peter's face and the opportunity to raise the fear and paranoia that festered within the Nazi hierarchy. Her bluff would keep Peter off balance and afraid to talk to other *SS* officers for some time.

Peter sat still, quite pale and drumming his fingers on his knee. "*Ja, ja*, I suppose I could drag my feet here for awhile, then take my time returning. I could waste time with incomplete or incomprehensible reports. During wartime, it is almost impossible to get rapid action on any matter unless it directly relates to the war effort."

He paused and sat contemplating for long moments before nodding his head slowly. "But I think it can be done."

"I'm sure you'll do your best," said Giselle dryly. "So, it's settled. I will make arrangements for the portal's activation and you will furnish the skull. We will meet here at *Villa Bethania* on March 10th."

"And you will lead me to the treasure before we use the skull?"

"If that's the way you want it. Are we agreed?"

"*Ja*," muttered Peter without looking at her. He rose to his feet and retrieved his black peaked hat and the pouch of Roman coins from the floor. As he walked toward the front door, he paused to see if anyone was moving to prevent his exit. No one stirred.

His mind was a turmoil of expectation and impatience. He now had the treasure within his grasp. And months from now, he could return without an army of scientists, he reasoned. He was also full of curiosity regarding the Star Portal. The implications of such power were staggering. He knew he could deal with Giselle at the first opportunity once the treasure and the portal were his. The thought that she was still alive grated on him.

"We will meet again," he said in a tone that suggested multiple interpretations. With a tight and humorless smile, he left.

As his big sandy-haired driver held the rear door of the *Kubelwagen* open for him, the man said, "I hope your business here was successful, *Herr Sturmbannführer.* You were inside for quite some time. Once I thought I heard something. Was there any trouble?"

"*Nein,*" replied Peter, absently toying with the pouch of gold coins, "no trouble at all."

CHAPTER 19

Southern France
March, 1944

THE FOUR CYLINDERS OF THE 1936 Mercedes-Benz 170V clattered with exertion as the small black car negotiated its way up the twisting hilly one-lane road toward Rennes-le-Château.

Sitting in the rear of the four-door sedan Peter felt cramped, wedged as he was between the right rear door and the massive body to his left. He was perspiring slightly despite a strong chilly March wind which caused the driver to constantly correct the veering car.

His emotions were mixed. The excited anticipation of recovering Solomon's Treasure and a fascination with the possibility of actually finding something like a Star Portal was dampened by fact that he was no longer in charge of the treasure mission. He felt lucky to be there at all, despite the great responsibility placed in him by *Reichsführer* Himmler.

Once again, as he had during the entire drive from Germany, Peter leaned forward and peered at the small steel strongbox resting on the passenger seat. Reassured that its invaluable cargo was secure, he eased his way back onto the cloth-covered rear seat.

He was not at all pleased with the turn of events. Even though he had managed to obtain the Skull of Fate, his own fate was in doubt. One more failure and he knew his position within the *SS* would be most precarious. Adding to his worries was the fact that his worst enemy was not only alive, but in a position forcing him to negotiate with her.

He smiled to himself but there was no humor in the expression. His thoughts had darkened. He would play Giselle's game until he was in possession of the treasure. Then he would take great pleasure in eliminating both her and her friends.

Peter tried to make himself more comfortable on the back seat only to be blocked by the big man beside him. *Verdammt!* He could no longer even obtain decent transportation.

He had hoped, in light of the importance of this mission, to have been assigned a big Mercedes, perhaps even one of the 770 *Grosser* convertibles. Instead, he was squeezed into the back seat of the cheapest, smallest model produced in Stuttgart with the biggest man in the world. He sighed. Considering the severe shortage of both vehicles and fuel, he knew he should be satisfied to even have a car at all to carry him back to southern France.

Peter had come a long way from the arrogance and pride he first felt upon being recruited into the Order of the Death's Head following his arrival from the Yucatan. He no longer felt confidence in his superiors or even the war effort. His years of close experience with the personal bickering and ambition within the top ranks of the SS had wiped away any illusions he had about unswerving patriotism.

He glanced at the big man riding beside him. Here was an officer for whom he still had considerable respect even though the man had been given command of what should have by all rights been his expedition. In fact, Peter harbored the very definite belief that, were it not for his role in learning about the Star Portal and the fact that he was the only person who might have knowledge of its functioning, he would not have been on this mission at all.

Looking over at his sleeping companion, Peter was filled with both awe and trepidation. The man was indeed big, both in stature and in reputation.

Standing 6-feet, 4-inches, *SS-Standartenführer* Otto Skorzeny was someone to be reckoned with, already world famous for his extraordinary rescue of the Italian dictator Mussolini. Peter gazed enviously at the Knight's Cross of the Iron Cross that hung around the sleeping giant's neck. It had been awarded personally by the *Führer*.

His awe stemmed from Skorzeny's remarkable record as chief of Germany's Special Troops, the nation's head commando and current darling. His trepidation came from the now certain knowledge that he no longer enjoyed full favor with *Reichsführer-SS* Himmler. He nursed doubts both as to his place in this new expedition and as to his future. He knew he could not fail again. And he continued to seriously wonder how he would be able to gain the treasure for himself under the nose of this famous commando.

Himmler had quite perfunctorily told him that Skorzeny would be in command only after the selection had already been made. Peter had not even been asked to help select members of this operation as he had the year previously. Peter knew Skorzeny was the right choice and he felt confidence in the commando's leadership. Yet, the selection of a national hero to conduct this new search for the treasure only underscored his own failure of the previous summer.

He had managed to take a look at Skorzeny's personnel file and had been greatly impressed with the man's accomplishments.

The son of an engineer, Skorzeny had been born in Vienna in 1908. Although a member of the conservative *Frei Korps* and *Heimwehr* after World War I, he did not join the National Socialist Party until 1930. Just before the war started, he became one of Hitler's personal bodyguards and, until his appointment as chief of Special Troops, Colonel Skorzeny handled secret agents for the *Reich*'s Central Security Office.

His name had become a household word the past fall when he led a daring daylight rescue of Mussolini from a hotel in the Italian Abruzzi Apennine mountains approachable only by cable car.

Soon after Peter had returned empty handed from Rennes-le-Château in late July, 1943, Mussolini had been deposed in the wake of Allied landings in Sicily and a terrific bombing raid on Rome. Anti-Fascist elements throughout Italy demonstrated in the streets and even attacked some Fascist leaders in their homes. Mussolini had been taken into custody by the officers of King Victor Emmanuel and his whereabouts had been unknown.

After hearing rumors that Mussolini was to be turned over to the Allies, Skorzeny had been hand-picked by Hitler to rescue his Axis partner. On September 12th, he and 18 troopers had crash landed on the mountain of Gran Sasso in a glider and rushed the hotel, which was guarded by more than a regiment of troops. They were accompanied by General Ferdinando Soletti of the Italian police. Recognizing both the khaki uniforms of the German commandos and the faithful Soletti,

Mussolini had leaned from a window and ordered the troops not to fire.

Quickly, Skorzeny and his men had disarmed the Italian troops and bundled the Italian dictator into a small German *Storch* light plane. The pilot managed to fly his passengers off the mountain in a death-defying short takeoff that barely missed dropping onto the rocks below. After a change of planes, Mussolini was flown to Vienna, then taken by train to Munich where he was flown to join Hitler at his Eastern Front headquarters at Rastenburg.

It was truly a remarkable achievement and the news of Mussolini's rescue flashed around the world. Despite his wounded pride over losing command of the operation, Peter knew that if any man could locate Solomon's Treasure, that man would be Otto Skorzeny.

He hoped, in light of his agreement with Giselle, to keep one step ahead of the big man. Or if that failed, at least he would know his every move and could still hope for a chance at the treasure himself. He had already made certain arrangements in Switzerland for the disposition of gold, silver and precious stones.

As the small sedan climbed the foothills of the Pyrenees, Peter sat contemplating the coming days. With Skorzeny's resourcefulness and SS troops to back him, Peter worried that the treasure would be found and shipped away before he had a chance to take it. His only hope lay in forcing Giselle to lead him to it without involving Skorzeny.

He also had grown less enthusiastic about her claims of a Star Portal but could not suppress lingering enthusiasm for the idea of gaining universal power for himself. What if the story were true? What if he indeed had an opportunity to conquer both space and time? In earlier years he would have scoffed at any such notion. His experience with the skull along with the seriousness given to the report he had submitted to Himmler had changed him and his views on such matters.

He leaned forward again placing both hands on the striped cloth covering of the seat in front of him and once more gazed at the strong-box riding on the front seat. Here was more cause for uneasiness.

Even Skorzeny did not know that the box contained the fabulous Skull of Fate. Himmler had been quite explicit on that point, explaining that a good portion of the security for the powerful talisman stemmed from the fact that no one knew of its presence. Likewise, Skorzeny knew nothing of the Star Portal. His mission was simply to locate the treasure and ship it into the *Reich*.

Peter turned as best he could and looked back at the convoy behind them through the small glass rear window of the staff car. A *Kubelwagen* mounting an MG-34 machine gun led more than a dozen huge Daimler-Benz LG3000 diesel trucks. Each carried a powerful winch installed in front of the radiator to ensure none would become mired in mud or soft earth.

Crammed in the trucks was a company of Skorzeny's *Waffen-SS* troopers, all hardened graduates of his famed commando training school at Friedenthal. This included a platoon of combat engineers capable of excavating for the treasure if necessary, as well as radio operators and all their pertinent equipment.

Bringing up the rear of the column was another machine gun-armed *Kubel* as well as a powerful armored car sporting a high-velocity anti-tank gun in addition to its MG-34. With the added firepower of this eight-wheeled *Sd. Kfz. 234/2 Schwerer Panzerspähwagen*, popularly known as a *Puma*, Peter felt confident that nothing could possibly interfere with their mission. After all, they were in German-controlled territory. The skull was perfectly safe.

He leaned back and tried to find a comfortable position next to his snoring companion. Despite the discomfort of bearing responsibility for the skull and his loss of prestige in Himmler's eyes, Peter had regained some measure of confidence in himself by convincing the SS chief to allow him to take the skull to France.

His empty-handed return to Himmler the past July had been only one disaster among several for the Third Reich at the time. Recently, the *Afrika Korps* had been forced back into Tunisia and by mid-May, British Eighth Army tank units had linked up with American forces there. By mid-July, Allied troops had landed in Sicily.

On the Eastern Front, on July 5th the German High Command launched Operation *Citadel*, an ill-fated attempt to pincer off several Soviet armies in a bulge in the front lines near the small town of Kursk. The massive attack by more than two German armies had been telegraphed for months, due to postponements, with an obvious buildup of forces. This had given the Russians plenty of time to prepare defenses many miles in depth. Despite foreknowledge of the attack by both sides, the Germans forced their way forward. Just as the battle hung in the balance, Hitler had rushed units from the fight to Italy to bolster Mussolini's failing power. As a result, the *Wehrmacht* lost three quarters of its mechanized forces in the swirling cauldron of armored battles around the town of Kursk and had not yet regained the initiative on the Eastern Front.

Peter understood that many officers suspected that the War in Europe had been decided by this gigantic tank battle on the steppes of Russia.

It was becoming clear to anyone who could follow a map that a ring of Allied men and equipment was now closing in on Hitler's *Reich*. It was no secret that Hitler's coffers were dangerously low and that an infusion of funds was desperately needed to maintain Germany's war effort.

All of this must have been on Himmler's mind when Peter debriefed him at the end of July. The dreaded *SS* chief had nearly dropped his pince-nez glasses while sputtering his anger and frustration at Peter's failure to locate the treasure. This failure was compounded when Himmler ordered Peter to further interrogate Otto Rahn and obtain more precise directions, only to learn of Rahn's death in Dachau.

He had narrowly escaped imprisonment or worse by giving his wrathful boss the full details of the Star Portal. Peter had wracked his brain trying to come up with a way to obtain the skull without imparting any knowledge of the portal but had failed to find any other convincing argument. But he had managed to keep Giselle's name and involvement with the skull out of his disclosures. He simply stated that he had gained his knowledge through Marie Denarnaud and had double-checked it with local Cathar leaders.

As he had hoped and expected, the superstitious Himmler had grown wide-eyed with his description of an ancient energy vortex to other realms. He had swiftly sworn Peter to secrecy concerning the matter. There had been several private conferences as the *SS* chief tried to ascertain the truth of such a claim.

After consulting a number of experts, including Haushofer and a strange inventor of circular energy generators named Viktor Schauberger, Himmler had became convinced that the stories of the Star Portal could be based on reality. And if such a portal truly existed, it certainly would be worth any effort to control it.

"I am told that one of our escaped scientists, a Jew by the name of Einstein, has advanced theories stating that it may be theoretically possible to manipulate both time and space," Himmler once confided in Peter.

Peter was not privy to what Himmler had said to Hitler to entice the dictator into giving up the skull, but he could well imagine the *Führer*'s enthusiasm for gaining universal power, especially considering his preoccupation with occult and mystical subjects.

All Peter knew for certain was that not long after New Year's Day, 1944, he had been summoned to Wewelsburg, where in a short and perfunctory meeting Himmler handed Peter the box containing the skull.

Himmler indicated that he felt the skull was in safe hands considering that Skorzeny and a company of highly trained commandos would be with Peter inside German-held southern France.

"With the Allies in Italy and an invasion of France imminent, time is of the essence," Himmler had said. Peering over his small pince-nez glasses, the *SS* commander had acted as though he was confident of the mission's success. But Peter could feel a sense of urgency about his demeanor. He wondered if his chief felt the specter of approaching defeat just as he did himself.

Looking up to see the gateway to Rennes-le-Château, Peter's thoughts again turned to Giselle. That he wanted her dead was certain, but not until he gained possession of the treasure and learned the secrets of the Star Portal.

He had learned from Otto Rahn's death that it was bad methodology to dispose of someone before they divulged all they knew. Thoughts of Rahn only angered Peter, both because of his premature death and because Peter was convinced the man had deliberately lied about the location of the treasure, either to protect it for the Cathars or to gain it for himself. It was ironic that now he himself planned to take the treasure even though the involvement of Skorzeny and his men had raised a considerable roadblock to this ambition, perhaps an insurmountable one.

It was for this reason that Peter had arranged for their arrival two days early. His plan was simple. When Giselle and her companions arrived for the rendezvous, they would be captured. With any luck, Peter could separate Giselle from the others and pry the location of the treasure from her without Skorzeny's knowledge.

As Peter sat devising his trap, the big man beside him snorted and looked about groggily. "Are we there yet?" Skorzeny asked with a yawn.

"Your timing is impeccable as always, *Herr Standartenführer*," answered Peter, glibly adding an ingratiating smile. "We have just passed the village gates."

Skorzeny flashed his now-famous toothy grin and said, "*Gut, gut.*

As I recall, you said you were supposed to meet your contacts here on March 10th?"

"That is correct, sir."

"But, today is only Wednesday, March 8th. We are early."

"The early bird catches the worm, as they say, *Herr Standartenführer.* I have reason to believe that my contacts are working with the French Resistance. Wouldn't it be impressive if we found the treasure and rounded up a group of dangerous Resistance fighters in the bargain?"

Skorzeny turned toward Peter and grinned. The excitement of anticipation made his eyes sparkle and the scar which reached from his left ear lobe to the center of his chin stretched wide to accommodate his smile. While Peter knew that his comrades called him "Scarface," he had not been able to bring himself to be so familiar with the national hero.

"*Ja*, that would be a nice touch. So where do we begin?"

"*Herr Standartenführer*, I think it would be wise to seal the village. Then when these people show up, we will simply arrest the lot and learn their secrets at our leisure."

"I like it, *mein junge*," said Skorzeny in a booming voice.

The convoy drove straight through the small village and circled in the large open area north of the Magdalena church and tower.

Skorzeny climbed from the small Mercedes and stretched. Walking to the low rock wall, he placed his wool M43 cap on his head. The service cap was a copy of the climbing caps worn by the elite *Gebirgsjaeger* mountain troops and was becoming very popular throughout the *Wehrmacht*. Skorzeny stood gazing at the panorama below. "An impressive sight, Peter, *nein?*" he said, still smiling.

Before Peter could answer, the tall man had turned and was shouting orders in a rapid staccato manner, "Seal off the village. Check all identity papers. No one comes in and no one goes out. Notify me of any intruders or anything out of the ordinary. Is that clear?"

"*Klar!*" shouted a burly sergeant in response. The men were boiling out of the trucks, laughing and joking as they formed ranks. They were relieved to be released from the hours of bumpy confinement.

Peter looked from the magnificent vista before him to the church and back over to *Villa Bethania* and felt a sudden sense of elation. He had more than 200 veteran SS troops with him led by the most famous and resourceful soldier in all Germany. He had enough firepower at hand to take on anything short of a fully equipped *panzer* division. All he had to do was scoop up Giselle and her friends when they arrived, force them to reveal their secrets and his problems would be at an end.

By Friday, March 10th, Peter's elation was at a peak, despite the fact that nothing out of the ordinary had occurred in the village. There was no sign of Giselle.

The impatient Skorzeny had left for Montségur with most of the troops the previous day. He had been in high spirits and Peter knew the commando leader was attempting to track the treasure on his own. Peter had begged off, explaining that he needed to wait for his contacts with a contingent of the troops. It was perfect. With the commando leader out of the way, there was nothing to stop him from securing the treasure and the portal, if such existed, for himself.

But by mid-afternoon, Peter was growing impatient. He had purposefully not visited Marie Denarnaud. He did not want to introduce her to Skorzeny and risk him learning the treasure's location. He decided to wait and gain what information he needed from Giselle and her companions.

Nevertheless, after Skorzeny's departure, he ordered a company of *Waffen-SS* troopers to surround the *Villa Bethania* and the adjacent church.

He waited until long after 4 o'clock, before his patience came to an end. After again looking at his watch, Peter stalked to the entrance and pounded on the door. After only a short wait, the ornately-carved wood door creaked open and Marie peered out at him.

"I thought it might be you," she said without any apparent concern. "Come in." The door opened wider.

Peter looked around nervously, wondering why the old woman would ask him inside so casually without the protection of Giselle and her male companion. He cautiously stepped into the house.

"*Madame*," he began, "I will not play games with you. The day is almost over and Giselle and her friends have failed to..." He stopped, frozen with surprise and shock.

Sitting alone on the very divan where Peter had tried to kill her was Giselle, acting very nonchalant. "Peter, I see you are right on time," she said with a blasé smile.

She was dressed demurely in a large, solid navy blue wool sweater and gabardine trousers thrust into high-top hiking boots. Standing nearby was the man called Michel. His right hand was in his jacket pocket and Peter did not have to guess what he was clutching out of sight.

Peter's apprehension returned. This was not good. No one had been observed entering the village, yet here sat the devil woman who had returned from the dead to torment him. And Skorzeny and the bulk of his men were kilometers away, busy with their own search for the treasure.

"But, how … how did you get here…" Peter's stammering was cut off by Giselle, who said through her smile, "Sorry, Peter, no time for chitchat. Did you bring the skull?"

"Yes," mumbled Peter, taking off his black officer's peaked hat and tucking it under one arm. "But surely you don't think I would have brought it here with me?" Now it was his turn to smile. His mind snapped into high gear. He was ready for this game of cat and mouse. Fleetingly, he wondered whether Giselle or he himself might be the mouse, but quickly put the question out of his mind.

"Can we go to the treasure now?" Peter said in a conversational tone.

Still smiling, Giselle responded, "Just as soon as I see the skull." Seeing a frown appear on Peter's face, she knew he did not have it with him. Climbing to her feet, she said, "It's getting late today. Shall we meet here in the morning for a fresh start? Say about 8 o'clock?"

Peter merely nodded, prompting Giselle to add, "With the skull?"

Peter gave her a piercing look and said, "Then you will lead me to the treasure?"

Giselle's smile tightened and it was her turn to nod in the affirmative.

"Then it is *au revoir* until morning," said Peter, placing his peaked hat on his head and leaving by the front door. He was scowling and deep in thought as he retraced his steps to the main square.

Giselle walked to the front door and stood gazing after Peter with a wicked smile. She knew he would agonize all night over how she got to Marie's house without being caught in his trap. She also knew that he would never find out, at least not from her. She would never tell him about the tunnel and the staircase leading from the ruins to the small church. It had been a simple matter to enter at the base of the hill, then slip from the church in the pre-dawn hours to Marie's back door. The hardest part was the daylong wait for Peter to arrive.

Her smile faded as she returned to the sitting room. She recalled how she and Michel had spent the morning hours reviewing both her plan to regain the skull and the months that had passed since her summer departure from Rennes-le-Château.

They had been hard months.

While operations of both the Sisterhood and the Resistance had been stepped up, so had the repression inflicted on the French people by the occupation forces. Identity checkpoints were more common and curfews had been tightened. Miscues and arrests had increased along with membership in the Sisterhood.

Throughout these trying times Giselle still had not fully accepted the loss of poor Charles and the fate of dear Gabby.

"More waiting?" Michel asked as she returned to his side on the divan. He was shaking his head in disgust. A man of action, the long wait for this confrontation had worn his patience thin.

Stroking his cheek, she said soothingly, "Patience, *mon cher*, things are working out nicely. There are not as many troops with him as I feared.

"I only wish that I did not have to take him anywhere near the treasure. But we cannot activate the Star Portal without him and the two are together. I will see that he comes alone. With luck, once I lead him there with the skull, we will signal the Resistance men. They should be able to overcome this handful of soldiers in short order."

"Well, I don't like it," he grumbled.

"Nor I, my sweet. But my thoughts are on the Star Portal. We must have Peter or someone with similar negative energy present to activate it. There must be the balance of good and evil present, just as there must be both male and female. We just have to make certain that he doesn't get his hands on the treasure."

Michel looked at her with hard eyes. "Oh, I will be happy to see to that after what those murdering swine did to Jean."

Giselle leaned against Michel on the divan and they both sat in deep contemplation.

Adding to her grief over Charles and Gabby was the tragic death of Jean Moulin. They had learned of his fate upon their return from Rennes-le-Château the previous July.

A member of his Resistance group had been arrested by the *Gestapo* but was released unharmed the next day. This turncoat arranged for Jean to travel to a park near Lyon where he was taken by Klaus Barbie. Poor Jean was tortured for days and had died while being sent to Germany for further abuse. Her heart still ached at the loss of the man most responsible for creating the French Resistance out of so many disparate groups.

But it was dear Gabby and Charles who brought the deepest heartache.

She still recalled the sense of horror and loss she had felt upon learning that Gabby and Charles had fallen into the hands of the Germans. Then she remembered the relief and elation she had felt when she was reunited with Gabby in Toulouse on the return trip home the past summer.

But it was not the same Gabby she had known. Her experience had changed her. Giselle's thoughts returned to her departure from Marie's home the past summer.

Heartsick at the loss of Gabby and Charles, she and Michel had stayed with Marie a further day to plan for the rendezvous with Peter. Taking back roads, they then drove the Nash to Toulouse where they planned to leave the car with Bernard. They knew its license number would now be on every *Gestapo* watch list and it was no longer safe to drive it. Giselle had hoped to have Bernard enlist some local Resistance men for a rescue attempt on both Gabby and Charles.

It was Bernard who had taken her to Gabby. Her delight at finding her young friend safe was tempered by the fragile creature she found waiting for her in Bernard's home.

Hollow-eyed and pale, it had taken some time for Gabby to haltingly tell of her experience.

"It's strange," she had replied to Giselle's question concerning what had happened, "but I honestly can't remember. Charles and I were arrested and taken to Montségur. Klaus Barbie himself was there and asking about a treasure. Then Charles was taken away and I…" Her voice faltered.

"You were left alone with the Butcher of Lyon?" Giselle's response was more a statement of horror than a question.

Gabbby nodded and sobbed.

Gently, Giselle asked, "He raped you?"

Gabby had looked at her with a haunted expression and murmured without emotion, "I only wish that was all."

Choking back her revulsion and anger, Giselle asked, "It's all right, my dear. You are in safe hands now. What happened after that?"

Between sobs, Gabby managed to say, "I really don't know. I was unconscious for a time. When I awoke it was morning and I was in the back of a truck with Charles. He looked terrible. His eyes were black-ened and his face bruised. There was a soldier with us armed with a machine pistol. I don't think he expected any trouble from a beaten old man and an unconscious girl.

"Charles looked relieved to see that I was conscious. I asked him where we were and he replied that we were just outside Carcassonne on our way to Barbie's headquarters in Lyon.

"When the guard ordered us to be quiet, Charles attacked him. It was a most uneven match but it gave me the opportunity to take his bayonet."

Through clenched teeth, Gabby said, "Brave Charles pinned his arms to his side and I stabbed him until he stopped moving."

Giselle had felt anguish that her young friend had had to suffer such trauma. She was further dismayed to notice the look of satisfaction in Gabby's eyes as she spoke of killing a fellow human being.

"Charles told me to find my way to the university in Toulouse and meet Bernard. When I insisted he come with me, he replied he didn't have the strength and was prepared to die. I was in no state to argue. When the truck slowed at the next sharp turn, I leaped out. I discarded my bloody sweater and eventually found a ride to Toulouse where I made contact with Bernard."

Giselle's joy at Gabby's return was diminished by the knowledge that Charles was still in German hands. Although, he could blame his companion for the guard's death, she knew there would be reprisals nonetheless.

Through Sisterhood sources she later learned that Charles was alive. He had been taken to a concentration camp in Germany, pos-sibly *Buchenwald*. Her efforts to gain a more precise location were still underway. Even some of the senior Nazi officers who courted Giselle's attention at Parisian social events could not tell her precisely what had happened to her friend. She got the definite feeling that they really didn't want to know. It was not just the French who were terrorized by the *Gestapo*.

Thanks to foresighted arrangements, she still had access to Charles' apartment and library, but she sorely missed his wise counsel and friend-ship. Often she considered the possibility of arranging an escape for Charles but always she rejected it as a hazardous waste of resources with no certainty of success.

In an effort to forget Gabby's trauma and the loss of Charles,

Giselle had buried herself in work for the Sisterhood. She daily followed the war news.

In the Pacific War, Allied forces continued to make headway in the island-hopping campaign, moving inexorably toward the Japanese home islands. The European Theater of War also was changing complexion.

The beginning of 1944 only brought more pressure on the German *Reich*. Just after the first of the year on the Eastern Front, Russian troops reached the former border of Poland and 50,000 American troops landed behind the German lines at Anzio in Italy. Aunt Fran and others within the Sisterhood had worked feverishly to aid the Allies there while Giselle stepped up her activities in France in anticipation of an invasion from England as daily it grew more apparent that there was no question if there was to be an invasion, only when and where.

And now, seated next to Michel in Marie's sitting room, Giselle again reminded herself to put the devastating loss of her friend and mentor behind her. She had more immediate matters to concern her.

She did not like the idea of leading Peter to the treasure, but could not think of any other way to get him and the skull to the cavern known as the Cathedral. Thank God she had at least convinced Peter and his superiors of its reality, at least enough to bring the skull within her grasp.

And she was still obsessed with the idea of opening the Star Portal.

During the intervening months, she had given considerable thought to the Star Portal. If such a device did exist and she could gain the use of it, it might prove instrumental in ending the war. According to the information she had received from Marie and Bernard, it indeed required a balance of energy to operate, both male and female, good and evil.

If this were true, she needed Peter to trigger the portal. The thought both appalled and fascinated her. It was ironic that she had told Peter the skull was necessary to open the portal when actually it was himself.

She had no doubt that once Peter knew the location of the treasure, her life would be subject to forfeit. But she had a plan to elude Peter's trap.

Before traveling south by train in the first week in March with Michel and Gabby, she had arranged for local members of the Resistance to meet with her and Bernard in Toulouse.

In a nighttime meeting in Bernard's home, she had laid her plans. Although she had agreed to allow Gabby to accompany them to the south, she had insisted that the young girl remain with Bernard and his Cathar followers.

"I need someone here, someone I can trust to see that my plans are carried out," she had explained. She did not want to admit she feared further capture and torture might unhinge her young friend. She could not bear the thought of losing her protégée a second time.

"I need you to act for me in my absence," she explained to her protesting companion.

Giselle had been greatly relieved when Gabby grudgingly agreed to remain in Toulouse to coordinate while Bernard and his followers led the Resistance men to the Cathedral cavern and awaited Giselle.

She had stalled for time to give Peter ample opportunity to acquire the skull and make the return journey but time was running out.

Peter returned to the headquarters at the base of Montségur to find Skorzeny in high humor.

"Peter, join me in a beer," he called, catching sight of Peter entering the room designated as both office and sleeping quarters.

Moments later, as Peter sank into a chair in Skorzeny's room with a bottle of *Schlossquell*, the big commando chief was brimming with excitement.

"We are making headway already, *mein junge*," said Skorzeny, taking a long pull on his beer. Wiping his small mustache with his sleeve, he continued, "Did you know there is a lengthy stairway leading from the ruins to the valley below?"

Knocking the wired porcelain cap from the mouth of his beer bottle, Peter took a swig and looked surprised.

"You didn't know about that did you? All those egghead scientists you brought here and you missed the stairway. We found the remnants this morning and I am now convinced the treasure is nowhere near here. I believe the Cathars must have taken it out through the tunnel even before the Papal Army arrived or early during the siege."

"How is that possible?" asked Peter. "For ten months the Pope's soldiers had Montségur surrounded."

"Aha!" laughed Skorzeny. "That's what the Papists thought too. But you see, Peter, no good commander would neglect to leave at least one avenue of retreat. Well, neither did the commander at Montségur. We found traces of an old footpath leading from the hidden entrance to the stairway. And tomorrow morning we will follow it. It leads to the northeast."

"But sir, the notes of Otto Rahn stated that the treasure was close to here. He believed this after closely studying the writings of Wolfram von Eschenbach."

"Eschenbach? That old lyrist who wrote about the Holy Grail cup? Think, *mein junge*. If Eschenbach truly knew the secret hiding place of the treasure, do you really suppose that as a Templar steeped in Cathar beliefs, he would have broadcast it to the world in his writings?"

Peter did not respond, instead contemplating Skorzeny's incisive question.

"Of course not!" continued the big colonel. "He would have directed searchers away from it."

Climbing to his feet, Skorzeny snarled, "Besides, what do I care what some idiot poet wrote 700 years ago? I am a practical man and I think in practical terms. I already have found a clue that you and all your scientific fellows could not. Let's get some sleep. We make an early start tomorrow. You will be joining us, of course."

"Actually, *Herr Standartenführer*, I still plan to round up those people I told you about. They may not present a problem but I would like to take a field radio and about 10 men with me. Good and dependable men," said Peter emptying his bottle. It had been a long and frustrating day.

Skorzeny scowled. "All my men are good and dependable," he growled while reaching for yet another bottle. The empties that littered the floor at his feet told Peter that the man was in no condition to be trifled with.

"Excuse me, *Herr Standartenführer*," said Peter. "I misspoke. I know your men are the best in all Germany."

Skorzeny smiled and relaxed, dropping back into his chair. He was in an expansive mood. "Yes, they are good men," he said. "In fact, the only man in this area that's questionable is that ass *Oberst* Fleischmann. The man actually wanted requisition orders from me in triplicate. From me! The man who was personally decorated by the *Führer*! What narrow-minded insolence. That's the problem in our nation today, Peter, too much paperwork and too little action."

"As you say, *Herr Standartenführer*," replied Peter absently. He was toying with one of the gold coins Giselle had given him and his thoughts were wandering. He was attempting to devise a plan to get for himself Giselle, the treasure and the portal all in one fell swoop.

Saturday morning, Skorzeny, looking fit and alert despite his drinking the night before, introduced Peter to *SS-Unterscharführer* Emil Kurzmann.

The dark-haired sergeant was shorter than most of the *SS* troops, but his barrel chest and muscular upper arms gave a good indication that he was a man who could more than compensate for his stature. Behind him were 10 troopers fully equipped with combat gear including mess kits and obligatory gas canisters. All carried MP-40 machine pistols slung over their shoulders except for two, who carried lethal looking *Gewehr 43* semi-automatic rifles with powerful *GW ZF 41* telescopic sights deadly up to 600 yards. One man also wore on his shoulders a field radio, its attached earphones hanging from his neck.

"Good hunting!" called Peter, waving as Skorzeny and the rest of the expedition pulled out in convoy, leaving Peter with only one truck and the small Mercedes sedan.

Turning to Kurzmann, Peter said, "*Unterscharführer,* load up, we are moving to Rennes-le-Château. You ride with me. On the way I will give you your instructions."

Kurzmann clicked the heels of his hobnail boots and almost shouted, "*Jawohl, Herr Sturmbannführer!*" As he turned and began barking orders to the men, Peter thought how thankful he was not to have been forced to train in the real military.

During the hour-long drive to Rennes-le-Château, Peter explained that upon arrival, Kurzmann was to take control of the village and be prepared to seize anyone Peter designated. The sergeant assured Peter that he understood the orders. Peter smiled to himself as the thought of Giselle and her companion trying to combat Kurzmann's trained veterans.

After arriving in the village, Peter ordered an early lunch for the men. Most men dug a handful of dry bread from their bread bags and some started up their small *Esbit* cookers to heat both bread and sausage. One man pulled a large field-gray metal can from the back of the truck and began distributing canteen cups full of steaming broth.

He scanned the activity as he strode to *Villa Bethania*. Before he could knock, he found Giselle and Michel exiting the front door to meet him. Marie, with a wary and concerned look on her face, peered from inside.

Giselle surveyed the troopers milling in the small square with disapproval. "We can't manage this mob in the caverns, Peter," she remarked curtly.

Peter shrugged. "I shall tell them to remain here and protect *Madame* Marie." His tone made Giselle realize that he intended to use Marie as leverage to gain the treasure.

"Tell them what you like, but they are not going with us and they are not to bother Marie Denarnaud. This operation will require absolute adherence to the formula I have been given to activate the portal. The slightest deviation from this ancient formula could make all our efforts ineffective, if not catastrophic."

"In fact, we should not start until Monday," she added matter-of-factly.

"What are you talking about, woman?" Peter was incensed. "We have everything we need. Skorzeny is already on the scent of the treasure. We must move quickly. There will be no games played here." His voice was sharp and his tone unswerving.

Giselle devised a small, secret smile and took Peter by the arm. Flinching at her touch, Peter allowed himself to be drawn across the town square, past the scattered *Waffen-SS* troopers at their midday meal to the low stone wall facing the valleys to the southwest.

Taking Peter by the shoulders she pointed him southward. His eyes took in the long line of a rocky ravine that cleaved the valley below. "There," said Giselle, pointing to a small dark hole on the far side of the bisecting ravine. "is the cave of Mary the Magdalene. That is where we must enter."

"*Unterscharführer*, bring me the field glasses," called Peter, squinting at the small dark spot on the other side of the valley. Taking the glasses, he surveyed the location for long moments. "The entrance is almost halfway down that steep hillside," he lamented. "It will take the better part of the day just to get there and set up ladders or ropes to make an entrance."

"That's why I said we should start Monday. There are materials we need, such as plenty of rope, lanterns and the like, not to mention food and water and sleeping gear. We may be in the caverns for more than a day."

"I can always radio for supplies," said Peter, his impatience evident.

She turned to Peter with an admonishing glare. "I doubt your radio will be much good to you deep underground. Besides, that treasure has been here for nearly a thousand years. One day won't make any difference, right?"

Peter bit his lip but he knew that she was right and he also knew he had to keep her appeased until the treasure was recovered. Grudgingly, he nodded his head.

"And you will come alone, understood?" she said.

Stalking off, he called over his shoulder, "Give the sergeant a list of our requirements."

Giselle stood and watched the slender black-clad officer walk away with a worried look. He could not know that she was stalling for time. There had been no word from Bernard or the Resistance fighters. She hoped they were in position. If not, her plan to take Peter and the skull would fall apart with unimaginable consequences.

By late morning, Monday, March 13, 1944, Giselle knew she could no longer postpone entering the cavern system. Surely Bernard and the Resistance men would be in position by now.

She, Michel and Peter, along with Sergeant Kurzmann and six of his men journeyed to the cliff overlooking the Cave of Mary Magdalene.

Shielding her eyes from the bright morning sun, Giselle could just make out the irregular outline of Rennes-le-Château on top of the hill across the valley. Glancing to her right, she saw Michel checking the straps on his backpack. Looking past him, she saw Peter with a metal case about 1-foot square lashed above his backpack. Her lips pinched together in anticipation as she felt certain this box contained the skull. Too bad the odds were not in her favor, she thought looking about at the armed troopers preparing to descend the cliff's face.

Michel had returned late Sunday and advised that he still had no word of the Resistance men. Giselle realized she would have to lead Peter into the tunnel system and hope for a chance to separate him from the skull. If only she could rid herself of the idea of activating the Star Portal, it would be a simple matter of disposing Peter, taking the skull and ending its power on behalf of the Nazis. But her curiosity concerning the portal and the temptation to use Peter to open it was overwhelming.

She had gone over in her mind the directions to the treasure. She was glad she had obtained them from Bernard. Marie would never have agreed to her leading Peter to the Cathedral. Now, if Bernard and his men were in place within the cavern, her trap would be sprung.

Giselle stood by Peter and watched the soldiers rig a pulley system that lowered a wide wooden plank to the level of the cave's entrance.

"If anyone is watching from the village, they will think we are window washers," laughed Peter. He seemed in good humor and very much in charge. His enthusiasm was lost on Giselle and Michel, who exchanged worried glances at every opportunity.

At last they were ready to enter the elaborate cavern system. One by one each treasure hunter was lowered until they could step into the cave.

Unterscharführer Kurzmann was the last to be lowered causing a clatter that reverberated throughout the cave system. In addition to his regular field kit, canteen and gas canister, he carried an MP-40 machine pistol slung over his shoulder. His arrival sounded like some itinerant huckster of pots and pans.

Wincing at the rattling, she said sharply to Peter, "I thought we agreed that we would go alone?"

He merely shrugged and replied, "You have your man, I have mine."

"*Merde!*" Giselle cursed under her breath but could not think of any legitimate objection.

"Is everyone all right?" One of the troopers was calling down from the top of the cliff through a chimney hole. Giselle could see his cap-covered head as a black silhouette jutting out into the lighted hole above them.

"We are fine. You may return to the village," called Peter. They all heard a distant "*Jawohl. Herr Sturmbannführer!*" as the remaining troopers moved off.

Glancing around at the remaining foursome, Giselle felt a surge of relief and hope. The odds were now even. There would be no opposition to her trap.

Despite the height of the sun, as the group moved further into the cave, the light grew more and more dim. Michel and Kurzmann knelt to light two large kerosene lanterns. Soon the cave was lit with a soft golden glow.

Looking about at the inky darkness beyond the reach of the lanterns, Peter said, "All right, which way do we go?"

Calmly, as though she were a tour guide addressing a troop of Boy Scouts, she pointed and said, "We go north."

"North?" asked Peter, knowing full well that Montségur lay in the opposite direction. "But the notes I have state the cavern we seek is near Montségur."

Giselle laughed. "And just how well have your notes served you up till now?"

Chastened, Peter changed the subject. "So what is to the north?"

"The 2,500-foot *Pech Cardou*," responded Giselle. "A sacred mountain that dominates this valley and to this day carries an aura of mystery and superstition."

"I have heard rumors concerning that peak," said Peter, more to himself than anyone else. "There are tales of strange lights, odd-shaped clouds and even things flying in the air. I always wrote them off as the overly imaginative product of rural dolts with too much wine on their hands."

Motioning to the steel case on his back, Giselle asked, "Is that what I think it is?"

Peter nodded, eyeing her with suspicion.

"Let me see it." The words came out sounding like an order. Peter backed up and shook his head.

"You will just have to trust me."

"Trust you?" Giselle could not hide the sneer with which she responded to the man who had twice tried to kill her.

"What assurance do I have that you will lead me to the treasure?" Peter countered.

Giselle's sneer curved into a malicious smile as she responded, "I guess you will just have to trust me."

"I thought you might say something like that," said Peter coldly. "I am not prepared to trust you on anything." He nodded to Kurzmann who promptly swung his machine pistol into a firing position.

Now it was Peter's turn to smile. Turning suddenly to Michel, he demanded, "Give me your weapon."

Giselle saw Michel look angrily from Peter to Kurzmann. They both realized he had no choice. Slowly, Michel withdrew his service revolver and placed it in Peter's outstretched hand.

Still smiling, Peter turned to Giselle. "Now you."

With anger and hatred flashing in her eyes, Giselle handed him the Luger.

"Now what?" she asked.

As Peter thrust the two handguns into his jacket pocket, he said evenly. "The time for games is passed. You will now lead me directly to the treasure…"

"Or what? If you kill me, you'll never find the treasure." Giselle's

330   the $\mathfrak{Sisterhood}$ of the $\mathfrak{Rose}$

voice was calm but her emotions were in turmoil. None of this was working as she had planned. Her only hope was that Bernard and the local Resistance group were waiting at the Cathedral as planned.

"Oh, I don't intend to kill you ... yet," Peter responded. "But I will kill your friend here and right now, if you don't lead me to the treasure immediately. And no tricks. At the first sign of treachery, your friend here will be dead."

Giselle looked at her dear Michel and sighed. This was not at all what she had foreseen. She saw no choice but to lead Peter to the treasure's cavern and hope that the ambush she had planned could come off before he killed someone.

"Very well," she muttered in a defeated tone. "As I said, go north." She pointed down the tunnel to their right.

Peter shifted his pack with the case containing the skull on his shoulders and held out a hand. "After you," he said and the foursome set off into the darkness of the cavern system.

As they moved forward, Giselle could only think of the terror and death this man had wrought in the Yucatan. Gritting her teeth in hatred and the desire for revenge, she grimly but mechanically put one boot in front of the other and tried to clear her dark thoughts. She knew her plan must work or she and Michel would never survive.

For several grueling hours the small group pressed on, stumbling over rock slides and pits which seemed to have no bottom. They dodged stalactites and stalagmites in every passageway and gallery.

They passed through caverns both big and small, some foul with dampness and mildew while others were dry and silent except for the scuttle of small unseen creatures.

There was no time in this dark and cavernous world. Only the bobbing lanterns and occasional speech indicated any human activity in this otherwise alien land of pitch black darkness and quietude.

Finally, at about 8 p.m. by Giselle's watch, she called a halt. No one objected. She suspected that the men were as bone-tired as she was but hadn't wanted to show weakness in front of a woman. She thought sadly of Gabby and for a moment wished she was with them. Gabby would show them what stamina really meant. She was thankful that her young friend was out of harm's way in Toulouse.

The thought of her friend's pain and humiliation at the hands of

Klaus Barbie rekindled Giselle's thoughts of revenge and she sneaked a look at Peter, who was unrolling his sleeping bag. Just a little longer and she would find a way to settle her score, she consoled herself.

Everyone was so exhausted they ate a light meal of cheese and bread washed down with water from a canteen and quickly fell asleep. Even their small fire was allowed to dwindle away until the inky blackness closed over them.

Giselle could feel the warmth of Michel lying next to her. She knew he must be feeling claustrophobic in the dark. She longed to turn and clasp him to her body. She too felt the need for some sense of reassurance and love. But she knew this was neither the time nor the place. Physical togetherness with Michel would have to wait.

Even with Michel next to her and knowing that Peter would not move against her until he had the treasure in his hands, Giselle still slept with one hand on a small rectangular German military flashlight. She longed for her Luger pistol.

Throughout the following day, the four spelunkers made their way single file through the stygian blackness. The only sound in this dark world was the soft tread of their boots.

Toward mid-day they came to a large grotto where icy water rushed through a crevice near the roof and cascaded noisily into a large pool near the center. Actually gratified to hear sound in the solitude of the cavern system, they stopped for a small lunch.

"We had better reach our destination soon or we're going to go hungry," noted Michel as he pulled apart the last remaining piece of French bread.

"We should be very close," responded Giselle. She had been unnaturally quiet the entire trip, not wanting to speak to Peter. She did not want to risk giving any indication that a trap was set at the end of their journey.

After a brief rest, the group continued their trek. It had been obvious from the start that they were not the first people to tread the silent passages of this immense system of interconnected caverns.

All along the way there were signs of excavations, even living quarters. Once they saw drawings on a cave wall that were similar to ones Giselle had seen in a *National Geographic* magazine. Those photos had been of drawings dated to pre-historic times that were found in French caves.

On occasion they came across some ancient tools, including a pick and a shovel with a broken handle, obviously abandoned once their usefulness was over. Once, Giselle found what seemed to be a Maltese cross, which she believed to have been left by one of the legendary Templars. Peter thought it looked more Celtic. Time and the elements had not been kind to the venerable object and they could not be certain.

Hours passed. How many? No one knew or cared. After all, it wouldn't matter and each of the four was too intent on thinking about what lay before them to be concerned with the time.

"What's that?" called Michel from behind Giselle. In the dim soft glow of the forward lantern, he was pointing ahead. "There's light ahead," he exclaimed. "Is it possible we are coming to the surface?"

Giselle peered ahead into the darkness. "I doubt it," responded Peter as he bunched up behind her. "By my calculations, we have been steadily descending, not climbing."

"Then what is it?" asked Michel.

"There's nothing to do but go and find out," quipped Giselle, stepping off into the gloom. The rest followed silently.

After about 100 yards the dark path widened and opened into an immense cavern with a high vaulted roof. Two tall stalagmites straddled the pathway like giant columns on a building. Several tunnels could be seen leading out of the cavern in different directions, black holes lining the circumference of the cavern.

"Why this looks like some sort of a…" began Michel. His thought was echoed by Peter, who spoke in an awed tone, "Cathedral."

The whole place indeed appeared like some gargantuan cathedral. There was a soft light pervading the whole structure. Giselle looked about expectantly but there was neither sound nor movement within the great chamber. Where were the men? What had happened to her ambush? Had she led Peter here for nothing?

As before, she had asked Jean Paul to follow the group to Rennes-le-Château and, although he had not made contact since their arrival, she felt he was close at hand. She only wished that he had followed them into the cavern system. But what if he had not? And, even if he had, what could one man accomplish?

Her grim thoughts were pushed aside as they moved forward into the lighted chamber.

Peter was fascinated with the light. Walking to the nearest rocky wall, he ran his hand over horizontal stripes of light running through the layered sediment. A glowing whitish waxy substance came off on his hand. "Phosphorus," he called. "There must be a strata of phosphate rocks among the limestone."

Peter paused, peering ahead. Something had caught his attention.

At the far end of the lighted gallery, the glow changed from a greenish tinge to something subtler, something more golden. The reason was quickly apparent.

As they moved forward, they saw the cavern walls converge to form a U shape. Within this cul-de-sac was an immense heap of irregular-shaped objects that reflected the glow of the walls. Oil lamps ringed the pile. Peter struck a match and placed it to one of them. Much to his astonishment the lamp flared with flame.

"They still contain oil," he commented as he continued to light the lamps. "Someone has been here and not long ago," commented Peter. Giselle and Michel exchanged knowing glances, knowing that their Cathar friends had been here only short weeks before.

"*Mein Gott!*" exclaimed Peter as he turned to survey the golden heap, now alight with a golden radiance. The other three gathered around him, equally stunned by the sight before them.

At one corner of this mass was a stack of bags that appeared to be made of dark linen. Many had split open over time and spilled their contents onto the rocky floor. Glittering in the glow of the phosphorescent light were thousands of gold coins, some crudely engraved, others with finely stamped images of long-forgotten rulers.

Toward the center were whole pieces of furniture, chairs, tables, rectangular seats, all apparently made of gold. Piled on top of them was a grand assortment of more golden objects.

Plates, various utensils, vessels, staffs, poles holding the tattered remains of flags or banners, candelabras, swords, menorahs, large and small bells, even a large harp, all made of gold or silver, were stacked higher than their heads.

But seeming to outnumber the objects of gold and silver were the jewels. Rubies, amethyst, diamonds, lapis lazuli, topaz, emeralds, sapphires, turquoise. Every imaginable precious stone was represented in abundance. They filled urns, vases, porcelain jars and variously sized clay pots.

The four stood transfixed at the sight of so much wealth in one place as the light from their two lanterns made the huge mass seem almost alive as reflections flashed and moved among the precious objects.

"We are all rich," muttered *Unterscharführer* Kurzmann, his eyes a blazing gold from the reflection of the pile before him.

"Not all of us," snapped Peter, with a quick motion to the sergeant. Before Giselle and Michel had a chance to react, the well-trained trooper leveled his machine pistol.

"I figured you would play it this way," said Giselle calmly as she slowly joined Michel in raising her hands. She continued to glance about expectantly but her hopes of rescue were fading. There was no sound in the huge chamber except their talking and movements.

Kurzmann nervously glanced at the wealth before him and back to Peter.

His eyes shining with excitement and triumph, Peter looked around as if to assure himself that this indeed was the treasure he had sought so long. Any thought of the Star Portal was pushed from his mind by the sight of the wealth spread before him.

With a slight nod of his head to Kurzmann, he ordered, "Shoot them. We have the treasure. These two are enemies of the *Reich*. Shoot them both!"

Giselle was stunned. She saw that if there was any hesitation on Kurzmann's part, his *SS* training prevented any outward demonstration of it. His left hand pulled back the bolt on the MP-40 with an ominous metallic click and his finger tightened on the trigger.

CHAPTER 20

Inside the Cathedral
March, 1944

"**WAIT!**" **GISELLE CRIED, LOOKING ABOUT** frantically as though she expected something or someone to intervene in what certainly seemed to be her last moments on Earth.

Kurzmann blinked, hesitated and looked to Peter.

Before Peter could respond, Giselle faced her nemesis and continued rapidly, "Peter, you are a fool. If you kill us now, you will never learn the secret for opening the Star Portal."

"What Star Portal?" he scoffed. Gesturing about him, he said, "I don't see any Star Portal here." He gestured toward the metallic box still on his shoulders with his thumb. "I think you simply made the whole story up as a ruse to get your hands on the skull."

With a wolfish smile, he added, "But I see the treasure and that's quite enough for me."

Giselle looked about frantically. Something was very amiss with her plans. She had overestimated Peter's ability to fixate on anything other than material wealth. And she had no idea where the Resistance men might be.

"You don't understand, Peter." Giselle's voice was now bordering on desperation. "The Star Portal is not a material object. It's not some gateway made of stone or wood. It is a convergence of energy frequencies, something like a radio, only of a much higher vibratory range. And I know how to provide the focus for such energy. But it will require all of us."

Peter looked at her blankly for a moment, contemplating. Although his face remained an impassive mask, a terrible and ominous coldness came to his eyes.

"*Unterscharführer*! Carry out my orders!" he barked.

Now it was Michel's turn to speak. "I wouldn't do that, Sergeant," he said. His gaze was directed past the sergeant with the aimed machine pistol. Both Giselle and Peter followed his look. Giselle made a small sharp sound deep within her throat as she gasped in surprise. Peter's eyes went wide with a combination of surprise and fear.

Kurzmann, seeing their reactions, spun on his heel, crouched and peered into the darkness outside the reach of the oil lamps and lanterns.

At first he saw nothing, but as his eyes grew accustomed to the gloom, he saw motion at the tunnel entrances. There was an amorphous shifting among the deep shadows, a conflicted movement of things large and human shaped.

Kurzmann's features twisted with fear as he sought to bring his MP-40 to bear on the movement in the darkness. He frantically shifted his aim back and forth.

"Put the weapon down!" The commanding voice was deep, masculine and came from outside the limits of his vision. Kurzmann, whipping the muzzle of his machine pistol from side to side, could find no certain target, only moving black shadows which seemed to be everywhere and nowhere at once.

Giselle and Michel stood still, looking quickly in every direction, trying to get a glimpse of the dark figures moving into the cavern. Peter began desperately fumbling with the small buckle on the hard leather holster at his side, trying to reach his Luger pistol.

"This is your last warning," came the voice again. "Drop your weapons or we will open fire." Suddenly the metallic sound of several bolts being cocked echoed through the chamber.

Peter froze. *Unterscharführer* Kurzmann, looking fearfully about at his unseen assailants, slowly lowered his MP-40 and placed it on the ground at his feet.

A dark figure stepped into the circle of light made by the lanterns and the lamps. They saw it was a tall man wearing a long, black woolen robe. His face was partially covered by a cowl. In his hands, he carried a submachine gun. Giselle recognized it as an Enfield-produced Sten Mark II, the type that the British were parachuting with increasing frequency into the occupied countries.

Behind the man other figures were now encircling Giselle and her three companions. She saw that they were both men and women and all were dressed in long black robes with heavy hoods masking their features. She saw that a handful of these people were carrying weapons. The unarmed remainder seemed to hang back as though grateful for the anonymity of the chamber's shadows.

A second figure stepped to the side of the armed man and the flickering light illuminated his features.

Involuntarily, Giselle cried, "Bernard!" She rushed to her Cathar friend and clasped him in a bear hug.

"Thank God you came in time. You were supposed to have been here waiting for us."

Bernard looked sheepish. "I am so sorry, *ma chère*. I have only been to this chamber twice before and my memory is not what it used to be. I'm afraid I became somewhat lost. I apologize for cutting it so close."

"Well, since we're still alive, I guess that's close enough," said Michel with a short laugh as he clapped Bernard on the back.

Both Michel and Giselle had stepped to the side of Bernard and the large man with the Sten gun. As they stood looking at Peter and his sergeant, Giselle said, "Bernard, I know your beliefs include a great distaste for weapons. To whom do we owe a debt of gratitude for saving our lives just now?"

She accentuated her question by bending slightly and peering up at the face of the large man. It was partially masked by his cowl. She was rewarded with a glimpse of a dark mustache slowly curling into a grin under a large Gallic nose, the centerpiece of a ruddy oval face.

"This is René Artois," replied Bernard. "He owns a small café in the town of Nouvion where he doubles as the leader of the local Resistance. I arranged for him and some of his people to accompany us as you requested."

"But how did you pass through this area?" asked Michel. He was thinking of his ill-fated hike to Montségur with Gabby and Charles. "We learned this area is off limits to civilian travel while these German pigs seek our hidden riches."

Bernard sighed. "That was another problem that contributed to our lateness. As you know, tomorrow will mark the 700th anniversary of the fall of the Montségur fortress. This day has special meaning for those of us still practicing the beliefs of the Pure Ones.

"I applied for permission to lead a pilgrimage of Cathari there, as we planned. But the military governor refused us permission. Something about an important expedition by the SS taking place here." He looked pointedly at Peter's black uniform with the SS lightning bolts and Death's Head insignia on his collar.

"But you are here," stated Michel.

"*Oui*. I knew the importance of honoring our agreement to meet you here with some protection." He again glared at Peter. "We decided to risk coming without proper authorization."

Bernard laughed. "We Cathari have never been overly compliant with authority," he added. There were soft chuckles from the robed figures lining the walls of the chamber.

"Then near Montségur, we encountered a force of SS troops. A colonel with a large scar was most accommodating. He said he didn't object to our religious pilgrimage, so here we are."

"Were you followed?" asked Michel.

"I don't think so, we haven't seen any signs of them." replied Bernard. With a look of concern, he added, "Is the treasure safe?"

"Yes, we just got here a short time ago," said Giselle. In a near pleading tone, she added, "Bernard, this is fabulous. Are you certain we can't take just a bit of this gold to finance our fight against the Nazis?"

Bernard looked stern when he replied, "Now, my dear, you know our agreement. You were allowed to lead this German to the treasure if it meant regaining the Skull of Fate. Nothing was said about looting the treasure that my people have protected all these centuries."

Then suddenly breaking into a wide grin, he added, "But, of course, I cannot imagine that our ancestors would object too strongly if a small portion of this hoard was used to end the reign of terror on the Continent."

Stepping to an earthen jar overflowing with rubies and diamonds, Bernard scooped up a handful and handed them to Giselle, who placed what she knew would amount to a small fortune into her pants pocket. Peter stood watching haplessly, his jaw locked tight in anger and his eyes blazing in helpless fury.

She took Michel by the hand and they both smiled back their thanks and appreciation. Then stepping forward, Giselle said, "*Monsieur*

René, if you and your men would be so kind as to prevent any more mischief from these two," She motioned toward Peter and Kurzmann, "I am anxious to begin working with Bernard on the ancient ceremony."

"Very well," said the tall Frenchman. He turned and commanded, "Louis, Antoine, watch these *Boche* buzzards. The rest of you can remove those robes and take turns at watch in the tunnels."

As the Resistance fighters among the Cathars moved toward the tunnel entrances along the walls of the Cathedral cavern, Giselle moved to Bernard's side.

"As a scientist, I am more than just a little intrigued to see if the Star Portal truly exists. May we start the proceedings?" she said quietly.

Bernard smiled beneficently and replied, "But of course, *ma chère*. This is the time that we agreed upon. And it is indeed propitious. The constellations are in the proper order and it is the 700th year since the fall of Montségur."

"What has the fall of Montségur got to do with it," asked Michel. "That happened so long ago."

"Yes," agreed Bernard. "But it has taken that many years for the constellations to arrive in just the right configuration. And there is a prophecy."

"What prophecy?"

"It was predicted centuries ago that, 'At the end of 700 years, the laurel will be green once more.'"

"But what does that mean?" Michel persisted.

Bernard stroked his chin and replied, "We can't be certain, but many believe that today will mark a resurgence of Cathari beliefs, that our philosophies can once more be heard in this land without fear of the stake or the rack. It might also mean that this is the time that an activation of the Star Portal may prove successful."

Stepping to the center of the chamber, Bernard pulled some papers from a black leather case he wore strapped across his shoulders. Holding them aloft, he called out in a loud voice to the two dozen or more robed Cathars who stood silently before him.

"Brothers and sisters, the time we have all anticipated has finally come. The laurel will bloom again. You all have practiced the chants that will activate the portal. And I have distilled the words passed down from our ancestors into these few pages. If you all will form a circle within this chamber, male and female alternating, we will begin. The 12 designated *parfaits* will form the pentagram and we will proceed."

"What about those two?" asked René, flipping his thumb toward Peter and Kurzmann. The sergeant was glaring at them with undisguised hatred. Peter's eyes were bright with anticipation. He had fulfilled his mission to recover the treasure and now it seemed he was on the verge of witnessing the reality of the Star Portal with a chance at unimaginable power. He believed it only a matter of time before he turned the table on his captors.

"They are necessary to the ceremony," explained Bernard. "Place them on one arm of the pentagram. Giselle, you and Michel stand at the other. Just as we must have balance of the male and female energy, there must be a balance of good and evil, the positive and negative opposite poles of energy."

As Peter and his sergeant were hustled into position on the forming geometric figure, Giselle noted he still wore the metal case containing the skull. But her excitement over the possibility of opening a gateway to another realm overrode her desire to regain the skull. As far as she knew, it played no role in opening the portal and she could retrieve it from Peter at any time after the ceremony.

Once everyone was in position holding hands, Bernard called for silence. Then he spoke in a clear and reverent voice. "We are gathered here today in the midst of world strife to pay homage to our ancestors who paid so dearly for defending their beliefs against an arrogant and murderous organization of men who called themselves servants of God. It is in their memory that we asked God to hear our cry for peace and justice on this world. Let us pray."

All heads were bowed as Bernard began to intone:

"Our Lord Jesus Christ, in whom we place our faith in deliverance from the death and tribulations of the material world, hear us, your faithful and obedient servants, as we pay homage to the Pure Ones of ages past who fell at the hands of those who worship Mammon, those who cause all manner of death and destruction in the name of Godliness.

"Give to us this day the mercy needed in a material and sinful world, a world in which the death of innocents is being repeated even in this modern age, an age when whole populations are being felled under man's destructive technologies.

"Give rest and absolution to those souls who must undergo the purgatory of man's brutality to man, amplified in this day by technology that has been twisted toward death rather than to life. And bless those whose bravery and courage every day advance the cause of peace and light in this dark world of misery and strife. Though not of our congregation, they are truly our brothers and sisters.

"We humbly ask that we shall overcome the sufferings of the world, as our Savior once did in casting off the darkness of death, and join with Him in receiving the welcome counsel of our Good Father in Heaven.

"To you, O Lord, we have gathered this day in honor of these saints, these Frenchmen who gave all for the certainty of their knowledge. They did not accumulate wealth, nor do we; they did not build empires, nor do we. They ministered to the soul and not the body, as do we, and they chose death rather than dishonoring their faith. But it was not the end of their existence, but a release as a bird from a cage. Their spirits took flight and, in that dark and terrible hour, they overcame the world, just as your son, our Lord Jesus did after the cross.

"Grant us some sign that the death of your faithful at Montségur shall not have been in vain, but that their descendants and followers could grow to be like them, remaining prayerful, pure and sanctified to the Gospel, in the name of our Lord, Jesus Christ. Amen."

"Amen," the word was taken up throughout the dim underground chamber. Giselle found herself mumbling the word and contemplating her own spirituality.

From all around the cavern, a long slow moaning rose in crescendo, a humming sound similar to that which Giselle had heard emanating from Hindu fakirs. This "ohm" sound grew in strength and intensity as Bernard now began calling out ancient chants and incantations gleaned from the tablets and scrolls mixed into the treasure hidden for so many centuries by its ancient protectors, the Cathari.

Her Jewish ancestry pushed itself to the forefront of her mind. Thoughts arose of the esoteric scriptures from the Kaballah and the Torah. She found herself chanting with the others, "*Kodoish, Kodoish, Kodoish, Adonai, Tsebayoth*! Holy, Holy, Holy, is the Lord God of Hosts!"

Long moments passed and Giselle stopped chanting. Instead, she found herself shivering and it was not from the usual chill of the cavernous chamber. The temperature had dropped noticeably and there was a subtle energy charge in the air. It brought the small hairs on the back of her neck to a standing position.

Giselle looked at Michel. His hand was cold and clammy. He glanced back and his face showed clearly that he too realized something unusual was occurring within this subterranean assembly and that it was frightening him.

Over the chanting of the cowled figures and the droning of Bernard's voice, Giselle thought she could hear a high-pitched humming sound, almost, but not quite, within the human hearing range. It was like a dog whistle her father had once used, perceptible but not audible.

She blinked in astonishment. In the center of the huge chamber a spot of light seemed to grow in mid-air, shimmering like moonlight reflecting off rolling water. The light was not bright but a peaceful glowing luminescence that moved, writhed and swirled.

The radius of this iridescent prism of light grew larger until it was more than six feet across. The ebb and flow of this effervescent energy slowly swirled and frothed like some giant amorphous one-celled creature trapped within a translucent Petri dish.

As the vibrational frequencies increased, the structured patterns of sound waves coalesced into a myriad of colors producing efflorescence in the air. Feelings of infinite love and warmth washed over her inner being.

She could not help but think of the Biblical story of Joshua and the power of his ram's horns and the people's shouting that brought down the mortared walls of Jericho. She had read papers on the capabilities of sonic frequencies and knew that it was an area that science had made little headway in understanding.

Despite her fascination and awe over this display of the supernormal, Giselle's innate scientific curiosity rose unbidden. She dropped Michel's hand while maintaining contact with the black-robed Cathar on the other side and stooped down.

Gathering a rock the size of a softball, she tossed it underhanded into the center of the colorful swirling energy where, much to her amazement and against every scientific law she had been taught, it halted, hanging motionless in mid-air.

Giselle saw Michel's eyes widen in consternation and disbelief but then a motion to one side caught her attention. It was Peter. While his two guards remained motionless, staring slack-jawed at the seemingly divine display in front of them, the blond officer had dropped to his knees. His eyes bulged from his head and she knew he too was dazzled by this profane and perverse attack on his practical scientific senses. His hand reached out, almost as though his touch might somehow explain the unexplainable.

A sudden reverberation swept through the chamber, breaking the spell of the moment. It was loud and sharp and was immediately followed by a distant shout. "*Alarme!*"

Everyone turned at the sound which Giselle quickly realized was a gunshot. She saw the rock she had thrown drop to the cavern floor as though some invisible hand had released it. The pulsating energy swirl grew dim and dwindled into nothingness.

More shots were fired, followed by the staccato sound of a machine gun.

One of René's men suddenly bolted through a tunnel entrance. A thin stream of blood poured down his face from a superficial head wound. "Germans! The *SS*!" he shouted, pointing down the passage behind him. To emphasize his warning, there was a rattling of automatic gunfire and a line of bullet holes stitched their way across the stone wall just above the man's head. An explosion rocked another of the tunnel passages. Smoke and dust billowed from the opening.

The huge underground cavern, which had been so silent when Giselle, Michael, Peter and Kurzmann first entered, was now filled with a cacophony of noise—the roar of German gunfire mixed with the sharp tattoo of the Resistance fighters' Sten guns, the shouts and screams of the terrified Cathars and the shouted orders of René and his men along with the fainter shouting of *SS* troop leaders. Amidst all this was the crisp crack of bullet slugs striking rock, ricocheting fragments of stone and steel, the dull explosions of hand grenades and the occasional crunch of stalagmites and stalactites crashing to the floor from bullet strikes.

Giselle and Michel dove for cover behind some of the golden furniture at the base of the treasure hoard only to find Peter and Kurzmann had beaten them to what appeared to be the only reachable place of safety in the giant treasure chamber. They could see the Cathars near the tunnel entrances falling back from gunfire within.

There were two large explosions in two of the entrances and, as suddenly as the firefight had begun, it stopped. Although there were still two or three more desultory shots fired, the fight was over.

The foursome behind the golden furniture slowly rose to their feet as the Cathar assembly poured back into the Cathedral chamber, pushed along by grim-faced *SS* troopers. From several of the tunnels walked René's Resistance fighters, several with wounds and all with their hands raised above their heads. They were herded into one corner of the cavern while the unarmed and unprotesting Cathars huddled in another.

Looking about, Giselle was surprised to see no bodies in the chamber, despite the fusillade of shots that had ricocheted throughout the gallery. Some of René's men were tending to the wounds of their comrades, but none appeared serious. The dead must have been left in the tunnel system.

Slowly the huge cavern filled with both men and light. The SS men must have been training for the Italian front, thought Giselle, taking note that their uniforms were the reed-green tropical field uniforms made for North Africa. They wore no helmets, but rather the light olive peaked M1940 field caps, many of which had been bleached to a near white by the sun. Obviously, these men had not expected a fight here in an area still free of Allied forces.

A group of engineers entered with a portable generator and soon the chamber was flooded with the brightness of two klieg lights.

Glancing up at a commotion at one of the tunnel entrances, Giselle saw a tall strapping officer wearing the same tropical uniform and a soft overseas cap enter the chamber. Men scurried to clear his way. He obviously was in charge.

Walking straight toward Peter, the big man held out his arms and said in a booming voice, "Well, well, well, look who we have here. *Sturmbannführer*, it seems I arrived just in time to rescue you from this ragtag bunch."

With a broad grin, he clasped Peter's hand and pulled him close. No one but Giselle standing beside him could hear his whispered greeting. "I'm sure you meant to contact me with your position as soon as possible, *nicht wahr?*"

Peter looked flustered. Before he could respond, the big officer stepped back and asked loudly, "Well, now, what have we here?" His eyes grew large and round as his men opened a gap in the ring of troops to reveal the treasure trove.

"*Gott in Himmel!* Would you look at this!" *SS-Standartenführer* Skorzeny exclaimed, surveying the mound of gold and silver objects and jewels. His eyes sparkled brightly in the golden glow now filling all but the most remote recesses of the giant cavern. "Eureka! We've done it! I thought these pilgrims might lead us to the treasure and so they have."

For the briefest moment Giselle thought she sensed the man's urge to seize the treasure hoard for himself. His smile faded and he glanced around as if to see what chance he might have in denying the find to his superiors. But there were too many men crowding into the chamber. Someone would talk. Word would get back.

His smile returning, he turned to Peter and clapped him on the back. Any suspicions he might have harbored were lost in his enthusiastic victory. "I will receive the Oak Leaves and Crossed Swords to my Knight's Cross for this," he gushed, "and I'm sure there will be something in it for you, as you initiated this search in the first place." He was beaming with the pride of accomplishment and apparently had lost all concern that Peter had gone off on his own with no apparent attempt to contact his superior.

After several minutes of examining pieces of the treasure mound, Skorzeny turned back to Giselle and Michel, the only two persons within any distance of the riches.

"And what have we here?" he asked Peter, who had stood by obediently while the colonel made his examination.

Seizing this opportunity to explain why there had been no contact, Peter quickly said, "*Herr Standartenführer*, I beg to report that these are enemies of the state. I had them lead me to the treasure and had taken them prisoner. But I was overpowered by those men." He pointed to René's small group huddled in one corner of the cavern.

Peter smiled and said in an ingratiating tone, "You indeed saved me, *Herr Standartenführer*. I will be eternally grateful."

A hint of suspicion returned to Skorzeny's eyes and he turned to Kurzmann. "Is this true, *Unterscharführer*?" Kurzmann clicked the heels of his hobnail jack boots and responded smartly, "*Jawohl*! *Herr Standartenführer*, this is true."

With that confirmation, any suspicions Skorzeny may have had regarding Peter's motives and actions were swept away and the excitement over his discovery returned.

"Bring the field radio," he shouted gleefully. "Send a message to Berlin. Just one word, '*Ureka*.' Sign it 'Scar.'"

Eureka. I've found it! That eternal cry of success. Giselle felt her entire body sag as the enormity of what had just happened dawned upon her. The Nazis had taken the world's greatest treasure. The thought was untenable when she began to think of what such wealth could buy—more tanks, more cannons, more guns, more war. It would purchase havens in other countries to carry on their warped view of genetically-pure Aryan superiority. It would pay for the continuation of their inhuman experiments in biochemical mind control. It could be used to create dummy companies across the globe to mask their ongoing plan for domination. Such power could spread far and wide, fueled by such a fortune.

Hours later, Giselle was sitting on a large rock, still morosely contemplating that Hitler and his minions now had virtually unlimited wealth to further their plan for a New World Order. Her mind was also reeling from worry over Michel and the knowledge that the Star Portal was real. She could think of only one consolation. At least poor Gabby was safe from all this.

The Cathars had been herded into a nearby grotto. But Michel had been taken away by the SS troopers, a prisoner along with René and his men. She knew that arrest would go badly for him, but she was in no position to help. He would eventually be handed over to the *Gestapo*, who undoubtedly would link him with Jean Moulin. Her heart ached at the prospect of his *Gestapo* interrogation. Was she destined to lose every love in her life?

Peter had requested that Giselle stay, arguing that her archeological knowledge might prove useful. He seemed quiet and withdrawn to Giselle, obviously still affected by the demonstration of supernatural power prior to Skorzeny's arrival.

He sat brooding nearby, straddling his metal case as though to protect it from being carted off with the rest of the treasure. Giselle began to understand that Skorzeny did not know what the case contained.

Giselle looked up to see the SS officer examining a large silver bowl ringed with gold inlaid plaques containing some sort of engraving. At least three large precious stones adorned the exterior of the bowl, which was cradled in a base made of a greenish mineral, perhaps emerald or jasper. Resting on its three-footed stand, the object looked like a large chalice.

As comprehension began to dawn on her, Giselle saw Peter follow her gaze and exclaim softly, "*Donnerwetter*! The Emerald Cup!"

The Emerald Cup, the Holy Grail, sought by so many for so many centuries.

Despite their enmity, Giselle's scientific curiosity was aroused. She whispered to Peter, "Do you think that's it? The real Grail cup?"

"I have no reason to believe otherwise," responded Peter in an awed tone. He stood helplessly while Skorzeny handed the cup to a trooper, who added it to a crate loaded with gold and gems. Soon it was on its way to the surface, carried by two strapping SS men.

Peter, perched on a rock seat, slumped forward listlessly. He became more and more dejected as he watched the great treasure hoard being carted off piece by piece by the *Waffen-SS* troopers. He saw his chance of everlasting wealth steadily slipping through his fingers. He didn't dare so much as pocket a coin or two for fear of being caught by Skorzeny. He had escaped the wrath of the big colonel once and did not want to push his luck.

One of the radio operators approached Skorzeny and reported, "*Herr Standartenführer*, we have placed an antenna outside and have established radio contact with Berlin. We sent the message you instructed and we have a reply," said the man snapping to attention.

"Yes, yes, what is it?" asked Skorzeny impatiently.

Reading from a scrap of paper, the operator said, "Well done. Congratulations. Watch the sky tomorrow at noon. Await our arrival. Signed, *Reichsführer-SS*."

Skorzeny grinned broadly, an act that accentuated his long scar. "Did you hear that? Himmler himself will meet us here tomorrow," he said to Peter, who tried to look pleased at the news. But Peter kept glancing at the large rock on the cavern floor which only a few hours before had unnaturally and mysteriously hung in mid-air, suspended by some inexplicable force.

Peter's world was in turmoil. His entire life had been one of self-centered pragmatism. Everything was orderly. His early training had only fortified his belief that anything anomalous was merely something that had not yet been scientifically measured and catalogued. Even his early disgrace carried a certain logic with it. Now he had to contend with something he could neither explain nor understand.

The experience with the rock had sent a chill throughout his entire being. The religious instruction of his youth crept unbidden into his thoughts. If things existed outside of his scientific knowledge then what if other matters were real. Religion? Spirituality? What if there was truly a God? Wouldn't that mean that there also was a devil? Was it possible that he indeed might be at risk of some everlasting fiery punishment?

Peter sat grappling with such thoughts as the weary troopers continued to heft all they could carry through dim passageways, lit only by flashlights augmented by some of the oil lamps, to the opening on the surface several kilometers away. They looked like a line of huge ants, each following the next with different sized bundles.

"*Herr Sturmbannführer*! Come take a look at this," the voice of Skorzeny echoed through the emptying chamber. "Bring the woman with you."

Peter slowly raised himself from his gloomy reveries and walked with Giselle to one corner of the treasure chamber. They peered down into the dim recess and saw pieces of rotted wood scattered on the floor. Apparently, at one time, the wood had formed a rectangular box of some sort. Engraved plates of gold that must have covered the box at one time were scattered on the ground. Two golden bands about four inches in width as well as four golden rings were lying amongst the wooden planks. Two poles made of a light-colored wood lay within the moldering pile of debris. Whatever the object had been had fallen apart when the wooden interior rotted and collapsed. Giselle stooped and picked up a handful of powder, not unlike flour, which lay scattered about under the remains.

Before she could ask about the powder, Skorzeny called out, "What do you make of this?" He stood farther into the alcove and his face, its scar highlighted in the omni-directional brightness of the klieg lights, shone with intensity. Giselle suspected he had an idea concerning this find but was looking for professional confirmation.

She knelt and poked around in the small pile of rotted wood, examining a small broken piece. Sniffing it, she opined, "It seems to be acacia wood. But I don't think you'll find any in this region. Strange."

Her voice dwindled away as she saw something glinting farther back in the recess.

"Give me your flashlight," she commanded the soldier standing by Skorzeny. In her scientific concentration, she forgot her prisoner status. The well-disciplined trooper reacted to her command and handed over his light without hesitation. Peter and Skorzeny both leaned in for a closer look.

Grasping the small metallic flashlight in one hand, Giselle held it toward the objects of her attention and gasped. There on the floor were two gilded kneeling figures, apparently angels judging from the wings that sprouted from their backs and curved toward each other. The centuries had dulled their gold plate but its luxuriousness was unmistakable.

"My God!" she whispered. "Can this be?"

Peter stood dumbfounded for some time before slowly turning to the expectant Skorzeny. "*Herr Standartenführer*, I believe we have found the final resting place of the fabled Ark of the Covenant!"

CHAPTER 21

"*Ausgezeichnet!*" exclaimed Skorzeny, stamping his booted foot. "Outstanding! The Ark of the Covenant. Just as I suspected."

Grabbing Peter by the shoulders, he said excitedly, "I will get diamonds with my Knight's Cross now."

"*Ja, Herr Standartenführer,*" mumbled Peter, stunned by the immensity of the discovery. "Our names will be on the lips of the entire world."

The big man stood silently for a moment, deliberating. "Perhaps not, *mein junge,*" he whispered quietly. His scarred countenance was contorted by a deep frown. "There are some secrets that were meant to be kept."

Seeing Peter's puzzled expression, Skorzeny added softly, "What the world does not know, it will not come looking for, *nicht wahr?* There is a time for military force and there is a time for quieter methods to achieve the same purposes." He touched one side of his long nose and winked.

Peter stood absorbing the import of Skorzeny's words. The Nazis did not mean to announce their discovery to the world. They intended the vast riches of Solomon's Treasure for more nefarious and secretive purposes than a public announcement would allow. Secret wealth meant secret power.

Skorzeny turned to Kurzmann standing nearby and ordered, "*Unterscharführer*, get some men and pack up all the metal here. Don't leave the smallest bit."

"But what about the white powder…" Giselle tried to ask.

"Never mind that dust." shouted Skorzeny. "Do as I say!"

Kurzmann saluted and hustled off to do his bidding. Giselle, her mind agog at what had to be the most important archeological find of all time, asked, "What will become of these remains?"

"Why it will all be melted into gold bars, of course," responded Skorzeny absently. "It will then be shipped out of Europe to fund the further activities of the *Reich*. To *Agartha* most likely."

Giselle did not recognize the name *Agartha*, but she knew that it meant a distant land, out of reach of Hitler's enemies. She felt the icy fear growing within her that she was witnessing the birth of some future *Reich*. Peter scowled, knowing that anything sent to *Agartha* was lost to him.

Staring at the sacred remains lying on the dusty floor of the cavern chamber, Giselle studied the exquisite filigree work on the gold plates. She saw on the *Kaporet*, the Ark's engraved covering, a miniature replica of the facade of the Khasneh, the famed Rose City temple at Petra. She instantly sensed the connection between that ancient temple of the Sisterhood of Isis and Rennes-le-Château.

She perched on a nearby rock and sat studying the etchings on the Ark with heartsick eyes. The symbols and hieroglyphics gave the very definite impression that they were some sort of map, a blueprint representing a key to the mysterious portal system. But she couldn't concentrate. She was depressed at the thought of such a find ending up as financial gain for these men, these monsters who pillaged history as well as whole countries.

She looked about as at least 100 armed men labored in the chamber. What chance did she have against such odds. Even if dear Michel was still with her, they could not prevent this looting of the world's heritage. And what of Jean Paul? She was concerned that there had been no word of her quiet but ubiquitous comrade.

Several hours passed and the line of soldier bearers never slowed. Rested men were brought in and the wholesale looting of the treasure chamber continued unabated.

Sergeant Kurzmann brought her a sandwich of processed beef and cheese on coarse bread, handing it to her without comment. She thanked him in a voice dull with worry and defeat.

She not only had failed to retrieve the Skull of Fate but had lost the world's greatest treasures in the process. The Ark of the Covenant, the Emerald Grail Cup, the Tablets of Testimony and who knew what else lost because of her scheme to regain the skull.

Perhaps it was just as well that her mind was dulled to the point of shutting down, filled with concern for Michel, Jean Paul and the others as well as anger and grief over the loss of Charles. She never noticed the hours that passed while the lighted chamber was emptied.

Full consciousness returned only when Colonel Skorzeny planted himself in front of her and called for Peter, who stepped to his side.

"What shall we do with her?" asked the big colonel.

"I'll take care of her," replied Peter with a hard and malevolent look on his face. Giselle felt a tension growing within her. Without the presence of his *SS* superior there would be no telling her fate at his hands.

"Very well." Skorzeny wore a cunning expression. Giselle felt sure he knew what Peter had in mind for her. But it was not his problem; in fact, it relieved him of her responsibility. "And the others too?" he added.

"Others?" Peter looked momentarily puzzled. "Oh, the Cathars. What do you advise I do with them, *Herr Standartenführer?*"

"Let them go."

"I beg your pardon?"

"Let them go. They are harmless. It was not them that shot at my men. In fact, I was the one who gave them permission to enter this restricted area. They did us a service by leading us to the treasure."

Pulling himself to full height, he said, "I am a soldier. I do not make war on women and clerics."

"Very well, *Herr Standartenführer,*" Peter clicked his heel as he rigidly gave the Heil Hitler salute. "I'm taking one of the weapons and *Unterscharführer* Kurzmann will remain with me. We shall meet you at field headquarters in time for Himmler's arrival."

Skorzeny checked his wristwatch and said, "That will be about noon, barely enough time to exit the tunnel system and arrive in Montségur. You'd better hurry with whatever you have planned." He smiled knowingly and walked off shouting, "Pack up the gear. Make one final search of the cavern. If I find one gold coin left behind, you all will celebrate Easter on the Eastern Front."

The klieg lights were doused and packed off. The giant cavern reverted to the dim chamber they had first entered. Giselle stood and watched the last of the *Waffen-SS* men leave the cavern and turned to find Peter holding an MP-40.

"Don't think you are getting out of this so easily," he said in a soft but menacing voice. "Go get the others and don't try anything. You know that I won't hesitate to use this and I will start with the Cathars."

As Giselle moved to Bernard and his followers, she heard Skorzeny call his farewell and heard the sounds of the German troops receding back into the tunnels.

Silently, she and the Cathars faced their captor.

"Are you going to shoot us all?" Giselle asked sullenly.

"Shoot you? Why no, my dear Giselle. In fact, you are going to assist me in a little experiment."

Seeing her questioning look, he continued. "We are going to resume the ceremony that was so rudely interrupted by that pompous ass." He nodded toward the tunnel that Skorzeny and the last of his troops had taken.

"Peter, please," said Giselle. "I think there has been enough damage done here today. Men have died and the world's greatest archeological finds have fallen into the hands of barbarians."

"Quiet!" cried Peter. "I should shoot you where you stand. But I have seen something today that I cannot explain. I want to see it again. I've lost the treasure. If there is the slightest chance that I might indeed acquire the power of a portal to other worlds, I am prepared to take it."

He laughed humorlessly. "I certainly will not be receiving any other compensation for my efforts to obtain the treasure. I'm sure Skorzeny will take full credit for the find.

"Now, this discussion is over. We will resume the ceremony." As if to punctuate his directive, he cocked the bolt on the MP-40. Behind him, Kurzmann took up a guarded stance. He too was armed with a machine pistol.

Peter and Kurzmann stood back to back cradling their weapons as Giselle and the Cathars formed a semicircle around them in the center of the now-empty treasure chamber. She noticed that Peter had the metal box containing the skull in front of him.

Bernard bared his head by pulling the hood of his robe back onto his shoulder and began, "O Lord…"

"You can dispense with the praying, old man," barked Peter. "Get on with the chanting."

Bernard glanced nervously around and commenced reading from his papers while his followers began their low repetitious chant. Again, the twelve chosen *parfaits* assumed designated positions to form a pentagram within the chamber while Bernard took Michel's place at one end of the formation.

Moments passed and Giselle felt her eyes closing. Unconsciousness stalked the outer fringe of her mind. She had been through too much with not enough sleep. The combination of sleep deprivation, worry, shock and excitement was causing a drowsiness she could not suppress.

But suddenly the strange glowing luminescence again manifested itself in mid-air, appearing as a swirling globe of energetic color. All colors of the light spectrum were represented within the circle of light. Again, a soft high-pitched whine was audible over the chanting of the Cathars.

There was the sound of rushing wind but nothing stirred within the cavern except for the rhythmic pulsation of the energy vortex, which oscillated and grew in a manner that was mesmerizing to all those viewing it.

Peter's eyes sparkled with a strange excitement as he watched in wonder at the energy vortex forming in the air before him. It was as though he saw distant galaxies and worlds within the swirling particles of energy. Worlds he now might personally dominate.

Quickly he knelt and opened the box at his feet.

Holding the crystal skull high above his head, Peter shouted above the rushing sound, "I want the power!"

Giselle's eyebrows bunched with concern that his request might be answered. Her anxiety was heightened as she saw the skull lift from Peter's hand and float toward the colorific sphere of light. Peter stood transfixed, disbelieving his own senses. Kurzmann, with his back to the light display, kept trying to glance back over his shoulder. His face was ashen and twisted with incomprehension and fear.

The men and women of the Cathari seemed oblivious to the events transpiring in the air before them. Their eyes were closed and the rhythmic tone of their chanting seemed to have placed them under a spell. They swayed to and fro as their chanting increased, both in volume and intensity. The physical presence within the now shimmering cavern grew ever larger and more substantial.

The Skull of Fate slowly moved to the very center of this pulsating energy force where it began to glow brightly, reflecting the myriad colors of the intense whirlpool of electrons.

To Giselle's amazement, the skull seemed to take on a life and movement of its own. There was a vague halo effect surrounding the skull, which began to take on the form of a human-like face.

Drooping down from this indistinct face, a flowing pattern of colorful light speckles began to form a human torso complete with arms and legs. But it was diaphanous, almost transparent. There seemed to be a great white light framing the figure which changed into multi-colored hues as the light expanded.

Peter shouted again. "I want the power!"

Time seemed to stand still as the translucent figure slowly turned toward Peter. The figure's hand reached out, stretching beyond all human capability. The filmy hand touched Peter's forehead and a giant white sphere suddenly formed behind his head.

As if it were some strange and miniature movie screen, Giselle could see fleeting images pass across the white canvas of energy.

Swastika flags and banners flapped in the breeze. German *panzers* rolled across open countryside, demolishing homes and public buildings. Deadly *Ju-87 Stuka* dive bombers with sirens screaming dropped their payloads on cities in Poland, Holland, Belgium, France, Norway, Russia and England. Old men, women and children were being rounded up by battle-hardened soldiers. Some were executed on the spot. Others were marked for transportation to detention camps. Lines of civilians wearing the yellow six-pointed Star of David on their clothing were transported by rail cars like cattle to grim and deadly places with names like Dachau, Buchenwald, Sobibor, Treblinka, Stutthof, Chelmno, Maidanek and Auschwitz-Birkenau. There were images of stacks of naked human bodies.

Giselle was horrified by the images that had been pulled from Peter's mind. Even though she had been fighting against the Nazis for nearly four years, she had never truly considered the enormity of their crimes against humanity. She had failed to see the scope of human suffering and death as being shown to her in the transitory images in this translucent energy matrix, projected from Peter's mind.

Suddenly, there was a voice, not so much heard as felt within her head. She could tell by the reactions of those about her that they heard it too. Bernard, along with several of the Cathari, had fallen to his knees and was sobbing with spiritual fervor. Peter was staring at the figure, his expression a mixture of hopeful reverence and frightened supplication. He could hear it too.

"You are undeserving of power." This message was seared into their minds.

Peter's face became a frozen mask of horror and fear. He made no movement, stiffly standing still in the face of a force he could neither control nor comprehend.

Slowly his entire body moved toward the figure within the circle of energy, moving smoothly without the normal subtle nuances of human movement. It was as though he was some stick figure, stiff and immobile, being drawn into a wind tunnel. Giselle was shocked to see that his boots were no longer touching the cavern floor. He also seemed to be diminishing in size.

Suddenly, Peter's body began to rotate as though he were practicing cartwheels in mid-air, except there was no effort on his part, only a horrifyingly slow rolling motion as he spun toward the energy vortex. Faster and faster he spun.

He began to scream. It began low but grew in volume, only to be swallowed up in the clashing colors and power of the pulsating circle. It seemed to Giselle that it came more from an intense and absolute psychic terror than from any physical pain.

Sergeant Kurzmann looked panic stricken as he watched his superior being drawn into the swirling mass of energy. He looked about wildly and rushed to Giselle.

"Make it stop!" he shouted over Peter's screams and the roaring of the energy vortex. Placing his MP-40 to her head, he commanded, "Make it stop or I will kill you."

Giselle was at a loss. She had no idea how to stop the process being played out before her. Michel and the Resistance men were gone. She was unarmed and surrounded by only the passive Cathars. At that moment, crushed by the loss of Michel and the treasure, she almost didn't care. All she could do was close her eyes and wait for her life to end.

When a shot rang out, she involuntarily flinched expecting pain and unconsciousness. To her amazement, she still lived.

Opening her eyes, she saw a thin arc of blood spurt from a small hole in Kurzmann's forehead. His eyes were wide and glazed as he slumped to the ground.

Not comprehending what was happening, Giselle could only stare at the body at her feet, then back to the spinning figure of Peter. It seemed to be falling into some deep horizontal chasm or pipeline made of swirling colors, dwindling in size as it moved. His cries grew dim and ended as he disappeared into the maw of unrefined energy. The vortex continued to ebb and flow. There was no sign that anything had passed through it.

The amorphous hand of the energy being now began to move toward Giselle. Frozen in place by some power other than her own, she watched the five fingers of pure energy reach for her head.

Somehow finding her voice, she cried out, "I don't want the power. None of us here want the power. We are unworthy of such power, especially today when millions of our fellow humans struggle to kill each other daily all over our world."

Finding her arms suddenly free, she raised both hands. "Take it back. Take back the power. Come back when we are better prepared to deal with such force. We beg you in the name of the universal God."

There was a murmuring all about her and she heard several shouts of "Amen."

The diaphanous hand slowly withdrew and soon the figure was proportionate again. The crystal skull, the only bit of solid material in that pellucid figure of energy, turned to face Giselle. It's visage eerily glowing in the reflection of the mass of raw energy. Its mouth opened wide.

No sound came, only the rushing of the electro-magnetic energy display being sucked in upon its self, as though water was being drawn down a drain. There was a brief flash and the skull was gone. The subterranean chamber was dark except for the few oil lamps.

Turning to her right, Giselle saw a diminutive robed figure step into the circle. One hand held a small *Walther* automatic. Bluish smoke wafted from the muzzle. Another hand pulled the black hood from the person's head.

Recognition came instantly and Giselle cried out, "Gabby!"

She rushed to hold the young girl in her arms. Gabby wore a grim smile full of satisfaction. Giselle realized that her young friend had found the opportunity to strike back at her Nazi tormentors.

"You saved my life," Giselle murmured as she hugged Gabby's small form. Pushing her away, Giselle frowned and said, "You disobeyed my orders. You shouldn't have come."

She was relieved to see the old mischievous smile return to Gabby's face as the young girl quipped, "Lucky for you I did. I couldn't stay behind knowing you might be in danger. I'm not a child any more."

Giselle smiled and shook her head. She turned and looked accusingly at Bernard.

The round *parfait* had an apologetic expression on his face. "I'm sorry Giselle," he said sheepishly. "I tried to make her stay behind but she was insistent. And like she said, she is not a child any longer."

Giselle pulled Gabby along until she was hugging both her protégée and Bernard. "You are forgiven, my dear friends," she said with a laugh. "We are alive and have witnessed a wonder here."

"A miracle from God," corrected Bernard.

"If you say so."

Bernard and Giselle looked at each other. No words were spoken. What was there to say? There was no sign of Peter, the skull or the energy being. Even in the years to come, none of those present would speak about the events of that day in the Cathedral cavern. It was too bizarre, too outré, too far outside their experience to discuss. Most simply dismissed the events as the hand of God and went on with their lives.

More than three hours later, Giselle along with Gabby and the Cathars finally made their way from the subterranean tunnel system into the light of day.

After trudging back along the route Giselle had first taken they found where Skorzeny's engineers had blasted a hole to the outside in a grotto near the *Pech Cardou*.

Emerging into bright sunlight, Giselle grimaced at its brilliance. After four days in near total darkness, the sunlight felt like knives piercing her eyes. There were cries of anguish from the Cathars around her. Gabby pulled her hood back over her face.

After some acclimation, she saw that the sun was at its zenith. Now that the initial pain had subsided, she welcomed the warmth of the March noonday sun.

Towering above them to the northeast was the mystical mountain of *Pech Cardou*. Giselle knew the treasure chamber had been somewhere under that enigmatic peak.

Looking toward the southwest, she could see the tiny village of Rennes-le-Château perched atop its hill and she knew that further west were the ruins of Montségur.

Putting her arm around Bernard, she said simply, "Well, *mon ami,* now you may resume your pilgrimage to Montségur, *non?*" He smiled and beckoned to his followers, who began to emerge from the stygian darkness into the light.

One of the emerging Cathars gave a shout and pointed to the sky.

As it was mid-March, the weather was not overly warm. But it was sunny this day with very few clouds in the sky. Far to the southwest, over Montségur, they could make out a growing line of white.

Shielding her eyes from the bright sun, Giselle tried to make out what was happening in the sky.

The thin white line continued to grow in length when suddenly it lurched to the right drawing the whiteness in another direction. Giselle was nonplused. What had they loosed? Could whatever power that came through the Star Portal have remained in this world?

Then faintly, she heard the sound of an airplane motor. Looking carefully, she saw the tiny dot leading the growing white line and realized it was an aircraft equipped with a skywriting apparatus.

Looking around at her companions, Giselle was amused to see some of the older Cathars crossing themselves and calling for God's protection.

Their cries became more insistent as the white lines in the sky came together to form a giant Maltese cross, plainly visible even from their faraway location.

"It is a sign from God," cried one woman. Another shouted, "God be praised!"

Even Bernard was not immune to the wonder of the moment. Standing beside Giselle, he said with great excitement, "The laurel is indeed blooming again."

Turning to Giselle, he said happily, "Don't you see? The Germans have been swayed to our cause. Even though they took the treasure, they have left us alive and unpunished. And now they paint a cross for us in the sky.

"I think this day, the 700th year anniversary of the martyrdom of our ancestors, will mark a resurgence of both our faith and our sect." He beamed happily as he motioned for his flock to continue their trek southward.

Giselle didn't have the heart to tell her spiritual friend that there was a good chance that the head of the dreaded Nazi SS, Heinrich Himmler, was in that plane and that the skywriting was merely his exuberance over gaining Solomon's Treasure for the coffers of the *Reich*.

Grimy and exhausted, Giselle stood beside Gabby basking in the warm rays of the sun. She watched Bernard and his congregation move slowly over the rugged hills of the Languedoc. Looking up, she studied the gigantic Maltese cross that was now almost complete over their heads. Her thoughts swirled as she considered the ordeal she had just endured. She thought of the vast underground cavern system and wondered if the legends of the subterranean world of *Agartha* might be true. After all, Skorzeny had used that very term. She also wondered about the white powder she had found lying about the ruins of the Ark. Could this mysterious powder have something to do with the power of the relic and even with the creation of the Star Portal?

And what had happened to the faithful Jean Paul? He was supposed to have provided extra security for Giselle.

Turning to Gabby, she asked, "Have you seen Jean Paul?"

"Why, no, isn't he supposed to be with you?" Gabby was sincerely perplexed.

Her words were interrupted by a loud familiar laugh from behind them.

A lone cloaked figured emerged and they saw a familiar face peering out from under the hood of the robe.

"Jean Paul!" Gabby and Giselle both shouted the name.

"I told you I would not be far away," said their friend as he reached their side.

Giselle scowled. "I almost died back there. I thought you were providing security."

Jean Paul smiled as he withdrew a pistol from beneath his robe. "I was. But our friend Gabby beat me to the draw." He and Giselle both looked at Gabby, who could only shrug.

"I was as fascinated with the portal as the rest," explained Jean Paul. "I have spent my entire life studying such things but it is only now that I know it is true. I have seen it with my own eyes. I managed to slip in amongst the Cathari and I thought it best to operate independently, so I did not alert Gabby to my presence. When we first entered the Cathedral, I stepped back into the shadows of one of the other tunnels. And don't look so dejected, Giselle. I may not have been the one to save your life, but I may have helped you in another way."

"And just how is that?"

Motioning for Bernard to join their group, Jean Paul said, "I had a premonition that the Nazis might get their hands on the treasure. So, some weeks ago I encouraged Bernard here to have much of the treasure—especially the ancient texts and scrolls—moved to another location. They are the real treasure. Gold and silver are only wealth. Knowledge is Power."

Bernard nodded. "This is correct." He looked a bit sheepish. "I'm sorry but I did not have time to tell you this in all the excitement."

Giselle had brightened considerably. "Oh, this is delightful news," she effused.

"And it gets better," said Jean Paul with a knowing grin. Giselle looked at him quizzically.

"You see, Solomon's Treasure has been protected all along. King Solomon himself invented the legend of a vast treasure hoard. He had a stockpile of wealth created from lesser items and he had beautiful reproductions made of most of the sacred artifacts. It was this treasure, the false treasure, that was taken by the Romans during the sacking of Jerusalem in 70 A.D. and later brought here by Alarec's Visigoths. All this eventually was added to the treasure brought here by the Knights Templar, who themselves pulled some sleight of hand.

"When the Inquisition was formed to bring down the Templars, their navy sailed away with much of the real treasure, leaving behind only the merest fraction, plus the fake wealth."

Her spirits renewed, Giselle was gushing with delight, "Oh, this is simply delicious. So Skorzeny did not get the treasure?"

"Not exactly, we saved the bulk of it but he still got a considerable sum for his trouble. That added to the immense wealth that Hitler has already looted from all of Europe will fund the Nazis for years to come."

Giselle was puzzled. "So what happened to the real treasure?"

Jean Paul looked more serious. "The bulk of the real treasure was entrusted to my organization, the Emerald Brotherhood. During the first century, my Brothers realized that the Jewish Revolt was doomed to fail so, posing as refugees from Palestine, they carried the treasure to southern France, the site of a thriving Jewish community."

"And the area where Mary the Magdalene fled with the family of Jesus…" mused Giselle.

"Exactly."

Giselle brightened. "Then Solomon's Treasure is still safe?"

"Even more so than before," answered Jean Paul. "Now the Nazis believe they have the treasure so they'll stop looking for it, *non?*"

"That's right," agreed Bernard with a self-satisfied smile.

"But what about Marie Denarnaud, René and the others?" asked Giselle, suddenly afraid that the Nazis might yet find traces of the treasure.

"It's quite all right," assured Bernard. "They believed they were protecting the real treasure hoard. No one but Jean Paul, myself and a few trusted *parfaits* know of the substitution and transfer of the real treasure."

"What must be done now to further ensure the safety of the treasure?" Giselle was still pensive, her nerves frazzled after the emotional roller coaster ride of the last few minutes.

Jean Paul lowered his voice. "Do not worry, the treasure is well guarded. The tunnel system you experienced is only the tip of the iceberg. The real treasure is protected by the true *Agartha*."

"But that's just a myth," Giselle blurted out. She was immediately sorry when she saw the look in Jean Paul's eyes. Real or not, he obviously believed in this legendary underground world where a subterranean people worked with peace and understanding within the harmony of nature.

Giselle tried to make amends. "That's the term I heard Skorzeny use," she said matter-of-factly.

Jean Paul appeared somewhat mollified. "That's right. But he was referring to a secret Nazi base. It may be in South America but we have reason to believe it is in Antarctica and only can be reached by submarine. The area is so remote that my Brotherhood's sources are not certain as to either its location or purpose. I myself think it is a retreat for ranking Nazis if the war goes badly for them."

"But Skorzeny called it *Agartha*." Giselle pressed the issue.

"That's true but he has no idea of the truth behind the real *Agartha*. You see, in prehistoric times, a great war sent a whole race of people underground. They survived and flourished there thanks to their great technology, much of which was ahead of what we know today. Thanks to this technology, the people of *Agartha* live fulfilled and peaceful lives. They have no use for a treasure such as Solomon's."

"Making them the perfect Guardians for the treasure…" Giselle was beginning to understand Jean Paul's words. "Have you been to *Agartha* and seen the treasure for yourself, Jean Paul?"

The young man looked solemn. "No and I doubt I ever will. It is not my place to go and seek the treasure. Only the Overseer of the

Brotherhood has contact with a representative of *Agartha*. And such meetings do not occur on our physical plane of existence. This is how these people protect the secret of their existence. Only rarely do stories concerning them reach the outside world, such as the legend of Shambhala or Shangri-La."

"So their technology includes Star Portals like the one we opened?" asked Giselle.

"Yes and much more. It could get very nasty if the Nazis were to gain access to their technology. This war could spread from our world to many others. And such Star Portals are not physical, as you have seen. They operate on a certain blending of sacred geometry and energy vibration. At the present time, humans require a certain substance to activate such portals as we are not yet spiritually evolved enough to use our own innate spiritual energy without assistance."

Giselle was standing deep in thought. She was beginning to put the picture together in her mind—the gold energizing designs on the floor of *La Coupole*, the words of Eva Braun concerning the white powder of gold and the strange dust surrounding the remains of the Ark.

"Of course!" she blurted out. "The white powder connected to gold, that's it. If you lay that out in the precise pattern of sacred geometry, you could open a Star Portal, couldn't you?"

Jean Paul only stood and smiled a deep and knowing smile. Stepping closer to her, he murmured, "Giselle, my dear, you really must be one of the ancient Sisters to have put all that together. But, perhaps we should keep this bit of knowledge to ourselves, *oui*?"

Giselle nodded slowly in agreement, her mind spinning with such new and unconventional concepts.

"We didn't use the powder but the portal activated," Giselle observed.

"I believe the Skull of Fate added enough focused energy to assist the sound vibrations from the chanting to activate the portal," Jean Paul replied.

"So, the skull was needed?!" Giselle said in wonder.

"Apparently so."

She shook her head. "What about the Grail Cup and the Ark of the Covenant? Were those real?"

"Yes and no. The remains of the Ark you saw was a replica created by the Templars. It was their coded message that you were reading.

However, their information was incomplete which is why they could never activate the portal. If the Nazis ever decipher it, it will be of no consequence. The Templars never had the real Ark.

"As for the Grail Cup, that was the cup of Abraham. It is valuable perhaps in terms of its antiquity, jewels and historical significance but not in terms of power or knowledge. The Brotherhood invented the legend of Abraham's Cup as being the Grail Cup as a diversion from the real Grail Cups," Jean Paul explained.

"Cups?" Giselle asked, not missing the plural reference.

"Yes. The real Grail Cups are the cups of Jesus and Mary Magdalene used at their wedding feast. They are symbols of love and the partnership, both masculine and feminine. The Grail, or matrix of life as we know it, is always comprised of duality. It is the essence of the Eternal Beloveds.

"The power of the two cups works only in conjunction with each other. And this must be done in conjunction with what has been known as the Philosopher's Stone, which is nothing less than the white powder of gold. Activation must be achieved multi-dimensionally on both the material and spiritual plane by audible frequencies applied to the electromagnetic optical spectrum in balance with the attendant human energy."

Jean Paul looked from Giselle to Gabby and Bernard. All were staring at him with glazed eyes and blank expressions.

He sighed and looked deep into Giselle's questioning eyes. "There is much more I could tell you about such technology and the Sacred Chalices but that is a story for another time," Jean Paul whispered mysteriously.

Gabby could contain herself longer. She had been standing listening to Jean Paul and growing more perplexed by the minute. "Jean Paul, how do you know of such things? I have known you for more than three years. We have attended the same university and some of the same classes. I have never heard you speak of such things. It's like I don't even really know who you are."

Jean Paul looked to Giselle as if to defer to her judgment on how best to handle the situation.

Placing a sisterly arm around Gabby's shoulders, Giselle leaned toward her and whispered, "I will explain everything later, dear Gabby."

Straightening up and taking Gabby's hand in hers, Giselle took one final look at the giant Maltese cross stretching across the sky and said in a loud voice, "Let's go home. I must find Michel and we still have a war to win."

Together, the friends set off on the first leg of their journey home to rejoin the Sisterhood of the Rose and finish the task they had undertaken.

Less than three months later, still grieving over her beloved Michel, Giselle saw the increasingly adverse effects on Hitler and the Nazis following the loss of the Skull of Fate. On June 6th, Allied forces from 26 nations stormed ashore in Normandy striking the weakest sector of Hitler's vaunted Atlantic Wall. There was quiet rejoicing throughout occupied France. The Resistance, now popularly called the *Maquis*, began intensifying their operations against the German occupation. Their activities now were synchronized with those of the American and British troops.

Giselle's days were increasingly busy as she coordinated Sisterhood activities from *Château les Fleurs*. Sitting at her desk one day in late June, she contemplated the events of recent months.

While the war was far from over, it was clear that a new day had dawned, a day of approaching liberation. Giselle knew the war would continue for some time. But she also saw that the Axis tide was receding.

With the Skull of Fate lost to Hitler, German military disasters were multiplying.

Since the Battle of Kursk, the Germans had been unable to launch any major offensive on the Eastern Front. The Soviets had slowly, but inexorably, pushed the Germans westward. In Italy, the Allies had landed behind the German lines at Anzio and were pushing slowly toward Rome.

It was just a matter of time before Hitler and his henchmen were wiped from the face of the planet. Even if the fabulous Treasure of Solomon was used to continue his twisted philosophies, he would be gone. The immediate threat would be ended. It would be up to future generations to finally stamp out his legacy of hatred, cruelty and notions of genetic superiority.

Giselle could not help but wonder how world events would have been altered had Hitler made different choices. With his interest in occult lore, art and architecture, what benefits might he have brought to the world if he had chosen to come from his heart rather than his ego? She thought of herself and the Sisterhood as well as millions of men and women all across the planet who had chosen to stand up to evil. Then she considered Peter and all the people like him, drawn to the dark side by greed, ambition and self-interest. It's all about choice, she concluded.

The ultimate disaster for the Nazis was D-Day. Both from sources in the Resistance and within the Sisterhood, Giselle had learned that the success of the invasion was guaranteed by the fact that Hitler had failed to authorize the release of his armored reserve. She knew only too well that if those *panzers* had been launched against the pitifully small beachhead, it would have surely spelled disaster for the invasion.

Strategists in both London and Washington were at a loss to explain Hitler's inaction at this most precarious moment in the war.

Giselle too wondered what might have caused Hitler's hesitation.

Her question was answered one day when a package arrived by courier. The stamps and markings showed it had been mailed in Germany, routed through Switzerland and on to the château.

Filled with curiosity, Giselle pulled open the packaging and stood shocked as she slowly became aware of the full import of its contents. Inside, there was no note or message, only two flowers—a long-stemmed red rose and a small white Edelweiss.

She realized that Eva Braun had sent it. It was her way of notifying Giselle that she too had done her part for the Sisterhood.

Giselle now knew why the Normandy invasion had succeeded. Allied Intelligence had made remarkable efforts to convince Hitler that the expected invasion would come at Calais, the point on the French coast closest to England. But she now knew that Eva may have played a significant role in assuring her *Führer* that the attack in Normandy was merely a ruse designed to draw his forces away from Calais.

Smiling, Giselle walked to one of the tall windows facing out on the garden. She could well imagine Hitler's fury over losing the skull and now the war. She felt the pride of accomplishment rising within her.

But her smile waned as she was touched by sadness and grief for all those who were sacrificed in this great struggle against tyranny and oppression. She was concerned that she might never again see Gabby exhibit the exuberance and enthusiasm of youth. And she sorely missed the serious, but always caring, Charles.

Most of all, she could not forget the loss of her dear Michel. She had lost Jim and now it appeared that she had lost Michel as well. Despite her best efforts, she could learn nothing of his fate. During the day, she immersed herself in her work. But, late at night, she cried often at the thought of Michel in the hands of her enemies. If he survived their torture, he would most certainly be sentenced to a concentration camp.

Yet she maintained a hope that she might yet rescue Michel or that he might survive the ordeal. And she was already scheming to recover the portion of the treasure taken by the Nazis.

But for all of her continued planning, she knew that she and the Sisterhood had already played a significant role in restoring peace and justice to a war-torn planet. And she knew that there was always hope, always another day to take up the struggle.

After her experience in the treasure chamber, it was a hope born of the certain knowledge that there was a power and intelligence beyond the three-dimensional world, a power that recognizes the difference between good and evil.

EPILOGUE

THE STORY YOU HAVE JUST read is fiction heavily laced with fact.

Celeste Levesque asserts that the story is a recollection of her past life. Amazingly, more than a half dozen others support this claim. They too claim memories of life within the world of the Sisterhood.

While there is no way to validate the reality of such memories, the account of the Sisterhood of the Rose makes for a great yarn. And much of the information is true. As with most medicines, a sugar coating helps it go down. Therefore, this tale can be called a work of "faction"—fact-based fiction.

This is nothing new. Hollywood has merged historical truth with dramatic stories for years. In fact, many people today believe there is more truth presented in music and films than in the corporate news media.

Celeste Levesque's research began after a near-death experience in the mid-1980s that led to an awakening of her deeper consciousness and spirituality. She also developed a keen sense that within her was a story the public deserved to hear.

She embraced new friends as well as new habits. She and an associate started a jewelry business and she became fascinated with gems and minerals. They seemed to release within her knowledge and memories of a life as an archeologist.

Her near-death experience had awakened dormant areas of her mind and psyche. She began having lucid dreams of distant times and places and her consciousness of the world about her expanded greatly.

Her knowledge grew considerably through reading and study on a variety of esoteric subjects. She came to realize that there were many worlds underlying the material world we consciously inhabit. She was constantly learning more and more, both about the universe and about herself. But she still had not learned what great purpose in life awaited her.

Her search for the truth behind her dreams began on a trip to New Orleans less than a year after her near-death experience. There, she realized this was the city she had spent time in as Giselle. Her Aunt Gez had maintained a residence here and New Orleans would play a major role near the end of her perceived past life.

Some time after that, she was riding in a friend's 1936 Mercedes Benz. Celeste suddenly had a vision, a flashback of her life as Giselle. She saw herself riding in similar vehicles throughout France, wearing the clothes of the period and images of people she worked with.

Then a friend in her current lifetime, who later told Celeste that she believed she had been Aunt Fran, gave her a silver compact with the initials "VV" engraved on it as a gift. This triggered even more memories. Each of the Sisters had given her items like this with cleverly disguised VV initials engraved on them. There was a compact, a cigarette case, and a moonstone necklace. In all there were twelve items. It is Celeste's hope that one day, these items will be found to further confirm the story of Giselle Tchaikovsky.

In the years following, Celeste continually thought of Giselle Tchaikovsky and her incredible story. Images of Mayan pyramids, wartime Paris, train rides, hidden treasure, evil Nazis and the fantastic Star Portal distracted her.

Was it all just a dream? Was it truly the memory of a past life? Did any of it really happen? Was Giselle a real person? What of Gabby, Charles, Jean, Michel, Marie, Aunt Fran, Jean Paul and Peter? Solomon's Treasure? The Star Portal? Was any of this real?

The questions lingered on long after her New Orleans vacation. They followed her as she returned to work and resumed her daily life.

She began to read and study the period of World War II. She made inquiries regarding Giselle and her story. She even visited upstate New York in the early 1990s in search of Giselle's childhood home of Skaneateles in the Finger Lakes region near Syracuse. She continued her research into the story including a trip to her beloved France and to the enigmatic Rennes-le-Château.

Evidence was scant and details hard to come by, yet Celeste felt there was something there. Perhaps the names were wrong or the time frame somehow distorted. Perhaps the story had taken place in some parallel dimension or timeline.

She also began participating in an ongoing series of past life regressions through both friends and professionals.

Over the course of several years, Celeste learned many intriguing facts that lent credence to the amazing story that she had first received in New Orleans.

In recent years, a spate of TV documentaries and books have detailed Hitler's obsession with esoteric knowledge and the occult. According to one of the Nuremberg prosecutors, the whole occult aspect of the Third Reich was ruled inadmissible in court because it was feared that such information might allow for a Nazi defense of insanity, since such ideas ran so counter to conventional thinking. Hitler himself once wrote, "I often go on bitter nights to Wotan's oak in the quiet glade, with dark powers to weave a union..."

A Professor Charles Richer of the Sorbonne was liberated by Allied troops on April 10, 1945, from the Nazi concentration camp at Buchenwald. He was strong enough, both in health and spirit, to give a tour of the camp to CBS Correspondent Edward R. Murrow.

Sophie and Hans Scholl did start an anti-Nazi movement at the University of Munich called the "White Rose." Both siblings were executed following a perfunctory trial.

The Allied acquisition of the German Enigma decoding machine was indeed one of the greatest and most secret weapons in the fight against Nazism. Often, Allied commanders knew of German plans and intentions even before the enemy. This amazing countermeasure was only made public in 1974. Credit for the initial success in acquiring and decoding the Enigma machine went to brave members of the Polish underground.

Jean Moulin did forge the disparate resistance groups in France into a formidable fighting organization, despite constant bickering between communists, socialists, democrats, supporters of De Gaulle and their enemies. Lured to a park near Lyon in early July, 1943, Moulin was caught in a trap laid by *SS Obersturmführer* Klaus Barbie. Taken to the dreaded *SS* headquarters in the Hotel Terminus, Moulin was savagely beaten for days but revealed nothing of substance to his captors. Placed on a train for transport into Germany for further torture and interrogation, he died en route from his injuries. He is still regarded in France as a great hero and martyr of the French Resistance.

SS Obersturmführer Klaus Barbie, known as the "Butcher of Lyon," was tried and sentenced to death after the war, but was never caught. American Intelligence agents helped protect him because of his "police skills" and his anti-communist credentials. Barbie lived in Bolivia until 1983, when he was finally deported to France where he was tried, convicted and sentenced to life imprisonment for his crimes. He died in prison in 1991.

Many female members of the French Resistance, such as Madeleine Braun, went on to greater achievements after the war, serving as role models for a new generation of young women who sought more from life than motherhood and housekeeping. Braun became the first woman elected vice president of France's National Assembly in 1946. Other heroines of the Resistance included Betty Albrecht, Lucie Aubrac, Germaine Tillion, Annie Kriegel, Evelyne Sullerot, Gabrielle Ferrieres and Genevieve de Gaulle, the niece of Charles de Gaulle.

British agent Ian Fleming left the secret service after playing a role in passing occult information to Nazi Deputy *Führer* Rudolf Hess and even advising President John F. Kennedy on how to end the rule of Fidel Castro in the early 1960s. After retiring to Jamaica, Fleming wrote fictional accounts of his spy work using the character James Bond. He died in 1964 during filming of the movie *Goldfinger*.

Svetlana Stalin, born in 1926, was the only daughter of Soviet dictator Josef Stalin. She caused an international sensation in 1967 when she defected to the United States, where she changed her name and became a writer.

Margaret Bourke-White, already an internationally known photographer for *Life* magazine, had in 1930 become the first Western photographer allowed in the Soviet Union. She was the only foreign photographer in Moscow when German forces invaded.

She photographed the conflict after taking refuge in the U.S. Embassy. She also was the first woman allowed to work in combat zones during World War II. From 1939 to 1942, she was married to novelist Erskine Caldwell.

Clara Petacci may well have helped sway Dictator Benito Mussolini away from the harsh anti-Jewish policies the Third Reich tried to force on Italy. Mussolini was lenient on Italian officials who consistently failed to carry out German orders to round up and deport Jews. Nevertheless, she was faithful to her lover. In late April, 1945, with nearly all the German generals in Italy secretly trying to negotiate an acceptable surrender to the Allies, Mussolini and Clara joined a convoy of German troops escaping north. The convoy was stopped by Italian Partisans, mostly communists and socialists, who recognized *Il Duce* and arrested him. Both Mussolini and Clara were shot and their bodies strung up feet first in a Milan gas station for public display.

According to new evidence from documents released in post-Communist Russia, Hitler was forced to launch a pre-emptive assault against the Soviet Union in June, 1941, to forestall an attack on Western Europe by Stalin in July.

Admiral N. G. Kuznetsov, who in 1941 was the Soviet Navy minister and a member of the Central Committee of the Soviet Communist Party, stated in his postwar memoirs that Stalin had made extensive preparations for an attack westward on a predetermined date. "Hitler upset his calculations," wrote Kuznetsov. Daniel W. Michaels, a retired U.S. Department of Defense official, stated, "The German *Barbarossa* attack shattered Stalin's well-laid plan to 'liberate' all of Europe."

The war was most certainly decided in Russia, where the intense and bitter struggle over the Volga city of Stalingrad ending in early 1943 marked the high-tide of German aggression, and the 1943 summer Battle at Kursk wrecked the German mechanized forces. But due to the enmities of the Cold War, Americans were unaware of this fact for many years and considered Russian statements to this effect to be Communist propaganda.

Eva Braun was finally married to Adolf Hitler the day before they reportedly died in his bunker under the *Reich*'s Chancellery in Berlin on April 30, 1945. Official history records that Eva took poison while the dictator shot himself in the head. However, controversy over this event has continued through the years. Eva could well have played a critical role in convincing Hitler that the Normandy invasion was a ruse to distract German attention from the true invasion point at Calais. It is well documented that the only reason the Allied invasion was not pushed back into the English Channel was that Hitler refused to send the German armored reserve units to Normandy, still believing the true attack would come at Calais.

Celeste found it interesting to note that the entire weight of the Allied invasion, utilizing the forces of 26 nations, faced only one quarter of the German Army. Three-fourths of the *Reich*'s military might was in the East desperately trying to stop the onslaught of the Red Army.

Marie Denarnaud continued to live in Rennes-le-Château but died of a stroke in 1953 at the age of 85, apparently without revealing the secrets she learned from Father Bérenger Saunière. Shortly before her death, Marie sold the *Villa Bethania* to a man whom she promised to tell a secret that would make him both wealthy and powerful. But the stroke left her vocal cords paralyzed and the secret was never revealed.

Although there have been many books and documentaries produced on the tiny village of Rennes-le-Château, mostly in Europe, apparently no one has fully solved its mysteries. One local travel brochure extols its "famous mysteries," while another quotes the Bishop of Carcassonne when he rededicated Saunière's *Eglise Sainte Marie-Madeleine*, the Chapel of Saint Mary Magdalene, in 1897. He told the gathered audience that the chapel presents a message from Saunière, who was an attentive priest yet posed a great dilemma for those searching for its secrets.

Celeste puzzled over whether Solomon's Treasure ever existed in the first place. She learned that this indeed was considered the greatest hoard of wealth ever accumulated in the world but was lost from history following the Jewish Revolt of 70 A.D.

She also learned that stories of hidden Nazi gold have circulated since the end of World War II along with rumors of a secret base in Antarctica funded and furnished by Nazis in friendly South American countries.

Celeste was shocked to realize that while the Germans were defeated in World War II, many top Nazis survived. (See Jim Marrs' *New York Times* non-fiction best-seller *The Rise of the Fourth Reich*.)

By early August, 1944, many within the Nazi leadership saw the writing on the wall. They knew the end of the war was only a matter of time.

Adolf Hitler, who according to captured medical records was on a roller coaster ride of euphoria and depression due to large daily doses of amphetamines and other medications to deal with advanced Parkinson's disease, increasingly lost contact with reality. However, the second most powerful man in the *Reich*, Hitler's deputy Martin Bormann, was not so incapacitated. On August 10, 1944, Bormann called together German business leaders and Nazi Party officials. They met in the Hotel *Maison Rouge* at Strasbourg on the border between France and Germany. Bormann explained the purpose of the meeting stating, "German industry must realize that the war cannot now be won, and must take steps to prepare for a postwar commercial campaign which will in time ensure the economic resurgence of Germany."

These "steps" came to be known as *Aktion Adlerflug* or Operation *Eagle Flight*. It was nothing less than the perpetuation of Nazism through the massive flight of money, gold, stocks, bonds, patents, copyrights and even technical specialists from Germany. As part of this plan, Bormann, aided by Himmler's black-clad *SS*, the central *Deutsche Bank* and the powerful I. G. Farben combine, created 750 foreign front corporations—58 in Portugal, 112 in Spain, 233 in Sweden, 214 in Switzerland, 35 in Turkey and 98 in Argentina. Through various combinations and partnerships with U.S. firms, these companies formed the modern multinational corporations that continue to dominate the economic world.

Several accounts of the recovery of a great cache of gold, silver and gems by the Nazis at the end of the war have circulated for years, as have tales of the Nazi *Agartha* base at the South Pole. Though not widely known to the public, these stories have never been fully disproved.

Celeste came to believe that the part of the treasure that Skorzeny got his hands on was the seed money for this tremendous financial empire that allowed top Nazis to survive and prosper. A silent partner in this monstrous scheme was the Vatican Bank, as revealed in several modern scandals including the P2 Lodge's attempt to overthrow the government of Italy in the 1980s. Also in the 1980s, President Ronald Reagan formally recognized the Vatican as a separate state with its own embassy in Washington, D.C., quite an accomplishment in a nation that prides itself on separation of church and state.

According to several unvetted sources, the treasure indeed ended up in the Languedoc region of southern France, a place of ancient and mystic secrets since the days of the Gauls, Romans, Goths, Celts, Merovingians, Carolingians, Cathars and Templars.

Following Otto Skorzeny's expedition to the Languedoc in March, 1944, the treasure reportedly was taken to the village of Lavelanet, where it was placed in crates and shipped by truck to either Toulouse or Carcassonne, then by rail to the small town of Merkers, some 66 kilometers from Berlin. It was then moved to Hitler's retreat at Berchtesgaden and placed within the deep tunnel complex there. Whatever was not melted down into gold bars and shipped out of Germany may still be hidden in the underground complex at Berchtesgaden or in caves in the surrounding mountains.

Gerta Buch Bormann, the wife of Hitler's deputy, Martin Bormann, was arrested in northern Italy at the end of the war. In her possession were 2,200 ancient gold coins thought to be part of the Treasure of

Solomon. It was learned that Bormann had sent a wealth of gold coins believed to be worth an estimated $800 million to Argentina by U-boat. There his fortune was placed under the personal protection of Eva Peron. Bormann himself was reportedly seen in South America for many years, even after West German authorities declared he died while trying to escape Hitler's *Führerbunker* in Berlin in the closing days of the war.

Reichsführer-SS Heinrich Himmler, the man most responsible for the search for Solomon's Treasure, tried to escape Germany after shaving his mustache, wearing an eye patch and assuming the identity of a discharged *Gestapo* agent. British authorities, under orders to arrest any member of the *SS* or *Gestapo*, took him into custody on May 21, 1945, near Bremen, Germany's second largest seaport. Before he could be interrogated, Himmler bit into a cyanide capsule and died instantly.

SS-Standartenführer Otto Skorzeny survived the war and was acquitted of war crimes by a tribunal at Dachau. After briefly working for the U.S. Army, Skorzeny, under the alias Robert Steinbacher and with funds from an undisclosed source, created a secret organization called *die Spinne*, the Spider. This group helped more than 500 *SS* men escape Germany. Many came to the United States under a secret program called *Paperclip*, which utilized Nazis in the Cold War. Skorzeny later moved to Spain where he operated a successful import-export business. He divided his time between his home in Madrid, a country estate in Ireland and a home on Majorca. He died in 1975.

But Celeste could never find any record of Michel Devereaux or of a Peter Freiherr von Manteuffel. It was as though the men never existed.

She continually sought to accumulate books, periodicals and news clippings that might be connected to the extended travels of Giselle as well as to the Sisterhood and its contribution to victory in World War II.

As the years passed, Celeste found she could not stop thinking about the story of the Sisterhood of the Rose and its contribution to victory in World War II.

Once, as she sat contemplating fact and fiction, truth and untruth, reality and unreality, she found herself absently stroking her hip, the site of a reddish-colored birthmark in the shape of a rose.

There will be those who, like Celeste, will ask, what is true and what is fiction in this account. Here is the story. Do your own research, search your own heart and soul memories and decide for yourself.

SISTERHOOD

OF THE

ROSE

SYMBOLISM

THE FOLLOWING IS AN EXPLANATION OF THE SYMBOLS THAT CAN BE FOUND IN THE FRONTISPIECE ART AND THROUGHOUT THE BOOK

 THE ANKH represents the continuity of life, the merging of the Staff of Ra with the Womb of Isis. The omega (shaped like an upside down horseshoe) represents the vessel or womb of creation in the feminine and the staff below represents the spark of life.

The **BLUE GRAPES**, also referred to as the Blue Apples, symbolizes the center of creation. Blue is the color that represents the center of the galaxy (or universe) and the home of the Great Central Sun. The roundness of the grapes represents the divine whole within which all creation exists.

 The **CHALICE** represents the fulfillment of the highest spiritual potential of human consciousness.

 The **COBRA BRACELET** was worn by Egyptian priestesses, especially the healing priestesses. It represents wisdom, healing, and protection. It also is associated with DNA and the divine blueprint.

 The **CRESCENT MOON** represents the natural rhythms and cycles of nature and life as well as the feminine polarity.

The **Dragonfly** represents the dreamtime and messages from spirit breaking through illusions, seeing truth, and embracing change.

The eight-pointed **Star of Isis** represents creation and the eternal flow of the cosmic cycles.

The five-pointed **Pentagram** represents feminine power and esoteric knowledge. Some secret male societies have distorted this symbol by turning it upside down.

The **Flag** represents national sovereignty. A flag that is hoisted by its end on a vertical pole represents a sovereign nation at war. A flag hung vertically from a horizontal pole represents a sovereign nation at peace, such as the flags raised at the Olympics. A flag that is adorned with fringe is symbolic of a sovereignty operating under maritime law.

The **Flower of Life** represents the sacred geometrical formula that is the divine blueprint for third-dimensional creation.

The **Labyrinth** with its eleven circuit circular pattern represents the calibration of and the re-calibration to wholeness, unity and the divine center.

The Merging of the five-pointed and six-pointed stars represents the **Light of God** at the moment creation meets the universal polarities coming together as a unified whole. Five is a feminine number and six is a masculine number.

The **Rose** represents the blossoming and transformation of the human spirit. The rose is considered to be the flower with the highest energy vibration. It generally has five inner petals surrounded by eight outer petals. Five and eight are both the numbers of the divine feminine and together they equal thirteen. Thirteen is the number of transformation, it is the activation of the twelve as seen in the twelve disciples.

The Rose **TRELLIS** is symbolic of the Sisterhood of the Rose and the Twelve Sisters. There is one rose for each of the primary Sisters. The number of roses, like the number of Sisters, is symbolic of the base-12 divine design found throughout creation.

 The six-pointed **STAR OF DAVID** or hexagram represents the balance between masculine and feminine, between the spirit world and the physical world.

 The **SKULL** symbolizes the human corporal body as a vessel for consciousness and a portal for the divine connection to God.

 The **STARGATE** is considered an energetic portal constructed of light that provides access or connections to different dimensional realities of creation.

 The **SWASTIKA** can be found in many religions including Native American. It can be traced back to at least the Phoenicians and is thought to originate in Atlantis. It represents the four corners of the Earth or the four directions as well as the four elements of creation: air, fire, water, earth. The Nazis distorted this symbol by rotating it forty-five degrees.

 The **SWORD** is associated with the Archangel Michael and separates truth from illusion and deception. In this sense it serves as the protector of Light and the true Word of God.

 The **WINGED ISIS** represents the divine feminine aspect of God, the Mother of Creation, and the Protective Mother.

 The **WINGED SCARAB** is an ancient Egyptian symbol representing the sun, the God of Creation, and immortality.

 The twelve **ZODIAC SIGNS** are astrological symbols representing the various aspects or expressions of creation and together they represent the totality of creation.